Praise for *Be*

'An intriguing thriller about
secrets' – *heat* magazine

'An intriguing novel about secrets, lies and the complicated
relationship between mothers and daughters, with a dark
mystery at its heart' – CL Taylor

'Sumptuously told, delivered in the most enthralling of
ways, *Beneath The Surface* absolutely blew me away' –
Becca's Book Blog

'Impossible to put the book down. I read it in one sitting...
a highly recommended read' – *bytheletterbookreviews*

'... proves that what a good thriller really needs is a well
thought out plot, realistic twists and well written
characters' – *A Novel Haul*

'The ending was perfect... I highly recommend this novel' –
Books, Chocolate and Wine

'The drama is SO well played' – *Little Bookness Lane*

'Filled with a sleuth of complex characters and unexpected
plot twists... I was hooked from the beginning' – Laura
Broadberry

'I'd highly recommend this if you enjoy themes of secrets
and lies within family settings, complex multi-layered
characters and moral dilemmas' – *Between My Lines*

Goodreads Reviews

'Brilliantly played out'

'Satisfying and authentic'

'All I can say is wow! I read this in one sitting'

'It kept me on my toes and made me want to continue to turn the pages until I ran out of them'

'*Beneath The Surface* plays its cards incredibly close to its chest as it poses disastrous dilemmas for one family under the microscope'

'Hooked does not even begin to describe how I felt about this book'

'From the first page of *Beneath The Surface*, I knew that this book was going to be a favourite of mine'

'Heidi Perks has smashed it on her debut, I can't wait for her next release'

'The twists and turns take you by surprise and I didn't want to put it down'

'A part-epistolary suspense novel, similar in tone and structure to Julia Crouch's *Tarnished*, exploring loss, family lies, and the repercussions of the actions of a manipulative and narcissistic matriarch'

HEIDI PERKS

beneath the surface

RedDoor

Published by RedDoor
www.reddoorpublishing.com

© 2016 Heidi Perks

The right of Heidi Perks to be identified as author of this Work
has been asserted by her in accordance with sections 77 and 78 of
the Copyright, Designs and Patents Act 1988

ISBN 978-1-910453-18-6

A CIP catalogue record for this book is available
from the British Library

Cover designer: Anna Morrisson
www.annamorrison.com
Typesetting: www.typesetter.org.uk
Printed in the UK by TJ International, Padstow, Cornwall

For my beautiful family: John, Bethany and Joseph.

And for my mum, who is thankfully nothing
like the mothers in this book!

April 2001

– One –

Abigail didn't know how she should answer the policeman's question. It was a simple one, and he had asked it with his head hung to one side, pen poised on his notebook as if expecting a quick response. But the fact was she didn't know if anything had been wrong in the last few weeks. Because she couldn't actually remember a time when anything was right.

When Abigail didn't say anything he rubbed a thumb over his stubbly chin and glanced at the policewoman sat beside him, eyebrows slightly raised as if to ask, *Where do I go from here?* The policewoman's face remained impassive and she didn't take her eyes off Abigail. She was the one asking most of the questions, the one who seemed to be in charge, just as she had the first time they'd met, two weeks earlier. Abigail had recognised them both as soon as she'd opened the door, and she suspected they did her, although no one had said as much.

'OK,' the policewoman said evenly, leaning towards Abigail. 'Let's go over it again. When you came home from school, tell us what happened. Was there anything you noticed that was different? Anything at all?'

Abigail shrugged. 'I don't know. I guess something didn't feel right.'

'How do you mean, not right?' she asked calmly.

'Well, they weren't here,' Abigail explained. 'They're always here. My mother is always in the kitchen and the girls are usually playing with their toys or watching TV when I get back from school. So I guess the fact that no one was in was odd.'

The woman nodded. 'And so what did you do when you realised they weren't at home?'

'Nothing much.'

The policeman sucked in his breath. Louder than he had intended, Abigail guessed, as she noticed his cheeks flush.

'OK, Abigail,' the woman said, shooting him a look. 'Take us through what you did, from the moment you came in from school and no one was here. Tell me everything that happened from that point.'

*****

Abigail didn't like going home from school. The thought of it made her mouth dry and her stomach churn. That afternoon she had put her name down to help the younger kids in the school play simply because it meant three days a week when she wouldn't be back until later. There was only one thing she enjoyed about getting home and that was seeing the girls, because they were always excited to see her.

Every night was the same. Abigail would turn her key in the lock and she would hear the girls shriek, *Ab-gail coming, Ab-gail home!*, and they would rush to the door, battling for hugs. She would pick each of them up and squeeze them, planting kisses on their soft heads and then they would rush off and play, or go back to sit watching the TV. Then her mother would call through from the kitchen in her cold, lifeless tone, 'Is that you?' and Abigail would think, *You know it's me, you've just heard them calling my name*, but instead would say, 'Yes, it's me.' That would usually be the extent of their conversation until teatime when she might still be ignored, but on the other hand could be fired questions that were usually badly hidden accusations. It was hard to tell what mood her mother was in until teatime and so Abigail made a point of keeping out of her way.

The last few weeks she had spoken to Abigail less and less and looked constantly distracted. She was always dropping something, often a plate of food that had slipped out of her hands, crashing to the floor and making her jump back to life. On one occasion Abigail noticed her mother staring into tomato soup bubbling away on the hob, one hand resting against the side of the pan. She had been about to point it out when suddenly her mother screamed, pulled her hand away and gaped at the burning red marks appearing on her palm. 'Aren't you going to put that in cold water?' Abigail had asked. 'Oh, yes,' her mother replied vaguely, as if the idea hadn't occurred to her.

Abigail shook her head at the thought. It summed her mum up: always away with the fairies.

But that afternoon there were no shrieks of *Ab-gail home!*, no TV blaring and no crashing of plates in the kitchen. The house was silent. With a sigh of relief, Abigail dropped her school bag to the floor and leaned back against the door, clicking it shut behind her. She couldn't remember a single time when she had come home to this – to nothing.

'Mum?' she called out as she walked towards the kitchen, glancing into the living room as she passed. 'Peter?' she shouted, though she knew her stepfather was unlikely to be there. 'Anyone?' Abigail called out louder.

Initially she had felt a little bubble of excitement that she had the house to herself and, grabbing a can of Coke from the fridge, Abigail went into the living room, flicked through the TV channels and settled on MTV. She put her feet up on the highly polished coffee table, which was an absolute no-no, and placed her can on the shelf beside her without even bothering to find a coaster. *Yes*, she had thought, *this is as good as it gets*.

But after a while of mindlessly watching TV, Abigail was restless. It was so unusual for there to be no one at home that she couldn't get comfortable. The room felt too quiet without the girls and suddenly she had an overwhelming need to have them back, snuggled up on the sofa with her. What if something had happened? She glanced at her watch. Had her mother told her where they were going but she just hadn't listened?

To pass the time Abigail pulled a notebook out from her school bag and started thumbing through its pages. There was so much coursework that term but she couldn't be bothered with it. Finding a bright pink pen, she started making a list of all the things she should be doing. But there was no point starting any of it because the girls would be back soon and then she could play with them before tea.

Although, of course, that meant her mother would be back, too.

Abigail stopped writing her list and clicked the lid back onto the pen because now she was thinking of her mother again, she couldn't concentrate on the list.

Her mother should have got her report card by now and it wasn't any better than the one she'd received at the start of the year. That one led to a row. 'Look at these ridiculous subjects you've chosen,' her mother had said, throwing the card on to the table. 'And you can't even be bothered to apply yourself to those anyway.' Abigail had planned what she was going to say to her mother this time – that she didn't stand a chance of doing well when every shred of confidence was ripped out of her. Cara had given her that line and she quite liked the idea of using it.

And yet she wasn't entirely sure her mother would even bother to read the latest report. And if she did, whether there would be a reaction to it. She could almost picture her mum's glazed eyes sweeping over the card before carefully putting it back on the table and turning back to whatever she was heating in the oven. Sometimes Abigail wanted to tap her on the head and ask if there was anyone at home. When she had sworn at dinner last week her mother had barely raised an eyebrow, and it was Peter who had slammed his fist on the table and told her to watch her mouth. Then, on the night Abigail had said she was going out at ten-thirty, her mother hadn't even lifted her head from the saucepan she was earnestly scrubbing. There was no more warmth than there had ever been, no more love than she was used to, but the comments were scarcer, the questioning less, the fights almost non-existent. In fact, the more Abigail thought about it, the more she realised she probably could answer the policeman's question because things had actually been very different over the last few weeks.

'Maybe now you're seventeen she knows you're old enough to do what you want,' Cara had said earlier that day. 'You know, it's like she's backing off 'cos we're adults,' she added, nodding her head wisely.

But Abigail didn't agree. She knew it was more likely her mother had given up. Lately she must have been so absorbed with the girls, or something else, that Abigail had dropped even further down her list of priorities.

'Aren't you pleased she's leaving you alone?' Cara had asked.

'Yeah, course I am,' Abigail had laughed. But she wasn't really – she preferred being shouted at to being ignored because at least then she didn't feel invisible.

Turning to the back of her notebook she pulled out a crumpled photograph of her dad and pressed it out, running her fingers across the creases distorting his face. It was the only photo she had of her beloved father. Things would be so different if he were still alive. Mum would never have married Peter, for a start. Her stepfather had never had time for Abigail. It was obvious he saw her as nothing more than an encumbrance. And she was sure her dark brown hair and olive skin, so obviously inherited from her dad, were just constant reminders to him that she wasn't his own flesh and blood.

*****

The girls' teatime passed. It was something they never missed, and the girls never ate anywhere but home in the week. There was a small chance they might have gone out, or even to a friend's house, but it was unlikely. Her mother didn't have many friends, and even fewer who were likely to invite them for tea.

The TV channels flashed in front of Abigail as she stabbed away at the remote control again, but she couldn't concentrate. The minutes ticked by loudly on the clock on the mantelpiece. There was still no sign of them coming up the path.

At six o'clock Abigail switched the television off and moved to the seat in the bay window. It was still light outside. She considered walking around the block, just to see if she could spot them coming back, because six o'clock was the girls' bath time and they never missed it.

She pulled aside her mother's unfashionable net curtains for a better look. The wire holding them up sprang against her touch. It would only take a sharp tug and she could have the whole lot down, she thought.

Her eyes scanned the line of semis on the other side of the road but she could only see as far as number 24. After that the road bent to the right and the oak tree that stood tall in their neighbour's front garden obscured the rest of the street. Her mother's bedroom window had a much better view. Abigail decided to check from that one, just quickly though in case they returned. Despite the uneasy feeling settling in the pit of her stomach, she still hated it that her mother would know she was worrying about her.

'Mum?' she called automatically as she reached Kathryn's bedroom door. As expected, there was no response and so Abigail tentatively pushed the door open, peering round it before stepping in. Something wasn't right, but for a moment she couldn't tell what.

Abigail stood by her mother's bed, running her fingers across the pale blue duvet cover when she noticed the throw wasn't there, the one her granny had crocheted as a wedding present for her mother's marriage to her real dad. Her paternal grandmother, of course – her mum's mum would never lift a finger to crochet.

Did its absence mean anything? Somehow it seemed to do so. Abigail backed out of the room and on to the landing, where she could see into her own bedroom and the bathroom. Both doors were open and she didn't need to go into the rooms to see everything looked normal.

'You're being stupid, Abigail,' she said aloud over the sound of her thumping chest.

'*So how come you feel so nervous?*' the voice inside her head whispered back.

The girls' bedroom door was closed. Not just pushed to, but someone had gone to the trouble of shutting it properly. Abigail's hands were clammy as she rested one against the door, where wooden letters spelt out the names Lauren and Hannah. She prayed she was overreacting; she was certain she had to be. But still she held her breath as slowly she pushed open the door.

Whatever Abigail expected it hadn't been what she saw. Throwing one hand to her mouth, the other clutched tightly onto the doorframe, her body grew numb; her legs felt like they would give way. Every hair on her arms stood on edge as she stared at the little girls' bedroom.

– Two –

Abigail took the tissue from the policewoman. Her hands shook as she wiped her eyes and blew her nose. She hadn't realised she had been crying until she'd seen the woman take the box of tissues off the mantelpiece and pull one out for her.

The policeman finished scribbling in his pad and looked up at her. 'So you haven't heard anything at all from your mother?' he asked.

'Of course not.'

'Not a note or a—'

'No,' said Abigail, 'I told you, nothing.'

The policewoman held a hand in the air, a gesture that stopped him asking more. He shrugged his shoulders and sat back in his chair, running a hand through spiky gelled hair. The policewoman then spoke again, asking more questions, questions that seemed futile, given the situation.

'Abigail, is there anything more you can think of,' she eventually asked, 'anything that might help us piece this together?'

They sat in heavy silence, waiting for Abigail to speak.

'Abi,' she said finally. 'People call me Abi.'

The policewoman nodded.

What should she say? There were so many things Abi could tell them. Like she didn't trust her stepfather, that she hated her controlling grandmother, or that her mother was so mad, she could have driven off the edge of a cliff. In the end she simply said, 'My mother obviously hates me.'

The policeman looked up at her under raised eyebrows. He seemed eager to wrap things up. She hadn't liked him the first time she'd met him, when Tasha was arrested for shoplifting. Abi was with her at the time but the police had no choice but to let her go as she obviously had no idea her friend had pocketed six packets of cigarettes. He'd flashed her a look on that occasion that seemed to say, '*I really have better things to do with my time than waste it on kids like you.*' She wondered why he had chosen a career in the police force when it obviously bored him.

'OK,' the policewoman said eventually. 'Tell us what happened next. When you opened the door, what did you do?'

Abi's heart pounded at the memory. What did she do? She didn't do anything, she told them; she just looked. Because what else could she have done? As Abi looked into the room she saw everything and nothing. Everything was gone. Nothing was left.

Every toy, every picture ... every little trinket the girls had accumulated in the two and a half years of their lives was gone. The pink cotton duvets with the embroidered fairies, the lamp that threw shadows of butterflies onto the ceiling, the books about princesses that Abi read to them every night, the pale blue china tea set she had found for them in a charity shop, the doll's house her daddy had made her when she was little ... All gone.

Abi stared at the room. At their bare matresses, at the drawers to the chest lying open, exposing their emptiness, no longer holding the little dresses, pyjamas and everything else that usually spilled out of them. At the empty shell of a room, only that morning so alive with the sound of the girls' laughter.

Their existence had been completely removed from the bedroom. It was as if they had never been there in the first place. But then Abi noticed something, tucked almost out of sight at the back of one of the beds. Wedged against the wall was Ted, Hannah's blue teddy that Abi had given her when she was born. The blue teddy Hannah slept with every night. As she pulled Ted free, Abi clutched him to her chest and cried because in her heart she already knew they had all gone, and had left her behind.

*****

'And so what do *you* think has happened?' the policewoman asked her.

'They've gone,' Abi said. 'My mother's left, and she's taken them away from me.'

The policeman shuffled in his seat and regarded Abi. A look of scepticism flashed across his face before he coughed and rearranged his features back to their blank expression.

But Abi knew that was what had happened; she just didn't know why. And the thought was unbearable because she had no idea where the girls were, but worse than that when she was going to see them again. She'd never spent more than one night away from them.

'Can you think where they might have gone?'

The policewoman's question broke her thoughts.

Abi shook her head. She had no idea and couldn't make sense of it. Why would her mother leave and take the girls and not her? Why hadn't she said they were going, even if she didn't intend to take Abi?

'Maybe we could go and see the bedroom?' the policewoman

suggested. Abi nodded and stood up at the same time as the doorbell sounded, startling them all.

'Are you expecting anyone?'

'No,' Abi said, going to the window to look out. 'Oh, it's my grandmother.' Her heart sank. Whatever Eleanor was doing here Abi had little doubt it would make the situation any easier. In fact it didn't pass her by that her grandmother's timing couldn't have been worse. What was she doing there?

'Oh?' The policewoman sounded interested. 'Do you want me to answer the door?' she asked, when the doorbell rang again and Abi didn't move.

'No, I'll go.'

Abi left the room and walked into the hallway. She knew everything would change as soon as Eleanor entered the house.

'What do you think?' she heard the policeman whisper. 'Something doesn't feel right. Do you think she's making it up? They haven't just gone on holiday?'

'And taken everything?' the policewoman said. 'I can't imagine that. Oh, I don't know,' she sighed. 'Let's just see what the grandmother has to say.'

Abi knew why they thought it didn't seem right. Why would they? Because surely no mother would just up and leave her daughter, taking her two youngest ones with her? Who in their right mind would do that?

Fourteen Years Later
June 2015

– Three –

Dear Adam,

I woke at four again this morning. I'm telling you 'again' like you know I've been doing that lately, which of course you don't. Sleep was something I found easy with you. Just the feel of your body lying beside me sent me into a deep, dreamless and peaceful sleep. But these days I'm restless. When I wake my body is wrapped so tightly in the duvet, like I've been wrestling with it, and my head is bursting with thoughts I can't rid myself of. They dance in my mind, prodding at me for attention. It's the same as it was all those years ago, after my mother left. I was gradually able to ignore them back then but these days I can't. Every time I manage to think of something else, my mind flicks back.

'Tell me what brought you to see me,' Maggie said to me this morning.

Maggie is my new counsellor. Truthfully, I hadn't wanted to see yet another counsellor; have someone else dig everything up again, leaving me raw with unanswered questions. Expose my lost hopes and dreams and my battered heart to yet another stranger. I saw three in the years after my mother left and none of them changed anything other than to make me feel even more alone and full of guilt.

I looked at Maggie quizzically because I had assumed she had all my notes. Dr Richards would have sent them prior to my appointment, and if she had them, she didn't need to ask why I was there.

She smiled. 'I want to hear it in your words,' she said as if reading my mind.

'Well, I guess it's because of what happened with Adam,' I said. 'I suppose that's the main reason I'm here.'

She nodded and waited for me to continue.

'But it's not just that. Adam and me, well – it's brought up other things too. Things I've tried to forget over the years.'

'Like what, Abi?'

'Other stuff I thought I'd managed to cope with. Like my mother and the girls.' There, I'd said it. 'Things I've tried to deal with but since Adam they've been coming back to me and I can't move them on,' I said.

Maggie is the reason I'm writing to you. After we had talked for nearly an hour she said she thought it would help me to write things down. I told her I wasn't sure that it would, but she told me to try anyway.

'So what do I do?' I asked her. 'Just write a list of everything I'm thinking?'

'You can do,' she said, 'or you could put it into a letter if you like. Personally, I think that's sometimes a better way of releasing what you need to say. You can be more honest and direct when you have someone to target.'

'But I wouldn't know who to write to,' I said. 'I don't have anyone.'

'Well, you can write it to anyone you like. And you don't actually have to send it,' she added.

I looked out of Maggie's window. We were in a room at the front of her South London flat, overlooking a quiet street with a park on the opposite side of the road. A man was walking his dog and another sat on a bench reading a newspaper. Both were oblivious to the people who shared their darkest secrets behind this window. Maggie had wooden shutters that were angled so it was hard for anyone to see in.

'I don't want to write to her,' I said eventually.

'Why's that, Abi?' she asked.

I shrugged and carried on looking out of the window, trying to show Maggie I simply had nothing to say to my mother, but already I could feel the anger bubbling up inside me, heating me up until I was sure it showed on my face. You always said I went red when I thought of her. You said, 'Why do you get so embarrassed, Abi? You aren't the one who should feel like that.' But that isn't it – it's pure rage I feel when I think of her.

'Maybe I'll write to Adam,' I said.

'If you'd like to write to Adam, then I think that would be a lovely idea,' she said. I saw her glance briefly at the clock on her coffee table. I had wondered why it was there when I first sat down, but then I realised it was so she could keep track of time without making it too obvious to her patient.

'Why don't you tell me about him? Let's talk about someone who makes you happy.'

'My time's nearly up,' I said.

At this she smiled at me and looking slightly embarrassed picked up the clock and turned it the other way round.

'I don't have any more appointments today. And I want to spend more time with you, if you would like that?'

Already I knew I was going to like Maggie. I nodded and she poured me another glass of water, pushed it across the coffee table towards me and waited for me to continue.

*****

We met six years ago. I was working in Morrisons in the evenings for the extra money. My supply of funds had dried up three years previously. I think I had squandered them much quicker than Eleanor had planned, but then she didn't know the dent alcohol and drugs could make on a London girl's money in her late teens with no one to answer to. That day I had sent off six applications for office jobs but I wasn't hopeful. Over the month I had applied for at least fifteen positions and hadn't had an interview for any of them. I was slowly resigning myself to a lifetime of working at New Look in the day and a supermarket at night, even though I'd always hoped for so much more when I was at school.

You were caught in the queue behind an old lady who was counting out her change coin by coin on the counter. I looked up at you and raised my eyes to say sorry and you smiled back at me and mouthed, 'It's fine.' I recognised you because over the last week you had been in every night, and I had caught you watching me, but you had never before come to my till.

'Thanks for waiting,' I said when the old lady had shuffled away. I grabbed your basket and scanned the items one by one. Four cans of lager; deodorant; cornflakes; a box of Dairy Milk ... My heart dipped a little as I packed the chocolates into a carrier bag. 'That's £12.78, please,' I said. I didn't look up at you as you handed me the money.

'So, are you on for much longer tonight?' you asked.
'No, thank God,' I said. 'I finish in fifteen minutes.'
'Busy night?' you laughed.
'I'm just very, very tired and I want to get to bed,' I smiled.
'Ah! Well, have a good one.'

You took the bag off me and I watched you walk out of the shop and stop just outside the door. The store was emptying out and I didn't have anyone else waiting at my till. I wondered what lucky girl was waiting for you and the chocolates at home, when you turned around and came back in, walking straight towards me.

'Did you forget something?' I asked when you stopped at the end of the conveyor belt.

'Yes,' you said. 'I, er … Look, I really don't usually do this but I just wondered if you fancied going out for a drink?'

'Oh,' I said. 'I don't drink.' Immediately I cringed at my response. 'I mean, I—'

'We don't have to drink,' you smiled. 'Maybe we could go to the cinema.'

'OK,' I said. 'But—' I glanced towards your bag. I'd assumed you had a girlfriend and by then I couldn't shake off the idea. 'Are you single?' I blurted out.

'Of course,' you laughed. 'Why? Ah, the chocolates, you mean? They're for my grandma. I'm visiting her tomorrow. I can promise you, I'm most definitely unattached.'

Nothing like the men I usually met, you were clean-shaven, tall and blond. In your striped shirt and jeans you looked like a rugby player; you were everything I dreamt of in a boyfriend. My head and heart were splitting me in two. My heart was doing a little dance of joy but my head was warning me not to get too carried away because things don't run that smoothly for Abigail Ryder. So in the end I said yes, then waited for something to go wrong.

It annoyed you that I always saw the glass half-empty, especially when you were an eternal optimist. We had been seeing each other for a month when you told me you were taking me for a picnic. I looked up at the sky and pointed out the clouds.

'There's rain coming,' I said. 'I don't think we should go.'

'Of course there isn't,' you said, loading up the boot, telling me to get into the car. 'Stop worrying.'

So I did as you said and smiled to myself as I caught you tucking a large umbrella under the picnic rug.

Sure enough, the rain came.

'It's going to be ruined,' I cried, throwing half-eaten sandwiches and sausage rolls back into the rucksack. I was annoyed that our day was spoilt but also that I had been right when I so wanted to be wrong. But when I looked up, you were laughing, arms outstretched and face turned to the sky, catching the rain on the tip of your tongue.

'How can you say our day is ruined when we're having so much fun?' you said, grabbing me around the waist. 'It's just a bit of rain, Abi. Who cares if we get wet when we're together?'

You always made me feel happy. You helped me see a glimmer of light rather than just a long black tunnel ahead. Over time I came round to your way of thinking that maybe things didn't always have to turn out bad. I pushed my demons even further down inside of me so they couldn't reach us and thought I could get away without facing them now I was with you.

Six months later I knew I'd fallen for you hard and I allowed myself to believe things were going well. Then one night we were sitting in your flat watching TV and I noticed you hadn't said much. You were absently rubbing your hand against my leg and I could see your head was elsewhere. I asked you questions and you either nodded or shook your head, but I could tell you weren't listening to me. Immediately my guard rose up in defence, and I cursed myself for foolishly trusting in us and letting you into my heart. I pulled my leg away so your hand fell into the space between us and hugged my arms around my knees.

'What's wrong?' you asked.

'What's wrong with me?' I snapped. 'Nothing! Look, maybe I should just go. I've got an early morning.'

I had at last heard back from an advertising company I had sent an application to, and they were interviewing me the next morning for an assistant account manager position. I had a sudden desire to get out of the flat – I thought I knew what was coming and I didn't want to hear it.

You sighed and hung your head back against the sofa, closing your eyes as you did so.

'Don't worry, Adam,' I said. 'I get the picture.'

You had met someone else. Or maybe you just realised you could do better than me, or you were bored or ... There were too many possibilities and maybe I was overreacting, but I was so scared you were about to break my heart and leave me.

At this you opened your eyes and sat up straight.

'What are you taking about?'

But I didn't answer; instead I just focused on gathering up my bag and shoes and trying to get myself out of the flat.

'Abi,' you grabbed me. 'Why are you suddenly leaving? Look, I don't know what you're thinking but whatever it is, I think you've got it wrong.'

'Then tell me why you're being like this with me,' I said. I could feel the tears stinging the backs of my eyes and I knew it wouldn't take much for them to well up.

'I've been thinking about things,' you said. 'About us, and where we're going. And I really love you, Abi. I want to be with you for the rest of my life, but there are things I want to know.'

I could have laughed: you had just said you loved me and you wanted to be with me.

'What do you want to know?' I asked, but by then I didn't really care what it was.

'Oh, I don't know,' you sighed. 'I guess sometimes I feel that I don't really know you. You can be such a closed book.'

'That's not true.'

'Yes, it is. We talk about stuff all the time, what we ate for breakfast, what's on the TV, who said what at work, but nothing important. Nothing that means anything. Every time I try, you change the subject.'

'I don't,' I whispered back, but of course you were right.

'Yes, Abi, you do. The other day I told you my parents wanted us to go to Scotland so they could finally meet you and you said, "Maybe you should go on your own, I'm sure it's you they want to see." I ask you what you want to do in life, and you shrug my question away and say, "I'll do whatever I end up doing." I haven't asked about your family after you very definitely told me you never wanted to talk about them. I don't know what to do, Abs. I really like you but I feel like for whatever reason you don't want me getting close to you.'

It was the first time anyone had pressed me on it. Probably no one had wanted to get close to me before and so they hadn't bothered pursuing why they couldn't. I felt that familiar burn under my skin and hadn't realised I was scratching at it until you grabbed hold of my arm. Now I was thinking of my mother and I so did not want to be. She had no place coming between us, and I was annoyed she was edging her way in. I pulled my arm away.

'I just want to know who you are,' you continued. 'I want to know everything about you, even the not-so-good bits.'

The room was closing in on me and I needed to get out, but you were holding onto me again and I could feel myself letting you pull me back. Don't put yourself through this, Abi, I was thinking. Don't let him open up your heart because you don't know what might drop out of it. But at the same time I wanted to tell you. Maybe you should know who I am. I let you pull me back onto the sofa and we sat for a while in silence, your arms

– 24 –

wrapped around me. It took me back to a time, so long ago, when I was only little. I was riding my bike along a promenade and fell over, badly grazing my knee. The skin stung like someone had cut through it with a knife. My daddy picked me up and we sat on the beach, him holding me tightly until I could no longer feel any pain.

'It hurts,' I said. 'Some things hurt so much I choose not to talk about them.'

'Just try, Abs.'

You looked at me with eyes pleading me to open up to you.

So I took a deep breath and said, 'My mother disappeared one day. I came home from school when I was seventeen and she was gone.'

'Oh, my God!'

Your face told me it was the last thing you expected to hear. I knew you were probably thinking the worst, that she had been abducted, maybe found dead. Sometimes I told people that because I thought it's what they wanted to hear – besides, it was better than the truth.

'It's not what you're thinking. She planned to go.'

'What?' I could hear the shock in your voice.

That's why I didn't usually tell people, because then they started to wonder what I'd done to make my mother leave me. 'The truth is I still don't know why. Fourteen years later I have no idea why she went or where. And that's not all of it. She took my sisters with her. They were only two.'

The word 'sisters' choked in my throat. I didn't talk about the girls. Ever. I couldn't, it wasn't possible to get through life if I let them into my world again.

'Jesus! And you haven't tried looking for them?'

'No, and that's why I don't talk about it. So I need you to drop this now. Please.'

'Of course, Abs, of course,' you murmured, and you wrapped yourself tighter around me like you would never let me go.

*****

'He sounds like a wonderful man, Abi. You obviously loved him very much,' Maggie said to me. 'I can see your eyes sparkle when you talk about him.'

'He was the only person who ever let me be who I was and who didn't push me into anything I wasn't ready for.'

*****

After I told you about my mother you didn't press me into telling you more. You had heard the worst and were still with me.

You made me feel safe again and I promised myself you were one person I would never let go. But then I didn't manage that either, did I?

Since what happened with us I started getting moments when I couldn't shake the past from my head. I had spent years burying memories deep within, but all of a sudden they were looming up inside me again.

The first time was one of those early spring days when the sun catches you out and it's warmer than you think it's going to be. I had wandered out to buy a paper and a coffee and sat outside on a bench in the park. Two teenage girls walked past me, arms linked together, their heads pressed in to each other as they giggled over something one of them said. I couldn't take my eyes off them – for all I knew, they could have been Hannah and Lauren.

I never have to work out how old the girls are. I've always

known exactly what their ages are at any given time over the last fourteen years. Now they are sixteen, soon to be seventeen. The same age I imagined these girls in the park were. Usually when I think of Hannah and Lauren, I quickly picture the happy scene I've drawn for them – the house in the country, the swings in the back garden, a dog by the fire ... Always they are laughing and teasing each other, and they are always, always both in the picture together. Then as soon as I have seen them clearly in my mind I can close the image down, knowing they are safe and happy, and then I forget about it again: it is the only way I keep going.

But on that day in the park I wasn't able to get them out of my head. I had conjured up my scene, thrown in some extras like the new outfits they were wearing, but then try as I might, I could not close down the image. I even tried mentally clicking the red cross in the corner of the picture to shut the file down, but still it kept springing back up. And every time it did so it taunted me with something that wasn't quite right. The swing was broken, swaying loosely by one rope. One of the girls was crying. Hannah was hiding behind a tree and when she appeared, her face was bruised and she didn't look like I thought she should. I was watching a thriller that my own warped mind was creating, but I couldn't stop it from playing.

This last year, every time I remember I've wanted to pick up a bottle again and get through it like I did when they left. I wanted to fill my head with alcohol or drugs until I forgot, but somehow I didn't. There are some days when it becomes almost too hard to bear, though, because a clear mind is a playground for the thoughts and memories you cannot control.

It was about six weeks after they left that I decided I wouldn't ever look for the girls. After all I had my reasons for believing they would be better off without me. I told myself they were fine. They were happy and oblivious so what did it matter what was happening to me? They were what mattered.

My own life was spiralling out of control and I didn't know what to do about it. I had all these questions about what had happened and how my mother could leave me. But I never got the answers I believed, and part of me didn't think I wanted them anyway. I decided the best way to cope was to forget – bury the layers of guilt, anger, sadness and fear deep down so I didn't have to face them.

Then along you came, and bit by bit I started to open my eyes to how I really felt and I realised I should never have let them go without looking for them. What if they weren't OK? I shouldn't have left them with her, plus I deserve to understand why she left me, don't I?

So after what happened with you and me I decided to look for Hannah and Lauren. I need to know what happened, Adam. I have to know why they left me, because something made my mother go, and it can't have been me.

– Four –

Hannah threw her bag onto the sand and used both hands to pull at one of the doors to open the hut. She knew it was most probably the heavy rain they'd had that spring making it stick. The same thing had happened the year before when Morrie had explained to her that dampness made the doors swell. Perhaps she shouldn't pull so hard, but it wouldn't open any other way. Morrie would be at the fishing sheds later. She could drop in on her way home and ask him to take a look before they got any worse.

Once the hut was finally open and the doors tied back with string Hannah turned to look for her sister. 'Come on,' she called, laughing as Lauren stumbled onto the sand at the bottom of the steps. 'What's taking you so long?'

Lauren scowled in response and held her arms up, shaking two carrier bags. 'Someone had to get the lunch as well, you know,' she muttered when she reached the hut. Neither of them ever wanted to do the food run – both avoided the corner store as much as they could. Once Theresa saw either of them coming into her shop, she clapped her hands with glee and started gabbling away about school, always dropping in how well her Maria was doing. Everyone knew her daughter was the brightest girl in the school but she was also the dullest.

'Fifteen minutes she held me there,' Lauren sighed, throwing the bags onto the decking. 'What a waste of my life!'

Hannah rummaged through the shopping, pulling out a box of tea bags and packets of biscuits, which she stacked on the small shelves in the corner of the hut.

'Doesn't look like we need to go back any time soon, at least,' she observed.

'Thank God! She tried to offer me a dinghy on my way out. Can you believe it? It had a head the shape of a crocodile.'

Hannah laughed. 'You should have taken it, it could have been fun.'

'I wanted to say, how old do you think we are?'

'She probably doesn't have a clue what normal girls our age are doing. Maria's most likely in the library all weekend swotting up on insects or whatever she's lately obsessed with.'

Hannah opened a packet of crisps and waved them in front of her sister.

'I'd better only have one,' Lauren said, peering into the bag and taking one out.

Hannah rolled her eyes and went back to unloading the food.

*****

It was the first hot weekend of the year. Already late June and they hadn't used the beach for sunbathing since last summer, but every spare moment she had Hannah went to the hut, unlike her sister, who didn't see the point of spending time on the beach if the sun wasn't shining. Lauren was like a weather vane. As soon as the sun came out, she popped up outside the hut in her bikini. But it didn't matter if it was sunny or not, Hannah was there all year round.

There were a dozen beach huts nestled amongst the dunes of the bay. When they were young, Hannah and Lauren loved running amongst the huts and hiding behind them. It always frightened their mum when she couldn't see them but it was never long before one of them shrieked with laughter and then she knew the other girl would be close by.

The best view of the huts was from the top of the cliff. Each one was painted in a different colour. It was an unwritten rule that no one should change the colour of their hut, but the girls were happy with theirs anyway – a cobalt blue. The nearer you got, the more apparent it was how shabby they were. Weathered by the salty air, only a few had been religiously repainted every year. But Hannah and Lauren loved them, and had thought themselves the luckiest girls alive when they finally had one of their own. It happened the summer they were eleven. For years their mum had been promising them that one day they would have one, but deep down they knew there was little she could do about it. If you owned one of Mull Bay's precious huts there was no way you gave it up easily. Owners kept hold of them for years and would nearly always pass them on to the next generation.

But one hot day that summer, the girls came home from the shops with their mum to find Morrie waiting for them on the doorstep. He had a huge smile on his face and was waving a rusty old key in the air. As soon as the girls saw it they both screamed with delight, knowing immediately what it meant. Earlier that year Mrs Partridge had died. Her death left a hole in the village community – most of the Bay's residents had known her all their lives, and the girls adored her. But after a couple of months people starting speculating about the hut. 'What do you think will happen to it now that she's gone?' they murmured. 'Of course, she has no family so there's no one to pass it on to.'

A meeting was called and it was decided the fairest way to determine the beach hut's fate was to put each family's name into a box and pull one out at random. Morrie had responsibility for the draw.

'We've got it?' they both shouted, jumping up at Morrie, who was laughing as he held the key just out of their reach.

'Mummy, look, we've got the hut!' Lauren shouted, turning to see Kathryn, who was smiling at them.

'I can't believe it, Morrie,' said Kathryn. 'Is it really ours?'

Morrie winked at Kathryn. 'It's yours all right,' he told her.

Lauren hadn't seen the wink – she was still looking at her mother – but Hannah had, and often asked Morrie if the beach hut was fairly theirs. If it wasn't, he never let on, although Hannah wasn't entirely sure he hadn't had a hand in it. Morrie was a good friend to all of them. He was older than Kathryn, although the girls didn't know how old exactly. His face was weathered by the sea, which could have aged him but didn't. Morrie had always looked out for the girls and they loved him like an uncle.

The beach was paradise to Hannah. It formed a perfect semicircle around the sea and was the heart of Mull Bay, the picture postcard fishing village where they had grown up in the North East of England. The girls had moved to the Bay when they were very young. They knew nowhere else and as children they had always thought there was nowhere else they would rather be. 'Who wouldn't want to live in a place like this?' their mother had drummed into them. 'It's beautiful. You're lucky to live here, there's no need for you to go anywhere else.'

Hannah had always agreed with her mother when she was young, when there was nothing better in life than swimming in the sea and playing on the sand. But in her teenage years she wasn't so sure. She still loved the beach, and spent most of her time there, but she no longer believed there was no point in seeing anywhere else. Of course there was. Hannah wanted to see the world. She'd made a long list of where she intended to go. Africa – where she would spend nights sleeping outdoors, listening to the sound of wild animals. The Pyramids; swimming in the Indian Ocean, where the sea was clear turquoise. And America, the bright lights of Vegas and the golden sands of California ... But right now she would be happy seeing London for the very first time.

Nowadays, her mother's words felt less like the wisdom she had always thought them to be and more of a noose around her neck.

Many of Mull Bay's inhabitants had lived there all their lives, rarely venturing outside its confines. Hannah knew it imprisoned them with its beauty but in turn it made them ignorant too. They were so sure the Bay was the most wonderful place to live that they didn't have the foresight to prove themselves right by going anywhere else. And it was making her feel trapped, an invisible prison. The other night they had watched *The Truman Show* on TV and it had left Hannah wondering if she flew high enough, could she touch the dome bubble encircling them?

As the kids of the Bay grew up, they divided into two camps. There were those who were desperate to leave as soon as they could, and the others who would happily stay for the rest of their lives. That year, twelve students were leaving Mull Bay Upper School. Nine had places at universities around the country, most of them in big cities they had only dreamt of visiting. The other three were boys who came from long lines of fishermen and didn't have the drive to think of other possibilities. That year was exceptional – there were normally much fewer leaving the Bay.

Hannah already knew which camp she fell into: she needed to get out. But she also knew there were two things standing in her way. First, her sister, who was less enthusiastic – in fact Lauren was so laid-back, Hannah already feared she would happily stay in the Bay for ever and doing anything without her sister didn't seem like an option. Second, a much greater obstruction was their mum. Hannah couldn't understand Kathryn's reasons, but whatever they were, she seemed hell bent on preventing the girls from having a life outside of Mull Bay. Hannah still remembered the first time she had asked to go out with friends in the evening after school. She was thirteen, nearly fourteen, and a group had arranged to go to the cinema. But Kathryn froze at the question. 'No,' she told her quickly, 'absolutely not.'

'But why not? We're all together, and the others are allowed to go and we won't be late—'

'It's not safe,' Kathryn said, her face drained of colour. 'Anyway, you're far too young.'

'Oh, come on, Mum, this is so unfair!'

'It's not unfair, it's completely reasonable and don't start arguing with me. I can't take it when you argue back.' Kathryn waved a hand in the air to stop the conversation and seemed shaken as she pulled out a chair to sit in.

As far as Hannah was concerned it was a ridiculous overreaction, but it wasn't all that uncommon. Often their mum would get flustered, panicked when she thought she was losing control.

'She's just concerned something's going to happen to you,' Morrie had explained to Hannah the next day. 'To her you're the most important thing in the world. I think she's just scared stiff something's going to go wrong.'

But to Hannah her mother's concern was smothering them. To her, Kathryn was so wrapped up in the two girls it was as if she wanted to live out the rest of their lives for them.

*****

Hannah glanced over at Lauren, sitting on a towel with its edges carefully smoothed out so the sand couldn't encroach on it.

'Are you painting your toenails different colours?' she asked.

'Yep, I'm seeing which one suits me best.'

'Do you seriously have nothing better to do with your time?'

'Not today,' she replied. 'Why, what are you doing, little sis?'

'Ha, ha!' Hannah grinned.

There was a five-minute gap between them, their mum was always telling them, but it was enough to give Lauren the licence to consider herself the older sister, although most people often thought it was the other way round.

'You can borrow a magazine if you're bored,' Lauren said, nodded towards the pile stacked up on her towel. 'I have *Heat*, *Grazia*, *Now* and *More*. There's everything you ever need to know about who's getting too fat or too thin, and who might only be getting fat because they're pregnant.'

'And you actually find that interesting?' Hannah shook her head. 'I worry about you. Anyway, I'm not bored. I'm thinking.'

'About what?'

'About a number of things. I'm planning something, although I'm not sure you'll be too keen.'

'What?' Lauren looked up and eyed Hannah cautiously, carefully unscrewing the top from a bottle of pink nail varnish.

'Well, I'm fed up with Mum saying we can't go away. She's using money as an excuse but I don't buy it. And so I'm thinking that some way or other we should try and go away on our own this summer.'

'Er, yeah, like she would say yes to that.'

'Well, obviously she's not going to be happy, but we should just do it. At least get some passports. We must be the only sixteen-year-olds who've never had one.'

'You're digging yourself a grave.' Lauren sighed.

'Maybe. But it's ridiculous. The others are all going away over the holidays. Sophie's going to Turkey again.'

'She's going with her parents, not on her own. And anyway, what's there in Turkey? It's too hot. Mum says sometimes it's over 40°C and I couldn't stand that.'

'What would Mum know? I doubt she's been anywhere near Turkey.'

'Talking of Mum, she wants us to go and see Grandma this weekend.' Lauren turned to Hannah, pulling a face.

'Oh, you've got to be kidding! We only went two weeks ago.'

Hannah's heart sank at the thought of going back to the home again so soon. She had always hated visiting their grandmother, but over the last year it had been even worse.

'It's her birthday,' Lauren reminded her. 'I don't think we have a choice.'

'Why can't she go on her own, why does she keep dragging us along, too?'

Lauren shrugged, 'I don't know. But it's something we've got to do, I guess.'

'Seriously, let's just tell her we aren't going this time.'

'Hannah, grow up! You know Mum will never let you do that. Just face it, we're going, whether we like it or not.'

Hannah stood up, pulling her T-shirt over her head to reveal her bikini top underneath. 'I'm going for a swim,' she told her sister, and walked away without asking if she wanted to join her. It made Hannah so angry that these visits were still dictated to them, as if they had nothing better to do with their time than look at the woman who barely spoke to them, and if she did say something it was rarely nice, or relevant. She would make a stand, she decided. That weekend she would refuse. Lauren could go if she wanted to be compliant, but Hannah wouldn't. She didn't care whether her mum liked it or not; she wasn't going to waste another day visiting Eleanor at that home.

The cold chill of the sea stung her skin as she submerged her body. It was just what she needed to clear her head. Hannah let her body float on its surface, kicking her legs only when needed. This was her therapy, looking out to the wide ocean and thinking, *I could just keep swimming if I wanted to. No one could stop me doing that.*

By the time Hannah got out of the sea she felt calmer. Lauren looked up when she saw her returning.

'What's all this?' Lauren asked.

'Jesus, Lauren, that's mine! What are you doing reading it?' Hannah snatched the notebook out of her sister's hands and threw it into her bag, which still lay outside the hut.

'I didn't realise it was stuff you wanted to keep from me. Anyway, I'm glad I read it, seeing that it heavily involves me anyway.'

'Yeah, well. I was going to say something. I just wanted to do some digging first, see what I could find.'

'Mum's going to hit the roof when she knows what you're up to, Hannah.'

'Mum is the reason I'm doing this in secret,' Hannah snapped back. 'If she could be more honest with us then I wouldn't feel the need to go behind her back.'

'But looking for our dad? It just seems too massive. And you know what Mum says about him. He didn't want anything to do with us when we were young.'

'Maybe. But that's all she has said. We don't really know what happened. Aren't you a little bit curious about why he left?'

'No, as far as I can see, he didn't want to know us and so I don't want to know him.'

'That's so short-sighted.' Hannah was annoyed her sister couldn't see her point, and even more frustrated she didn't share her passion for finding their father. She wanted to know what he looked like, what features she'd inherited, if they shared a sense of humour and all the little things they might have in common, like preferring warm milk on Weetabix. There were so many things Hannah didn't know about her past, and the only person who could tell her was reluctant to do so.

'I imagine him having dark hair like me,' Hannah tried. 'What do you reckon?'

Lauren sighed. 'I don't know and I don't care. He's probably bald. And he's probably living with a young woman and their three snotty-nosed kids. And then Mum would be devastated.'

Hannah sighed. She knew when to stop: Lauren was definitely more sensitive to their mother's needs than she was, and she didn't want to hurt her sister.

'Lauren, have you put any sun cream on?' Hannah touched Lauren's shoulder, changing the subject. 'You're already burning.'

'Damn it! I did put some on earlier, Factor 30 as well.'

Hannah silently handed Lauren her T-shirt and went into the beach hut to grab a towel. She wouldn't mention their dad again, at least not until she had something concrete to tell her. Hopefully then Lauren would be intrigued enough to help her find him.

– Five –

Kathryn had been planning a little treat for the girls. It was to be a surprise, something to keep them occupied for a bit over the summer. It was all in her head still, she hadn't thought through the details, but she was thinking the three of them could go away to a little B&B, maybe somewhere up the coast, just to get away. She had intended to mention it over dinner the other night but then Hannah had started her persistent questioning about Peter and the whole thing had gone right out of her mind. Now she came to think of it, she could no longer see what the attraction had been in the first place: far better to stay in the Bay, where she knew where everything was, and besides, the thought of packing always seemed so stressful.

Kathryn was sitting at the kitchen table filing her short nails even shorter and wondering what she should get her mother for her birthday when the sound of the letterbox clanging with the post made her jump. She glanced at her watch: it was already past ten. Why so late that morning? Pushing back her chair so she could see through the kitchen window, Kathryn could just make out the boy, must be a new lad, pulling at the gate, trying to get the latch to click. And then when he couldn't get it to catch, he just left it swinging. Turning on his heel he was about to walk away with her gate left wide open.

Kathryn raced to open the front door and called out in a sing-song voice which suggested she was jollier than she felt:

'You just need to pull it up first then it will catch. It's a bit fiddly but I would appreciate it if you could always close it behind you.'

The boy looked up at her but didn't speak.

'Here, let me show you,' she started, walking down the path, her slippers scuffing along the paved stones.

'No need, I've done it,' he said gruffly as he lifted the gate, closed it and mounted his bicycle that lay on the side of the road in front of the house.

'Thank you,' Kathryn called out as he cycled down the lane, waving his hand in response.

She didn't like change; it made her wary. She hoped the usual postman would be back and thought she might even call in at the post office later to ask where he was. Things rarely changed in Mull Bay, so it was difficult when they did. The previous year the café on the high street announced they were selling up and for weeks Kathryn was on edge, wondering what might take its place. Every time she passed the 'For Sale' board she felt herself tensing up. Was it the not knowing, she wondered. Meanwhile there was plenty of talk about who might take it and what they would do with the café. Mostly the residents spoke of two young men from London who wanted to turn it into a wine bar, a thought that sent a cold shiver down her spine. She was surprised when some people said they were open to the idea, saying it would bring more money to the Bay. But for Kathryn all it represented was more youngsters to lead her daughters astray with their late-night drinking. Thankfully the café owners had a change of heart and didn't sell. On the day Kathryn heard the news she opened a bottle of wine and drank the lot in one evening. The sense of relief was amazing.

Turning back to the envelopes in her hand she flicked through until she saw one with a familiar scrawl across the front. Dropping the rest of the post onto the shelf, her hands trembled slightly as she held it. There was nothing to fear, of course. He hadn't let her down yet. But every time she knew there was the chance he might not have enclosed the cheque. Or worse, he had written to her, wanting to see her again; and that she really didn't think she would be able to face.

Kathryn looked up at the mirror hanging in the hallway and leaned forward as she began to peel the envelope open. 'You're beginning to look like an old woman,' she told her reflection. 'You look more like Mother every day.'

In reality she didn't look her fifty-six years. Kathryn actually looked very good for her age, but there were definitely signs of ageing that hadn't been there a year ago. Dark shadows beneath her eyes made her skin look thinner and her eyelids were more hooded as if she hadn't managed a good night's sleep in a while. Flecks of grey were springing up at the edges of her hairline. People always commented they couldn't believe she didn't colour her hair. Good genes, she told them, her mother didn't go grey until she was in her sixties. Kathryn ran a hand through her hair. It was cut short, almost cropped, but she hadn't had it trimmed for a few months and the ends were hanging over her ears. The sea air of the Bay had served her well over the years, but lately she was definitely looking older.

Turning back to the envelope, Kathryn pulled out the cheque, read the amount and silently thanked Peter. He had proven himself over time and in turn she had come to trust him, but she still hated relying so heavily on her ex-husband.

She peered inside the envelope but this time there was nothing else. Occasionally he included a short note. The last cheque, the one just before Christmas, had had one attached. It was written on a piece of lined paper ripped out from a pad and on it he told her he was now living in Liverpool, was doing extremely well for himself, and that he hoped she and the girls were well. The notes lacked substance and she would prefer he didn't send one at all. Kathryn wasn't bothered by his lack of emotion or interest – it was easier if there was none at all.

For years she had worried that Peter might turn up on her doorstep. Before he moved to Liverpool he was living in a town just a two-hour drive from the Bay. Mother always sighed whenever Kathryn voiced her concerns, almost rolling her eyes before telling Kathryn he had no interest in unsettling her life. Eleanor always seemed so sure about that and she told Kathryn it was pathetic to keep worrying over him. But she was worried: what if one day he announced that he wanted to see them again?

Kathryn had told Lauren and Hannah she had no contact with their father. In one heated discussion she had even said she thought he was living in Australia, although afterwards she couldn't remember exactly what she'd told them and berated herself for not remembering because Hannah was likely to pull her up on something. Lately her daughter was questioning her a lot about her father, and how she wished the questions would stop.

Thankfully Peter had never turned up, and eventually Kathryn stopped imagining he might. Now she was grateful he continued sending the money, as promised, and appeared to want nothing in return. Right now she needed the money more than ever as it was the only source of income she had. The hefty fees for the care home were rapidly draining her mother's funds, which meant Kathryn's whole future and existence in the Bay were completely dependent on Peter. They hadn't realised until after her father's death that despite his apparent wealth, he had accrued a lot of debt. Morrie often hinted she should reconsider the care home Eleanor was in, but Kathryn couldn't bring herself to do so. Her mother would hate to be anywhere else and she didn't have the guts to think about it, even though, as he had carefully pointed out, Eleanor wasn't in much of a mind to argue.

Soon she would need to do something about money but for now she could continue putting it off. Besides, other things concerned her. The girls, particularly Hannah, were putting more strain on her. They were growing up and demanding more independence. One day they would grow their wings and fly away and then what would she do?

And then there was her mother. Of course Kathryn could see it, she wasn't stupid: as much as they tried to tell her Mother was doing fine, she knew she wasn't. Eleanor was her world. The only person who had always been there for her, and Kathryn was scared, because losing her mother was like losing her own mind.

*****

Tucking the cheque into her purse Kathryn slipped on a pair of shoes and headed straight for the bank. She had a number of errands in the high street that she needed to do and one was to find something special for her mother's birthday.

When it came to buying her mother a present Kathryn was still panic-stricken even though, as Hannah once said, it really didn't matter anymore. She had shouted at Hannah when she said that but her daughter was right, and though Kathryn would never say it aloud, it gave her a little relief that her mother could no longer judge what she gave her.

It had started on a school trip when Kathryn was nine and she had bought her mother's birthday gift with her own money. Carefully choosing a brightly painted ceramic pot, Kathryn had been thrilled with what she had done for her mum. But when Eleanor unwrapped it, she had screwed up her eyes and said, 'This is a little garish, isn't it?' and the pot was cast to one side. Kathryn could still remember the sinking feeling, the utter dismay that as always, she had got it so wrong.

She wasn't looking forward to seeing her mother at the home that weekend, not that she would ever say as much to the girls. The journey was long and she tried to avoid driving far as much as she could, but since Eleanor couldn't get to Mull Bay, the journey was a necessity.

It was obvious Hannah didn't enjoy the visits although she had never said as much. Whenever they saw Eleanor, she was snappier than usual and barely spoke to anyone while they were at the home. Kathryn had given up prodding her daughter to speak to her grandmother in the residents' lounge. It was tiring enough trying to be jolly herself without having to encourage Hannah to do the same. In the end she ignored Hannah's bad moods and instead counted her blessings her other daughter was chattier. Lauren was always positive, telling Eleanor what they were doing, even though she got nothing in return.

At first she tried not to blame Hannah. Kathryn was well aware the trips were anything but fun, if they could ever have been called that. Whatever anyone thought, Kathryn wasn't blind to her mother's ways, but she still loved her. No one else had held her together when she was falling apart and she needed her. But over time Kathryn began to feel annoyed when she watched how Hannah behaved with Eleanor, rolling her eyes at Lauren and shaking her hands dramatically to the gods when she didn't think Kathryn could see her. It made her angry, and it reminded her of the way Abigail had been.

Kathryn shook such thoughts out of her head and focused instead on what Mull Bay's gift shop had to offer. Browsing the shelves she recited the shopping list to herself. It was a neat little trick that concentrated her mind on what it could manage: birthday present, groceries, watch battery. *There was something else*, she thought, muttering through the list again. *That was it, a joint of pork.* After she had found a gift, Kathryn would go straight to the butcher's. A habit inherited from her mother, they always had a roast on a Wednesday. When she was a child, Wednesday was the night her father, Charles, invited business associates and their wives for dinner. Eleanor was right in thinking that ordering their cook to roast a joint mid-week impressed the guests. The wives often murmured comments like, 'This is really so splendid, Eleanor. I don't know how you manage it all. Bringing up a child as well.'

Kathryn had liked it when they said things like that because Eleanor always made a show of how easy her daughter was to 'bring up'. As if she actually enjoyed having a daughter, which as Kathryn knew, wasn't remotely close to the truth.

Whilst Kathryn didn't match cook's culinary skills, she still thought it right to impress such little things upon the girls. Sharing dinner together as a family every Wednesday was one of them.

That night she served the pork with roasted vegetables. It was a simple dish but Kathryn knew the girls loved it. She had intended to make an apple crumble that afternoon too, one of her mother's recipes. She knew exactly which one she wanted to recreate and that morning had told Lauren she was making it. But when the time came she could no longer remember how. Two hours were wasted that afternoon trying to recall the recipe. She just had to hope that Lauren had forgotten.

In the end none of it mattered. The evening was ruined when Hannah started on at her again, although this time it wasn't about Peter.

'Can we ask you something, Mum?' Hannah said tentatively. 'Run something by you?'

'Can *you* ask, you mean,' Lauren muttered.

Hannah gave her sister a sideways glance before looking back at her mother and continuing. '*We*,' she paused, adding emphasis to the word, 'we were wondering if we could go away this summer, just Lauren and me. Maybe?'

Kathryn carefully rested her knife and fork on the table and looked at Hannah, who in turn briefly dropped her gaze to the table before puffing herself up and attempting to smile. Suddenly Kathryn had lost her appetite.

'What do you mean, like a trip?' she asked.

'I know you won't want to go anywhere,' Hannah went on, 'I mean, what with Grandma being ill and all, but—' She paused and Kathryn waited for her to continue, to see if she had thought through what she wanted to ask. Already she could feel the butterflies gnawing away inside her gut.

'So maybe just Lauren and I could go somewhere. Out of the Bay,' the words came tumbling out. 'Not abroad or anything, and not for long, just to go somewhere else for a bit. Maybe. Mum?'

Kathryn opened her mouth to speak, but couldn't form the words she wanted. What she would have liked was to calmly tell her daughter that the world was too big a place for children of their age. Hadn't she told them enough times the Bay was all they needed? But she feared her voice wouldn't sound calm and rather thought she would instead scream the words, which might push them still further away from her.

Fear was bubbling inside her. How she wanted to grab hold and never let them go. Didn't they understand how much she loved them? How much it broke her heart to think of them somewhere she couldn't see them and know what they were doing? Still, she knew how insane that would sound if she were to try to explain to anyone how she felt: her overwhelming need to keep them close and prevent them from getting into trouble. She had spent years building them a safe life in Mull Bay and now they wanted to break free. Kathryn closed her eyes and silently begged her mother to tell her what to do but no words came back from her.

'Mum?' Lauren's voice broke her thoughts. Her daughter sounded worried. Kathryn snapped her eyes open and took in the two of them watching her, their faces blank, gaze unmoving. Maybe she had spoken her thoughts aloud.

She shook her head. 'I'm sorry, I can't talk about this right now. I have too many other things to think about. And we have Grandma's birthday this weekend and—' Her voice drifted off.

'We're sixteen,' Hannah muttered. 'We're going to be seventeen this December. We're old enough to be trusted.'

Don't say that, Kathryn thought. *Don't tell me you're nearly seventeen. You're still babies, children who need me. And don't question what I say.* She could so clearly remember Morrie once saying to her that she needn't worry about her children when they were tucked up safely in the bedroom next to hers. 'Wait till they're older and you don't know where they are, or what time they'll be home,' he had joked. But he hadn't understood the enormity of those words. What she feared most was the girls growing up and not being able to have any control over them anymore.

'Leave it,' Kathryn said as calmly as she could. 'Please just leave it.' Standing up, she started clearing away the dishes, signalling the end of the conversation. 'I hope you have both remembered Grandma's birthday present,' she added as she left the room and went into the kitchen.

The air was thinning and she needed to grab onto the counter to steady herself as she moved to the sink. She couldn't go through it all again as she had all those years ago: she didn't have the strength. Scrubbing hard at a pan, Kathryn tried to shake off the thought that she was losing another piece of control, only this time she had no clue as to what to do about it.

– Six –

Dear Adam,

There were things that happened, Adam. There were secrets in our family so tightly compressed into concealed packages that sometimes I forgot what the truth was. They taught me to lie, but I never wanted to do so with you. I never intended to, but still I did.

For three years and ten months we were blissfully happy and I thought nothing was going to ruin that. We had married in a registry office in Scotland, a quiet ceremony with only your parents there. It was the happiest day of my life. I was so grateful you easily accepted that I didn't want a big wedding even though I had a feeling you would have liked one. We spent lazy holidays in Greece and Italy, reading books and dozing in hammocks. Our weekends were taken up with long brunches, afternoons wandering around museums or seeing your friends. Life was pretty close to being perfect.

But then one Saturday morning I woke to see you grinning at me like an excited little boy.

'Let's do it,' you said. 'Let's try for a baby.'

My heart stopped.

'What?' I sat up, pushing the pillows behind my back and stared at you. 'What do you mean? We've never spoken about babies before.'

'No, I know.' You were still grinning. 'But it's obviously something I've always wanted. And I think, why not now? Everything's going so well for us. Things couldn't be better.'

Yes, I wanted to say. Everything was going so well for us so why spoil it by talking about having babies? And was it that obvious you'd always wanted them? It certainly wasn't to me.

Your face was so full of hope and excitement. I knew if I told you I didn't want children it would shatter you and I couldn't do that. I had promised you I would do anything to make you happy, because that was all you had ever done for me. But this was not on my radar. The thought of trying for a baby left me cold. I kissed you on the forehead and told you I was going for a shower. 'OK,' you said as I got out of bed and walked to the door. 'I love you, Abi. I'm so happy right now. I can't believe we haven't done anything about this before.' I let the cold water wash over my body as I fought with the dilemma of staying true to myself or giving the man I loved what he wanted.

*****

One year later you were getting ready to go back to work after the Christmas break. It was January 7th, 2013, the day after your thirtieth birthday. You looked tired and I noticed for the first time lines appearing around your eyes. They weren't sparkling with life as they usually were. 'Didn't you sleep well?' I asked.

'Not really.' You shook your head. 'I've been thinking we should go and see someone, a fertility doctor. A girl at work was talking about this guy, Dr Richards. She said he's really good.'

'Oh?' I really didn't want us to go down that route and so I tried to play down the idea.

'You don't sound keen,' you said.

'I think we should give it another couple of months,' I said. 'I don't know if I like the thought of seeing a doctor yet.'

You smiled in return and said, 'OK,' but I could tell you were getting impatient.

Then three days later you came home from work and told me you had booked us an appointment. 'I know you said not yet, but he's the best guy around,' you beamed. 'We're lucky to get in so quickly. He has a cancellation for next week and I said we'll take it. I don't see the point of waiting any longer, do you, Abs?' Suddenly life had returned to your eyes.

'I don't understand how it's so soon,' I said. 'Isn't there a waiting list or something?'

'What's the point in not going private if you can afford it?' you replied. You rarely used money as a solution but I hated it whenever you did.

I felt my body tense with annoyance. 'There's plenty of other things we should be spending the money on,' I said. 'The car needs a service and we could do with a new dishwasher. That one barely gets the dishes clean anymore. I'm forever taking dirty bowls out, still caked in porridge.'

You grinned and grabbed my arms, 'Abi, I will buy you a new dishwasher if that's what your heart desires. But we can afford this, too.' You kissed me on the forehead, still grinning at me foolishly.

I should have said no to you there and then but I couldn't. Your face was lit up like it was Christmas morning. You thought Dr Richards would be the answer to our problems. So I went along with your plan until the morning of our appointment, when I tried to cancel it. I was at work and hadn't concentrated on anything for two hours. Lucy asked me if I was ill but I couldn't tell her I was sick to the stomach with nerves. She would want to know why, and no one knew that.

Instead I called Dr Richards' office and spoke to the receptionist – I was going to tell you they had cancelled us. 'I'm afraid I can't do anything without speaking to Adam Lewis,' she told me. 'He's the one who's booked and paid for the appointment,' she added. 'Plus he said it was urgent when he called last week and I've done everything I can to squeeze you in. If you really need to cancel I won't be able to refund your money.'

I hung up. You'd told me they had a cancellation. You'd lied to me but I couldn't say anything because then you'd wonder how I knew the truth. I had no option but to show up as planned.

I didn't eat anything all day and felt empty and nauseous in the waiting room. I saw you glance at me when I refused a cappuccino out of their posh machine, but you didn't say anything. When Dr Richards appeared at the door of his room and called our names I froze. 'Don't be nervous,' he smiled, flashing his bright white teeth at me. He was older than I expected. The flecks of grey in his hair and the creases on his face were oddly comforting.

He stood aside and gestured us into his office, where a real oak desk and cream leather sofas dominated the room. Oil paintings hung on the French-grey walls and a fireplace was stacked with logs on the far side. It all spoke money and I flashed you a look to let you know I wasn't happy.

'So, what's brought you here?' he asked, looking at me. I wanted to say, what do you think has brought us here? I would have thought that was obvious, us being in a fertility clinic. But I didn't say anything; I couldn't articulate myself. And when the silence was too much you jumped in.

'We wanted to talk to you about the fact we've been trying for a baby, but it hasn't happened for us,' you explained clearly. 'We're worried that something's wrong and if it is, we want to know what that might be so we can do something about it.'

Dr Richards nodded and continued to smile but he kept looking at me, like he assumed I was the one who wanted this appointment.

He leaned forward in his chair and placed his elbows on the desk, resting his chin on his thumbs. 'And how long have you been trying?' he asked me. When still I didn't answer I watched him slowly move his gaze to you.

'Just over a year,' you told him.

He nodded again and asked more questions, about our general health, pressures at work, and whether either of us considered ourselves to be stressed, even how often we had sex. I swam in and out of the conversation. He asked more and more questions and each one you answered succinctly. Occasionally he glanced at me, probably to check I was still alive. I still hadn't spoken and it crossed my mind to get up and walk out of the room – leave the adults to discuss why we hadn't yet managed to conceive a child.

At one point everything became blurred and I thought I might faint. I've never fainted in my life and don't know why I thought I might have done so then, but the room was spinning and I was suddenly unbearably hot and dizzy. That's when I noticed you both looking at me. I was busy fanning myself with a leaflet I had taken from his desk and hadn't heard what had last been said, but you were obviously waiting for me to answer.

'I was just asking how you feel about all this?' Dr Richards prompted, still smiling. 'We haven't heard from you yet.' His eyebrows furrowed and he looked at me seriously. 'Can I get you a glass of water?'

I shook my head and still you waited.

'I don't know,' was all I could think of saying. 'How I feel about it, I mean.'

If you were annoyed with me you didn't show it.

His bright, wide smile was slowly fading. We have a strange one here, he must have thought. He'd probably seen nothing like it before: a woman who had no idea what she thought about not getting pregnant.

I knew he wanted more and I wanted to say something that would satisfy you both so the attention would be taken off me. I could feel the heat of you sitting next to me. You were shuffling in your chair and I didn't want to let you down any more than I already was. 'I guess I feel the same as Adam,' I spluttered, hoping this would suffice, but of course it didn't.

Dr Richards' smile had disappeared by then. You grabbed my hand and gave it a squeeze in a show of solidarity. Did you think this is just Abi being Abi? Whenever you took me to your office Christmas dinners I would stand in front of the latest person to be introduced to me, trying to figure out something amusing or intelligent to say. By the time I had thought of it the topic had moved on. You would then sling an arm over my shoulder and say, 'Did you know Abi works for an ad agency? Joan, isn't that the same as your husband?' And then Joan or whoever was left to make conversation with me would turn and ask me something I could happily answer. You always had a knack for filling my silences.

Dr Richards had seen more than nerves, though. At the end of our allotted time he said, 'Abi, I'd like you to come and visit me on your own, if you would be happy to?' The smile had sprung back. 'Maybe next week?'

'Is that necessary?' you asked, shuffling forward so you were a barrier between him and me. You knew it would be the last thing I'd want to do.

'Not if Abi doesn't want to, but I'd like to have the chance to chat with her on her own,' he said. 'If that's OK, Abi?'

I nodded because more than anything I couldn't find the right way to say no.

'Adam put Dr Richards on a pedestal,' I later told Maggie. And you did, didn't you? You were buzzing when we left his clinic that day. 'It's going to happen,' you kept saying to me. 'I can feel it, I really think he can do something for us.' You leaned over and squeezed my arm. 'Sharon at work was saying that as soon as she and her husband saw him he started them on this treatment and it took just three months before she fell pregnant.'

You were so wrapped up in the bubble of prospective parenthood you couldn't see what was going on right in front of your eyes.

– Seven –

Hannah sat on the back seat of her mother's car idly drumming her fingertips against the window. She could sense Lauren staring at her and knew she was irritating her sister, but she was bored and irritated herself. She wanted her mother to hurry up so they could get the day over with as quickly as possible.

'Will you stop doing that?' Lauren hissed. 'It's so annoying!'

Hannah tapped again, louder this time before stopping and turning to face her. 'What's that you're reading anyway?' she asked, nodding at the book Lauren held in her lap.

Lauren turned it over to show Hannah the cover. 'It's about a boy who's deformed.'

'Sounds uplifting.'

Lauren rolled her eyes. 'It is actually, you should read more.'

'Where is she?' Hannah asked, looking past her sister and towards the house. 'Why's she taking so long to get out when she told us to be ready ten minutes ago?'

'I've no idea, probably stressing about forgetting something.'

'We're only going for the day, it's not like it matters if she does,' Hannah sighed.

'Well, you know that doesn't make any difference,' Lauren said, turning back to her book.

'At last,' Hannah muttered when Kathryn appeared in the

doorway. She clicked her seat belt into place. 'And can you imagine how slowly she's going to drive with that bloody cake on the front seat? It'll take us a lifetime to get there.'

Lauren stifled a giggle as their mother opened her door to the car and peered at her daughters in the back. 'What's so funny?' she asked. 'And have you both got everything? I don't want to turn back at the end of the street because one of you needs to go home for something.'

'Mum,' Lauren interrupted, 'we have everything. Please, let's just go.'

Kathryn slid into the driver's seat and looked at them in the rear-view mirror. 'And have you got your presents for Grandma?'

'Oh yes, indeed we do,' Hannah smiled back, shaking the box of Quality Street she'd grabbed at the store that morning. The hint of sarcasm was lost on Kathryn, who had by then turned her attention to checking the lid of the cake box.

'Maybe one of you should come and sit upfront and hold this instead,' she suggested, fiddling with its catches. 'If I brake suddenly the whole thing will go flying into the windscreen and be ruined.'

'It'll be fine,' Lauren sighed. 'Put the seat belt round it if you're concerned.'

'No, you're right,' Kathryn sighed, turning the ignition and jamming the gearstick into first gear. 'I'm sure it'll be fine.'

Hannah shook her head at her sister and mouthed, 'Oh, my God!'

Lauren smiled, turning back to her book. It was going to be a long day.

Hannah always dreaded visiting her grandmother. Even when they were young, staying with their grandparents had not been the treasured experience it should have. As soon as her mum mentioned spending the school holidays at Grandma's large, rambling house in Yorkshire, Hannah felt sick. She hated Lordavale House, where the days dragged and the nights lasted forever.

Lordavale was the type of place where you might expect to bump into the Famous Five: long corridors and hidden passageways, a multitude of rooms behind closed doors. It all gave the impression of being the perfect spot for childhood adventures, with lots of places to hide and things to explore. If anyone other than Charles and Eleanor had lived there, Hannah and Lauren would have loved it.

The house was a former boarding school, a notion that always seemed so apt to Hannah. She often wondered if they had left Grandma behind when it closed down. Eleanor perfectly fitted the bill for an old school mistress, pounding her cane on the stone floor for attention, sending the girls to bed without their supper if they spoke out of turn. Instead of being exciting, the house felt eerie. Many a night the sisters had huddled together in one of the single beds, imagining they could hear the voices of small children calling out to them from the eaves.

There were no toys at Lordavale except for an old doll's house. Three storeys high with nine rooms, each one was as meticulously furnished as the next. 'This was mine when I was a little girl,' their mum once told them, as she peered into one of the miniature bedrooms, brushing trembling fingers gently over a tiny bed. At that moment Hannah had thrust Barbie onto the roof and Kathryn let out a yelp, pulling it away.

'No, just be careful, this isn't a—'

Hannah could still remember how her mother had stopped herself from finishing the sentence.

'Isn't a what, Mummy?' Lauren asked repeatedly. 'Isn't a *what*?'

'Isn't a toy,' Kathryn murmured, staring at the house. Then, when their grandma's voice boomed that lunch was served, she had ushered them out of the room, closing the door behind them. They never saw the doll's house again.

Lordavale boasted a drawing room. Eleanor took great pride in declaring they would have tea in the *draaawing room* whenever guests appeared, elongating the word to sound more impressive. It always made them giggle. Once the guests had seen them and admired their pretty dresses, the girls were shooed to another part of the house and they would run off laughing and whispering *draaawing room* to one another.

In hindsight Hannah could appreciate the room's beauty. Mahogany panelled walls surrounded a wide open fireplace, big enough for Hannah and Lauren to hide inside when they were younger. It had a stone wall at the back and all the trimmings you would expect to see: the iron guard and pokers sticking out of a pot to the side. Leaded windows hung almost floor to ceiling, overlooking the large Koi pond in the garden. But the room was spoiled. When Hannah closed her eyes she could still see the oversized oil painting of Eleanor sat regally in a deep blue velvet chair, hanging above the fireplace. From that painting Eleanor's eyes watched her, burning into her, her gaze following her every move; ready to pounce if she did something wrong. As a child the painting had freaked her out and she couldn't understand why no one else seemed as bothered by it as she was.

But Eleanor didn't only dominate the drawing room: paintings and photographs of her adorned many of the walls and side tables around the house. They were mostly portraits of a younger Eleanor in the days before she had that hideous scar running down her left cheek, which must have been before the girls were born because they always remembered it, her face so layered in powder trying to conceal it.

'She needs to be able to see everything we do,' Hannah once whispered to Lauren as they edged past her pictures and up the staircase. 'Like she's omnipotent.'

'Omni*present*,' Lauren had murmured back. 'Omnipotent means she is all-powerful.'

'Exactly,' Hannah sighed. 'That's exactly what she thinks she is.'

Eleanor certainly seemed to exert a power over their mum. Hannah could remember clearly how, during their visits to Lordavale, Kathryn seemed to become someone else, almost as if she wasn't their mother at all. Even to a child the difference was apparent. When they were on the beach and it was just the three of them, Kathryn would laugh and hug them and play games. She only told them off if they went out of her sight, telling them never to go where she couldn't see them. But at Lordavale she was different: she didn't smile, she didn't laugh, she just drifted around the house like a ghost. It always used to take her a couple of days to settle once they had returned to the Bay, and then she was back to her normal self again. Or at least as normal as Kathryn ever was, Hannah thought now.

Nowadays Kathryn didn't smile as much. More and more she was morphing into a ghost mother, one whose face was plastered into an uptight expression, always looking as if she expected something to jump out and bite her. On the days when they visited Grandma now, she would apply a jolly appearance, almost in contrast to the way she used to be on visits when Hannah and Lauren were children. But the act didn't fool Hannah. She could see that beneath the fake smile and shrill laugh the nurses would see later, her mum wasn't comfortable visiting Eleanor any more than she herself had ever been.

If her grandmother was once all-powerful, she should see herself now for she was a far cry from being lady of the manor anymore. And she was far from present in her own mind, let alone anywhere else.

Once upon a time Eleanor had been a glamorous woman. She was tall and held herself so upright the girls used to imagine there was a pole attached to her back. They rarely saw her without make-up, her eyelids coated in a steely grey powder and a thick layer of red painted onto her lips. Her hair was always set into a position that never moved and a string of pearls hung around her neck, sticking out where they caught the sharp points of her collarbone. Eleanor had never looked like a grandma, or even an old woman. Always she was immaculately presented to the outside world. But since she had been in the home they had watched everything that had ever made her elegant rapidly ebb away.

*****

The sound of her mother's fingers tapping against the steering wheel in a monotonous drum was beginning to grate. Since the start of the journey, when Kathryn was fretting about everything, she hadn't spoken a word. Her eyes remained focused on the road ahead, her rigid body arched forward as if prepared for an animal to spring out in front of the car. Occasionally she glanced towards the cake but then her head would snap back into position. Refocused. It was hard to imagine what she was thinking about. Aside from the obvious – worrying about her own mother's ailing health, worrying the girls might do something outrageous like want to go on a date, or come home past ten at night. Aside from all that, it was almost impossible for Hannah to guess what went on inside Kathryn's head.

Only that morning Lauren had asked her if she was OK and how she felt about visiting Grandma. Kathryn had swung around, a U-shaped smile glued to her face, and said, 'I'm fine, why wouldn't I be?'

'But Mum, you must be wondering how she's going to be today or—'

'Oh, nonsense! Of course not, I'm looking forward to seeing her,' she murmured cheerfully. 'Now, where is your present for her, Lauren?'

'It's right here,' Lauren muttered.

Hannah wanted to shake some sense into her. Anyone with half a brain could see she wasn't looking forward to it. If only she would tell them how she really felt about Eleanor maybe they would get somewhere close towards knowing what made her tick. Was Kathryn scared Eleanor was ill and might die? Was she angry that she was no longer the mother she used to be? Did she even like her? Hannah wished she would stop wasting time trying to shield them from everything and be honest. She was so busy building up barriers, she wasn't letting the girls get close to her.

But denial was a happy place where their mother lived. The day she told the girls their grandma was moving into a home, she wrapped the news up in shiny paper and added a bow to the top – 'It will be lovely for her, lots of other people her age to befriend and play Scrabble with.' They had never seen their grandma play Scrabble in her life. Why she would want to take it up in a nursing home was anyone's guess. At first the girls thought their mother was acting that way for their sake, to protect them from knowing the truth, but now Hannah considered it was more likely she simply hadn't accepted it.

Kathryn could be so childlike in her ways, and the way she idolised Grandma was odd. On nights when they were staying at her house, the girls would sit on the marble landing where the double stairways met and listen. Hanging their legs through the balustrade they could hear Eleanor chipping away at their mum below. 'I would never allow those girls to do half the things they do if they were my children,' she once said. 'Running around the halls, screeching. And they have no manners.'

'They do have manners, Mother. It's just children these days aren't the same as when I was younger.'

'Nonsense! It's you, you're too weak with them. You let them run all over you. If you aren't careful, you know what will happen.'

The girls had looked at each other and shrugged. They had no idea what might happen but they didn't like the threat in Eleanor's voice. Hannah reached over and squeezed Lauren's hand and they tiptoed back to their beds, desperate to hide beneath the covers and shield themselves from her. She sent fear running through them, and Hannah hated that their mum allowed it.

Shuddering at the memory she put her headphones on. Grandma wasn't a threat to them anymore. In an attempt to zone out for the rest of the journey to Elms Home, Hannah focused instead on what she wanted out of the summer, mentally listing: Leave the Bay; Look for my dad.

She glanced at Lauren, who was still engrossed in her book, and wondered how her sister appeared to switch off. Lauren didn't like Eleanor any more than Hannah, but she never wound herself up to the same extent. 'Lauren is much more placid,' she once heard her grandmother remark to an afternoon guest at Lordavale. 'Hannah is the fiery one.' She preferred the notion of having fire running through her veins – it meant she was likely to do something with her life. She wouldn't settle for Mull Bay for the rest of her days, as her mother hoped she would.

*****

'Here we are, girls!' Kathryn sang out as they turned into the sweeping driveway.

Elms Home was a beautiful house, too good for Grandma, Hannah always thought whenever they drove slowly through the gated entrance and over the speed bumps. They got out of the car and waited for their mum to carefully lift the birthday cake from the passenger seat. It wasn't a homemade cake but purchased from a bakery the day before. Hannah was grateful they hadn't been made to invest an afternoon up to their elbows in flour but she wouldn't have been surprised if the cake was passed off to the nurses as one of their own: little things like that showed more love and care. Apparently.

'Come on then, let's go in.' Kathryn smiled at the girls and then up at the building. 'I expect Grandma is waiting for us all,' she added wistfully, the words catching ever so slightly in her breath.

Hannah glanced at Lauren, who shrugged in return. Both knew their grandmother would be doing nothing of the sort.

At the door they were greeted by Patricia, the nurse in charge of Eleanor. In her fifties, she looked every bit the cliché of a matron. If she hadn't chosen to be a nurse, then one way or another a nursing home would have found its way to her. She was always delighted to see the girls, bombarding them with questions about what they were up to. Hannah often wondered what bad things Patricia must have done in a past life to end up looking after Eleanor.

'Here come the girls!' she called from the doorway, her face beaming. 'How lovely to see you all, good journey?'

'Wonderful, thank you,' Kathryn beamed back.

Hannah and Lauren both stepped forward, allowing Patricia to kiss them on the cheek. 'And how are my favourite twins today?' she asked. 'You look more alike every time I see you.'

Kathryn carried on grinning inanely as she prodded the girls into the hallway. 'Where is Mother today?' she asked.

'She's in the living room.' Patricia nodded towards the doors at the far end. 'We have the patio doors open in there as it's such a lovely day. You can take her through to the garden later, if you'd like.'

'Oh, that would be lovely, girls, wouldn't it?' Kathryn exclaimed enthusiastically, walking towards the lounge. 'Oh yes, I can see her already. Look, there she is, by the window. And could we have some plates, please?' She turned to Patricia. 'I've made a cake for Mother.'

Patricia nodded. 'I've even laid out some games to play, if anyone's up for it,' she called out behind her as she retreated to the kitchen.

'Oh, that sounds perfect, doesn't it?' Kathryn said.

'Yes, a perfect little birthday party for the old witch,' Hannah muttered under her breath.

Eleanor had her back to them as they entered the living room. An apt way for her to greet them, Hannah considered.

'Hello, Mother,' Kathryn called out as she walked around to face her. 'Happy birthday! We've brought you some gifts and a cake, look.'

Hannah and Lauren shuffled alongside their mother and Hannah held her breath as she waited for the inevitable. It was hard to know what Kathryn expected because she always looked so foolishly hopeful.

Eleanor held her gaze, looking out beyond them into the gardens as if not even aware of their arrival. When finally she moved her head she stared at each of them in turn, not smiling, her face registering no emotion at all.

'Who are you?' she asked eventually, fixing her focus on Kathryn.

Hannah and Lauren both turned to their mum, who continued smiling. *How brave*, anyone else would think. *What a strong woman*. But neither of them missed the signs: the sharp intake of breath, the hand gripping the side of the chair Eleanor sat in, the eyes clouding and blinking hard.

'There must be a ton of emotions boiling up inside her,' Lauren confided in Hannah later. 'I would just want to scream if I was Mum.'

'Yet she never does,' Hannah observed, which always made her wonder what might happen when those emotions eventually boiled over.

– Eight –

The morning it was confirmed to Kathryn that her mother had Alzheimer's was one blustery autumn day the previous October. She remembered it well because she had gone to the home on her own that time. The girls were at school, and Joanne Potts, Elms Home's manager, had called her the day before, asking to see her. It was important, she told her, and it would be better if Kathryn could make it that week.

Kathryn made a point of murmuring and flicking through her diary but eventually said, 'I suppose I could move a few things around and come tomorrow, if that suits?' They agreed a time and Kathryn wrote the appointment onto the blank page. She kept her voice light as she said goodbye; she didn't want them thinking she was unduly concerned, but meanwhile her insides were doing somersaults. Of course she knew what was coming.

At the end of the visit Kathryn closed the door to the home behind her. Her face was the blank canvas it had been when she arrived an hour earlier. As she walked towards her car, the gravel crunching beneath her feet, the wind suddenly picked up and leaves whipped around her as if in some kind of frenzy. Kathryn stood still and held her arms out to her sides; she lifted her face to the sky and let the world spin around her. The whole scene seemed quite fitting and she was almost comforted by it. It felt as if the universe was balanced, the turmoil inside her mother's brain was recreated outside. But on the other hand, she realised how great her own sense of turmoil was becoming, because if her mother was no longer able to command her, she had absolutely no idea what direction she should be heading in.

The nurses hadn't understood her analogy about the universe. They appeared anxious when they came out to check on her. Twenty minutes they said she was standing there, without moving. Of course it hadn't been that long. They were always exaggerating.

'Are you sure you're OK, Kathryn?' they asked, their faces perfecting a look of concern. 'Do you want to come back inside for a moment?'

'I'm fine,' she insisted. 'I'm perfectly fine.'

But of course she wasn't fine. How foolish of them to even ask. She didn't trust the nurses who worked there, particularly Patricia, who always seemed far too happy and too interested in their lives for her liking. She also didn't like the way they treated her mother, like a child who didn't know her own mind.

*****

The night of Eleanor's birthday, once both the girls had gone to bed, Kathryn sat on the stone seat at the end of her back garden and took a cigarette out of its packet. Her thin fingers shook as she held onto it, placing it between her lips as she fumbled to flick the lighter with her other hand. Once lit, she drew a deep breath, inhaling the smoke, and for the first time that day felt like she could breathe again. She wished she could relive that feeling she had had last autumn. The universe no longer felt balanced. Every day that passed meant another fragment of Eleanor's mind was chipped away. Lost for ever. It didn't make sense that a mind, once so strong, could end up like that.

Eleanor's birthday was a particularly difficult visit. Her own mother not recognising her – she might as well have risen from her chair and kicked Kathryn in the stomach. A small part of Kathryn wished she had let her guard down, even for that one moment. It would have been such a relief to scream, 'What the hell do you mean, asking who I am? I'm your daughter, who has visited you every week since you've been in this home!' Or even to cry and let someone else pick her up and carry her off, tell her everything was of course going to be OK and this was what they were going to do about it. But she hadn't done either of those things. Instead she had stood there smiling back at her mother like an idiot, like it was the most obvious question in the world to be asked, and it didn't bother her one bit.

Why did she do that? It was a question that had been asked of her over the years. Why did she let her mother turn her into a shadow of the woman she could be? They told her she was foolish, some of them, that she was weak. They told her many things. But no one knew Eleanor like she did.

Some days were easier; some days her mother knew who Kathryn was. Some days they held conversations, although increasingly they were about trivial and irrelevant things. Like the one they had had a month ago when Kathryn asked her advice about whether or not she should let Lauren go out in her friend's car. The girl had only passed her test three weeks before and it was blindingly obvious to her that Lauren shouldn't go anywhere near it. But still she wanted to do the right thing, to make sure she wasn't alienating her daughters by giving them some freedom. As always, Kathryn had driven to the home with hope in her heart. Hope that Eleanor would be communicative. And at first it had seemed like she was going to be. But no sooner had she asked her opinion than Eleanor began talking about Maureen, who, by all accounts, had worn the same shoes for so many months she had worn holes in the bottom of them. And no one was doing anything about it.

'Who is Maureen, Mother?' Kathryn asked patiently.

Eleanor shrugged. 'What does it matter anyway?' she sighed.

What did any of it matter? Long gone were the days when Eleanor told Kathryn what she should do. Her mother had always been her pillar of strength and decision. Even when she was little, people had laughed and said that one day she would need to be surgically removed from Eleanor's skirt tails. But they didn't understand that if you had a mother like that, there was little you could do about it even if you wanted to.

Wrapping the lighter into a handkerchief, Kathryn tucked it back in her dressing gown pocket. She finished her cigarette and stubbed out the end on the stone beside her, folding a tissue around the butt before throwing it in the bin. Lifting her hands to her nose, she grimaced at the smell because actually the thought of smoking disgusted her. *It's a horrible habit*, she drummed into the girls. They knew well enough there would be consequences if she caught either of them with cigarettes.

Kathryn went into the house and scrubbed her hands with vigour until the scent of rose and jasmine almost masked that of stale smoke. It would be her last, she decided, her thumb rubbing against the lighter in her pocket. It would be best just to throw the whole damn lot away, she could deal with things some other way. But Kathryn had never been much good at dealing with anything.

But she had been feeling better and the searing burn of anxiety that shot through her stomach like a knife had all but gone. Then she started to feel its familiar sting once again. The morning after that blustery day she awoke with a sense of unease and it had since rarely left her side. Nowadays nearly every morning she woke with a feeling things were slightly off-kilter. It was never a good thing, to start the day with a sense of dread.

Now Kathryn felt exposed to the world again. She had never had to worry about thinking for herself because Eleanor always did it for her. To the point where she was happy for her to do so because from an early age she had realised her opinions counted for little anyway.

'I'm thinking of becoming a nurse,' Kathryn had said when she was twelve.

'Don't be ridiculous,' Eleanor snapped. 'You would never make a good nurse; you need to have more backbone. I could cut my hand right here and you would run away, screaming.' She had held up her right hand and made an action of slicing it with the other.

Kathryn returned to her bedroom and crossed off 'nurse' from her list. Of course her mother was probably right. She didn't really think she would relish the sight of blood, although she couldn't remember ever seeing much.

And so that was the way it always was. Kathryn made a suggestion and if Eleanor didn't agree, she accepted it. What was the point in fighting someone who was always going to win?

But it wasn't like that any longer. Eleanor could no longer even tell her what time of day it was and so suddenly Kathryn felt like she was facing the world and all its problems on her own. She had a future she was uncertain how to handle and a past she constantly feared would catch up with her. Being so exposed meant having to answer her own questions – like Abigail. That was one that kept cropping up lately. Images of Abigail were taunting Kathryn, and it scared her. Now her mother couldn't give her the answer. Every time she saw Abigail's face she found herself asking, 'What have I done? What if I didn't do the right thing because I never properly thought about it?'

And no one answered her.

*****

Kathryn jumped when the phone rang, in turn burning her finger on the edge of the pan. She had been boiling milk on the hob to make hot chocolate.

'Hello,' she answered, glancing at the clock, wondering who could be calling so late.

'Kathryn, it's only me,' Morrie said. 'I'm sorry it's late but we have a situation at the beach. Some youths came by tonight and dumped bottles and rubbish all over the place. It's disgusting down here. I was wondering if the girls could come by tomorrow, we need helpers to clear up the mess.'

'Of course,' she said, running her finger under cold water and shaking her hand to ease the pain. 'I'm sure they'd be more than happy to.'

'How did it go today?' Morrie asked. 'I bumped into Hannah this morning and she told me it's Eleanor's birthday.'

'It was fine,' Kathryn sighed.

'OK, well, you know where I am. You know, if ever you want anything.'

'Thanks, Morrie, I'd better go. I'll send the girls down first thing.'

Kathryn hung up the phone and went back to stirring the milk, scooping the skin off the top with a wooden spoon and laying it over the side of the pan.

Dear Morrie, she thought. Sometimes her heart was bursting to tell someone what was really on her mind and if she ever chose to, it would be him. He had known her and the girls since they moved to the Bay in 2001. The first time she saw him he was trawling a net of fish out of a boat, just one of the local fishermen. He was only nine years older than her, but his weathered face made him look much older. She couldn't believe it when someone told her his age. After that she saw him occasionally, whenever they were near the beach. He waved at them if they passed by, and smiled at the girls when they were toddling about on the sand, but nothing more than that.

She couldn't even remember if she had spoken to Morrie before a time, almost a year later, when she had taken the girls to collect shells on the beach. It was early spring and the sun was shining brightly. They stopped by the huts and Hannah was poking a rockpool with a net.

'Don't disturb the fishes,' Kathryn told her daughter.

It felt like a matter of seconds that she had taken her eyes off Lauren, focusing instead on Hannah's unsteady jabbing, but in that short time Lauren had wandered off and was climbing over the rocks at the edge of the Bay.

'Lauren, come back now!' Kathryn called, spotting Lauren's head bobbing up above the rocks. But the small child carried on clambering until she slipped and lost her balance. Now Kathryn could no longer see her, she could only hear her cries.

'Lauren!' she shouted out in fear. 'Lauren, where are you?'

Morrie had heard her cry and had run along the beach and straight for the rocks. He climbed them with swift confidence until he reached Lauren and carried her back to Kathryn.

'She's not hurt,' he told her, handing Lauren over, 'maybe just a bit shocked. Although not as much as you, by the look of it.'

That evening he had come by the house to see how they were all doing.

'You could have got to her,' he told her kindly. 'She wasn't in any danger.'

'That's good.'

'Was it just that you were frightened?'

'I can't swim,' Kathryn admitted.

Morrie smiled. 'You're going to have to learn if you're to live in the Bay,' he said. 'And the girls must, for sure. I can teach them if you like?'

And Morrie stayed true to his word. He took the girls under his wing and made them into waterbabies. But Kathryn never set foot in the water. And since the girls had grown up, she barely ventured to the beach, either.

From that day on, if Kathryn needed someone to fix a leaking pipe, or put together some shelves, Morrie appeared with a grin and a toolbox. And when he was there, he played with the girls, showing them magic tricks and promising them something he would always fulfil, like taking them out on his boat.

Over the years, on occasion Kathryn allowed herself to consider the possibility of more than friendship with Morrie.

She knew he was keen – he hadn't said outright, but it was obvious he liked her. But a relationship with another man was the last thing she needed. Look where the last one had got her. She should have followed her heart then, she'd known it wasn't right. No one would fill the gap in her heart Robert had left, especially not Peter, yet she had married him anyway.

But some nights, alone in bed, she felt lonely and she would let her mind wonder what it would be like to be with a man like Morrie. With his mop of coarse grey hair and thick eyebrows, he wasn't textbook handsome. The sun had aged his skin and deep lines had set in around his eyes and mouth but he made her feel safe and he never asked anything of her.

Kathryn dismissed the thought. Even if Morrie asked her outright there were reasons why she wouldn't let anything happen. Three reasons, she counted. First, no one could get that close to her family, it was too risky. If her past ever got out … And two, there was Peter. She couldn't risk him finding out there was a new man in her life and stopping the cheques or worse still, turning up on her doorstep. But more than any of that was reason three, her mother. The comments she had made over the years, such as, 'I see that fisherman is here again. You'll have two daughters working with fish, if you're not careful.' No, Eleanor would never approve of her having a relationship with Morrie.

Three reasons that made it out of the question. And so Kathryn put the thought to the back of her mind every time. Besides, she didn't know if she could love him. Not like she had Robert.

Instead she played out in her head the conversation she could have had with Morrie that day.

'Ever since my mother was taken into the home I feel like I'm dying with her,' she started. It was something she thought about a lot recently, whether she actually was. Dying inside. She rolled the words around her mouth, savouring the way they felt. Some days it was too hard to make all the parts of her body work together as they should. All she wanted was for all of it to go away. Maybe her mother was the lucky one – she didn't have to think about anything anymore.

– Nine–

Dear Adam,

On January 5th, 1990, Kathryn took a call that changed the course of our lives forever. That day runs clearly through my mind as if I watched it on TV yesterday, the memory playing like a reel in slow motion. When anyone asks me about my dad, that day is still the first thing I remember.

My mum was in the kitchen cooking his tea. She was singing to herself and was in a good mood because he had phoned that morning to say he was coming back early from work. He had been away for three nights and she was so excited to see him, it was like he hadn't been home in weeks. She had on her favourite yellow jumper, and the pearls he had bought her for Christmas, and I could smell her perfume drifting in from the kitchen, mingling with the smells of chicken casserole.

I was happy, too – I loved seeing my daddy. I was lying on the living room carpet, drawing him a card to say 'Welcome Home'. It had three stick people on the front and flowers all around the edge, and I had been so absorbed with drawing it, I hadn't heard the telephone ringing until my mother came in to answer it. When she saw me she frowned and I knew she wouldn't be happy that I was using my felt tips near the carpet, but she didn't say anything.

She answered 'Hello?' into the receiver and I watched her, trying to guess who it was. Then she threw her hand to her mouth and slowly crumpled to the floor. Dropping the phone she shouted, 'Abigail, get your coat!' I sat there, looking at her, and she said, 'Now, Abigail, quick! We have to go to the hospital.'

'Can I wear my nurse's uniform?' I asked.

'No.'

'Oh. But—'

'I said no, now please just do as I ask and get your coat on. And your shoes, where are your shoes?'

I cried all the way to the hospital, wailing that I wanted to be a nurse. She told me to stop going on, saying she couldn't deal with my screaming. She never said why we were going. I don't even remember her telling me who was in the hospital but at some point I must have found out it was my dad.

She drove fast and every time we stopped she slammed on the brakes so hard I fell forward in my car seat. We pulled up outside the door of the hospital and she hauled me out of the back of the car. 'This is where disabled people park,' I sobbed, thinking I was being helpful. 'Look, there's the picture of the wheely chair. Daddy says we shouldn't park where—'

'There's no time,' she said.

I followed her, running through corridors and swinging doors, hanging on to her hand and trying to keep up. When we reached the place where my dad was, one of the nurses held me back as my mother pushed open the door and left me behind.

'I want to go with Mummy,' I cried.

'No, you come and have a look at what we've got in here,' the nurse said. I expected the room to open into Narnia. Instead there were a few boxes of plastic toys, dolls with matted hair and a pram with a wobbly wheel. I refused to play with any of it and sat in the corner while they offered me unwanted squash and digestive biscuits.

As soon as my mother appeared in the doorway I knew something awful had happened. Her hair was a mess, as if she had been tugging it. Black streaks ran from her eyes to her chin *and she said nothing, just looked at me, rubbing tears away with the back of her hand.*

When she held out her hand I stood up and took it and we walked back to the car in silence. I knew better than to say anything – I think I knew I didn't want to hear what she might tell me.

Once we were inside the car I eventually spoke.

'Why are you sad, Mummy?' I asked.

She clutched her hand against her mouth and threw open the door, throwing up onto the car park.

'Mummy?'

When she finally turned around, she reached out and put her hand on my knee. 'It'll be fine,' she said. 'We'll be fine, don't you worry.' As she spoke she stared at me with lifeless eyes and I could feel her whole body shaking through that hand against my leg. Even at six I knew everything was not OK and that we wouldn't be fine.

'Mummy, what's happened?'

'Your daddy had a broken heart,' she told me, 'and they weren't able to fix it.'

*****

Maggie asked me to talk about my dad today. 'I want to know how he fits into yours and Kathryn's pictures,' she said, asking me to think about all the memories I have of him. I told her it was funny but I couldn't think of my dad as a whole, more a series of events I strung together until I formed the person I thought he must have been. Of course I didn't know him for long but there are definitely bits I picture clearly.

The only issue I have is how difficult it is to remember my dad without immediately thinking of Kathryn too. The two of them went hand in hand in my childhood. I always remember them being so in love. I was sure he loved her, as much as he did me, yet now I can't imagine what a man like my dad must have seen in her.

I told Maggie I think he was a passionate man. He had a collection of classical music LPs he used to play at dinner and on Saturday mornings he took me to art galleries, where he showed me paintings of men and women, saying, 'Look at their faces, Abigail. Think how they are feeling, look how in love they are by the way they look at each other.' I later learned he met Kathryn when he was working at the Musée d'Orsay in Paris. I was so excited when you took me there just after we got engaged because it meant I could drag you around it, which you did obligingly even though I know you weren't as interested as I was.

I wonder if he would have stayed in Paris if it hadn't been for my mother. She told me once he only came back to England because she refused to live in France. Did he question what he had given up the day he returned? I sometimes heard her joke, 'Robert, you should have stayed in Paris if you don't like my cooking.'

'I gave up food for love,' he teased her back.

My grandmother used to call him a gypsy. I first overheard her say it to my mother when I was supposed to be in bed. I must have been about four or five and I hadn't heard of one before. The next morning I asked my mother what a gypsy was and she squinted her eyes at me and said, 'Where did you hear that word?'

'Grandma,' I told her.

'Were you listening in on our conversation, Abigail?' she asked. 'You know it's rude to eavesdrop.'

She never told me what a gypsy was and I forgot about it until three months later when the fair came to town. Dad was urging her to take me, saying how much I would love the lights and the music and riding the carousel.

But Kathryn was adamant she didn't want us going. 'It will be swarming with gypsies and the like,' she said. 'I don't want to spend the evening watching my bag in case one of them tries to steal it.'

I couldn't believe Eleanor must have thought Dad was a thief and I wondered if he'd stolen something of theirs. There were enough nice things for him to take, and I started imagining finding piles of my grandmother's jewellery in his bedside drawer. One night when my mother was putting me to bed I asked her if Daddy was a bad man. She looked at me, smiled and said, 'No, your daddy is the best.'

Of course in later years I knew that wasn't what Eleanor meant. She was simply letting my mother know Dad wasn't good enough for her.

Eleanor didn't see the man I saw. The father who sat with me in bed if I had a nightmare, made chicken soup if I was poorly, and rubbed calamine lotion over my body when I had chicken pox. One Christmas he spent hours making paper chains that he strung all around the house, interwoven with fairy lights, until my mother made him take them all down, saying they were a fire hazard.

*****

I think you would be the kind of father he was, Adam. I can see you gathering up a brood of children and reading them stories, running with them on the beach, and letting them tackle you to the ground over and over again with endless patience. I hope you know it was never you I doubted, I hope you know it was me.

The following week I didn't try to cancel my appointment with Dr Richards but when you left me at the door I considered running. We agreed to meet an hour later in the bar around the corner, you wished me luck, kissed me goodbye and walked away. I waited for you to disappear but you kept turning to wave at me. Did you know there was a chance I wouldn't go in? As soon as you were out of sight my foot wavered on the step of his surgery.

I had never understood people saying a switch had been flicked until that moment. I thought, Abi, it's time to stop running. So I turned and went into the waiting area, announcing my name to the sullen receptionist. Then I knew there was no turning back.

Dr Richards asked about my week and we discussed work. Then he deftly turned the conversation onto you and me. He asked me a few things I was sure you'd already told him. When did we meet? How long had we been married? How long had we been trying for a baby? I wondered if he was testing me, seeing whether our stories matched. It was almost as if he'd completely forgotten I was in the room the week before. But they were the easy questions. The hard one came next, when he asked how I felt about trying unsuccessfully for a baby. I think I just shrugged because then he asked about our relationship instead. His eyes looked through me when he spoke – I imagined him seeing right into my soul.

I told him you were the one who made me try mussels for the first time and I realised they were my new favourite thing; that for our first-year anniversary you blindfolded me and took me to the theatre, where you'd booked tickets for Miss Saigon. I told him every Christmas morning we sat in bed opening our stockings while sipping champagne and eating mince pies. And that whenever you went away with work you left me love notes hidden around the house, and you told me you loved me every single morning and every evening without fail. Just to make sure I always knew.

Actually, I didn't tell him any of those things. Not 'our' moments. In reality I think I said, 'It's good.'

The funny thing is I didn't tell him anything worth knowing until I was leaving his office.

I was surprised when my time was up. I didn't think he could have got much out of our meeting but I stood up, shook his hand and headed for the door. When I reached it, I was angry, though. I was annoyed with myself for slipping away from the truth yet again, the truth that was tearing me up inside.

I must have paused because he called my name and said, 'Are you sure there's nothing else you want to discuss with me?' He was holding my arm, not tightly, but enough to make me think he didn't want me to leave. 'I don't want to waste your money if this isn't the route you want to take. Many women don't like the thought of putting their bodies through IVF, and even if it's something your husband wants but you don't—'

'Stop,' I said. I didn't want to hear any more, especially when he was getting it so wrong. 'We aren't even trying,' I told him. 'I'm on the pill, I always have been.'

He waved his arm towards the chair and silently I sat back down again. I bowed my head towards my lap because I didn't want him to see the flush of red rising up my throat, its burn constricting me like someone's hands around my neck.

'I take it Adam doesn't know?' he asked after a moment.

The tears ran down my cheeks and I brushed them away roughly with the sleeve of my coat. I felt fraudulent crying but once I had started, I couldn't stop. I felt so guilty; I was crushing every hope you had for a family and you had no idea.

When you and I met an hour later at the bar you asked me how

I felt, meeting him on my own. I told you I hated it, that I wasn't comfortable without the security you gave me. But, strangely, that wasn't true: I felt liberated.

'Let's get something to eat,' I said, picking up a menu. 'We can talk about it tonight.' You looked at me and I knew you wanted to ask more but you didn't, and instead sat back as I called the waiter over.

But I didn't tell you the depth of my deception that night, or even the night after. In fact I didn't tell you for another month. I wanted to, Adam, more than anything. But every time I tried to find the words my mouth dried up. As soon as I thought about it, I imagined losing you and the reality slapped me in the face.

The following month, when I got my period, you looked so sad. I asked why you seemed more bothered than usual and you said, 'I don't know why, I just hoped it might be different this time.'

I knew then I couldn't drag you through another month. 'There's something I need to tell you,' I said.

*****

I paused and looked up at Maggie but she was still watching me with the same non-judgemental expression.

'Don't you think that's awful?' I said. 'Because I do. I can never forgive myself for lying to Adam.'

'I think you were probably desperate, Abi,' she said. 'I don't think you're awful.'

I didn't think you would ever understand, Adam. I couldn't contemplate bringing another life into this world. I was so frightened I would make a bad mother like the line of mothers who have gone before me, and you deserved so much more than that.

When I told you the truth you didn't react as I thought you

– 85 –

would. I expected you to get angry, not to hit me of course, but at least to hit something. It was so much worse: you remained calm. At least if you'd shouted I would have got what I deserved.

'I can't talk to you about this right now,' you said. 'I will do, but not yet.'

I watched you sling your washbag and clothes into a case.

'Where are you going?' I whispered.

You shrugged. 'Probably up to Mum and Dad's for a bit.'

'Will you tell them?'

'No.'

I followed you as you took your case down the stairs and let yourself out of the front door.

'Adam?' my voice cracked as I called after you.

You turned around and said, 'I need time, Abi. I need to work out what this means.'

When you left me that night my whole world fell apart once again. This time there were no nasty surprises, I knew I was being left. This time I knew why, and I understood I was definitely the reason.

*****

I had lost the love of my life just as my mother had all those years ago. Only hers wasn't her own doing. I think back sometimes to how it was after my daddy died, and how Kathryn must have felt. Amongst my anger and bitterness I sometimes feel a pinch of sympathy for her but it always passes quickly, when I remember something else about her. Like the time a few weeks after my dad died when I came home to find all his photographs missing. I stood in front of the wall, staring at the bright patches of paint where they once hung.

'Where's Daddy?' I asked when my mother came into the room.

'We've talked about this,' she said. 'Daddy's gone to Heaven.'

'No, he's gone from the wall,' I said.

'Oh, yes, well …' She was flustered, ushering me into the kitchen, where she pushed me onto a chair and pointed to some jam sandwiches. 'It's probably better if we put them away for now. Then we won't get sad.'

'But I still want to see Daddy,' I said, the tears splashing down my face and onto my plate. 'If I don't see him, I might forget what he looks like.'

My mother turned her back to me, busy at the sink, cups and plates clanging together. I could see her shoulders shaking but she said nothing more. I slipped off my chair and crept out of the kitchen, trawling the house for anything I could find. Eventually I found just one photo tucked inside a book: a photo of my daddy's face, smiling, tanned and happy. I ran into my room and hid it under my mattress so no one could take him away from me.

*****

Not long after that Eleanor said something to my mother. I think of it as days later but it could well have been months.

'The girl needs a father figure in her life,' she said.

My grandfather was there at the time. I didn't see Charles often; he rarely made an appearance. He was forever working away, or if he was in the house he was holed up in his office until Eleanor called him down to dinner.

'Eleanor,' he snapped, 'it's too soon.'

'I'm just saying she shouldn't let the grass grow under her feet,' she hissed back at him. 'She's almost thirty-two.'

I don't remember my mother saying anything in return. She might have protested but if she did, I didn't hear. Then Eleanor mentioned a man called Peter, who had apparently never married even though he was thirty-five, she said, making it sound like a good thing. 'Peter works for your father,' she told my mother in the tone she reserved for showing off. 'And he wants to get into politics with Charles.'

The next morning at breakfast I heard his name again.

'Charles, have you heard from Peter lately?'

I looked up at her and then at my mother, whose head hung low, looking down at the breakfast table as she slowly circled her spoon around her cereal bowl. I didn't know why but I had a funny feeling in my tummy that day. I didn't like Eleanor talking about this man even though I had no idea then how much he was going to affect my life. I waited and hoped for my mother to say no, but of course she never did.

I'm sure Kathryn can't have wanted to meet him. It was Eleanor pushing him onto us, but my mother let her. I wish I could go back to that day and shake her to life, tell her not to let him come into our lives and pull apart everything we had. Why didn't she say no, why did she let them take away the memory of my daddy so easily?

Two weeks later I came home from school to find a strange man in our kitchen.

'Abigail, this is Peter,' Kathryn said. 'He's my new friend.'

Peter was leaning back against the counter, an arm resting on it, one hand cradled around a mug of tea and the other in his trouser pocket. He had dark curly hair and wore wire-rimmed glasses and was only slightly taller than my mother. He pushed a curl away from his thin face, set down his mug and held out his hand to me. I stared at it – I was seven years old, I didn't want to shake his hand, and all I could see were hairy knuckles and spindly fingers that weren't my daddy's.

'Why?' I asked Kathryn.

'What do you mean, why?'

'Why do you want a new friend?'

She giggled nervously and said we were going to be spending quite a bit of time with him, so it would be nice if I liked him.

'What do you think? He's going to take us to the seaside tomorrow, for a day trip. That'll be fun, won't it?'

'What do you think?' she asked me again at the end of our day in Bournemouth. 'Do you think you like him?'

Peter had bought me an ice cream and paid for us to play crazy golf although he always passed on his turn, waiting with a bored expression for us to finish. We walked to the pier and he handed me a pile of cash and told me I could spend it at the amusements. I ambled into the arcade, amongst its flashing bright lights and the beep beeping of fruit machines, but I had no desire to waste the money on the slots. My daddy had never liked them – he always said they were for fools. So I pocketed the money and wandered back outside, where I saw my mum being pawed at by Peter. She was giggling again and neither of them noticed me sitting on the bench, waiting for them to finish.

So of course I didn't like him.

'He's OK,' I shrugged.

'Is that all?' she asked.

'I don't want a new daddy,' I replied.

She looked at me and took a deep breath. 'No one's going to replace your daddy,' she sighed.

My mother asked me a lot over the next couple of months: 'So, Abigail, what do you think of Peter? Do you like him?'

I have no idea why she wanted my opinion; it was obvious it counted for little.

'He's OK,' I would say. And that was all I felt: he was OK. He never once asked me what I had done at school, or what my

– 89 –

favourite subjects were. He never played a board game with me, took me to the park or sat at the table while I ate my tea. He brought me a gift occasionally but it was never anything I wanted. Often I heard him ask her when I would be going to bed. And then when I was in bed I would hear him murmuring and her tittering and I would pull the covers over my head to block out their noise.

One day she asked me again. 'What do you think of Peter, Abigail? Do you like him?'

'He's all right.'

'Oh, Abigail, he is more than all right! He is a very nice man, and he's asked me to marry him. What do you think, Abigail? Isn't that wonderful? I'll have a new husband.' She smiled at me with a tight jaw and dead eyes.

No, it wasn't wonderful. I felt sick to the pit of my stomach. My dad was all I wanted, not this new man. Not Peter who barely registered my existence. I stared at my mother and cried. And she stared right back at me. Then she shook herself and said in a very jolly voice, 'Right, fish fingers for tea?'

*****

I sometimes wonder where Peter is now. I have no idea whether or not he still lives with Kathryn and the girls, but I hope he isn't in their lives. Peter was only ever interested in one thing and that was looking after number one. I still wonder what Eleanor's reasons were for bringing him into our family.

– Ten –

The exams were over. Hannah and Lauren walked to the diner perched at the edge of the clifftop overlooking the bay. It was usual for most of the students from Year 11 upwards to go and they expected at least forty to turn up. This was an informal invitation, always arranged by someone in the final year. That year it was Donna Morton.

Donna was already at the diner when the girls arrived. Her blonde hair piled high on top of her head didn't move as she flung her arms about her while she talked. She wore a white, low-cut top with denim shorts that were probably too short but still looked good on her long, tanned legs. One of the boys leaned over to whisper something in her ear and she threw her head back and laughed loudly, her large white teeth on show. Afterwards she stole a quick glance around the diner just to check everyone was watching her.

'Oh, hello, twins!' she called out when she saw the girls entering. 'Have a mocktail,' she winked as she scooped juice from a punch bowl into plastic cups, handing one to each of them before whispering, 'If you want anything added, then go and see Becky. She's out by the barbecue.'

'I swear she doesn't know who's who,' Lauren whispered as they walked outside, into the heat of the early evening sun. 'I don't think she's ever called me by my name. If you aren't around, she just refers to me as Twin A.'

Hannah laughed. 'Well, obviously she has more in her

boobs than her brain. Did you see the size of them? She must have implants, no one's are that large naturally.'

'Sophie says she has. Apparently her dad bought them for her for her eighteenth birthday. Can you believe it?'

'Not really. That's probably just what she's told everyone.' Hannah looked around to see if she recognised anyone. 'It makes it sound like her dad is cool. Look, there's Becky.' She pointed towards the small group gathering by the barbecue area. 'What do you reckon?' she waved her plastic cup. 'Do we see what she can add to this?'

'I'm not sure.'

'Oh, come on,' Hannah tugged at her sister's arm. 'It's not as if we'll be here for long anyway. Might as well have a bit of fun while we are.'

It was the first year Hannah and Lauren could go to the end-of-exams party. Every year it took place at the diner, where parents could rest assured a watchful eye would be cast over potential underage drinkers. But every year a Donna or a Becky would manage to sneak in bottles of vodka and gin they had stolen from their parents' houses.

The party at the diner usually ended early. There was no licence to serve alcohol and no one in the Bay was keen to encourage teenagers to hang out at the beach and drink. That didn't mean there weren't those who still did, but on the whole, once they attended the sixth form, and if their parents were lenient enough to allow it, the students headed out of the Bay and into the nearest town, half an hour away.

'It's a bloody prison!' Becky was laughing as they neared her with their cups of juice. 'They could film *Big Brother* here, there are that many eyes looking at you.' Whatever she was pouring into the gathering mass of cups was coming out of a large water bottle. 'Better to be safe,' she added, holding up the bottle. 'Extra water?' she shouted loudly.

Becky was a carbon copy of Donna. Except for her dark brown hair, which she once tried to dye blonde but failed dismally, they looked like clones of each other. Becky's shorts were white, and her vest slightly less revealing, but other than that they dressed and sounded the same. And they were both as dumb as each other, Hannah thought, as she held out her cup.

'I think she's had enough *water* already,' Lauren sniggered after they had topped up their cups and were sitting down at one of the benches.

Hannah slipped her sunglasses down to cover her eyes, shifting on the seat so that she could keep one eye trained on the path leading up to the diner from the road.

'Who are you looking for?'

'No one.'

'Come on, Hannah. I'm not stupid. Is it Dominic?'

'No.' Hannah could feel the burn in her cheeks and gulped down the rest of her drink. The strength of whatever alcohol Becky had added made her gag and spit it out onto the grass in front of her. Then, just as she looked up, she saw him. Dom was walking towards them, an arm casually slung over the shoulder of one of his friends, a boy called Cal, and they were laughing. She didn't know if it was at her; she didn't think Dom would do that but then she didn't know him well enough to say for sure. They had spoken a number of times; he had always been friendly but there was never more than that, despite Hannah hoping there might be.

He nodded in her direction and saluted before disappearing into the diner with Cal.

'What a nob!' Lauren gave a suppressed laugh.

'No, he's not.'

'Oh no, Hannah is properly in love!' Lauren sighed, rolling her eyes.

'He's just so good-looking,' Hannah said. 'Don't you think?'

'No, he's not my type at all.'

'And what's your type, dear sister?'

'I don't know really. Less stereotypical, I guess,' Lauren said. 'He's too surfer dude for me.'

'You can't say a toned, tanned body isn't attractive.'

'His eyes are too close together.'

'Oh, for God's sake!'

'And I prefer dark-haired guys.'

'Like Cal maybe?'

'Jesus, no!'

They both laughed. Cal was known as a player but neither of them could understand why. He was shorter than Dom by at least a head and what he lacked in height he made up for by being loud and brash. Hannah didn't know why Dom hung out with him other than to make himself look even better.

'So tell me,' Lauren said, turning to face Hannah, 'have you been thinking any more about what you mentioned the other day?'

'Which bit?'

'Looking for our dad.'

Hannah was shocked her sister had brought the subject up. It hadn't been mentioned since the time on the beach, and she was struggling to think how she could say anything to Lauren, given her previous reaction.

'Yes,' she said, sitting forward on the bench. 'I've been writing a list of everything I know about him. Or at least everything Mum has told us, which of course we can't take as gospel.'

'OK, go ahead.'

'Really?' Hannah was excited. It was more than she could have imagined, having Lauren on board so easily.

'I'm not saying I agree with what you're doing, but I don't want to be left out either.'

'Well...' Hannah held out a hand and started counting off her fingers. 'We know his name is Peter Webb. We know he must have left us in about 2001 because that's when we came to the Bay. We don't know how old he is but guessing he's about Mum's age, then he's in his late fifties. And we think he might be in Australia.'

'Do we?'

'Well, probably not. Mum once told me that but I'm not sure I believe her. It's a bit clichéd to come up with Australia, isn't it? I think it was just the first thing that popped into her head. She didn't look as if she knew what she was talking about.'

'And is that it?'

'Yep, major stuff to go on, eh? Looks like he'll be found in no time,' Hannah added sarcastically.

'So where are you thinking of starting?' Lauren asked, sipping at her drink. 'This stuff is disgusting, I can't drink any more of it.'

Hannah reached over and tipped it into her own cup. 'It's not that bad. Anyway, I like the buzz it gives you.' She had noticed Dom coming out of the diner and watched him as he made his way to where Becky was still laughing loudly, attracting a group of students around her who wanted whatever taste of alcohol they could get their hands on.

Becky was inching away from the group and making a beeline for Dom. 'Look at the way she flicks her hair and pouts her lips at him. She's so obvious. Surely he doesn't fancy her, does he?'

'Don't all the guys? Anyway, back to us.'

Hannah sighed. 'I have to get my hands on someone's iPad. I thought of using Morrie's computer but I can't risk him telling Mum. And I tried at school but social media sites are blocked and Facebook must be the easiest place to start looking. Can you believe in this age of technology, it's nigh on impossible for you and me to search the internet?'

Kathryn had been clear she didn't want them having access to the web. 'There's too many people out there who'll pretend to be someone they aren't,' she told them. 'It's safer walking the streets than being in some chatting room.'

'Chatroom, Mum. And even thirteen-year-olds can use Facebook,' Hannah retorted.

'I don't care! They're not my daughters.'

Eventually agreeing to buy them mobile phones, Kathryn had spent ages choosing ones that didn't have access to Wi-Fi or 3G connections. Hannah had thrown the phone in her bag in disgust when she had been given it. She wasn't going to let anyone at school see she didn't have the latest iPhone – they'd be laughing stocks.

'Hey, girls!'

Hannah looked up to see Dom walking towards them, Cal slinking behind as always, trapped in his shadow. Dom was smiling directly at Hannah, a smile that heated her up, and she prayed she wasn't blushing. She took another large mouthful of her drink and, getting used to the taste, managed to swallow it without flinching.

'Do you mind if we sit with you?'

'Actually, I've just seen Sophie,' Lauren said to Hannah. 'I'm going to talk to her. I'll be back in a bit, OK? And we'll need to go soon,' she added, looking at her sister pointedly.

Hannah sidled up the bench to make room for Dom, handing Lauren's empty cup to Cal, who'd said he was going for refills.

'So, are you going into town later?' Dom asked.

Hannah shook her head. 'I doubt it,' she said. 'You?'

'I'd rather not but I imagine Cal will drag me down there later. It's a shame you're not coming, I might enjoy myself a bit more if you were there.' He smiled at Hannah and she took another gulp of her drink. Was he coming on to her? Hannah had never had a boyfriend, and she had no idea how she was expected to act.

'Maybe we could get our drinks and go for a walk on the beach instead?' he asked.

'I don't know.' Hannah felt the heat spreading down her neck. She knew she must be the colour of beetroot by now. She saw her sister with her back to her, deep in conversation with Sophie. She would have to tell Lauren if she went off with Dom, she couldn't just slip away. But if Lauren ended up going home without her then there'd be hell to pay. 'I mean, my mum's expecting us back and I don't know—' Hannah stopped, annoyed she was still letting her mother dictate what she did. Dom wouldn't be interested in someone who ran back to her mummy, not when he had Becky ready to pounce on him, given half a chance. 'OK,' she smiled. 'Let's do it.'

'Great! I'll tell Cal if he ever gets back with the drinks, but by the look of it he might be a while. I think Becky has snared him, poor guy. He's probably in his element, though I can't imagine why he would be.'

'Oh? You don't think she's pretty?'

'Becky?' he asked, turning back to look at the group, who were by now dancing and singing loudly. 'She's OK. Bit too plastic-looking for me,' he laughed.

Hannah smiled. 'I'll go and tell Lauren we're going,' she said. She knew how her sister would react and was prepared for them to fall out over it, but their arguments never lasted long. Hannah wouldn't be late and as soon as she got home that night and into bed, Lauren would be fine with her again. It was her mum who would take more careful handling, but right now all she could think about was being alone on the beach with Dom. It was a risk worth taking.

'You have to be kidding,' Lauren said. 'Mum is going to be furious. She'll probably go out looking for you.'

'Then just don't tell her where I am. Tell her I'm with Sophie, or one of the others. Please, Lauren. I promise you I won't be late. I'll only be an hour or so then I swear I'll come home.'

Lauren shook her head. 'Fine, but don't say I didn't warn you.'

*****

Hannah didn't notice how late it had got and when she looked at her watch and realised two hours had passed, she told Dom she was going to have to go. He insisted on walking her back to her house, but they stopped at the corner of the lane, where he held her face between his hands and kissed her gently on the lips, then told her that he would like to see her again if that was OK with her. Hannah hadn't been kissed before, and when she quietly closed the front door behind her, she leaned back against it and touched her lips gently: she was in love.

'What do you think you're doing?' Her mum's voice made her jump. Hannah turned and saw Kathryn sitting at the table. 'You said you'd be home at ten, and it's nearly eleven. Where have you been?'

'I didn't realise the time,' Hannah said calmly. She knew her mother was angry but she didn't care. Nothing could ruin her good mood. 'I was just talking to the others who didn't go into town, and I forgot the time.'

'Were you with a boy?'

'There were boys there.'

'Don't be smart. I'm asking if you went off with a boy, Hannah. You're too young to be doing things like that.'

'Actually I'm not, Mum. I'm perfectly old enough to have a boyfriend if I want one.' Hannah started walking up the stairs. This was getting ridiculous, she was sick of being treated like a child.

'If I find out you're lying to me—' Kathryn shouted as Hannah got to the top of the stairs and closed the bedroom door behind her.

'You'll what?' she muttered to herself. There were plenty of threats but Hannah wasn't ever sure they would come to anything. Besides, there was little her mum could do to stop her seeing Dom.

'You still awake?' she whispered to Lauren, crawling into the single bed next to her sister's.

'Just.'

'Dom's amazing,' Hannah sighed. 'I was really nervous

going down to the beach with him but he was so lovely. We did nothing but talk, it was so nice.'

'I heard Mum waiting downstairs for you,' Lauren said.

'He asked me out,' Hannah giggled. 'We're meeting up next Thursday, as soon as we break up.'

'Seriously?'

'I *know*,' Hannah giggled.

'Mum will freak, of course.'

'Of course.'

'Does she know how old he is?'

'He's only eighteen, Lauren. He's hardly a dirty old man,' Hannah sighed. 'He's gorgeous. And he's so into me, asking loads of stuff about me, like what I'm going to do after school, if I want to go to Uni. "What are your dreams?" he asked!'

'Sounds like a prick.'

'You're just jealous. Anyway, guess what? He's going to lend me his iPad. He says he'll help look for our dad. He seemed really into the idea.'

Lauren rolled over and stared at her sister. '*What*? You told him you were looking for our dad? What the hell did you do that for, Hannah? Now it's going to be all over the Bay.'

'It won't. He said he wouldn't tell anyone.'

'You're unbelievable,' Lauren said, rolling back and closing her eyes. 'Now shut up and let me get some sleep. And Mum's pissed off with you, by the way.'

'So what's new?' Hannah said, plumping the pillow beneath her and lying on her back. She lay awake for a while. There were too many exciting things to think about and suddenly the summer seemed like it was full of possibilities she hadn't imagined a week ago. With Dom's help she could find their dad. Since planning to look for him the thought of it had been burning away inside her. He was another piece of her jigsaw. Yes, she got that he left them when they were children, and she could see why Lauren might not be interested in giving him a chance, but Hannah wanted to. Because what if they had some connection she had been missing out on all her life? What if he was the parent she actually got along with? They could spend summers and Christmases together, and he could drive her to places and listen to what she was up to, and tell her to follow her dreams rather than trying to suppress them, like her mum did.

She listened to the gentle slowing of Lauren's breathing and knew when her sister had fallen asleep. Listening to her was like the familiar ticking of a clock. Hannah blew her sister a kiss, and closed her eyes. She couldn't imagine being able to sleep if Lauren wasn't in the bed next to her, but the more she dreamed of bigger things, the further she felt she was slipping away from her.

– Eleven –

There was a time when Kathryn was eight that she remembers clearly. She was walking with her mother, holding hands. It was autumn and the pavements were heavy with leaves. Brown, gold, red … Kathryn couldn't take her eyes off the colours as she watched them tumble over her shoes. Cars were swooshing past her, but she was trying to concentrate on the crunch of the leaves underfoot. It was a busy road and that was why her mother had such a tight grip on her, one that occasionally felt too tight on her hands.

'Walk carefully.' She felt a yank on her arm. But the leaves were so beautiful and she wanted to run through them and kick them high into the air. Kathryn started to skip. She was still in step with her mother, knowing not to go ahead. 'Stop it,' her mother hissed. 'Stop skipping,' her voice louder that time. Kathryn's hand was pushed away and she no longer had anyone to hold onto, no one keeping her safe, and suddenly the roar of cars was louder than the crunching of leaves. Her mother had already started walking ahead of her, and Kathryn had to run to keep up with her. Head down, she knew she was being punished by no longer having her mother's hand to hold but she couldn't understand why. Was it her happiness that annoyed Eleanor?

Lately memories were flooding back, ones she hadn't given any thought to for years. It was almost like a valve had opened up in her head and was allowing dribs and drabs of her past to seep back in when she had thought she had managed to keep them out.

Kathryn pulled the duvet off. It was too hot in the bedroom and she was sweating under the covers. It was the fourth night that week she hadn't been able to sleep and she considered asking for more tablets from Dr Morgan, although he was often reluctant. He didn't believe medication was always the answer for Kathryn and had asked her to come in and see him about some things soon. She had agreed, what harm could it do? Her old doctor was dead now and she had to get used to someone else taking care of her.

Slowly easing herself out of bed, Kathryn realised how drained she felt. All she wanted to do was get back into bed and sleep for the rest of the day. But her eyes, despite their heaviness, were wide open, as if searching for something. Her body might be telling her to sleep but her mind wasn't at rest.

Hannah hadn't come home until eleven the previous night even though she had promised she would be back by ten. Kathryn could hear her mother's voice telling her she couldn't control her own daughters. She feared Eleanor was right about that too and there was little she actually was capable of.

Knowing she wouldn't get back to sleep, Kathryn crept down the stairs and into the kitchen. She filled the kettle and sat at the breakfast table, waiting for it to boil. Her fingernails were in a state, she noticed, inspecting her hands that were splayed on the table in front of her. Bitten like a child's. She must have been absent-mindedly chewing them again. The nail on her right thumb had been gnawed so low the flesh was starting to bleed. 'Damn,' she muttered under her breath as she looked for a plaster, pulling out kitchen drawers. She knew she had bought plasters the other week, only it wasn't obvious where she had put them. Everything in her kitchen had a place. Her plasters had a place. The girls would joke about how organised it was, yet now she couldn't for the life of her think where those wretched plasters were.

The more she looked, the more aggravated Kathryn got. Heat was rising at the back of her neck, bubbling under the surface of her skin. Even in her thin nightie she felt the need to flap the top of it to cool herself down. It was all so stupid. The blood on her thumb had already dried up, but the fact she couldn't find the plasters made her determined not to stop until she did.

'Mum?'

Kathryn heard the voice but didn't stop pulling out drawers and opening cupboards. They had to be somewhere; plasters didn't just vanish.

'Mum, what are you doing?'

'I'm looking for something,' she muttered.

'What are you looking for?' Lauren asked. 'Mum!' she grabbed Kathryn's arm, causing her to swing round and face her. 'What are you looking for?'

Kathryn stopped and stared at Lauren, wondering why her daughter looked concerned. Then out of the corner of her eye saw the chaos she had created. The room was usually so pristine; if she hadn't been standing in the middle of the mess she would have assumed they'd been burgled.

'Well, who knew we had so much stuff?' Kathryn said.

Lauren stared at her in disbelief. 'It's not usually tossed around the kitchen. What were you looking for anyway?'

'A plaster,' Kathryn said, holding her thumb up.

'For what?'

'It was bleeding.'

Lauren grabbed the thumb and held it up to her eye. 'Bloody hell, Mum! I can't believe you made all this mess for that.'

'Please don't swear.'

'Have you even looked in the medicine box?' Lauren said as she started packing everything back into the open drawers.

Ah, the medicine box! Of course, that was where they would be. How silly she hadn't thought to look there.

'Yes, although only quickly,' Kathryn said. 'Don't do that, Lauren. I'll tidy this away.'

'How old is some of this? Do you throw anything away?' Lauren held up a postcard and looked at the back. Kathryn recognised the picture: Morrie had sent it from Scotland three years ago. She took the postcard out of Lauren's hand and shoved it back into the drawer.

'I said please don't worry about it, Lauren. I can tidy up.'

'Maybe we could sort through it, then you'll know where everything is.'

'I do know where everything is,' Kathryn replied. 'I don't need to sort through any of it.'

'Seriously?' Lauren asked, gathering papers and tins and boxes from the floor. 'You know what's in every one of these?'

'Paperclips, elastic bands, pens, stamps … Yes, I know what's in every one of them, Lauren. I'm not losing my mind, thank you,' she snapped.

'I didn't say you were,' Lauren sighed. 'And what about this?' she added, holding up a faded brown manila envelope that had fallen out of the back of the larder cupboard. 'What's in here?'

Kathryn's eyes widened. She hadn't seen that for years. Maybe not since they had moved to the house. It was the middle of the night when they had arrived in Mull Bay. She had taken the girls' sleeping bodies up to their room, one at a time, and laid them carefully in their beds, Lauren on the right and Hannah on the left. She could remember the night as if it were yesterday. The Bay had felt eerie, and she was alone. It had been so frightening; she had had no idea how the following day was going to pan out, let alone their whole future. Just her and the girls in a new home, where she was supposed to be spending the rest of her life, and all she could do was trust the people who'd told her to go. She couldn't believe that was fourteen years ago, and they were still living in the same cottage. Her mother had been right: things had turned out as she had said they would. Her mother was always right.

Kathryn had stuffed the envelope at the back of the cupboard that night. The girls were too young at the time to reach the top shelf of the larder cupboard, and she had always planned to move it when she found a more suitable place but had forgotten all about it. She lurched forward, reaching for the envelope as Lauren pulled her hand back.

'Uh-uh,' Lauren laughed. 'Not until you tell me what's in it.'

'Give it here now,' Kathryn demanded.

'Of course I could always have a look,' she said, pretending to peel back its seal.

'I said give it here now,' Kathryn stood up. 'That's personal and you have no right looking at it.'

'Fine,' Lauren said, handing her the envelope. 'I was only mucking about.'

Kathryn turned back to the kettle that had now boiled and poured hot water into a mug. As she did so she could feel her daughter's eyes penetrating the back of her head. She was sorry she had snapped at Lauren but now her hands were shaking and all she wanted to do was get out of the room, and be on her own.

'What are you doing up so early?' she said, but when she looked around Lauren had already gone.

With a deep sigh Kathryn finished making her mug of tea. The envelope needed a safer place, not stuffed at the back of a kitchen cupboard. It was a foolish error on her part, but she hadn't had any need for the papers inside since they'd arrived in Mull Bay. If the girls ever saw what was there, though ... A safe box was needed, she decided, climbing the stairs, back to her room. That or something else she could lock. She would get one from the hardware store that morning.

At the top of the stairs Kathryn could hear the girls talking in hushed tones behind their bedroom door. She could imagine Lauren telling Hannah about the state of the kitchen and how Kathryn had snapped at her. Hannah would be rolling her eyes in response, muttering something about how typical that was, and why hadn't she looked in the envelope; she would have.

She had always taught the girls it wasn't right to eavesdrop but they were talking so quietly, Kathryn needed to know what they were saying. Carefully treading on the carpet to miss the creaks in the floorboards, she edged closer to the door and leaned in as far as she could.

'I really wish you wouldn't,' Lauren whispered.

Silence. Then Hannah mumbled something she couldn't grasp. *This was ridiculous*, she thought, and was about to back away when she heard, 'Mum's going to find out, you know. And when she does, she'll stop you doing anything about it.'

About what?

Kathryn edged a little closer.

'She needn't know if you don't say anything,' Hannah replied.

Kathryn's eyebrows furrowed. What were her daughters talking about?

Lauren sighed. 'Of course she has to know. She'll find out at some point anyway. You're being stupid if you think you can do this without her hearing about it.'

There was silence until Lauren spoke again. 'I really wish you'd forget all about it.'

'I can't,' said Hannah. 'Now I've started thinking about it, I know it's exactly what I want to do.'

What do you want to do? Kathryn wanted to shout through the closed door. *What is this secret I'm going to hate?*

'I'm going to find our dad,' Hannah said. 'And when I do, I'm going to ask him what really happened in our past, because sometimes I have a feeling Mum isn't telling us everything.'

Kathryn froze. She would have liked to slip away to the safety of her bedroom but her legs were like lead, anchoring her feet to the carpet outside her daughters' door. *Oh no*, she thought, *this can't be happening!* Her heart was beating too fast, and clutching a hand to her chest, in turn she dropped the mug of tea, its dark brown liquid spreading across the carpet, splashing against the skirting board.

She stared at the mess. *Get a cloth*, a voice inside her screamed. *Clean it up before it stains!* Her head was pounding at the thought of Peter, though, and how there was no way she could ever let the girls find him, and all she could do was sink to the floor and watch as the fibres of her cream shag pile soaked up what was left of her tea.

– Twelve –

Dear Adam,

I shunned the idea of looking for the girls on Facebook over and over again. I knew all it might take would be a few clicks and I would see their sixteen-year-old faces looking back at me. But every time I considered the idea, I became paralysed with fear of the unknown. As soon as I saw them I'd be opening up a Pandora's box that I would never again be able to close the lid on.

At least that was how I felt until this morning when a rush of courage swept over me and before I could talk myself out of it I started searching. I typed in their names – Hannah and Lauren Webb, but nothing. I tried Eleanor's surname, Bretton. I even tried my own, Ryder. I couldn't imagine why Kathryn would change their names to my dad's but it was worth a shot. I searched the endless photos of Hannahs and Laurens around the UK but the more faces I looked at, the more I wondered if I would even recognise the girls now. Maybe I pass them on the street every day and I don't know it. Maybe they've been standing in front of me in a queue and I could have held out my arm and touched them, but I didn't see their little rosebud mouths or freckly noses in their teenage faces. I have no idea what the girls look like any more and now what I want, more than anything, is to know.

Sometimes when children go missing people do special pictures of them years later, showing what they might look like now. I want to see them, Adam. I can't bear that I have no idea what they look like any longer. The only pictures I have are in my head, of the way they looked at two years old. How would I ever recognise them now?

The night they left I opened the door to my grandmother. She was draped in a long fur coat that skimmed her ankles. It made me feel sick to look at her, no interest in what animal suffered to dress her. She nodded to the police car on the road and asked why it was parked outside our house. I told her they were inside; I said my mother had disappeared.

'Say that again,' she said slowly.

I told her again that Kathryn had gone, and the girls too. We continued to stand on the doorstep. I could hear the two police officers talking in the living room and saw Eleanor look over my shoulder and into the hallway beyond. She hesitated, then looked back at me. 'Do you know where?'

'Of course not,' I said. 'Why do you think the police are here? I'm scared,' I added suddenly, though hating to admit it to her. 'Where are they?'

She looked at me again with her hard cold eyes and then pushed me aside and strode into the house, full of purpose. I wondered what she was going to say to them, whether they would recognise her from the newspapers. I had a sudden feeling that everything would be taken out of my hands and I didn't know if that was a good thing or not.

I left my job today. Maggie asked me what I plan to do with my time and I told her if I were better qualified, I'd love to study. She said it was a great idea – many mature students were learning new crafts later in life – and asked why I thought I needed to be better qualified. I told her that I had dropped out of school at the age of seventeen with only a handful of GCSEs. I wasn't sure I was cut out to be a student.

'How many GCSEs do you have?' she asked me.

'Five,' I said. 'All grade C.'

'That's not bad, Abi.'

'Considering, you mean?'

'No, not just considering.' She paused. 'Why don't we talk about what was happening at that time, at home?' she suggested hesitantly. 'Your last couple of years at school.'

We'd touched on this time in my life twice before, a while back. But both times I'd clammed up and she hadn't brought it up since. She says she knows when I don't want to talk about things because I start biting my bottom lip. I hadn't realised I did it until one occasion when I bit so hard it bled.

To be fair, it was a miracle I managed to get five of anything. But there was a time before that when I really enjoyed school: learning excited me.

When I was thirteen our art teacher, Miss Jennings, asked us to collate a picture made from scraps of rubbish. I wanted to do it well because I was keen to get a good grade. Miss Jennings suggested I took Art as one of my options for the following year and I liked the thought of it so I made an extra effort with the collage. It became a map of the world. I carefully chose materials to represent countries. Italy's heel was filled with dried penne and the sea made out of labels from tuna and sardine cans. She gave me an A* and asked me to show it to the headmaster, who told me he was impressed with such a show of originality. I was so excited! I rarely took much home to show my mother but of course I wanted to take that.

As I approached the house I heard raised voices. I didn't often hear her and Peter arguing but that evening they were. I made a big deal about closing the front door, wanting them to know I was back so they would stop shouting, which they did. I went into the kitchen, where my mother stood by the sink with her back to me.

'Mum ...' I approached her. 'I got an A* for this at school today.'

She turned around to look at what I was holding but she wasn't smiling. She took the picture out of my hands and stared at it. I wanted to take it back – I was scared her eyes were going to burn a hole right through it.

'Huh,' Peter muttered. 'Art. That's not going to get you anywhere in life.'

He swirled his whisky around in its glass, downed it and then left the kitchen, slamming the door behind him.

My mother threw my picture down and called after him. I think she aimed for the table but it slid past it, ending up on the floor. 'Peter!' she shouted. 'Peter, don't do anything rash!' And then she was gone, running up the stairs after him.

I picked my picture off the floor and held it between my hands. I was so angry, with them and with myself for feeling like I would cry. Art might not get me anywhere – it didn't get my dad anywhere – but I wasn't going to stop because of what Peter thought. I contemplated my picture, how I had foolishly hoped it might take pride of place on the fridge. Then I ripped it up, sending the tiny pieces scattering like confetti. After that I was even more determined to do what I wanted and didn't bother taking anything else back to show my mum.

Later that year the school were holding a parent and students' evening, but Cara had got us tickets to see the Backstreet Boys on the same night. We were only thirteen but I wasn't surprised when she told me her parents didn't mind her going. They believed Cara should 'be free and explore herself'. They didn't realise she was letting half the school explore her too, and I don't think they would have been quite so liberal had they known how free Cara was with cigarettes, alcohol and boys.

My mother disliked her and never tried to hide it. I saw the way her eyes narrowed whenever I brought Cara back to the house, following her, waiting for her to do something wrong. As soon as Cara left she would tut and say, 'I don't trust that girl. She thinks too much of herself.' Kathryn knew she was a bad influence and she was right. But Cara was fun and I enjoyed being with her. Plus she was popular and I didn't want to pass up the chance to be best friends with one of the cool girls.

So I decided to sneak out to the concert with Cara and didn't bother telling my mother about the parents' evening. I knew she'd come down on me hard when she found out I'd omitted to tell her about the school meeting. They would send a letter, asking why they hadn't heard back from her. It was the first time I'd taken such a risk but I chanced it because I didn't really care.

If she ever noticed, or if she ever got a letter, then she chose not to say anything to me, but I was so sure she'd find out that I found myself waiting for a punishment that never came. I told Maggie that was probably the start of it. Of me thinking that if she couldn't be arsed to reprimand me, then I couldn't be bothered to do as she told me.

Maggie wanted to know more about Cara. 'She sounds as if she was influential,' she said.

'She showed an interest in me,' I told her. 'I was going to take that anywhere I could find it.'

'So did the two of you stay friends for a while?'

I nodded. 'Until just after my mother left, then I went off the rails a bit and her parents eventually noticed what their little girl was up to, too. When Kathryn left, I stayed in the house for about six weeks, but as soon as my grandmother gave me a chunk of money, I moved out and rented a room in a shared house. That's when I started living life a bit more freely and Cara's parents decided it was too much. They shipped her off to a private college where she could take her A-levels without me screwing things up for her. I didn't hear from her again.'

'Why did your grandmother give you money?' she asked. 'Was it much?'

I nodded. 'It was more than a teenager should have responsibility for anyway. She handed it over in an envelope and said it was up to me how I spent it but I wouldn't be getting any more. It lasted me just over a year. I kept it in its envelope under my mattress. I was lucky no one ever found it as I didn't have another penny from her after that.'

'It's funny really, isn't it?' I said to Maggie after a while. 'That I was the one considered a bad influence on Cara in the end.'

'Take me back to that turning point,' Maggie said, 'the term before Christmas when you were thirteen. Your mother started showing signs of indifference towards you. Did that become the norm until she left?'

I shook my head. 'No, there were times when she was all over me and I could hardly breathe.'

'In what way?' Maggie asked.

'Controlling. Making sure I adhered to the rules.'

'Her rules?'

'I doubt it. The rules passed down from my grandmother more likely.'

My mother was like a puppet, with Eleanor pulling the strings. This was particularly the case when things went wrong. Kathryn would throw everything into a suitcase and pack us both off to the house her parents had just moved to in Yorkshire. My mother was usually running on empty by that point. It happened just *after my daddy died. I was only seven but I felt like neither of my parents were around. Daddy was no longer there, and while my mother was still there, she might as well not have been. She could barely bring herself to cook us tea. After having tinned ravioli six nights in a row I told her I couldn't eat it anymore. Even now the smell of it reminds me of those weeks after he died.*

My mother bathed me, got me dressed for school, sometimes took me to the park, but all of this was done with minimal conversation. Her eyes were like glass. She used to stare right through me as if she could no longer see me. I wondered if they had taken her to the same place as my daddy had gone. Or maybe she just wished they had. She certainly wasn't the same after his death.

That was when Eleanor came along and changes were made. We no longer spoke of him; his photographs were taken down. My mother was allowing Eleanor to cleanse us of his memory. But all they had done was remove the good bits of our lives, and either my mother couldn't see that or she didn't have the energy to fight it.

It happened every time Kathryn came across an obstacle. She would mutter, 'I need Mother,' and we would traipse up to Lordavale. When Eleanor saw us at the door, her eyes would roll to the back of her head. She looked like she wanted to scream but she never did. Usually she grabbed my mother's arm and pulled her into the house, pushing her into a room where she raised her voice and talked at Kathryn at length. I often wandered around the gardens until they were finished. Often the doctor would be brought up to see her, a strange, squat-looking man who looked like a weasel, I always thought. I didn't like him. To me he looked shifty, and I was glad I'd never had to see him when I was a child.

My mother would then emerge, injected with a new surge of

power, and once Eleanor was happy Kathryn could function in a manner deemed acceptable we were sent back to London. I wouldn't be surprised to learn Eleanor was performing her own lobotomy on my mother on those occasions.

'Do you think your mother suffered any mental issues?' Maggie asked when I told her that.

I shrugged. 'I think she was caught under Eleanor's spell. And she was very weak. But I don't know, maybe she did. I was never told.'

'It certainly sounds as if Eleanor had a way of manipulating Kathryn.'

Eleanor had the ability to manipulate everyone around her. My mother was pliable; she would bend into any shape Eleanor wanted. But I never thought I would, not until the day they left, when Eleanor later convinced me it was in my best interests to stay away. For a while I believed her when she said it would blow over, and my mother would be back as soon as she was better. 'Give her time,' she told me, 'and once this has all calmed down, it will work out.' She never told me how. But then as the days became weeks and I was more demanding with my questions, my grandmother could see I was becoming a bigger threat to her than she'd anticipated. 'Take this,' she said, desperately thrusting the money at me. It was more money than I'd ever seen. I thumbed through the banknotes, adding up thousands in my head, and then eventually found my first piece of solace at the bottom of a bottle of vodka.

'Yes,' I said to Maggie. 'She has a way of dealing with everyone, once she finds their vulnerable spot.'

I only pray she isn't looking for it in the girls.

– Thirteen –

Hannah decided to tell her mum she was seeing Dom that Thursday. They were meeting in the café on the high street and so she knew it was only a matter of time before it would get back to Kathryn. The gossip would run like a river through the lanes of the Bay until it reached her. *Oh, Kathryn, we saw your daughter in the coffee shop today with that Dominic boy. No, Hannah, of course. Isn't he older than her? What do you think about it, Kathryn? Personally I'm not too sure about the Wilson family. Did you ever hear...?* Then they would add a pinch of gossip that was most likely made up, because things like the truth didn't seem to matter to the women of the Bay.

Hannah said Dom was helping her with a school project that had been set for the summer holidays. Kathryn didn't react at first, making her wonder whether she could just slip out of the room unnoticed. When Kathryn eventually asked what the project was about and who had set it, Hannah surprised herself at the speed at which the lies came out of her mouth. The story sprung to the tip of her tongue at pace. Lauren was within earshot and she knew her sister would back her up, if need be. She could almost feel Lauren's disapproval boring into her back, but knew she would never do anything to drop her in it.

She wished she didn't have to lie. It would be so much better if her mum were the type who sat her girls round a table and wanted to know all about their boyfriends. Got nervous with them if they were waiting for a call and excited when they were finally asked out. Asked the boys over for dinner, and laughed with them, wanted to know what their interests were, winked when they left the room and admitted she thought they were good-looking.

But her mum wasn't like most, her own dating experience being so limited. Kathryn had told them she was thirty-one when she met their dad and, as far as they knew, there hadn't been anyone serious before him. And then he ended up leaving her on her own to raise two small children in a village where she knew no one. Hannah supposed that went a long way towards accounting for her mum's odd behaviour.

Dom was already in the coffee shop when she arrived. His chair was facing the door but his head was bent forward, an expression of concentration fixed on his face as he tapped his thumbs on his mobile. The bell on the door rang as Hannah walked in and he automatically lifted his head before standing up to pull out a chair for her.

'What can I get you?' he asked.

'A skinny latte, please,' Hannah smiled.

Dom came back with two lattes and a slice of Victoria sponge, which he cut in two, pushing one half towards her. 'Don't tell me you're the type of girl who says no to cake,' he said.

Hannah grinned and picked up a fork from the plate. 'I never say no to cake.'

Dom laughed. 'Good! I can't stand girls who are forever saying they're on a diet. It's boring.'

Hannah wondered how many girls he knew well. Someone as good-looking as Dom had probably been on many dates. She knew of at least three ex-girlfriends who would be bitching about her once they knew she was going out with him.

Dom ran his fingers through his mop of curly blond hair and grinned at her. He was a surfer and had the look to suit. His hair was bleached with sunlight, his skin golden brown. She imagined the shape of his toned body underneath his T-shirt. She'd seen it many times before, when he stripped down to his shorts on the beach. Dom was always one of the first to rip his top off and run into the sea, whatever the time of year. But Hannah preferred fantasising about its contours hidden beneath his clothes.

'Let's drink these up and go somewhere else,' Dom suggested.

'Like where?' Hannah was surprised. She hadn't thought they'd go anywhere but the coffee shop.

'I dunno. The beach?'

Hannah shook her head. 'I'm always there. And besides there'll be plenty of people we know.'

'Then I've got an idea,' he said, standing up and holding out his hand for Hannah to take. 'Come on, let's go.'

*****

Hannah had never been in a convertible before. When Dom took her back to his house and told her to wait in the drive she hadn't expected him to come out dangling his dad's car keys and suggesting they go for a drive. She wasn't entirely sure he had permission and couldn't imagine many fathers happily handing over the keys to their year-old Mercedes to their eighteen-year-old sons.

'It's fine,' Dom laughed as he started the engine, when she'd asked him for a second time if his father knew. 'He's cool about it.'

'Are you sure?'

'My dad works for a car dealership,' Dom shrugged. 'It's not even his. And I'm insured. So please, don't worry about it.'

Hannah smiled and leaned back against the cream leather seat. As Dom accelerated and drove out of the Bay, she could feel the wind whipping through her hair. She felt wild and free, and it was exhilarating.

'What are you smiling at?' Dom asked, his voice rising above the sound of the wind and the engine.

'I feel alive!' Hannah shouted, throwing her arms into the air and laughing.

'I need to get you out more.'

'I want you to drive forever,' she said. 'If you kept going, where would we end up?'

'I dunno. Eventually the South Coast, maybe Brighton. But it would take us a long time to get there.'

'What's in Brighton?' she asked.

'A pier, a beach … I've got no idea, I've never been. Why? Do you want to go?'

'Yes, I want to go to Brighton!' she laughed. 'I want to go everywhere. I want to go to London and Cornwall and Liverpool too. I want you to drive me all around the country in your car and we won't come back until we've seen all of it!'

'You're mad,' he laughed. 'But it's a deal. This summer I'll take you to one of those places. You choose where you want to go the most.'

Hannah looked over at him and smiled. The best-looking boy in the world was sitting next to her and he had just offered to take her out of Mull Bay. Dom was the start of the rest of her life.

'London,' she said. 'Let's go to London one day.'

Twenty minutes later they pulled off the road and onto a stony lane. Dom stopped by a gate, where he pointed to the grass on the other side and Hannah got out of the car, waiting for him to get a picnic blanket and drinks from the boot. 'It was all I could find,' he shrugged, passing her a can of Coke and jumping over the gate. Hannah followed him and waited for him to lay the blanket down for them to sit on.

'I'm impressed you packed a blanket,' Hannah said.

'I didn't. It was already in there,' he admitted. 'And I'm sure you'd be more impressed if I popped open a bottle of wine.'

'No, I don't even like wine.'

'You really are different to most of the girls I've dated,' Dom smiled.

'Oh?'

'That's a good thing, trust me.'

Hannah watched him lay back on the blanket and close his eyes, a gesture that seemed so self-assured. She lay down next to him but couldn't relax. They were in the middle of a field. It was a strange place to bring her, and she didn't feel entirely comfortable being there. The heat of the sun was burning down on them and she started to feel her stomach rumbling. The cake wasn't enough to fill her up and it was past lunchtime.

'Can't you relax?' he asked without opening his eyes.

'Yes, of course I can.'

'Do you wish I hadn't brought you here? Would you rather we stayed in the Bay?'

'God, no!'

Hannah spent her life wanting to get out of the Bay so she couldn't work out why she felt so uneasy now they had.

Dom propped himself onto his elbow and looked at her. 'Let's talk.'

They talked about the Bay, surfing, their friends and school. He told her stories about Cal that made her laugh, and she realised she didn't want to be anywhere else but in the middle of a field with Dom.

'Have you thought any more about looking for your dad?' he asked.

'A little bit,' Hannah admitted. 'To be honest, Lauren's so up and down about it, I really don't know what to do. One minute she's interested, the next she's worried about Mum.'

'But what do *you* want to do?'

'I want to find him,' she insisted. 'But I'm also worried. Like Lauren says, he wanted nothing to do with us, so what if he still doesn't?'

'You talk about Lauren a lot,' Dom said. 'I can't imagine what it's like, having a twin.'

'It's wonderful,' Hannah smiled. 'She's the other half of me.'

'Don't you ever argue?'

'Course we do. But we always get over it.'

'You're very different to each other,' he said.

'In what way?'

'She seems a bit more,' he waved his hand in the air. 'I dunno, stand-offish with me. I wouldn't know what to say to her. I find you easier to talk to.'

Hannah laughed. 'That's probably because you haven't tried talking to Lauren. You didn't talk to me much until the other night.'

'That's true,' he smiled, still watching her.

Hannah wondered whether she was in heaven. She could

be. As she closed her eyes then and felt the warmth of the sun touch their lids she wasn't hungry anymore.

'I'm going to have to go back soon ...' Dom suddenly broke the silence.

Hannah's stomach sank. She'd never been so aware of the movements inside her gut as she had been that day. It was too soon to be leaving the sanctity of the field they'd made their private camp.

'Do we have to?' she whispered. 'I like it here, away from everyone.'

Dom laughed. 'You sound like you don't get out much.'

'I don't.'

'Is your mum really as bad as people say?'

'What do you mean?' Hannah asked, opening her eyes to look at him. 'What do people say?'

'Nothing much, just that she doesn't let either of you do much on your own.'

Hannah didn't answer.

'Has she always been like that?'

'I suppose so. She's anxious about everything. It's like she thinks we're still kids, and she doesn't want us to grow up. Sometimes I wonder if it's because Dad left her, and she's worried we'll do the same. But it can be suffocating, and the tighter she grabs hold of me, the more I want to break free.'

Even thinking about the way Kathryn smothered them made Hannah angry. Both she and Lauren had always been good, never given their mum anything to worry about. She wished she would trust them enough to make some of their own decisions rather than try and control the way they lived.

'So did your dad live with you in the Bay, before he went?'

'No, we moved right after, I think. We used to live in a

house in North London, but I can't remember it. We were only two when we left.'

Hannah once learnt that a child doesn't have any memories before the age of four, but she didn't agree. There were certain things she could recall that she knew must be memories. Lauren could back her up on most of them too. Like they both remembered getting a second-hand bike for their third birthdays. Hannah's was purple and Lauren's was pink, and Hannah distinctly remembers crying because she wanted Lauren's. Apparently Lauren said she didn't mind Hannah having it but she couldn't remember that bit.

Then there was the time Lauren fell off a swing, which Mum confirmed wasn't long after they moved to the Bay. Hannah could still hear Lauren's piercing scream and see her sister lying on the grass beside the swing, her leg bent at an angle that shouldn't have been possible.

'You're bound to remember things like a broken leg,' her mum said.

But Hannah wasn't convinced you'd remember it when it wasn't your bones that had broken.

She couldn't remember the house they used to live in before they moved to the Bay, though. However hard she tried, Hannah couldn't bring to mind its rooms or the way it looked from the outside. It didn't help that there were no photographs of it. The house itself drew a complete blank.

Yet there was something else, a little fragment of memory in the corner of her mind that never went away, although this was one Lauren couldn't back up. Hannah swore blind she could remember someone else living with them. There were times when she pictured it clearly: someone else in the house who played with them, cuddled them, loved them.

'It must be our dad,' Lauren had said on one of the many occasions Hannah mentioned it.

'It isn't him, I know it's not.' Hannah was certain about that.

'Well, there wasn't anyone else there. Not that I can remember, anyway.'

Hannah knew it wasn't their father because the presence she remembered was female. It first came back to her when someone once walked past her and the smell of White Musk lingered. It was such a strong feeling and she had to hold onto it to believe she was right. One time she asked her mum but Kathryn snapped at her, telling her not to be ridiculous, before laughing it off. Hannah was certain it wasn't her imagination, though. There was someone else in their lives and whoever it was, she was certain it was someone she and Lauren had loved very much.

– Fourteen –

Kathryn waited by the kitchen window. She had pulled the shutters halfway down so she could see out but could also inch backwards without being seen when either of them approached the gate. Both of her girls were out, Lauren careering around the Bay in a car driven by a seventeen-year-old who had barely passed her test. Kathryn, of course, was none too happy about that. The facts screamed at her – young drivers were the most dangerous threat on the roads today.

But Hannah was causing her more concern. There was no summer holiday project. She had known that as soon as the lie spilled from her daughter's mouth. When was the moment she had lost her? The moment when Hannah believed lying was easier because what she was doing was so obviously wrong? Kathryn hated that her daughters didn't think they could tell her things. This time around she had tried doing everything right, letting them know she was always there, watching out for them, worrying about them. Wasn't that all any normal mother would do? She was trying her best, but often she felt it might never be enough.

Kathryn wasn't sure about any of it anymore. Faces and thoughts were coming back to her, distorting her perception of reality. Hannah was talking about things and wanting to know too much, and Kathryn didn't have all of the answers. At least not the ones she could share with them. She was whipping up the past. Peter, Abigail, even Robert had appeared in her dreams again, all of them circling her like horses on a carousel. And how she wanted to stop the music and get off the ride, but it just wouldn't stop. It kept spinning and spinning until it blurred into one jumbled mess and she couldn't break any of it apart.

Kathryn reached for the tablets the doctor had grudgingly prescribed, and took two more. They wouldn't knock her out. It took more than Temazepam to do that, it seemed, but they helped slow the ride down temporarily at least.

Dr Morgan had acquiesced to give her something to help her sleep, though anyone would surely see in her eyes she had been awake most nights. Eventually he had tapped out a prescription onto his computer, leaning forward as he waited for it to print.

'You were on medication for a long time, Kathryn,' he noted. 'Prochlorperazine.'

'Yes, it was for sickness. I had dreadful sickness as a child,' she explained, although as she replied she realised she couldn't remember a time when she had ever been violently sick.

'Right, so how are you doing now, generally? Aside from the problems sleeping, of course.'

Kathryn shrugged. She hadn't known Dr Morgan for long, not properly. She had only been going to the surgery regularly for just over a year, after Dr Simmonds had died and her mother hadn't been aware enough to find a suitable replacement. Anyway, it made sense that she found a local doctor now, but she still didn't like to open up too much, especially when he seemed to doubt Dr Simmonds.

Edgar Simmonds was a family friend. Kathryn had seen him since she was a young child. He was also Peter's uncle, a fact she hadn't found out until a while after they met. Peter didn't see him often but still it kept Kathryn from going to Edgar's funeral in case they did meet again.

She remembered seeing Edgar Simmonds quite often as a child, especially in her early teens. He came to the house and spoke with her in the drawing room, her mother always lingering in the corner. It's funny how that had seemed the norm, that they had never visited his surgery, as most people would do.

Kathryn suspected that was down to her parents. Lord Charles Bretton, her father, was a member of the House of Lords, and an outspoken member of certain select committees. Her mother, famed in her own right for being his elegant wife, had appeared in many magazines in the fifties, showing off the glamorous lifestyle of the wealthy, and promoting herself as the perfect housewife. Image was everything to Eleanor, and Kathryn always knew she would never be part of the portrait Eleanor desired.

She was a pretty child, and when she was very young Kathryn had also been brought out for family photographs, smiling on her rocking horse, playing sweetly with a doll in the corner of the living room while her mother perched on the edge of the chaise longue, a glass of martini in her hand. But then she reached an age when she was 'an awkward girl', 'a constant disappointment' and even 'an embarrassment' to her mother – Eleanor's own words, which had stung hard until Kathryn believed them to be almost certainly true.

Kathryn knew Eleanor didn't want children, but had agreed to try for a son, an heir to take over the business and inherit the title. That was one particular conversation she wished she hadn't overheard.

Meeting Robert had changed her life because he had stopped her from feeling like she was a failure, like she didn't belong. He had shown her that she could be loved and he had done that every single day until the day he died. Eleanor didn't like Robert, he wasn't the son-in-law she hoped for, but by the end of Kathryn's teens, it seemed Eleanor was ready to hand over her daughter to anyone who would have her.

She had died with Robert that day. Someone had come along and taken her too, leaving an empty shell on earth that her mother had scooped up and filled with all the strange parts that made up Kathryn. She didn't know why she loved Eleanor as much as she did. Many had asked her. She knew it wasn't a love that was returned, but still her mother had been there for her. Without her she didn't see how she would be here now.

*****

Kathryn flicked up the blind and peeked out. It hadn't taken long for the news to reach her that Hannah was with Dominic Wilson in the coffee shop. At least she could tell the gossips she was aware of the meeting, that much she knew. They had apparently shared a slice of Janice's Victoria sponge.

'It all looked very sweet,' Theresa from the corner shop giggled. 'Young love, eh?' she said, handing Kathryn a loaf of Hovis and her change.

Young love indeed. Kathryn did her best to smile back, although it most likely came across as a grimace.

'Of course they weren't there long,' Theresa droned on,

loving the fact she had something to tell Kathryn about her own daughter. 'They both left the café and went off somewhere together, although I'm sure you know all about that.'

'Yes, of course,' Kathryn flushed as she stuffed the change into her pocket. If the corner shop wasn't so convenient she would shop elsewhere. Every time she saw Theresa's permed blonde mop springing up and down as she bounced around the store Kathryn's blood would boil. She had never liked the woman.

Dominic Wilson ... She didn't know that much about the Wilson family. The mother seemed pleasant enough. They would acknowledge each other and occasionally exchange a few words in the queue at the bank but they didn't have much in common. Rosemary Wilson was the mother of two boys. Her eldest, Benedict, was twenty-one and he was in and out of the police station like he was on a piece of elastic. Only minor offences, people said, but of course once you were tarred with that brush it took a lot for the people of Mull Bay to forget. Kathryn guessed that was why Rosemary kept her head down – the shame of having a son in trouble with the police. While Dominic was the better behaved of the two boys, it didn't amount to much, given his competition.

Kathryn was about to leave her post at the kitchen window when she caught sight of Hannah unlatching the gate. She quickly sat down at the table, clenching her hand around a mug of cold tea, and tried to appear collected. Maybe the tablets she had taken earlier were beginning to have a calming effect. She felt a little less jittery than she had done.

'Hello, darling,' she sang out as she heard the front door close. 'How did your little date go?'

Hannah appeared at the doorway and Kathryn could see her shuffling her feet.

'It wasn't a date, Mum,' she mumbled.

'Oh, don't be silly, a handsome lad like that! And you've been gone for hours. Where have you been, darling?'

Hannah didn't respond, but continued nervously stepping from one foot to another.

'Come on, you can talk to me.'

She could see Hannah's shoulders loosen. 'We just went out for a bit and talked. We didn't do anything else.'

'I'm not saying you did, honey. I just wondered where you'd been.' Kathryn was sure her voice sounded almost shrill but she couldn't seem to help it.

'Just outside of the Bay, not far.'

'So how did you get there?'

'Oh, Mum,' Hannah sighed, 'what does all of this matter?'

'It matters to me, Hannah. Just please tell me where you went. Please. I need to know.' Kathryn knew she sounded desperate. But she was: desperate to have her daughters where she could see them.

'Just out. I have no idea what the exact co-ordinates were,' Hannah snapped as she backed out of the kitchen, her footsteps heavy on the stairs.

Kathryn was momentarily speechless. 'Don't you speak to me like that, Hannah! Come back down and apologise,' she called out, following her out of the kitchen, standing at the bottom of the stairs.

Nothing.

'This is that boy's influence on you, isn't it? Two hours in his company and you're talking to me like this. You won't be seeing him again.'

The girls' bedroom door opened and Hannah appeared on the landing. 'You can't stop me from seeing him, Mum. I'm sixteen years old.'

'And while you're living under my roof—'

'Oh, please,' her daughter spat, retreating into the bedroom and slamming the door behind her. 'Fine, I'll move out!' she shouted from the other side of it.

*****

It was quarter past midnight and yet again Kathryn couldn't sleep. For the last two hours she'd been tossing and turning from side to side; the heat was too much, despite the night air drifting in through the open window. Her head was cluttered with thoughts, the movements in her mind too rapid. The same questions were haunting her over and over as they had since she'd overheard the girls' conversation. What would happen if Peter came back into her life? Would the girls find out the terrible thing she had done all those years ago? How could they ever forgive her? Of course they couldn't when she would never forgive herself. She had accepted it was the right thing to do at the time, that she had no choice and that it was best for her and the girls – but what if it wasn't?

Kathryn crept quietly down the stairs, pulling on a sweater over her pyjamas and putting her cold feet into the boots by the front door. She didn't know what it was about her feet, or her hands, for that matter. The rest of her body was so hot but coldness pricked at them even in the middle of summer, making them tingle.

Plucking her keys from the rack, she stuffed them into the pocket of her sweater, slowly opening the front door and pulling it carefully behind her. The air was fresh. There was a slight chill in the breeze, so Kathryn wrapped her arms around her waist, scrunching her toes to keep the blood circulating.

She had no idea where she was heading to but started walking anyway: out of the gate, turning right and down the lane, so quiet at this time of night. The first time she had seen a sky lit with so many stars was the night she arrived in Mull Bay. Few street lamps lit the lanes and she was always amazed by how beautiful and clear it was. But despite this, Kathryn felt queasy at the thought of that first night. Whenever the memory came to mind she brushed it away as swiftly as she could. She had done what she was told and moved away, but was it right?

Robert used to say, 'How does your gut feel?' when she couldn't make up her mind about something. That night, if she were truthful, her gut had felt all wrong, but still she hadn't done anything about it. It wasn't so easy to sweep away the memories anymore. Partly that was down to Hannah quizzing her all the time but it was also because her mother was no longer giving her the answers.

Kathryn turned left at the end of the lane and followed the road, past the store, past the post office. She realised she was heading to the beach, although she hadn't been planning to; the roads were just taking her there. The Bay seemed different when she was the only one around. It was nice to think she could do anything she wanted and for once wouldn't be spotted and talked about.

At the corner Kathryn crossed the road, barely looking for cars as she strolled to the other side, but no one was driving anywhere at this time of night. It was an exhilarating thought. She could run down the path that led to the clifftop, her arms stretched out either side of her, shouting if she wanted to, and there would be no one around to catch her doing it. She could leap down the steps and onto the sand; the adrenalin might even take her into the sea and there would be no one to stop her. Keep going once she was in the water, if she wanted. How long would it be until someone realised what she had done? Hours? Days?

Of course Kathryn wouldn't go down to the beach. Even in the daylight the vast expanse of sea scared her. At night it was as black as ink and when she stood on the clifftop, her eyes scanning as far as she could, she froze at the thought of being near enough to the water for it to carry her off somewhere. She crouched on the grass at the edge of the cliff and looked down at the beach.

'Talk to me, Mother,' she called out to the sea. 'Tell me how to get through this.'

*****

By the time she left the cliff to go back home, the first shards of light were beginning to crack through the sky. She must have been there for hours. Kathryn felt a little lighter by the time she reached the cottage because she had made a decision: if Hannah was so intent on looking for her father, then she was going to have to make sure she failed. And the only way to do that was to see Peter herself. But before she called the man she hadn't spoken to for fourteen years, she needed to speak to her mother. There were things Kathryn needed to know, needed to face up to, and she had a feeling Eleanor was the only one who had the answers. All she could do was hope there was some way of getting them out of her.

– Fifteen –

Dear Adam,

My mother didn't have friends – I don't think she got the point of them. Kathryn always made comments to me about how mine weren't a good influence. I knew they weren't, but then neither was she. My mother had let Peter into our lives and yet it was plain to see she didn't want him near her. She had buried the memories of my daddy inside his coffin even though he was the one she truly loved. What kind of influence was someone who could ignore her own feelings?

Cara could persuade me to do things, and sometimes I'd do them because I knew Kathryn wouldn't approve. Maybe I liked to annoy her or maybe it was just to test her reaction. It was the school year in which we were turning fourteen and we thought we knew everything. Cara came to school one day with a 10-inch gap between her knee-high socks and the hem of her skirt. I couldn't believe she'd got away with it and of course I wanted to wear mine the same. That night I took the scissors out of my mother's sewing box and cut off a strip at the bottom of my skirt.

When Kathryn saw it the following morning she screamed at me. In the cold light of day I could see the ragged, fraying hemline and realised it looked nothing like Cara's. She tried to stop me from leaving the house 'looking like trash' but I ran out anyway and didn't turn back. I knew I'd made a mistake but I didn't want her knowing that. Besides, Cara had told me the day before to do it, so there was no way I wasn't wearing my new short skirt to school.

'Shit, Abi!' Cara had laughed when she saw me getting off the bus. 'Why did you hack your skirt off? You look like a tramp!'

I could have cried with shame but I bit my lip and swallowed down the lump inside my throat. 'How come yours looks OK?' my voice cracked.

She pulled up her un-tucked shirt to reveal the bulge of skirt, rolled over at the waist. I stared at her, my cheeks and neck burning with the pain of humiliation.

'I can't believe you were so stupid!' She was laughing loudly and I could sense people stopping to see what all the commotion was about.

I wanted to run home but I couldn't give my mother the satisfaction. Then as I stood by the gate, wavering with indecision, I heard someone shout at me from across the playground. 'Hey, cool look, Abi!' I knew the voice. It was Tasha Abbot, the tallest, skinniest, most popular yet most terrifying girl in our year. I wanted the ground to swallow me up until I realised she actually meant it. Cara looked confused, shocked. She looked angry.

I turned to look at Tasha, who was smiling at me. Not mockingly, but genuinely approving of the look I'd rocked up to school in that day.

And that was it. That was the defining moment where I took myself and Cara into the heart of the coolest group of kids in our year. Where dressing like a Spice Girl and getting your belly button pierced were essential. The 'wrong crowd', as my mother referred to them.

Being in Tasha's gang was fun. We got to discuss the sex they were all having. And if we weren't having it ourselves, we made it up. I didn't let on that at thirteen I was still a virgin. I had no desire to have sex with any of the boys at school but it seemed to be the done thing for Tasha's gang. Don't get me wrong, Adam. I knew it was wrong, and I knew my new friends were by far the minority, but they were so cool. Everyone wanted to be them or be friends with them – or at least that's what I thought.

Hanging out with Tasha meant I started getting back late, sneaking out of the house at night, smelling of cigarettes and drinking Diamond Whites in the park on Saturday nights. I was everything a thirteen-year-old girl shouldn't be. Maybe I was every parent's worst nightmare, but the fact was I had a disillusioned mother who thought she was making a happy family with a stepfather neither of us liked. She in turn took orders from my grandmother, who was almost frenzied in her approach to parenting: laying down rules that went out in the fifties, and which were all for her own gain. And above all else, a daddy I missed every single day, but who everyone else seemed to have forgotten ever existed.

Kathryn had no idea how to handle me. Eleanor was phoned on a weekly basis. Whenever she was in town, she would turn up to 'knock some sense into me' or would tell my mother what to do over the phone. I always knew when Kathryn had spoken to her because my mother would start mimicking her tone. 'I will not have my daughter speak to me like that', or 'I will not tolerate such behaviour in my house'.

I hated living at home. Kathryn was either screaming at me or in denial, and my stepfather couldn't care less. I was turning into an angry, confused teenager and the only positive I had in my life was my new friendship with the scariest bunch of kids in school.

Then just before we broke up for Christmas a new boy joined: Jason. He had dark hair, which hung down either side of his face, and a scar running across the top of his lip. The word was that he'd got it fighting but he would later tell me he'd fallen off his bike when he was six.

He almost glided across the playground, he was so smooth; his jeans hung beneath his pants and he wore headphones, which he removed when he got to the door but kept draped around his neck. Three other boys from our year had fallen into step beside him but Jason towered above them. I was in love with him – my only problem was so too were Cara and Tasha.

That Christmas we stayed with my grandparents for a week. Peter joined us for the duration, although I sensed he didn't want to be there. His face was set in a permanent grimace and whenever my grandparents weren't in the room, he was scowling at Kathryn about something. During the first two days he made frequent retreats into my grandfather's study, where they sat smoking cigars, drinking Cognac and talking politics. It didn't seem to bother my mother, him spending so much time without her.

Kathryn used those visits to soak up Eleanor's wonderful parenting tips on how to control a daughter. She certainly had her own in place so must have felt qualified to offer up advice. I would catch them whispering in corners of the house, my mother's shoulders hunched forward, head nodding dismally, eyes shining like a rabbit in the headlights when she finally noticed me standing in the doorway.

On Christmas Day, once lunch was over, Peter and Grandpa retired to the study again, this time to drink port. (No, it wasn't Downton Abbey, this was the nineties.) I was left sitting at an oval mahogany table designed for twenty guests with only my mother and Eleanor for company.

'You should know, Abigail,' my grandmother stated, 'that if your behaviour continues in this manner, you will be sent away to a boarding school in Scotland.'

I waited for the punchline that never came. It seemed she was serious. I looked at my mother but her head was hung so low, I thought it was about to clunk against the dining table.

'If what behaviour continues?' I asked.

'You are a disgrace to this family and your antics will not be tolerated any further. No grandchild of mine will act in this manner. Do you understand that?'

'Mum?' I asked my mother, who remained mute and almost unconscious at the table. 'What do you mean, a boarding school in Scotland?' Now I was scared. For a long time now I hadn't felt wanted in our home, but to be sent away to a boarding school – and so far away. I looked at my mother, silently pleading with her to say something, to promise me she wouldn't send me away, but she said nothing. 'Do you mean it?' I asked her.

'Yes, we do,' Eleanor replied, standing up to leave the table.

'Mum?' I asked again. Why wasn't she saying anything?

'That's all on the subject, Abigail,' my grandmother told me. 'It's your decision how you want to act but I will not have you embarrass me. And I fear that is what you will do.'

Embarrass her. That was what everything boiled down to. Always so concerned with their precious image, how it would affect Charles, how she herself would look. Eleanor let people see what she wanted them to see but if only they knew the person she was behind closed doors. How I longed to show them the Eleanor I knew. Her popularity angered me, but it seemed only I could see how fake and self-centred she was. Eleanor didn't care for her so-called friends; she cared only for herself.

Charles's success was also Eleanor's weak spot. I didn't realise it then, but I would later, and I would try to use it to my advantage. My grandmother was cloaked in the fear that we would step out of line and damage her precious reputation, and she was willing to do anything to prevent that happening.

You might have thought the threat of boarding school would have worked, but it didn't. Back at school that January I not only continued seeing my friends, I started hanging out with Jason too. I was angry with Eleanor for thinking she could dictate my life and even more bitter towards my mother for not having the backbone to stand up for me. She was slowly abandoning me, I felt, and so my friends were my only source of comfort.

'So, d'you wanna go out with me, then?' Jason asked me one day. Of course I did! I adored him. No one else in the school could strut like he did.

My mother didn't know. There was no way I would let her into this little secret of mine and have her do everything in her power to make sure I never saw him again.

Jason and I didn't do much but hang out. In the early evenings I watched him skateboard around the empty park. I waited on the sidelines of football pitches, freezing cold, with no idea of what was happening in the game, and then went back for my tea. But I didn't push my luck with Kathryn. I started to play the game so she didn't realise I was still hanging out with Tasha or Cara, or seeing Jason, because the threat of boarding school still hung in the air. She didn't take much interest by then, though. As long as nothing I did demanded anything of her, I was pretty much left alone.

I was convinced as soon as we got home from Christmas at my grandparents' house that Peter would leave. In my eyes their marriage was a farce – any fool could see neither of them wanted to be in it. I spent most of that month waiting for the day I found Kathryn in tears because he'd walked out. But he never did; he was still lingering and if anything appeared to be making more of an effort with her, even if it was killing him to do so. Sometimes I caught the expression on his face change when she left the room.

The smile he had plastered on for her benefit dropped when he thought I wasn't watching. I often wondered why he was so angry and miserable when he could have done something about it.

For Peter was everything my daddy wasn't: Peter was a career man. He would sit at the kitchen table talking into his mobile phone, just because he had one. One leg slung over the other, he would run a hand up and down the creases at the front of his trouser legs, a permanent frown on his face as he barked into the phone, 'Well, just get rid of him, then. We can easily find another man happy to get his wages.' Peter was climbing a ladder, but it was obvious Eleanor was holding it for him. He was trying to find his way in politics, using my grandparents to get there. They must have known a weasel like him was using them and I still couldn't understand what they were getting out of it. My mother, however, seemed oblivious to what was going on. She was too busy painting on her own face, one that said, 'I am happily married'.

At dinner Peter regaled her with stories about women in the office and how relentless they were in their requests for more money they didn't deserve. And my mother laughed along with him like a fool. I would stare at her in disgust. I despised her for being too blind to see what a jerk she was married to, or too weak to do anything about it. She was morphing into someone I didn't recognise: if a person could become their own shadow, she was definitely an example of it.

Occasionally I tried to do something about it. I remember one night, March 20th, because it was the night before my fourteenth birthday. Our relationship had been stretched as far as I thought it could go, each of us pulling one end of a piece of elastic, and I was waiting for it to snap. I was annoyed because Jason had a football match he refused to cancel the following night and so I had nothing to do on my birthday. Meanwhile, Tasha was distancing herself from me, spreading rumours I had dumped my girlfriends for a boy. Her jealousy was infectious and Cara had caught the bug, too.

My mother hadn't asked me what I wanted to do for my birthday so I didn't suggest anything, but that night Peter didn't come home from work at the usual time and she suggested making me a cake.

'Don't bother,' I said, an automatic response for the teenager I had become, although inside all I wanted to do was shout, 'Yes, please make me a cake! That's exactly what I want for my birthday.'

She gave me a look of resignation and sighed as she walked out of the room and into the kitchen. I listened hard, hoping to hear signs of baking, but there were none. Eventually I followed her in under the pretence of making myself a drink and found her sitting at the kitchen table, staring into space.

'What are you doing?' I asked.

Nothing.

'Mum?'

Her skin was so pale I remember it as almost blue, and her eyes were glazed over as if a film had been pulled across them. I continued to watch for any sign of movement, but none came. She was motionless except for the twitch of her hand, clutched around something so tightly her knuckles were white.

'Mum, is that a bottle of pills in your hand?' I asked. Still nothing. I grabbed her hand and tried to prise the fingers apart until they eventually fell open, releasing the bottle and sending tiny white tablets scattering across the floor.

'Jesus! Have you had any of these?' I shouted.

She snapped out of her trance and stared at the floor, where I was gathering the pills and tipping them back into their bottle.

'Yes, I've had two,' she replied with clarity. 'They are paracetamol, Abigail. I have a headache.' She snatched the bottle out of my grasp and screwed the cap back on, placing them back on the highest shelf of our cupboard.

'You don't have to stay with him, you know, Mum,' I said. 'If he doesn't make you happy, we can always leave.'

When she looked at me her face was softer. I swore she was about to tell me what was really going on inside that mixed-up head of hers and agree that yes, we should definitely leave. She opened her mouth to speak and then clamped it shut, turning to look out of the window and after a moment back at me. Her face had changed again; there was none of the softness I had seen only seconds before. Instead the glazed look was back and she eventually spoke in a cool, even tone.

'Abigail, I love Peter and he loves me. I do not ever want to hear you suggest anything so preposterous again. Do you understand me?'

My heart sank, taking any hope I had with it. Had my mother's soul been taken away and replaced with mechanical parts? I wouldn't have been surprised.

'You're pathetic,' I spat at her, angrily. 'He doesn't love you. Anyone can see that.'

I can still feel the sting of her hand across my face.

– Sixteen –

Something woke Hannah at a quarter to five. Her body jolted with sudden alertness and she lay listening for a clue. Then came the slam of a car door and the low rumble of an engine ticking over. She knew it was her mum's Peugeot before she'd even made it to the window to watch Kathryn drive down the lane, turn the corner and disappear out of sight.

'Lauren, wake up.' She shook her sister by the shoulder. 'Mum's just driven off somewhere.'

Lauren groaned and stirred but didn't open her eyes.

'Lauren,' Hannah said louder.

'What's the matter?' Lauren hissed.

'I said, Mum's just driven off somewhere. Do you know where she's gone?'

'What's the time?' Lauren asked, rubbing her eyes.

'It's not even 5 o'clock,' Hannah said, grabbing her watch from the bedside table and checking it. 'That's my point. Where's she going at this time of the morning?'

'Go downstairs and see if she's left a note,' Lauren said sleepily, rolling out of bed to look out of the window herself. 'If not, we'll try calling her.'

Unable to find a note, Hannah picked up the phone and punched in the numbers for her mum's mobile. They hadn't spoken much since she'd threatened to leave the house the week before. Hannah had tried to keep out of her mum's way, and in turn, Kathryn hadn't said anything more about Dominic. She didn't have any intention of leaving, it wouldn't come to that, but for now she was pleased the threat had appeared to subdue her mum's constant questioning.

The phone rang out at the other end and clicked into answerphone. After the beep, Hannah left a message: 'Mum? I just saw you drive off. Where are you?'

Hannah poured two glasses of orange juice and took them up to the bedroom. Neither of them would get any sleep now that Mum had apparently gone AWOL.

'She didn't say anything to you, then?' she asked Lauren, passing her one of the glasses and getting back into bed.

'Not a thing,' said Lauren. 'Where do you think she's gone?'

Hannah yawned. 'No idea, nor has she, probably.'

'I'm worried about her.' Lauren looked at her sister earnestly. 'She's doing strange things again.'

Hannah flicked at the remote control to turn on the television that sat in the corner of the room. 'There's nothing decent on.'

'Of course there isn't. Most people don't get up this early.'

'Most normal people, anyway. What do you mean by strange things?'

'She doesn't seem to know what's going on, she looks like her head is constantly somewhere else entirely. Oh, I don't know, it's just like she's not with us half the time. Do you know what I mean?'

Hannah nodded, still gazing at the TV as she flicked through the channels. 'She went out in the middle of the night a couple of nights ago, too. She doesn't know I saw her, but I'd gone to the loo and clocked her through the window, coming home about this time.'

'Why didn't you tell me?' Lauren asked, propping a pillow against the headboard and sitting up.

'It slipped my mind. Blimey, *The Jeremy Kyle Show*'s on!' Hannah laughed.

'Turn it over,' groaned Lauren, reaching for the remote as Hannah pulled her hand away.

'Let's watch the news, then. She might turn up on it.'

'Why? What are you thinking she's done?'

'I'm thinking that if she's not thinking properly at the moment,' Hannah said, 'she could be doing anything right now. Maybe she's standing in her pyjamas, holding a poor man hostage behind a petrol station counter.'

'Don't say that, now I'm going to worry.'

'I'm only joking,' Hannah laughed. 'She's fine. There'll be an explanation.'

Lauren sighed. 'She's got a lot on her mind, what with Grandma and—'

'Go on, say it,' Hannah interrupted. 'Me and Dom.'

'She's worrying about you, that's all.'

But Hannah didn't think it was that. For a while her mum's strange moods had been bubbling under the surface. She was always on edge, snapping at one of them as soon as they tried stepping away from the precious life plan she'd carefully mapped out for them. Increasingly, Hannah had felt her mum knew exactly what she wanted from her and her sister. What bothered her was how far Kathryn would go to make sure she got what she wanted.

Grabbing a packet of face wipes, Hannah pulled one out and rubbed it over her skin. 'She's trying to stop me from seeing him.'

'Well, clearly that's not working,' Lauren said. 'And that's gross! Look how much make-up's come off on that. You should take it off before you go to bed.'

'But Dom's a good guy. Mum has no right, or reason, to not want me seeing him. Why isn't she happy I've found someone decent?' Hannah turned to her sister. 'And why don't you like him, Lauren? I want you to like my boyfriend.'

'I don't *not* like him.'

'But?' Hannah asked.

Lauren shrugged. 'I just don't like the way it's causing this atmosphere in the house. I'm treading on eggshells every time I'm at home. You and Mum, tiptoeing around each other, it makes me feel uncomfortable.'

'And you really think that's all come about since Dom's been on the scene? Come on, Lauren, her moods are nothing new.' Hannah clambered off the bed and peered out of the window but there was still no sign of their mum returning.

Lauren picked up the remote control and carried on flicking through the channels, pausing when she came across Jeremy Kyle again. 'At least we aren't as bad as them,' she said, pointing the remote at the TV.

'We're not far off!'

*****

At 9.30 a.m. the girls heard a car pull up outside the house.

'She's back!' Hannah called as she went to the window to look out. 'Oh my God, Lauren! You'll never guess what she's brought back with her.'

'What?' Lauren asked as she ran down the stairs.

'Grandma.'

Hannah opened the door and watched Eleanor, who was holding onto the gate with one hand and gesticulating with the other. Their mum was gently pulling her mother's right arm to remove her from the gate.

'Come on, Mother,' Kathryn urged. 'You must remember the Bay? And our cottage?'

Lauren joined Hannah at the door. 'What's she playing at? There's no way Grandma will remember it here.'

'I can't believe they let her out,' Hannah whispered. 'Do you think Mum stole her?'

'No! Do you think she did?' Lauren gasped. 'Do you think we should call them?'

'No, let's see what she says … if they ever get in the house.'

Kathryn finally encouraged her mother up the path, Eleanor barely looking up as she walked past the girls into the living room, where Kathryn plumped up cushions in the armchair and made a fuss of settling her into it, turning the chair so she could look out of the window. The girls hovered by the door and waited for their mum to come out of the room.

'Why's Grandma here?' Lauren asked, following her into the kitchen.

'Because I thought she could do with a nice day out,' Kathryn responded casually. She might as well have said, *I thought I would have Weetabix this morning.* 'Maybe we could take her to the beach later?' she added.

'But she hasn't been out of the home for a year,' Lauren continued.

'I know that,' Kathryn snapped, 'and that's why I thought it was time for a trip.'

'Do they know she's here?' Hannah asked.

'Of course they do.'

'And they don't mind?'

'She is my mother,' Kathryn said, raising her voice, before taking a deep breath and adding more calmly, 'and if I want to take her out, then I will do.'

'So, they do mind,' Hannah muttered under her breath. She watched as her mother set about the kitchen, humming quietly as she made a pot of tea, arranging biscuits on a plate and reaching far into the cupboard for cups and saucers, laying it all on a tray. Hannah didn't even recognise the white porcelain decorated with delicate blue birds her mum had produced. Kathryn was engrossed in the particulars of this little tea party charade, as if she believed that alone would solve all of their problems.

'When is it lunchtime?' Eleanor called from the living room.

'Not yet, Mother,' their mum sang out.

'Did she bring a bag in?' Hannah asked her sister once Kathryn had taken the tray through. 'Do you think Mum plans to keep her here or do you reckon she'll be going back tonight?'

*****

By 11 a.m. Kathryn was noticeably agitated by Eleanor's relentless requests for lunch. 'Fine,' she snapped. 'I'll make it now.' Sandwiches were presented on the everyday plates from Marks & Spencer and they sat around the table in the garden. Eleanor silently ignored the lunch she had been offered, a fact that in turn Kathryn tried to ignore as she continued to spout everything that came into her head. Hannah had long since ducked out of the pantomime playing out in front of her. She wished she didn't have to watch it unravel further. Her mum's anguish was embarrassing.

By midday, their grandmother was back in the armchair, looking out to the lane she clearly had no memory of. Waiting. For what Hannah couldn't tell. Probably to be taken back to the home; to see something or someone that meant something to her because sitting in their cottage in Mull Bay she looked completely out of her depth. Eleanor had worn the same confused expression on her face since they had first seen her at the gate.

'I really think she wants to go back soon,' Lauren said, pulling her mum to one side.

'Nonsense, she's having a lovely day.'

'Mum, she's got no idea where she is.'

'Let's go the beach. A little sea air does everyone the world of good.'

They watched as their mum coaxed Eleanor to stand up, struggling to put her cardigan on her. Every time Kathryn reached out to take hold of her mother's arm, Eleanor batted it away as if swatting a fly. Kathryn's patience was wavering. It seemed obvious to Hannah sea air was not what Eleanor wanted. Eventually the cardigan was slung back over the arm of the chair. Another pot of tea was made, this time served in mugs with tea spilling over the edge as it was placed heavily on the coffee table.

'Fine,' Kathryn said eventually. 'I'll take you back to the home.'

Eleanor almost sprang from the chair she'd been cocooned in all day, wobbling only slightly as she pulled her cardigan over her shoulders and announced she needed the bathroom.

'Do you want us to come with you to the home?' Lauren asked her mum as they waited in the hallway.

Hannah threw her sister a look and Lauren shrugged in return.

– 150 –

'I just wanted it to be a special day for her,' Kathryn said, leaning against the bathroom door. 'I wanted her to see the Bay. I was sure she always liked it here, I thought she'd remember the cottage.'

'Mum, it was a sweet idea.' Lauren took hold of her mum's arm. 'I'm sure she still enjoyed herself.'

'I thought if she was back here, she might start remembering more. I could turn back time.'

'Well, you don't know how much she's taken in,' Lauren tried. 'It might have helped more than you think.'

As Kathryn grabbed hold of Lauren's arm, a determined look flashed across her face. 'I think that home is repressing her,' she said, leaning in close for fear of Eleanor hearing. 'I've been thinking maybe I should move her in with us.'

'Mum, you can't,' Hannah gasped.

'Why not? You think I can't look after my own mother? I could do a better job than they're doing. I don't trust those nurses.'

The bathroom door opened and Eleanor shuffled out. In that moment it struck Hannah, watching her grandmother struggle to pull the light cord, how she was a shell of the woman she had once been. Her mum might not see it, or perhaps she didn't want to, but despite the way Eleanor had been it was still a sad thing to see. It wasn't possible for her to dictate anyone else's life anymore, she couldn't even control her own; her words no longer meant anything. *Maybe it wasn't such a bad thing Mum had done that day*, she thought. *All she had wanted was for her own mother to see a piece of the life she'd once enjoyed.*

Eleanor had stopped and was clutching the bannister at the bottom of the stairs, looking intently at Hannah. Her eyebrows were arched in concentration as she stared at her granddaughter, but for once Hannah no longer felt frightened by her.

'Is everything all right, Grandma?' she asked.

'What are you doing here?' Eleanor asked, her long bony fingers curling and uncurling over the wooden post.

'I live here.'

Eleanor shook her head, and Hannah could feel the stillness around her. Everyone had stopped what they were doing; the air was heavy with anticipation, each of them waiting to hear what Eleanor was going to say next. The moment of tenderness she had felt towards the old woman was passing.

'And what have you been up to this time?' her voice rose. 'No good, I expect. Thinking you can come in here with those ideas of yours, ruining things for everyone.'

Hannah squirmed and turned to look at her mum, her gaze imploring her to come to the rescue. But Kathryn was rooted to the spot, frozen in the moment, her mouth hanging open in shock.

'Mum?' Hannah whispered. 'What's going on?' It was clear her grandma didn't know what she was talking about but it was unnerving, and she was desperate for Kathryn to step in.

'Well, I won't let you, girl! Do you hear me?' Eleanor was saying, leaning in closer.

'Grandma, I don't know what you're talking about,' Hannah said. Eleanor seemed to believe so powerfully in what she was saying, even though it made no sense to anyone else.

'Mum,' Lauren said from behind her. 'Say something, what's Grandma talking about?'

But still Kathryn didn't answer.

'I'll make sure you don't ever breathe a word of it,' Eleanor continued, stooping forward and looking Hannah directly in the eye.

'That's enough!' Kathryn finally snapped to. 'We're going back to the home now, Mother.' She pushed Hannah out of the way and reached past her to grab Eleanor's arm, dragging her towards the door as quickly as her frail legs could take her. Ushering her mother down the path, Kathryn didn't look back at the girls standing in the doorway, both confused but relieved their grandmother was leaving.

They had reached the gate when Eleanor turned to look back at them.

'Abigail,' she said nodding, as if the name had just come back to her. 'That's who you are.'

'Abigail?' Lauren asked. 'Who's she talking about, Mum?'

But Kathryn, who had by then manoeuvred her mother through the gate and onto the lane, didn't bother answering.

'What was all that about?' Lauren said, turning to Hannah, who was still watching them clamber into the car.

'Search me,' she replied, but Hannah was shaken. There was something about her grandmother's tone, something in the way she had looked at her. Whoever Eleanor thought she'd seen in that moment, she truly believed it was someone called Abigail.

Abigail, Hannah rolled the name around in her mouth. *Ab-Gail*. She knew the name, she was sure of it.

– Seventeen –

Kathryn tried keeping her mind on the road ahead because getting her mother safely back to the home was something tangible she could focus on. On the one hand she wanted it to be over as soon as possible, but on the other she had an hour with her mother to herself and talking to her had been the main reason behind bringing Eleanor back to the Bay. She had hoped that a change of scenery, a place that might trigger memories, would relax her mother into opening up to her. But then Eleanor had thrown Abigail's name into the pot and now Kathryn could feel herself slipping deeper, much deeper, into the hole in which she had been sinking these past few weeks, and she knew she would have to pull herself out fast if she was going to confront her mother.

Eleanor's shoulders were scrunched forward, and her face screwed so tightly it made her look as if she were deep in contemplation. *Oh, to be inside her head*, Kathryn thought, and to know how her brain was functioning. She could be anywhere right now, miles away from the storm she had just stirred up for Kathryn back home.

Think. What was it she had set out for that morning? Peter. She needed her mother's help so she could stop the girls finding Peter. She needed to know what she knew about him, how much Eleanor really had to do with their marriage, because she had a feeling she didn't know the half of it.

Why did Peter suddenly leave me, Mother? That was what she would ask.

Why were you so intent on bringing him into my life but were happy for him to duck out when things got really tough?

And why did you just say Abigail's name?

'Peter,' she blurted before she could stop herself. However much Kathryn wished she could shut her eyes and blank out everything around her, she knew the journey would come to an end soon. This had to be done.

Eleanor lifted her head slightly, her gaze now focused on the road rather than her lap.

'Do you remember Peter?' Kathryn asked tentatively.

'Of course I remember Peter,' Eleanor answered sharply. Yes, perhaps she was remembering a lot more today, which was good. Maybe this was all going to be OK.

'The girls want to see him again, Mother. And I don't want them to. When we moved to the Bay, you told me he was out of our lives. Do you remember?'

Eleanor didn't answer, and so Kathryn carried on. 'I really don't know why you introduced him to me in the first place. You must have known he wasn't my type.'

Eleanor made a small noise, resembling a grunt.

'What was that, Mother?'

Eleanor said nothing, but turned away from Kathryn to look out of the window to her left.

'He wasn't exactly Robert,' she tested, taking a deep breath to quell the swirly feeling starting up in her stomach. Kathryn hadn't wanted another husband, especially not Peter. Yet she had gone along with it, swept up in her mother's desire to find what she described as a suitable husband for her daughter.

'Peter had good prospects,' Eleanor murmured, almost making Kathryn jump. 'Big plans.' She nodded. 'Your father was getting older. He didn't have a son to pass it on to.' She almost spat out the word 'son'.

'But you knew I didn't love him.'

Eleanor shrugged, a gesture Kathryn chose to ignore.

'He wanted to leave me, just before I got pregnant,' she went on. It was something she had always wondered about. Not the leaving but rather what in the end made him stay. Peter had come home from work to find Kathryn making the bed. Without taking off his suit jacket, he had walked into the bedroom and told her, 'I can't do this anymore, Kathryn. I've had enough and I don't want to be with you any longer.'

Kathryn had stared at him as he pulled a suitcase off the top of the wardrobe, throwing it open on the bed she was trying to make.

'I don't care what happens, I'm not happy,' he went on.

'Where are you going?' she'd asked, looking from him to the suitcase and then back at his face.

'I've, erm ... I'll get a hotel room.'

'Is there someone else?'

He'd shaken his head, mildly. But she didn't believe him. She knew he probably had another woman, yet she really didn't care. Instead she watched Peter open the wardrobe doors and pull starched white shirts off their hangers, throwing them into the case, avoiding her stare. And as she watched, she considered that his leaving might not be a bad idea after all.

When the doorbell rang, he stopped abruptly.

'Who's that?' he'd snapped.

'Probably my parents. They're coming for dinner tonight. Daddy was meeting some other MPs at the club in London today. Had you forgotten?'

At this his face had turned ashen. 'Shit!' he cursed, slamming the wardrobe door shut and sinking onto the bed next to the case, burying his face in his hands.

'I'll let them in,' Kathryn had said and left him in the room.

Three hours later, her parents came into the kitchen to say they were going. She had left them talking to Peter in the dining room so she could wash up (Abigail had long since retreated to her bedroom). As soon as they'd left, Peter followed her up to the bedroom and gave her a brusque apology.

'I didn't mean what I said earlier,' he muttered as he threw the shirts out of the case and into the bottom of the wardrobe, pushing the door closed with his foot. 'I won't be leaving.'

Kathryn looked at her mother. 'I'm sure you reminded him what he could lose if he left me. I'm not stupid, Mother. I knew he was in it for his career, to take over Daddy's business.' Still Eleanor didn't speak but Kathryn had a feeling she was taking it all in.

'But what I don't get is why he suddenly went. When I came to the Bay and everything came to a head, he walked away without hesitation.' Kathryn paused. 'It doesn't make sense. What changed? And then of all times.'

Eleanor turned to look at her daughter.

'The girls want to see him again,' Kathryn pleaded. 'And I don't know who or what I'm dealing with. I just want to know the truth.' Kathryn held her breath and waited. 'Mother?'

'I have no idea who you are talking about,' she said finally.

Kathryn gripped the steering wheel tightly. The anger coursed through her body. *Yes, you do*, she wanted to scream. *You know exactly what I'm saying*. Why did her mother shut her out when she needed her more than ever? *Because it suits her*, the answer fired back, *because it's always about her*. Kathryn wanted to reach out and grab Eleanor and shake her; to make her see that yet again she was turning her back on her only daughter. *Why are you doing this to me, Mother?*

But she said none of it to Eleanor. Instead she took long slow breaths, rolled her shoulders in an attempt to release the tension and, as always, let her words build up inside, stacking one on top of the other ready for the day she would erupt like a volcano and it would all pour out of her. Then everyone would know that she was astutely aware of everything that was going on around her, but she had just chosen not to react. She wasn't naïve; she just never had the guts to face it.

*****

They pulled into the Elms Home car park and Kathryn switched off the engine, turning to face Eleanor, who was already unclicking her seat belt. It didn't seem to matter how many times her mother rejected her, Kathryn realised, she still felt an overwhelming, almost pathetic need for her to want her, to love her or even just to accept her. The anger came and went but always she was left with the same thing: a desperate longing for her mother.

Kathryn placed one hand over Eleanor's, half to stop her mother from getting out of the car, half to steady her own nerves. The touch of Eleanor's skin beneath her fingers surprised her and she couldn't help but look down at it. Often she held her mother's arm, mostly to direct her to where they were going, but when was the last time she had properly touched her, felt her flesh? The skin was papery, a sheer film covering the bones underneath. Shocked, Kathryn moved her hand away, scared the skin might rub away if she pressed too hard. It wasn't that it felt different to how she remembered, it was more that she barely remembered holding her mother's hand.

'Aren't we going in?' Eleanor asked.

Even as a child, her mother never showed her love. Kathryn couldn't recall a single time when Eleanor had held her on her lap, wrapped her arms around her or cuddled her when she was upset. She wanted to reach out and touch her again, hold her mother's hands in her own and feel them against her skin. Kathryn focused on a liver spot between Eleanor's thumb and forefinger. *How long had that been there*, she wondered, raising her own finger to touch it. This simple need to feel her mother was still as overpowering as it always had been. Kathryn had always done everything her mother told her to, in the hope that one day Eleanor would reward her with a warm smile or embrace her and tell her she was loved. Yet her fingers hovered, because Kathryn knew what her mother's reaction would be. And when Eleanor snatched away her hand, she would only be left feeling more rejected than she felt in that moment. Placing her hand back in her own lap, Kathryn avoided the risk.

'I said, are we going in?' Eleanor barked, breaking her thoughts.

Kathryn looked up. 'Why are you like this, Mother?' she said, surprised at her sudden courage, 'when everything I do is to make you happy. Like today, I did it for you. Did you have a nice day today?'

But Eleanor looked at her blankly with tired eyes. Her

shoulders had slumped even further forward, as if her body had given up.

'Did you enjoy seeing the girls?' she went on.

'I really want to go in now,' Eleanor sighed.

'I don't know what else to do, Mother,' Kathryn whispered, letting the dampness of fresh tears slide down her cheeks. 'I must have got it all so wrong as a child, but I don't know why.'

*****

Patricia was waiting at the entrance as she and her mother slowly walked towards the building. Eleanor picked up speed once she saw the open door.

'I don't think this was a wise idea ...' Patricia stood aside to let the two women through. 'Have you had a nice day, dear?' she said to Eleanor.

Eleanor grunted and Patricia called a young girl over to take her through to the dining room for tea. The girl didn't look old enough to be out of school. Kathryn hadn't seen her before and hesitated in letting go of her mother. The girl wore a badge: 'Janie, Student'.

'Bye, Mother,' Kathryn said, kissing Eleanor on the cheek. 'I'll see you again soon. I enjoyed our day.'

Once they had gone Patricia turned back to Kathryn. 'You shouldn't have done this, it's too unsettling for her.'

'I just wanted my mother to come back to my home, a place she used to love,' Kathryn snapped. 'I can do that, can't I?'

'If she wants, then yes, but that's the point: it wasn't what she wanted.'

Kathryn could feel the irritation bubbling beneath her skin. Unaware, she started scratching at her arm. How dare

Patricia scold her, tell her what she should or shouldn't do with her own mother. It wasn't her place. She wanted to tell Patricia she should watch what she said to her, they were paying her salary after all.

'Kathryn? Are you OK?'

Of course, now she felt the guilt. This was why she didn't make decisions, she never managed to get things right. Not only had her mother hated the day, most likely Kathryn had caused a decline in Eleanor's health.

'Kathryn?'

The room started to swim around her again and the air was so thick. Had they closed all the doors? It was far too hot. They were making it difficult for her to breathe.

'Joanne, can you come out here a minute?' Patricia's voice sounded far away. Had she gone somewhere?

The other patients had to feel it. They must be hot too. Her heart was beating very fast now. She could feel its thump, thump, thump drumming a tattoo inside her chest. The tips of her fingers were starting to tingle again. *Concentrate on wiggling them*, she thought, and taking short, sharp breaths. But the heat was getting too much, it had gone straight to her head. Could no one else feel it?

'Hold her other arm. Quick, get her to the chair.'

A damp flannel was placed against her forehead. That felt good. It sent a shiver through her spine that made her want to giggle. And whatever it was they had given her to breathe into was doing the trick. The air conditioning can't have been working if they had special equipment to hand.

'Are you OK, Mrs Webb?' The manager, Joanne, was peering over her.

Kathryn nodded, her breathing slowing, returning to its

normal pace. They took the equipment away from her mouth. A paper bag, she noticed. Was that all it was?

'Patricia, get Mrs Webb some water, please.' Joanne's voice was kind. Kathryn was grateful she was there – there was something about Patricia she didn't like. 'Shall we go through to my office?' Joanne asked, nodding towards the door behind them.

Joanne held out a hand and Kathryn took it, slowly standing. Her legs wobbled slightly as she walked towards the office, although she was already feeling better. Once in the office they both sat facing each other across a desk. Pulling her chair forward, Joanne leaned her elbows on the desk, linking her fingers, stretching them out and then curling them back down again. It was almost mesmeric watching that movement, those perfectly manicured nails, little white tips filed into squares.

Joanne smiled at Kathryn.

'Mrs Webb ...' she started.

'Please, call me Kathryn.'

'Kathryn, of course,' she nodded, her blonde ponytail swishing at the back of her head.

Joanne Potts didn't look the type to be running a nursing home. *How did she have the time to look so well groomed*, Kathryn wondered. Of course, she didn't have children. Just a fiancé to look after, and by the size of the diamond wrapped around her ring finger, it was he who was looking after her.

'Are you feeling any better?'

'I am, thank you,' Kathryn said. 'I didn't eat anything at lunchtime,' she added, by way of explanation.

Joanne nodded again. 'Of course. Only we do know how difficult this can be for the relatives, and we're always here for you if ever you wish to talk about anything.' She paused. 'It's just that I was a little concerned this morning when Patricia told me you'd taken your mother out for the day. I'm not too sure it was,' she paused again, 'appropriate.'

Kathryn sighed. She was bored of the subject now. Joanne shifted position in her leather chair, making it squeak. It sounded funny in the silence of the room. Kathryn fought the urge to giggle. There was nothing funny about being summoned to this young girl's office but all of a sudden she couldn't think of doing anything but laughing.

'What's funny, Kathryn?'

Kathryn didn't know anymore, but the look on Joanne's face – surprise mixed in with a pinch of horror – made the whole situation even more amusing. She was laughing so much she'd begun to cry. Only now the laughter had petered out but the tears were still flowing.

Joanne pulled a tissue out of the pretty pink box sitting on her desk and handed it to her.

'I wanted her to see the sea again,' Kathryn said. 'I thought she'd like it. I thought she'd remember it.'

'That sometimes happens, but not always.'

'I wanted to get her back to my house and for everything to be like it used to be.'

Joanne nodded. 'I understand that.'

'I doubt you do,' Kathryn muttered.

'I see a lot of relatives going through the same thing as you, and—'

'It's hardly the same thing,' Kathryn snapped. 'It's not the same as having your own mother staring at you, never knowing what she's thinking, what she might say next. Whether she even recognises you.'

Joanne didn't speak. Her mobile vibrated on the desk and she glanced at the screen before switching it off. At the same time, Patricia came into the room with a glass of water. It was enough to make Kathryn stop talking. Only little things, but reminders that day-to-day life went on for other people. They really weren't interested in what was happening to her and her mother.

'I think I'll go,' she said, standing up and walking towards the door. 'Thank you for your time, Joanne.'

'You have all the time—' she was calling after her, but Kathryn had already left the office. All the time for what, she didn't know. In fact, time was the one thing Kathryn was running out of. Time certainly wasn't on her mother's side; its passing would only make things worse for her. And time was making her daughters grow up too fast, taking them away from her, allowing them to spread their wings, make their own decisions and potentially bring Peter back into their lives. No, time was the one thing she didn't have on her side, and right then she knew the only thing she could do was find Peter and get to him before the girls did. She had to find out what really happened and make sure he never saw her girls again.

– Eighteen –

Dear Adam,

At fourteen the last thing I wanted was to find out my mother was pregnant. But that's what happened.

It was constantly being drummed into us at school – the practice of safe sex, and how not to get yourself knocked up. A girl from Year 11, Paula, had left school the previous year, six months pregnant. Then after the Christmas holidays she came back in to show everyone her baby. It was a little bundle of blue, a baby boy called Tyler. At first everyone was cooing over him, but then Tyler started screaming and didn't stop. I watched Paula's face; she was trying so hard to smile but I could see the tears of frustration she blinked away as she rocked him harder and harder in his pram. As soon as she left, everyone was murmuring, 'Thank God that wasn't me' and 'Her life is so over now'. I think the teachers were secretly pleased Paula had brought Tyler in for us all to see – it was the perfect lesson in what happened when girls weren't careful.

I wasn't talking to Cara much by then, or rather she wasn't talking to me. She was still jealous that Jason liked me more than her. Jason and I weren't having sex. There was pressure to, from people like Tasha, and definitely from Jason, but I really didn't want to. I was only fourteen and the thought frightened me. Not that I had anyone I could confide in. Although I was beginning to worry Jason would lose interest in me, what put me off even more was my mother getting pregnant.

I found out by mistake when I saw a pregnancy test in the bin beside the toilet. It was half-wrapped in tissue but I could see the end of the stick poking out. I pulled it out of the bin and unravelled the tissue, gawping at the two bright pink lines in the window. It took me a moment to flick my eyes to the writing at the side that confirmed my fears my mother must be pregnant.

How I hated her. I hated that she was going to bring another child into the world when she didn't have time for the one she already had. It wasn't jealousy; I was angry with her. Angry that she thought she was such a good mother she could warrant doing it all again, and that she even wanted a child who wasn't my daddy's.

I was so angry I took the stick and went downstairs to find her. She was in the kitchen, as ever, this time staring into a cup of tea. I shook the stick in front of her face and screamed, 'I can't believe you've done this!'

Her face turned chalk-white. She didn't have any words to defend herself.

'Have you not heard of bloody condoms?' I shouted. 'This is so embarrassing!'

Still she said nothing but began fidgeting in her seat, her discomfort angering me more. 'I hope you're going to get rid of it,' I spat.

'How dare you,' she said eventually. 'How dare you even suggest such a thing!' I knew there was no way my mother would have an abortion. She was brought up Catholic; and there were certain beliefs my grandmother had instilled into all of us, and valuing life, whatever your age, was one of them.

'You're too bloody old to be having a baby!' I shouted. 'Everyone's going to laugh at me.' I started crying.

'Oh, this is so typical of you, Abigail,' she spoke calmly. 'Always thinking of yourself and not about anyone else. I should have known you wouldn't be happy for me and Peter.'

'And is he happy?' my head snapped up to look at her. I was sniffing like a child, wiping snot from my nose.

Her eyes flickered momentarily. 'Of course he's happy. He's thrilled we're having a baby together,' she told me in the even, lifeless tone I'd come to expect from her.

*****

Maggie asked me how I had felt deep down.

'Lonely,' I recalled. 'Does that sound stupid?'

'Absolutely not,' she said. 'Many people feel lonely and a lot of the time they're surrounded by people. Some people feel lonely in their marriages, like your mother might have done.'

'I never felt that way with Adam,' I said. 'In fact it was the opposite. Even when he wasn't with me I knew he was only a phone call away. I never felt like he was far away, even if he was in a different country.'

Maggie smiled. 'That's a beautiful way of summing up your marriage,' she said.

I told Maggie about the time you were staying in Surrey for a conference when I was lying in bed and heard a crash downstairs. I thought it was a burglar and I could literally feel my body freeze with fright. It was 3 a.m., that horrible time when morning is still distant and you don't want to be awake because everyone else is sleeping. I called you and you answered straight away. I could hear the panic in your voice even though you tried to hide it. You told me to call the police and said you'd come home and then I felt calm enough to turn on the lights and creep downstairs first rather than dial 999. Thankfully I did because it was just a broken shelf that had sent saucepans crashing to the floor.

Maggie laughed when I finished the story. 'I don't think I could do that now, though,' I said. 'Now I'm on my own I wouldn't have the nerve to confront potential burglars.'

I feel lonelier now than ever. Wasn't it Tennyson who said, "Tis better to have loved and lost than never to have loved at all"? I don't think I agree with him. Loving and losing you, Adam, sometimes feels harder than if I'd never met you at all.

*****

I was living in a house with two people I didn't like. Peter, who had never wanted anything to do with me, and Kathryn, who was rapidly spiralling that way too. On top of that, I'd surrounded myself with friends who made me feel empty. Great if you wanted fun, but no use if you needed more. When I tried talking to Tasha about my mother once she told me to stop moaning – 'Abi, d'you really think I want you hanging around if you're going to get all depressed on me?'

Over the following weeks Eleanor was around much more than usual. Charles had business in London, on some select committee or other, discussing wronged politicians or rather ones who had done something wrong. Eleanor made the most of the opportunity – meeting wives in Harvey Nichols for coffee, manicuring her talons, purchasing new clothes to hang off her ageing body. Then she would come to the house armed with her own special kind of first aid repair kit, intending to plaster up the cracks of a household threatening to fall apart any moment. She wouldn't have let it reach that point, of course. But the first time she arrived, after my mother had told her the happy news of the pregnancy, I could see alarm shining out of her eyes.

If she'd been the type of granny yours was it would have been wonderful to have her around. Granny Vee would have made endless cups of tea and knitted blankets and booties for the new baby. It would have been the happy household of a family expecting a new arrival. Not like the one I was living in, masked in fear and silences. Everyone drowning in their own worries, neither time nor desire to find out if anyone else in the house was keeping their head above water.

And enter Eleanor. Eleanor didn't come to make anyone feel better, she was there to make sure it didn't get worse because she must have known my mother wouldn't cope.

On her first visit, Peter was in a particularly bad mood. It was three days after I'd found the stick in the bin. I hadn't said anything to him about the pregnancy and neither had he to me. We were both pretending it wasn't happening.

My mother had barely spoken to either of us. Most of the time she was either throwing up in the bathroom or lying in bed. Her morning sickness lasted all day but I was more inclined to believe she used it as an excuse to shut herself away from the world spinning around her. I was angry with her for doing that: she couldn't face the music and so she went to bed. It was all I wanted to do too – to close the door to my life and pull the covers over my head until I could hear nothing.

Peter was slamming about in the garage, muttering away to himself as he sifted through boxes. I watched him through a gap in the door but could only see part of him. The previous night my mother had told Eleanor and he wasn't happy about it.

'Why have you told her already?' he growled when he thought I was out of earshot.

'She's my mother,' Kathryn said. 'She needs to know.'

'You need her to know, more like.'

'Why are you being so bitter about it? I thought you'd be happy to share the news.' My mother had an edge to her voice, trying to make it sound jolly, but I could tell it was strained.

'I just wanted us to keep it quiet for a bit longer,' Peter said.

My mother started crying. She didn't often cry. You would think she would be the type to do it more but she wasn't and I often wondered if she was so devoid of emotion that half the time she didn't even consider it an option. But that night she cried and Peter tried to placate her in his brusque, clumsy manner.

'Come on, Kathryn, don't get upset now, it's all fine,' he chirruped, practically slapping her on the back.

Stiff upper lip and all that.

*****

That night when the doorbell rang Peter stopped in his tracks in the garage, a box in one hand. He waited for someone else to answer the door and I knew I should go, but I couldn't stop watching him. Eventually my mother shuffled down the stairs, her purple dressing gown pulled tightly around her.

'You look awful,' Eleanor told her when Kathryn opened the door.

Peter swore quietly, dropped the box and straightened his back, so I quickly moved away from the door to sit at the table. He was surprised to see me when he came out of the garage and if Eleanor hadn't appeared in the doorway at the same time he'd probably have questioned me.

'Peter,' Eleanor nodded in his direction. 'Isn't this wonderful news?' she asked in a flat tone. She hadn't thought it wonderful at all. Babies were of even less interest to my grandmother than the children they grew up into. More likely she was wondering how another grandchild might adversely affect her life. And with my mother obviously not coping, it was just one more thing for her to have to deal with.

He brushed his mouth against her cheek and said, 'Yes, Eleanor. We're all thrilled.'

Out of my mouth came a noise resembling a snort. I hadn't meant to – I'd wanted to sneak away from the circus that was unfurling and go up to my room, unnoticed.

'What was that?' Eleanor said to me.

'Nothing, Grandma, just agreeing we're all absolutely delighted Mum is having a baby. It's just the perfect thing. Exactly what we all wanted.' I left the room before anyone could say anything, but not before I heard her say, 'Let's hope you bring the next one up with more manners.'

*****

So my mother was pregnant with a baby that at the time I didn't want her to have. I didn't like the thought of another child being brought up by those two – it didn't seem fair.

'I want to know how the girls have turned out,' I said to Maggie today. 'Sometimes I try drawing what I think they look like. But I could draw hundreds of pictures and I wouldn't have a clue.' It's hard to imagine when your mind is such a blank canvas. 'But it's not just what they look like, I wonder if Hannah is the loudest, because she always had more tantrums. Does Lauren giggle all the time like she did when she was a toddler? Does she now play the piano because she always loved this little plastic keyboard she had, or have they both had every ounce of fun and imagination torn out of them over the years and now they're just shadows of the little girls they once were?'

Maggie waited a moment and then asked me, 'Have you thought about all the things that could go wrong when you look for them? Or, of course, when you find them?'

'Like what?'

'Well,' she said cautiously. 'Most likely they know nothing about you. Or they might, but they might not want anything to do with you.'

'I thought you were on my side,' I said, taken aback. Maggie had always been supportive of everything I told her.

'Oh, Abi, I am on your side. That's why I'm saying this. You don't know what's happened over the last fourteen years or what they've been told.'

'I know that. But that's why I'm doing all this, isn't it? Going through it all again? Reliving everything that happened before she left me, so I can find out what happened after?'

Maggie nodded. 'Of course it is, Abi. I don't mean to worry you. Anyway, carry on with your story.'

Eleanor moved into Claridge's so she could come to the house nearly every day. Not bearing gifts, or offering to help: she came with words of steel and an eye that roamed over us to ensure everything was operating smoothly. I don't know who by then she was keeping the most tabs on: Peter, my mother or me. We were all capable of doing something crazy.

Peter acted like a puppy whenever she was there – 'Yes, Eleanor', 'No, Eleanor'. Then as soon as she was out of the house he looked fit to explode. A few times I caught him swinging an axe at stumps of wood at the end of the garden. One time I even saw him dig a large hole in the middle of the lawn, filling it up again the next day. He obviously had no idea what to do with the hole once he'd made it but I liked to imagine he was planning on throwing my grandmother into it.

One Sunday he came home from the pub at lunchtime, a few whiskies inside him. It was two o'clock and my mother had been cooking a roast dinner. In itself that was unusual and she'd obviously omitted to tell Peter, because when he came in and smelled the charred chicken, he told her he wasn't hungry and had only come back because he had forgotten his phone.

Five minutes later he left the house again. I was probably smirking because Kathryn said, 'What do you think is so funny?'

'Nothing.'

'You think I enjoy cooking all this for people who don't appreciate it?'

'Then go and tell him.'

The pans crashed against the sink as carrots and beans were drained, water cascading down the side and onto the floor. I watched as her slippers began to soak up the water. 'I meant you,' she said eventually.

'You're so lame,' I snapped back.

'What was that?' she turned to me. 'What did you call me?'

'LAME,' I said the word slowly. 'He doesn't want this baby, and you're pretending not to notice. It's pathetic.'

*****

'Do you think I was horrible to her?' I asked Maggie.

'No, you were a teenager, and you had a lot going on. Of course she was the one you would take it out on.'

'Sometimes when I think about what I used to say to her I feel bad.'

'Really?'

'For a moment. Then I remember everything else, and I think she deserved it.'

'You were only fourteen, Abi. Kids say stuff like that to their parents all the time.'

'But I saw something in her eyes that day. She knew Peter

– 173 –

didn't want a baby. She must have known it was the worst thing to happen to her.'

'You sound like you regret what you said.'

'I guess I just wonder if things could have panned out differently,' I said. 'Maybe I was too hard on her.'

Occasionally, Adam, I would ask you if you thought that. Often it was when I felt sad about something completely different, and then all of a sudden I couldn't shake off the thought of my mother abandoning me. 'Do you think it was my fault?' I would ask.

'God, no! No way, not at all.' You were always so adamant. 'It was never, ever your fault and don't even think it was. Only she was responsible for her actions.'

Was she, though? She was a mess. In truth, I don't think she had responsibility for anything in her life.

Maggie moved in her seat and watched me, waiting for me to go on but I didn't say any more.

'What happened after that?' she asked.

'My mother told me to get out of the house,' I said.

I went to the payphone at the corner of the road and dialled Jason's number. I told him I needed to see him but he said he couldn't get out for another two hours as all his family were round. I said I'd wait for him and I walked to the shopping centre, killing time by window-shopping and drinking Diet Cokes in the café. When the shopping centre closed, I moved to the steps outside and waited some more. I was beginning to think he wasn't going to show, but I still didn't want to go home.

Three hours after I'd called him he finally appeared, his pockets bulging with bottles of alcohol taken from his parents' drinks cupboard. We went to Hampstead Heath and shared three bottles of beer and the quarter bottle of his dad's Jack Daniel's. It was April 25th, a date I remember clearly.

– Nineteen –

'OK, there are obviously thousands of Peter Webbs, and that's just in the UK, but I thought I'd start there,' Dom told Hannah. 'So then I added dates, and put in schools in London between 1965 and 1975, and got it down to thirty-four. We obviously have no idea how old he is, but it's a good guess. You definitely sure he was from London?'

'Not definitely.'

'This is going to take for ever,' he sighed. 'We need to think of a different angle. How did they meet? What did he do for a job? Try and think of anything at all, even if it's just a guess.'

Hannah twirled her fingers in the sand and looked over at his iPad. 'I don't know any more. I wouldn't even know if you showed me a photo and said, "This is him".'

'Well, let's do it differently. We can start googling your family and see where we go from there.'

'My family? What's that going to do?'

'Haven't you ever googled yourself before?' Dom laughed. 'Give me the full names of your grandparents and your mum.'

'This isn't going to work,' Hannah sighed as she reeled off the names and watched as Dom started tapping. 'It's a lost cause.'

She loved that Dom had agreed to help but she couldn't imagine them getting anywhere, not when she knew so little. Lying back on the sand, she closed her eyes, letting the sun warm her skin, and had almost drifted off when suddenly he spoke.

'Actually it might not be a lost cause – you never told me your grandfather was a lord. There's loads of stuff on here about him.'

'Let me see.' Hannah sat up and pulled herself closer. 'Wow, he looks so much younger!' She pulled the iPad towards her. 'I knew he was, but I never really took much interest. Mum never seemed to know what he did. Can I read it?'

Hannah scrolled down the page, her eyes skipping over the words, most of them going over her head. She didn't know much about her grandfather, Charles. He had died four years ago, when she twelve, but when he was alive he hadn't been a big part of their lives. He was a peer of the House of Lords, she read, a member of the Committee for Privileges and Conduct, whatever that meant.

They flicked through articles, skim-reading them. 'Looks like he was quite the man,' Dom joked. 'Go back a page, there's something about your grandma.'

'Look at all those photos, it looks like a shoot for a house magazine! I didn't realise she was some mini celebrity in her own right. Blimey, that's her all right, though! You can still see the coldness in her eyes. Even in those she looks like she thinks she's God's gift.'

'This one talks about his company,' Dom said, grabbing the iPad back. 'Bretton Inc.' Hannah nodded as he continued to tap his fingers against the screen. 'You know what, Hannah? I think we might just have hit the jackpot.'

'What do you mean?'

'Peter Webb, Director of Services,' he read out, 'takes over Bretton Inc. It looks like your dad not only worked for your grandfather, he took over when the old man retired.'

'What? But it might not be the same one. I guess it might not be my dad ...'

Hannah couldn't believe they had found him. It was too easy, too unreal.

'It has to be. It's too much of a coincidence. I think I might have to become a private investigator,' Dom said. 'I've only gone and got you a photo of your dad.'

*****

Hannah stared at the screen, at the stranger in the photograph smiling back at her. Dark, curly hair, round glasses that made his eyes look small, clean-shaven, wearing a smart navy suit and a red tie. He was shaking hands with a man who stood at least a head taller than him. The photo was taken in 2000, the year after he left. She willed herself to remember him or at least to recognise some small feature, but nothing came.

She shook her head. 'I don't feel anything. I thought I would, but I don't.'

She continued to look at the man who had to be her father, taking in every inch of his face again. 'I don't think it can be him, because I would feel something, surely? Nothing about him looks remotely familiar.' She looked away. 'It's not him.'

'Hannah, it has to be. You're not going to recognise him, you haven't seen him since you were two.'

'But I thought I would feel it,' she said again, clenching her jaw to repress the lump in her throat. She didn't want to cry about a man she didn't even think was her dad, but she suddenly felt so sad. This wasn't what she had expected at all. Looking at the man in the picture made her feel ...

nothing. 'I thought I'd look at him and know in my heart, but this is just a stranger, and he looks nothing like I imagined he would.'

She pushed the iPad back to Dom and held her face in her hands. 'God, it all does my head in.'

Hannah stood up. She couldn't look at his face anymore. Her head was telling her it had to be her father but something in her heart was rejecting the fact, and she knew that didn't make any sense. 'I'm going in the sea,' she announced. She needed the icy-cold water to take it away. Dipping her head under would erase these unsettled thoughts if only for a moment and then she'd be able to think again more clearly.

'I'll come with you,' Dom said, draping his towel across their things. Together they walked towards the sea, stopping at the edge. Hannah dipped her toe in but pulled it back as soon as the water bit. However much she was used to the feel of the sea, its first touch of the day always made her shiver.

They stood for a while, looking out to the water. It was as if Dom understood her need for silence, waiting with her without saying a word, then eventually he reached out for her, taking hold of her hand and squeezing it.

'My grandma called me Abigail the other day,' she said eventually.

'Who's Abigail?'

'I don't know. And normally I wouldn't think anything of it,' she said. 'It's not as if much that she says makes sense at the moment.'

'So what's bothering you?'

'There was something about the way she said it, like she knew what she meant. And the way my mum reacted,' she replied, 'you could tell she wished Grandma hadn't said the name.'

'You know what?' Dom said after a while, 'I believe everyone comes to the Bay to escape something, or someone.'

Hannah felt the grip on his hand tighten and she looked up at him.

'So what did you escape?' she asked.

'Not me, but my family – my oldest brother,' he explained. 'Nathan, he died when he was seventeen. He would have been thirty last week.'

'Your brother?' she gasped. 'I never knew you had another one.'

'I was only five when he died, but I can still remember him. He had left home but came back nearly every day for his tea, and every Sunday he brought a bag of washing for Mum to do. "Nathan," she would say, "When are you going to learn to start cooking and cleaning for yourself?" But she always said it with a smile on her face. She never minded.'

'So how did he die?' Hannah asked, watching Dom's face tighten. It obviously pained him to talk about a brother she had no idea existed.

'He was in the wrong place at the wrong time. Some guy started a fight in a club and one of his mates got caught up in it. They dragged him outside and started beating him up and Nate stepped in. By that point there were about ten guys involved. According to witnesses you couldn't tell who was on whose side by the end of it. I think some of them just joined in for the fun of it.'

'Your poor family.'

'Mum swears Nate wasn't like that, wasn't a fighter. Course you never really know, do you?' he said. 'One of them

– 179 –

pulled out a knife and Nate just happened to be at the other end of it. Five seconds later the cops turned up but by then it was too late for him. His mate ended up badly bruised, but Nate was dead. Mum couldn't get her head round that.'

'I'm not surprised.'

'She blames herself. No one can tell her there was nothing she could have done to protect him, but I guess that's what mums do.'

'I guess.' She couldn't imagine how her mum would cope if she lost one of her daughters. These days her mum couldn't cope if she clicked on the wrong wash cycle. It put into perspective how little Kathryn had been through compared to Mrs Wilson, yet to look at them, you wouldn't believe it was that way round.

'You know, I still hear her talking to him sometimes, when she thinks no one's about. She tells him what's she done that day, even if it's boring stuff like going to the supermarket.' Dom glanced at Hannah. 'My dad's not around that much, he works a lot, and she never says any of it to me. It makes me wonder if she thinks Nate's the only one who'll listen to her.'

'Your mum must be so strong to keep looking after you all like she does.'

He shrugged. 'Anyhow, my point was, the Bay is an escape. If you weren't born here, and you don't fish, then I reckon you need a pretty good reason for finding your way here.'

'I never thought we had one. I always thought Mum just liked the sound of it.'

But now Hannah wasn't so sure. Maybe they had escaped here. Certainly there were things her mum wanted to hide from them. She had always thought it was just her dad, but now she began to wonder if it was more than that.

'Look around you,' Dom continued, gesturing towards the near-empty beach behind them. 'It's so bloody isolated. Every kid here's desperate to get out at some point. I bet most people in the country don't even know it exists. I'm telling you, you come here because you don't want to be found.'

Hannah looked around the bay. Dom was right, and it was nothing she hadn't already felt herself, but it was still a sad thought. Mull Bay was beautiful, yet it was holding her in its clutches, and more than ever she felt the need to break free.

'I do want to look through the rest of those articles,' she said. 'I have to find him and I need to know what happened. I just don't feel up to it right now.'

'OK, we will,' he said. 'Sleep on it tonight, and we can crack on with our search tomorrow, if you want.'

Winking at Hannah he added, 'We'll do it together.'

– Twenty –

Peter had never wanted children. Having a family meant putting another person's needs before your own and that didn't fit his make up. All he cared about was how many people he had working for him, how big his next bonus was, and who he needed to impress to further his career. Consequently, Kathryn hadn't planned to get pregnant; she hadn't intended to bring an unwelcome child into the world. But she had made a mistake, forgotten to take the pill and had unwanted sex with her husband just to placate him one night.

When the test read positive her heart lurched. After she told Peter his face set like stone: he gave her no reaction, no emotion, simply strolled out of the house, briefcase neatly tucked under one arm, mobile phone clutched tightly in his hand. Back then she had hoped that he might change and learn to want and love what was growing inside her. Now all she hoped for was that he hadn't, and he still wanted nothing more to do with the girls.

Eleanor introduced Peter to Kathryn a month after he started working for Charles. 'I have someone wonderful I would like you to meet,' she had said. Kathryn should have followed her instincts. She wasn't ready to meet anyone so soon after Robert. No one could fill the hole he had left in her heart.

'I don't know, Mother. It's so soon.'

'Nonsense! You can't continue to revel in your own misery, Kathryn. It's unhealthy.'

'Fine,' she sighed.

She didn't have the fight in her anyway. Robert's death had left her empty. Most days she wished she didn't need to get out of bed and she was sure she wouldn't have if it hadn't been for her mother sniping at her to get on with life.

'Think how it affects me seeing you like this,' Eleanor told Kathryn. 'Do you really think I can bear to see my daughter waste her life?'

The sentiment had surprised her until she added, 'Anyway, you can't go on being a single mother for much longer. It doesn't look good.'

The first time Kathryn met Peter he took her to a fancy restaurant that had recently opened. She endured an evening of his bragging, how he had managed to secure the best table for them, and how he would of course order the wine because he knew a lot about that kind of thing.

'I'm doing exceptionally well at work you see, Kathryn,' he told her over dessert. 'I have nineteen people working under me right now, but of course I expect that to double once I take over the project team next year.'

He took a drag on his cigarette and blew the smoke out of the corner of his mouth. Kathryn smiled politely as he continued.

'Your father sees what I can do, of course,' he said. 'To be honest, I don't think he'd know what to do without me now. I've turned that place around since I got there.'

'Really?' Kathryn said with feigned interest.

'Yes. It was in need of some fresh eyes and sharp thinking,' he said, tapping the side of his head. 'I think he knows I'm the man to watch,' he winked. 'Of course, in return I'm rather hoping your father will help me too. I see myself as prime minister one day,' he chuckled. 'I'd be quite good, don't you think?'

Why her father was watching him, Kathryn wasn't sure. But Charles was an intelligent man, so he must have found something appealing. Kathryn would need to keep looking for it, she considered.

'I'd like to take you out again,' he said at the end of the evening. He hadn't asked her, rather assumed she would want to go on another date with him as if she had nothing better to do. Which it turned out she hadn't because to her frustration she found herself agreeing to see him again.

They had nothing in common but Eleanor's interest was sparked whenever his name arose and Kathryn felt an unbearable need for her mother's approval. Ever since she had lost Robert her days were getting darker and she found herself clinging, like a life raft, to Eleanor. So if Eleanor liked him, Kathryn thought she probably would too one day.

As time went on and she continued seeing him, Peter spent more and more time talking about work and taking her to places she didn't particularly wish to go to, such as fancy wine bars, shows, the opera. Then when he asked her to marry him, she couldn't really think of a reason to say no. Other than the fact she didn't love him, or particularly enjoy his company, but for some reason that didn't affect her answer.

Kathryn knew she shouldn't have agreed and that he didn't love her either, but she had already lost her soulmate and she would never love another man anywhere near as much as she had Robert, so there was no point in waiting for anyone else. She might as well make do with Peter.

*****

Kathryn lay on the bed facing the ceiling. Whenever she closed her eyes she felt the nausea washing over her. It came in waves, rolling across her body and then subsiding, making her believe it was over only for another bigger swell to drown her again. It was better to keep her eyes open.

Her hands rested on her stomach cradling the piece of paper with Peter's number on it. He had sent it to her a year ago, attached to a cheque. She had been tempted to throw it in the bin when she'd pulled it out of the envelope. His brief note explained he had changed his number and thought she should have it, just in case. Just in case of what, she had no idea. Just in case they moved maybe. Just in case she didn't need his money any longer, or needed more. Instead of throwing it away, she had tucked it at the back of her bedside drawer. Just in case.

Kathryn didn't conceive that one day she'd be calling that number. For over an hour now she had been lying on the bed, playing out the phone call in her head and second-guessing his reactions. Taking a deep breath, she picked up the phone and slowly tapped in the numbers. Her heart thumped as she listened to the ringtone. She could feel its force beneath her chest, almost burning through her skin each time it pounded. Pulling herself up, she leaned back against the pillow and waited for him to answer.

'Hello?'

The sound of his clipped tone took her by surprise. Had she tried to remember how he sounded she wouldn't have been able to, but as soon as she heard his voice it was like they had spoken only yesterday.

'Hello?' he asked again, the edge to his voice showing faint irritation. 'If this is some foreign call centre—'

'Peter,' she eventually said, 'it's me, it's Kathryn. I need to see you.'

*****

Three days later, Peter was sitting on a sofa at the far end of Costa Coffee. His face was obscured by *The Times*, which he shook as he turned the pages, but Kathryn recognised him as soon as she entered the coffee shop. The top of his head was visible above the paper, his hair bouncing in curls both greying and receding. As he bent his head forward she could see a balding patch. How confident he must be, not needing to look out for her, when he knew she would be arriving any minute.

Kathryn steadied herself by gripping a chair. *Half an hour*, she reminded herself. *That was all this needed to take*. Then she could be out of there and never see him again. For the last two hours she had been telling herself that over and over as if it were a mantra: get what you need and get out.

Peter dipped his paper and gazed up at her, holding up his hand in a half-wave when he saw her. Although he stirred in his seat as if about to stand he remained seated. He wasn't smiling, and so Kathryn didn't smile back, just walked towards him muttering under her breath, *Get what you need and get out*. On reaching him she saw the hint of an amused smirk and it crossed her mind she had been talking aloud.

'Can I get you a coffee?' he asked, gesturing to the chair opposite.

'No.' Her voice shook. She needed to compose herself but

already she could feel the heat rising beneath the light shirt she had chosen to wear. She needed to flap its collar and cool herself down, but then he would know how uncomfortable she was, so instead Kathryn sat down on the seat opposite and took deep, steady breaths.

'Straight to business it is, then.' He smiled at his own joke, eyeing her carefully as if she might do something strange any moment. 'You look ... well.'

But Kathryn had noticed the dark shadows under her eyes that morning, the gauntness of her cheeks. She didn't answer Peter.

'So, it's been what, ten, eleven years and you don't have time for pleasantries?' he asked, raising his eyebrows.

'Fourteen years, Peter. It's been fourteen years. The girls will be seventeen this December.' She winced at her mention of the girls. She hadn't wanted to say anything personal about them so soon.

'Seventeen. Wow! Have you got any photos?'

'No, I don't, I'm afraid,' she replied coolly.

He nodded. 'So how are they? Are they why you're here?'

'They're fine,' she said, volunteering nothing more.

'Well, come on, Kathryn,' he said, leaning forward, placing his elbows on the coffee table between them, clasping his hands together as if in prayer and resting his chin on his fingertips. 'What is it that's brought you here so urgently?' His eyes widened mockingly as he said the word *urgently*. 'Don't keep me in suspenders.'

That awful expression he used. It had always irritated her. How quickly a few words had taken her back to a time she didn't want to be in. Already Peter had knocked her off-balance and she had to pull herself together to regain control.

– 187 –

'I need to know something, Peter,' she started, 'the truth about us.' Kathryn waited but he didn't respond. Shuffling in her seat she tried to focus. *Get what you need and get out*, she told herself again. 'How come you suddenly left us when we moved to the Bay?'

Peter leant back into the sofa, his eyes wide, his head hung to one side as he contemplated her.

He's got a wonky mouth. Abigail's words came flooding back to her. *Two thin lips and when he opens them up his mouth looks as if it's filled with crooked tombstones.* She had scolded her daughter at the time for being so rude but as she regarded him now she could see what Abigail meant. Peter wasn't attractive when you broke his features down into separate parts. His mouth was a strange shape and his eyes were too round and small. *They look like buttons that are the wrong size for his face.* She couldn't remember where this ranting of Abigail's had come from, but it was making the process easier for her now. Really, why on earth had she married him? It wasn't his money. And his ambition had driven her mad, all those nights listening to how successful he considered himself to be.

'And why's the past so important to you now?' he asked, breaking her thoughts.

'I just want some answers.'

'Because Eleanor can't give them to you anymore or because she's been saying things you don't want to hear?'

'What do you mean?' Kathryn gasped.

'I know she's in a home, Kathryn. I know what's happened.'

She could feel the sting of tears pricking her eyes. Maybe this wasn't a good idea – she would never have the upper hand over Peter and it really was getting unbearably uncomfortable.

'Maybe I should go,' she said, grabbing her handbag from the floor.

'Oh, Kathryn, you've only just got here,' he laughed. 'But if that's what you want ...' He waved a hand in the vague direction of the door. 'Remember me to your mother, won't you?'

Kathryn stopped. 'Do you know what, Peter? I've never asked much of you. I put up with everything you threw at me. You wanted to leave me, fine. You could have. You changed your mind, fine. I let you stay. Then you decided you'd go again and that was no problem either. You went. All I'm asking of you is to tell me the truth. What actually happened?'

'OK, take it easy,' Peter said through clenched teeth, leaning in and glancing around at the few customers engrossed in their own conversations. He paused and seemed to consider his answer. 'You weren't too bothered by my leaving, Kathryn. Neither of us were happy, were we?'

'I'm not talking about how happy we were. I'm not saying it wasn't the right decision, I just want to know how come you were suddenly confident it wouldn't affect your career?' She knew she was right about him only staying in the marriage for his own good, yet once she had moved to the Bay and he had left, Peter had still taken over Charles' business. And that's what Kathryn had never understood. 'What did my mother have to do with it?' she asked.

Peter picked up his coffee cup, swirled it around in his hand and then settled it back on the table without taking a sip. He gazed up at her, even had the decency to look slightly ashamed, she thought.

'I'm not proud of myself,' he said. 'I didn't intend to hurt you. When they introduced us I thought you were beautiful, you know. I didn't ever expect to have a wife that looked like you. Of course I knew they were keen for us to get together. Eleanor wanted a son-in-law to take over the business and the fact they knew my uncle—' He paused and looked back at his coffee cup. 'I had hoped we might work out but obviously we didn't. We're far too different really, aren't we, Kathryn?'

She waited for him to carry on, not knowing how to answer him.

'I knew you'd never love me. You never stopped loving Robert, did you? Only I soon realised I didn't like being married to someone who wasn't really there half the time.'

'What do you mean by that?'

Peter shrugged. 'We didn't talk, you showed no interest in me or being with me. You were more like a housemate than a wife.'

'This isn't what I came for,' Kathryn said. 'I don't need to know why the marriage went wrong.'

'I never liked the way you let your mother control you,' he went on. 'I always wished you would stand up to her, but we both know what she's like, don't we? I let her control me too in her own way.'

'Because you were getting something out of it,' Kathryn added. 'My father's business for one thing.'

'Yes of course there was that,' he said. 'But with you –' he shook his head – 'I always wanted to do more but I'm afraid I never did.'

'I don't understand.'

'I wanted to tell you what she was doing but I couldn't. I would have lost everything.'

'Tell me what? You're not making any sense,' she said.

Peter pushed his cup away and shuffled in his seat. His eyes flickered between Kathryn and the table as he took a deep breath. 'The reason I still took over the business was because we made a deal. She let me go and I promised I wouldn't tell anyone what I had found out.'

Kathryn opened her mouth to speak but he held up a hand to stop her. 'Just let me finish now,' he said. 'There was a time when I couldn't take any more of your moods, the way you regressed into yourself, wouldn't let anyone near you. At first I put it down to grief or depression.' He shrugged. 'I had no idea what was going on with you but it was getting me down too, so I went to see my uncle about you. Of course Edgar wouldn't talk to me, told me he couldn't, patient confidentiality and all that, but I knew there was something he was keeping from me. He was too similar to my own father, an appalling liar.'

Kathryn shifted nervously. The hairs on her arms were beginning to stand on end; she had a feeling she didn't want to hear what Peter was going to tell her.

'So I started to look into things myself, like the drugs you were taking. The ones they told you were for sickness. Things just didn't feel right and then you got pregnant, and I went back to see Edgar again, begged him to tell me the truth. I said I was worried about how the drugs might affect the pregnancy, that I'd spoken to a doctor friend of mine who told me that sickness wasn't the only thing they were used for. Edgar told me that when you were twelve, he had diagnosed you with schizophrenia, Kathryn.'

'What?' Kathryn's mouth dropped open. 'You're making this up.'

'I'm not, I'm afraid. Less was known about it then and your

mother freaked out, saying she couldn't let it get out she had a daughter with such an illness. As always, Eleanor was consumed by what people would think of her. So Edgar agreed to hide it. Keep it from the world and the press. They told you the drugs were for sickness.'

'But...' Kathryn didn't know what to say, what it all meant. Whatever she thought he might tell her it wasn't that level of deceit. 'I don't believe you.' She shook her head. It couldn't be true, there was no way her mother would have hidden the fact she had an illness from her for all those years. Not just because she was ashamed.

'I'm telling you the truth,' he said earnestly.

'No.' Kathryn shook her head again, the air around her was thinning and even the motion of moving her head was making her dizzy, but she had to try and focus. 'I can't be, I don't even know what it means. Isn't that when you have two personalities?'

'No, it's nothing like that,' said Peter. 'You need to talk to someone and get the facts, get the help you need—'

'No. I don't believe you,' Kathryn cried. 'Why the hell did you never tell me?'

'I believed it was under control. And I knew if I said anything my uncle would lose his job over it. I'm sorry,' he said. 'Like I said, I'm not proud of all my decisions.'

'Jesus.' The air was closing in on her again, she didn't want to have another panic attack, not in the middle of Costa, not in front of Peter. Flapping herself with a napkin, Kathryn made a move to get up but her feet couldn't hold her steady and she fell back onto the sofa.

Peter stood up, leaning over the table, and reached for her arm to help steady her. 'I'm sorry, Kathryn,' he said again.

'Get off me.' She whipped her arm away, cursing herself that she was getting into a state. This was the last thing she needed. 'I need to go outside for a bit,' she said, carefully pushing herself back up. 'I need some air.'

'OK, well shall I come with you?' he asked, his eyes curiously watching her.

'No,' she said. 'No, stay here.' She moved, unsteady on her feet, and grabbing hold of the sofa turned to face him before she went outside. 'Just do one thing for me,' she said. 'I need you to promise me something involving the girls.'

*****

Once outside, Kathryn leant back against the wall. Her head was thumping, a blind pain shooting across it and making her need to close her eyes. She wiped her damp palms across her top and waited for the feeling to pass, wondering whether she would make it back inside again or not. Peter had agreed that if Hannah, or even Lauren, ever knocked on his door or called his phone he would tell them he didn't want to see them. He agreed he would do that for her, at least.

But the other things he had said – she had an illness that her mother had covered up. It couldn't be true. Surely.

Her head felt as though it was caught in a vice gripping her tighter and tighter. The same thoughts were prodding at her now, ones about moving to the Bay, about leaving Abigail. If her mother had hidden that from her what else had she manipulated?

'What have you done, Mother?' Kathryn cried out. 'Tell me he's lying. Oh God!' She felt so sick; she was going to need to find somewhere, to get off the high street at least. But all she could see were crowds of people rushing back and forth, back and forth. 'What the hell have I done?' she cried out.

A woman pushing a pram stopped and stared at her, frowning. Then she spoke to her, but Kathryn couldn't hear the words.

'My daughter,' Kathryn said. 'I left my daughter.'

She clutched at her mouth. Now she really was about to throw up, and all over the woman's pretty blue shoes.

'Is this woman OK?' someone else was asking.

'She says she's left a daughter somewhere.'

'Daughter?' The other sounded surprised. The two women were gazing about now, one of them pointing into the coffee shop, both talking at her with too many words.

Run, run, a voice said. And so she ran, and kept on running down the street with no idea where she was going, but she had to get away from the people who started crowding round, staring at her as if she was losing the plot.

– Twenty-One –

Dear Adam,

The night you left me I thought you were never coming back, but I didn't blame you. Why would you want to be with someone who lied to you, made you think you were trying for a precious child, when really all they were doing was everything they could to prevent that from happening. You texted me the following morning to say you were staying at your parents, and that you would call in a few days. 'Give me some space to think,' your text read.

Three weeks after that you came home. I hadn't expected to see you in the kitchen when I got back from the shops. You jumped when you saw me, like you hadn't expected it either, but I think you were so lost in thought you hadn't heard the door open.

'Adam!' I cried. I dropped the shopping bags on the floor and made my way over to hug you.

'Don't...' you held up a hand and I stopped, rooted to the spot. You'd never held back from me before, and suddenly I felt a new wave of grief washing over me. Of course you weren't there because you wanted to be with me; you'd probably come back for your belongings.

'We need to talk first,' you said. 'I have to know why you did this.'

'First', you had said 'first'. That meant there would be an after. And that meant there was hope. I started to allow the jittery feeling I had in the pit of my stomach to bob about in its bubble of optimism.

You pulled out a chair for me and I sat at the table.

'Go ahead, Abi. This is your turn to talk.'

Your voice was commanding, but it wasn't stern. It was soft and gentle, pleading with me to make you understand why I had lied. Only then did I look at you properly, and I saw all the hurt I'd caused you darkening your eyes, making them lose their sparkle. Your face was drawn – had you not slept since you'd left me? I wanted to stroke your cheek, rub out the tiredness, turn you back into the Adam you were, full of life and joy. And I wondered if I could ever give that back to you.

That moment I had to decide whether to tell you the truth or let you go.

*****

'April 25th, 1998,' Maggie reminded me today. 'You said that was a date you remembered well.'

It was the day I lost my virginity to Jason. We only had sex the one time, although he was more than ready to do it again after that, just not with me. He now had his sights set on Tasha.

Two weeks after that I skipped a period but I didn't give it much thought because I had other things on my mind, like Jason barely speaking to me. Whenever I saw him in the playground or the canteen he was joking with a bunch of mates, Tasha hanging onto his arm and throwing her head back in riotous laughter when he said something mildly amusing. Cara, however, glad my short-lived relationship was over, was happy to be friends again. And so a month later, when I skipped another period, it was in her that I confided my growing concern I might be pregnant.

It was Cara's idea to steal the pregnancy test from the chemist. I made a scene at the counter about the price of their chewing gum while she slipped a test into her pocket. An hour later she stood outside her parents' bathroom while I peed on the stick and then came in and sat with me as we waited for the test to display its pink lines.

There were two. By then I knew what I was looking for, and I knew without hesitation I was pregnant.

'Oh … My … God,' Cara said. 'Oh no, Abs! What are you going to do?'

I started crying and Cara put her arms around me, soothing me with, 'Shit, your mum's going to kill you!'

That made me cry harder.

'Didn't you use condoms?' she asked.

'He said he preferred it without.'

'Yeah, well, don't tell your mum that bit.'

'She's pregnant too,' I blurted out.

'Holy crap, that's hilarious!' she laughed before straightening her face and saying, 'Of course if it wasn't so hard for you. Poor Abs.'

I could see her trying to stop giggling and I knew that Cara would never be a true friend, but right then she was the only one I had.

We were still sitting on the cold tiles of the bathroom floor when her parents came home. Cara gasped when she heard the door open and looked at me in mock horror before sprinting to the landing, calling, 'Mum, can you come here a second?'

'Cara, what are you doing?' I cried.

'She'll find out sooner or later,' she shrugged.

'No, she won't, tell her something else.'

'Mum,' Cara said when her mum appeared at the door and caught her breath at the sight of me crying on her bathroom floor. 'Abi's just found out she's pregnant.'

Cara's mum made me sweet tea and gave me three chocolate digestives. She didn't look particularly happy at the prospect of her daughter's fourteen-year-old friend being with child, but said

– 197 –

nothing to make me feel worse than I already did. I was beginning to appreciate Cara telling her when I heard them in the kitchen.

'I bet you're glad that's not me, aren't you, Mum?' Cara said.

'I know you wouldn't put yourself about like that, love,' she replied.

*****

So, Adam, that's what happened. I had a baby. I have a baby. Somewhere.

I know what you must be thinking:

'Five years we were together, and you couldn't bring yourself to tell me that?'

No, Adam, I couldn't.

'Yet you managed to tell Maggie in what, three months?'

Yes. Though it wasn't easy. And to be fair, she is a professional. And to be fairer still, I probably saw her every week with the intention of telling her even if I didn't admit that to myself at the start.

'Why couldn't you tell me?'

I couldn't tell you for a number of reasons. I could lie now and say it was a repressed memory, but it wasn't. I've never forgotten, I just learnt to manage it by blocking it out of my head. If I never told anyone it happened then it didn't matter. I could live without it scarring me. Or at least that's what I thought.

'But you were prepared to lose me?'

I was prepared to do what I needed to do to stop myself from going insane. But I prayed and prayed that it didn't mean I had to lose you.

I like playing out our conversation in my head: I can make you sound more reasonable. Plus it gets to go my way.

*****

Maggie suggests that when my family left I put the memories of my baby into my subconscious memory. She said when that happens it can sometimes trigger a warning sign. It's how she tries to explain why I lied to you about being on the pill: my subconscious was warning me it wasn't a good idea for me to have children.

After you first mentioned us trying for a baby I woke up that night drenched in sweat. My grandmother's words were eating away at me, reverberating in my ears, 'You are too self-centred to be a good mother, Abigail. Look at how you're acting, not putting anyone first but yourself. You would never be able to keep a child safe or give them what they need.' They were thrown at me so often I haven't ever been able to shake them off. I grew from a child myself into a woman, still believing them to be true.

I justify it by reminding myself I already have a child that I haven't been able to keep safe, so I couldn't become a mother to your children because I couldn't bear to think I'd screw things up like I did the first time. And I can't bear the thought of possessing any of the maternal genes that run through my family – ones that would turn me into the type of mother Kathryn was – or worse, Eleanor.

So that's why I lied to you, Adam. I pretended I'd stopped taking the pill. I let you believe we were trying and I was giving you everything you wanted. I didn't tell you the truth because I didn't want you trying to persuade me otherwise.

*****

Back then it didn't take long for the news of my pregnancy to reach my mother. Cara's mum called her a week later – 'Just to let you know, Kathryn. In case Abigail hasn't said anything.'

Of course, my mother was furious. 'How could you do this?' she kept saying to me, her hands shaking wildly as she ran her fingers through her hair. 'What happens now? What do we do now?' She was questioning it over and over in a feverish rant, but of course neither of us had the answers.

I hadn't wanted it to happen, but of course that didn't feature on my mother's radar. I tried pleading with her to help me because I was frightened. Already I had a baby growing inside my tummy and I had no idea how we could make it stop. I almost begged her to hold me and tell me it would all be OK, and together we could work something out. But instead she was going round and round in circles, shaking her head, her eyes betraying her fear, practically shaking me to give her the answer. And so I stopped asking.

*****

That night the cavalry arrived in the shape of my grandmother. I opened the door to find her standing on our doorstep, fury burning in her eyes. She pushed me aside and walked into the house without speaking to me.

'What is this family coming to?' she hissed at my mother, who was cowering behind a stack of books she'd decided to clear out of the loft. 'And what the hell do you think you're doing, Kathryn?'

'I'm just having a sort out,' she chirped.

'What is wrong with you?' Eleanor continued as she kicked the books to the side of the room. 'No wonder your daughter is in this mess when you can't even focus on the matters at hand.'

My mother began packing the books back into the boxes that moments earlier she'd taken them out of.

'I just don't know what to do,' she whimpered.

'Well, that's why I'm here, isn't it?' Eleanor snapped. 'Because sure as hell we aren't letting this get out: we will tell everyone you are having twins.'

*****

It was the middle of June and I was nine weeks pregnant. Eleanor was making decisions; plans were crystallising. No one else would ever know about my situation. 'Apart from Cara and her mother, of course,' Kathryn chipped in solemnly. That same evening Eleanor paid the Whites a visit, and to give them their due they never let it slip. (The following week Cara told me her mother had booked a holiday to Spain in August. They had never been abroad and she couldn't believe her luck that her parents could suddenly, somehow, afford it …)

It was determined I would stay at school until the summer holidays. 'You'll need to loosen your clothing and you'll just have to tell everyone you are eating too much,' Eleanor told me.

Subconsciously, my hand moved to my stomach. It felt no different, just as flat as it had always been.

'In the meantime,' Eleanor told my mother, 'we need to get the word out.'

The following day my grandmother dragged me to the post office. We stood in the queue and I waited for her to announce, loudly, to the cashier, 'I would like to set up two accounts in my name, please. Yes, it's all very exciting: my daughter saw two babies on her scan, she's expecting twins!'

The three old women in the queue behind us gushed what a

blessing that must be and Eleanor agreed that yes, she was very lucky, before turning back to the cashier and winking, tapping her nose and saying, 'Keep it to yourself though, dear, won't you?' Everyone knew Cheryl was a gossip. She lived at the end of our street and took notes on all the comings and goings so she could 'discuss' them at length with her customers. Head held high, my grandmother left the post office, one more thing ticked off her list.

The day after school finished Kathryn drove us to my grandparents' house in Yorkshire, where we would spend the next six months. Eleanor called my headmaster to say I wouldn't be returning until the spring as she was taking me on a trip to Africa, where I would be home schooled. He of course knew who my grandfather was, so bought the whole story and wished us well, saying he looked forward to hearing all about it when I returned. Grandpa had lived in Africa for seven years. It gave him plenty of opportunity to drill into me everything I needed to know, on Eleanor's command.

In reality I spent the next four months in their house going out of my mind with boredom. Eleanor was constantly buzzing around, questioning my mother and me as if we were in an interview, making sure we got our stories straight until she was satisfied neither of us was going to say or do something stupid at the last minute.

My mother swung like a pendulum. One minute she was relaxed with Eleanor in charge and would come back from the shops laden with bags full of baby toiletries, white babygros and vests, sleepsuits, little bits for a nursery and books on parenting as if she were a first-time mother. Sometimes she almost whipped herself into a frenzy of excitement and I could never work out if she was truly happy or going completely mad. But at other times she locked herself in her bedroom, only emerging for dinner when she would barely speak to anyone, her face expressionless and unreadable.

I, on the other hand, kept out of everyone's way as much as possible. Every few weeks I would meet with Dr Edgar Simmonds, who knew the depth of our lie. But apart from that, I spent hours drawing pictures and sketches, just to keep my mind occupied. I did it because it made me feel closer to my daddy, and right then more than ever I needed someone who was on my side.

As my belly grew bigger I started to feel like I wasn't alone so much. Every time I felt a flutter or a kick, and eventually my baby turning its whole body inside of me, I grew to love the little person I carried within me. It was all mine, my precious baby, and I had an overwhelming need not to let it go. Some nights I lay awake imagining what I could do to escape, how we could run away and live together on an island far away so no one would find us, but always I landed back in reality with a deafening thud. I knew I had given up any options a long time ago.

My mother's due date came and went. Eleven days later she went into labour and on December 15th the first of the 'twins' was born. Although not due for another month, in the early hours of New Year's Eve I felt the first pulling pains of what I guessed were contractions. I screamed out in terror: the pain had taken me by surprise, and I didn't like what was happening to my body. Eleanor came into my room, picked up my bag and ushered me into the car. I could see my mother watching me from her bedroom window, holding her own baby close to her chest as we drove into the night to the hospital.

The hours passed and the contractions grew stronger. Dr Simmonds arrived, along with a midwife called Mae, who Eleanor had paid for. Mae told me I was doing well and that my baby would soon be born. I screamed at her to get it out of me, clutching her tightly in fear because I didn't want her to go. She was the only person I wanted to get me through it, I thought, because she had kind eyes. I wanted Edgar nowhere near me.

Eleanor remained in the hospital, only occasionally coming into the room to see how I was doing. Every time she appeared, I looked away – I couldn't bear to see her watching me in so much pain. Right then I was blaming her for making me go through with it.

By evening I was desperate for pain relief, begging Mae to help me. I asked her to give me anything that would take away the agony but she told me there wasn't time: my baby was on its way.

I screamed and cursed and pushed until I heard her exclaim that she could see a head. And at thirty-five minutes past midnight on New Year's Day my daughter was born.

They handed her to me and I took her in my arms. She was tiny and slippery and her eyes were scrunched tight, making her nose wrinkle up. Her head was covered in soft, dark hair. I wrapped my sheet over her and pressed her naked body against my own, and as my tears fell onto her little face I didn't take my eyes away from hers: my daughter. I was holding the most precious thing in the world and I had a burning need to look after her for ever.

'The first baby girl of the New Year!' a nurse exclaimed, coming into the room. 'We'll have to take a special photograph for our wall.'

'You'll do nothing of the sort,' Eleanor said sharply, following her in.

My grandmother leaned over to look at my baby and nodded. I didn't look up at her; I didn't say anything to her. I just wanted Eleanor to get out of the room and leave me alone with my daughter again. Once she had left, Mae came back over and sat next to me, rubbing my arm. 'Is everything all right, Abigail?' she asked. 'Are you OK?'

I nodded, tears still spilling from my eyes as I held my little girl against my chest and nuzzled into her head. I would have breathed her in if I could.

'She's perfect,' I whispered.

'She is,' Mae smiled. 'But here,' she took hold of my arm and loosened my grip, 'don't squeeze her too tightly.'

I looked down at the black downy hair covering my daughter's head; her tiny chubby fingers gripping my thumb so tightly. The nappy Mae was putting on her that was too big for her. I studied every inch of her little body and I could still describe it to you perfectly.

I didn't know how I was ever going to let my little girl go, yet I knew I had no choice. I should have run out of the hospital that day like I'd wanted to, but I didn't – I was too scared I might lose her completely.

'What are you calling her?' Mae asked.

'Hannah,' I replied.

'What a pretty name.'

'I read in a baby book it means "God has favoured me",' I said. 'I like that. I want her to always be looked after.' And as I held Hannah close against my chest, I knew that was all I wanted for my baby girl – for her to feel safe and happy and loved. Looked after like I never was.

*****

There was no ceremonious handing over of my baby because of course I still lived with her new mother. On January 31st, 1999, Kathryn and I and the two girls, Hannah and Lauren, went back home. It was a clear-cut plan. I did as I was told and as soon as I got back to London, I returned to school, where I got to live the life of a teenager again.

Only no one accounted for how I would feel. Every night I spent hours staring at the babies. Once they were safely asleep in their cots, I crept into their room and lay my hand on Hannah's tiny tummy so I could feel the comforting movements of her breathing. Then I would do the same with Lauren, my little half-sister, because I didn't like the thought of her missing out just because she wasn't my own.

They were both beautiful in their very different ways. Hannah's hair was getting lighter but was still a dark brown, and she had chubby cheeks that reminded me of a hamster. She was slightly bigger than Lauren, with podgy little arms and legs. Lauren's fair, downy hair made her look almost bald. People of course accepted they were twins because that is what they were told. Why would they believe any different? But when I looked at them I couldn't imagine how anyone could be so gullible. They barely looked like sisters, which of course they weren't: Lauren was Hannah's aunt. The thought messed with my head so much whenever I watched them sleep soundly together in their cots that I dreaded to think how it might affect them if they were to ever know the truth.

I don't know if Kathryn was ever haunted by such thoughts. It won't come as a surprise to know that we never discussed it, but I was sure she wasn't always handling it as well as she tried to make out.

'Lauren goes on the right,' my mother shrieked at me one day when I had settled them down to sleep. 'What are you doing?'

'It's not as if you need to tell them apart!' I snapped.

I had no idea why she did those little things but I wondered if she was trying to instill some 'twin-ness' into them. Making up for them not sharing a womb.

– Twenty-Two –

Hannah looked at her mum in disbelief. She hadn't mentioned her dad's name since reading the article about him, and until that morning Kathryn had clammed up whenever his name was mentioned. Now all of a sudden her mum seemed not only willing to tell them about him, but she was adamant they must hear it right then.

Kathryn was already dressed when she appeared in the kitchen, wearing a cream cashmere cardigan over a sundress. She had obviously made an effort, and she almost passed it off until Hannah noticed the buttons had been fastened all wrong, and where one shoe was pink, the other was red. About to point these out, Hannah stopped when her mum held up her hand to speak. And suddenly she was more than happy to tell them about their dad. In fact she insisted they know all about the kind of man Peter Webb really was.

Peter. His face flashed up in Hannah's mind as Kathryn drew her own ugly portrait of him. 'I fell in love with his charm,' she said. 'He had everything I was looking for in a man: ambition, intelligence, looks. Then I fell pregnant and everything changed. He told me he'd never wanted children, that he wasn't a family man. And after you were born, true to his word, he wanted nothing to do with you. He started to …' She stopped and waited for Hannah and Lauren to nod their encouragement. 'He became a bit violent, never with you, just me. And so I finally told him he had to go. I was scared he might hurt you too. And that's why I don't want you looking for him. I don't want you having anything to do with him. You understand that, don't you? You mustn't go near the man. You can't trust him.'

Hannah listened intently, and along with Lauren she nodded that no, of course they wouldn't go near him, not if that was the type of man he was. But there was something odd about the earnest look in her mum's eyes imploring them to believe her. Hannah couldn't help but feel there was something amiss.

Once Kathryn was satisfied with their assurance that they wouldn't ask about him again and would never go looking for him, she left the house.

She was meeting Morrie, or so she said.

*****

Lauren looked ashen. Hannah could imagine what her sister must be thinking.

'He sounds like a monster,' Lauren said.

She could tell Lauren was fighting back tears because her back was arched rigid and her fingernails were digging into her palms, making little white semi-circles in the flesh. It was something she had always done since they were young, a distraction to stop herself from crying.

'Yes, well,' Hannah said eventually, 'I certainly wasn't expecting that.'

Lauren shook her head. 'Can you believe what Mum's been through? It must have been awful. I just don't understand how someone doesn't want to know his own daughters, and then to be so violent too. My God, Hannah, it doesn't bear thinking about.'

'No.'

'It makes my skin crawl to think someone like that is our father. Doesn't it you?'

Hannah nodded. 'Where are you going?' she asked as Lauren got up and picked her bag off the floor.

'I need to do something, something normal. Sophie's going to the shopping centre today and I'm going to go with her. I can't sit here thinking about him right now. Come too.'

But Hannah shook her head. 'No, you go. I don't fancy it.'

Lauren didn't need telling twice. She was out of the door in minutes, leaving Hannah to mull over what she hadn't wanted to say, that there was definitely something not right about her mum's story. The way she so readily proffered information, a story so carefully structured that it left Hannah wondering what was really going on. She was surprised when her mum had started talking the moment they appeared in the kitchen, and had watched her closely as the facts unfurled. It felt more like Kathryn was reading a script but without the expression of a talented actress: her tone flat, her speech relentless until she'd finished what she wanted to say. Even when Lauren asked a question, she'd held up a hand to stop her.

And the truth was, Hannah didn't believe a single word she had said.

*****

On her insistence the girls forget all about their father, Hannah had of course agreed just to get her out of the house. As she had listened to her mum and watched her nervous gestures it reminded her of something Lauren had told her a week earlier when she had found Kathryn in a state, frantic over some envelope she had obviously not wanted anyone to see. Hannah had thought nothing of it at the time. Her mum's odd behaviour was part of everyday life but now she wondered if there was more to it. And as she had the house to herself she was going to find whatever it was she was hiding.

Hannah started searching in Kathryn's bedroom, pulling out drawers from the chest, carefully rifling through make-up, underwear, balls of socks and then putting everything back in its place. Inside the wardrobe she removed shoes and bags and opened shoeboxes. She then ran her hand along the top but found nothing. Pulling up the crocheted throw, she peered under the bed, moving a suitcase to the side of the otherwise empty space. Pausing briefly, her eyes took in the room and settled on the bedside table.

Something was jamming the drawer and she needed to tuck her hand inside and push it down to release it. Once open, she stared at the number of things stuffed inside, so unlike every other organised drawer in the house. She started thumbing though receipts, photos, a notepad and passports until right at the bottom she noticed a brown envelope.

Hannah prised it out. 'Private and confidential' was written across the top in block capitals, underlined twice. The seal had come unstuck and a line of tape hung loosely over it, so old it had turned brown and lost its purpose. She took a deep breath and tentatively opened it, peering inside. Nothing; whatever was in it had been removed. Her heart sank. She'd been so full of anticipation that suddenly she felt like crying. About to put the envelope back into the drawer she absent-mindedly dipped her hand inside, a final sweep, and felt something tucked at the bottom. Clenching her fingers around the paper she pulled it out and unfolded it, once, twice, three times until it was laid flat across her lap: it was a page from a newspaper. She scanned both sides, looking for something that made sense, but nothing seemed relevant. So she started again, this time looking closer, reading each line, searching for anything to do with her mother.

And that's when she saw it: a small article tucked into the right-hand corner at the bottom of the page. An article that made her heart stop but made no sense whatsoever.

– Twenty-Three –

Kathryn hadn't intended to lie so much about Peter, but she hadn't been able to stop the words from spilling out of her mouth once they started. Still, she was pleased the girls had bought the story, and had promised her they wouldn't continue the search for him. At least she could put that to rest.

She had a missed call from Peter that night. He had called her at midnight and left a message, asking her why she had run off, saying he had more he needed to tell her. He mumbled something to do with the truth about Mull Bay, but it wasn't clear what he meant. Kathryn didn't know how much more she could take, but at the same time she knew he might be the only one who could give her answers.

Kathryn stopped at the clifftop, where she intended to call him back. Hopefully the girls wouldn't see her, but even if they did then she could tell them a story: that she was still on her way to Morrie's.

Dipping into her pocket, she realised she had left her mobile phone on the bed. Damn, she didn't want to go back for it but what if he called again and one of the girls answered? Reluctantly, she turned round and walked back to the cottage.

The girls must have left, it was so quiet when she went in. Kathryn dropped her keys on the hallway table and began to climb the stairs. But as she neared the top she heard a rustling from her bedroom, and when she reached her door and slowly pushed it open she saw Hannah crouched on the floor, beside her bed.

The sight threw her.

'Hannah?'

Kathryn looked at Hannah and then at the drawer of her bedside table, half out, and then back to her daughter before her eyes settled on the newspaper cutting in her hand: the news the hospital had leaked to the local press, that Eleanor had thankfully never seen. The cutting she had kept all about the first baby of the New Year because it was the only piece of truth she had.

Hannah turned slowly. Colour had drained from her face. Kathryn's fingers gripped the doorframe tightly, steadying her as she swayed towards it, and her eyes bulged as they flicked from Hannah to the newspaper and then back to Hannah. Her mouth opened into an 'O' and then clamped shut again.

This was it, the moment she had dreaded for the whole of the girls' lives.

'What are you doing?' Kathryn eventually asked, the words little more than a hoarse whisper.

'What does this mean?' Hannah asked, holding up the newspaper. 'It doesn't make any sense, Mum. I don't get it.'

'It's, erm …' Kathryn's brow furrowed. She was thinking hard, but no words came out.

'I mean, it's my name, isn't it? Which means it must be me, right? But yet it can't be, can it, Mum? What about Lauren? What about the date? That's not even my birthday.' Hannah tapped her finger against the paper. 'And I don't get why it says I was born in Leeds when I thought it was London. So is it someone else?'

Kathryn continued to stare at Hannah.

'Are you going to say anything?' Hannah shouted. 'Just tell me what this is, Mum. Just be honest with me. Please.'

'*Ohhh,*' the noise Kathryn heard coming out of her own mouth was a groaning sound, like an animal in pain. She threw her hands to her head, her fingers splayed as their tips dug into her scalp, and she saw Hannah watch in horror as she sank to her knees onto the carpet.

'No, no, *no!*' she mumbled through her sobs. 'Ohhhh, *God!*' The words stretched out interminably.

Her world was falling apart and none of it had been her doing in the first place.

– Twenty-Four –

'Mum …' Hannah's voice shook. 'Please just tell me what it is. I can handle it, it can't be that bad.'

She had seen her mum like this before. The day they had taken Grandma to Elms Home her mother had stood in the hallway of Lordavale House and howled like a wolf.

'It's OK, girls,' a nurse had told them. 'It's just the shock. She'll be right as rain in a moment, you both go and wait in the other room.'

But this time Hannah couldn't walk away and let someone else deal with the hysterical state her mum was getting into and it was beginning to frighten her.

'It's OK,' Hannah tried to sound calm. 'Just tell me what it is. You'll feel better once you do.'

'I never wanted you to find out, Hannah,' Kathryn cried out.

'Find out what, Mum?'

'What happened,' she said, grabbing the sleeve of Hannah's top and twisting it into a tight ball. 'I was doing it for you. For you and Lauren.'

'Doing *what* for me?' Hannah shook her arm free. 'Mum? What did you do?'

'I'm not—' she started. 'I'm not—'

'Not what?' Hannah cried. 'You're not *what*? Just say it.' Although she was beginning to realise she probably knew the answer.

Kathryn's head was shaking back and forth as if she had lost all control.

'Are you my real mum?'

'Oh God!' Kathryn murmured, clutching at her throat with one hand. 'I'm so sorry, Hannah. I'm so sorry. You should never have found out.'

'Who—' Hannah paused, her voice cracking. 'Who is my mum?'

'Abigail.' She had to strain to hear her mother's words. 'Abigail is your real mother.'

'Who the— But that's who Grandma called me the other day.' She wanted to reach out and grab her so-called mother by the hair and scream at her to shut up and stop telling her sick lies. Beg her to tell her she was making it all up, was confused as she sometimes got. She wanted to slap her with such force that Kathryn would stop blubbering on the bedroom floor and spit out whatever it was she had to say. But Hannah's body was paralysed, her arms heavy at her sides.

'Who is Abigail?' Hannah's voice was barely a whisper.

Kathryn placed her hands on her knees to steady herself and appeared to be calming a little.

'Abigail's my daughter,' she said eventually. 'And your mother. I adopted you. She was too young and she could never have raised you.' She shook her head again. 'I wanted to bring you up as twins and—'

'Lauren?' Hannah asked. 'Tell me you adopted both of us, didn't you? Not just me?'

But Kathryn squeezed her eyes tight, covering them with her hands.

'Mum,' Hannah shrieked, 'tell me Lauren's my sister!'

Kathryn's head barely moved but gave a glimmer of a shake, so small but enough to tell Hannah what she really didn't want to know.

'Lauren is mine,' she whispered.

'Oh God!' Hannah shouted, feeling as though she was about to be sick. She pushed Kathryn aside and ran into the bathroom.

'Hannah, wait!'

'Where's Abigail now?' she screamed, clutching the bathroom sink. Kathryn had followed her and was leaning against the door, pulling at her cardigan as if she were about to rip it off.

'She's—' Kathryn looked up at the ceiling, letting her eyes roll back. Hannah had never seen her mother look like this before. It was disturbing to watch yet she had to know. 'She's ... I don't know,' Kathryn said eventually, shaking her head.

'You don't *know*? What do you mean, you don't know?'

'We lost touch when we came here.'

'Lost touch? How do you lose touch with your own daughter? None of this is making sense, Mum,' Hannah cried out. 'Or whoever you are,' she added. 'Oh, my God, you're my grandmother!'

'Hannah ...' Kathryn reached out to touch her, but she pulled away sharply.

'Get off me!' she screamed. 'So what happened? Did she run away from you?'

Kathryn was crying again, shaking her head and covering her face with her hands.

'Tell me the truth.'

'We had to get away,' Kathryn cried out. 'We had to go. We had to ... *I* had to.'

'You left your own daughter?'

Hannah really thought she was going to throw up there and then. She had to get out, to get away from this hideous liar; she couldn't take any more. Her mother was sinking to the floor, curling up into a ball. Hannah felt an urge to kick her, to get the whole truth out of her, but she also needed to get out, to get away from her. There was a whole army of questions twisting her thoughts until she couldn't think at all. Questions she would soon be desperate to ask, but right then all she could think of was getting away from the person she had believed was her mother.

Hannah's whole life was a lie. She had been betrayed by the one person who was supposed to be there for her, no matter what; the person who had taken her away from ever knowing her real mother.

*****

Within minutes, Hannah was at the clifftop. She had tried calling Lauren and then Dom but neither had answered their phones, and somehow she had to get to Lauren. She spotted Dom in the sea, flat out on his surfboard, arms dangling either side of it and engrossed in conversation with Cal. The water would be cold. Despite how much had already happened that morning, it was still only nine o'clock and the sun hadn't had time to warm it up. The wind was picking up and she knew that meant Dom would spend most of the morning surfing. Running down to the shore, she called out his name. He looked up and held up his hand in a wave, then turned back to Cal.

Hannah cupped her hands around her mouth and called again, waving at him to come in. This time he grinned and gave her a thumbs-up, then pointed out to sea and turned away as he and Cal started paddling away from her.

'Dom!' she called out again. 'Come back, I need to speak to you.' But she knew it was useless: he hadn't heard her and they were moving further away. Hannah wiped away tears with the back of her hand; she had no idea what to do next. She needed him, wanted him to take her to Lauren, and now the wind was blowing stronger and she was shivering in only a thin T-shirt and shorts. But she couldn't go home, she hadn't brought the keys to the beach hut and Morrie would be fishing. She really didn't know where to go and she desperately wanted Lauren.

Running over to the pile of clothes the boys had discarded on the sand, she picked up Dom's sweatshirt, held it briefly against her face to breathe in his familiar, comforting smell and then put it on. She could feel keys in the pocket and looked back up at the clifftop. She hadn't noticed before that his dad's car was parked at the top. Still shivering, she decided to wait for him in the car – she would be able to see when they came out of the water. Tapping out a text to him, she told him that she urgently needed him to take her to Lauren at the shopping centre. That she had just found something out about her mum. Then Hannah left the beach and walked back up the steps.

She sat in the driver's seat so she could put the key in the ignition to start the heater. Leaning her head against the window she closed her eyes. 'My mum isn't my mum,' she tested the thought aloud. 'That's someone called Abigail. And that isn't even the worst bit,' she cried, tears now spilling down her cheeks and falling onto her bare legs. 'No, do you want to know what the worst bit is?' she called out to no one. 'She only gave birth to me. Not Lauren, just me. So Lauren isn't even my sister. And the really screwed-up bit, the bit that would make bloody great TV, is that Abigail is actually my mum's daughter,' Hannah started to laugh hysterically. 'My mum is my grandmother!' she shouted. 'What kind of freak show family are we?'

The depth of Kathryn's deceit was so great. Their whole lives were stacked with lie upon lie and Hannah had no idea if she would ever know which parts were true. Did Lauren know any of it? Surely not, she thought, although who could she trust now? Nothing her mother said would matter to her again. Nothing she herself did mattered. She could run and run, and whose business was it to ask where she was going or to tell her that she couldn't do it? No one's – that was who. Her whole life Kathryn had told her not to do this, not to go there, not to stay out too late ... For Hannah to tell her every single thing she was doing or thinking, or planning. For as long as she could remember, Kathryn had gripped onto her so tightly – and for what? To protect the web of lies she had created? And she had stopped her from ever knowing Abigail, her mother – Kathryn's own daughter. What kind of sick person would do all that, and why?

Hannah grabbed hold of the steering wheel, both hands gripped so tightly she would have felt the pain if she hadn't been crying so hard.

'God!' she called. 'And you, Dom, why the hell aren't you with me?' she added, looking out to sea. He was still paddling around, he and Cal circling each other like sharks waiting for a kill. Hannah screamed until she felt some of the tension leave her body, but it was no good, she couldn't sit there any longer. She needed to get out of the Bay, find Lauren, talk to the only person who would have any idea what pain she was feeling at that moment. But also she had to find out if Lauren already knew. The need to get to her sister was beginning to drive her crazy.

Picking up her mobile she tried calling Lauren again but once more it went straight to answerphone. She was angry with everyone now. Angry with Lauren for having her phone switched off, and angry with Dom for mucking about in the sea when she needed him. And then her phone started to buzz. *Home* flashed up on the screen.

She had no desire to speak to her mum, but a tiny part of her, and something she didn't like to admit, was nervous about what Kathryn might do. And with the small possibility it could be Lauren, Hannah pressed the green button and tentatively answered, 'Hello?'

'Darling?'

'I don't want to speak to you,' she cried.

'Hannah, please come home. We need to talk. Is Lauren with you?'

'Oh, that's it, isn't it?' Hannah let out a strangled laugh. 'You just want to make sure I don't get to Lauren first!' she shouted.

'No,' Kathryn said slowly. 'No, that's not it, but—'

'Oh my God, yes, it is!' Hannah cried out and hung up, tossing her phone onto the passenger seat and banging her hands against the steering wheel. 'Oh my God, what do I do?'

Cursing Dom, she looked out to sea again but she knew he wouldn't be coming out any time soon. And so she weighed up her options, which whittled down to taking a bus or calling a taxi. But in her rush to get out of the house she had left without any money, so she considered one final option as she ran her fingers over the keys dangling from the ignition. It wasn't one she should even entertain and had she not been so hell bent on getting to Lauren that nothing else mattered, she wouldn't have given it any more thought.

Turning the key a notch further, she held her breath as the engine rumbled. The only thing against this crazy idea, other than the fact she was essentially stealing, was that she'd never learnt to drive. Not properly anyway. Morrie had taken her out in his own car on many occasions. A couple of times he'd driven to a large open parking area that was always desolate in winter and let both girls have a go behind the wheel.

'You take to it well,' he once told Hannah. 'I think you're a natural. Now just don't tell your mother what we're doing,' he added, laughing.

Without giving the idea any more thought, she thrust the gearstick to Drive, gave one more cursory glance towards Dom's figure bobbing in the sea, and drove off, across the gravel and onto the road.

The car sped off through the roads leading out of the Bay far too quickly. Her manoeuvres were jerky, her braking too hard and often too late. She didn't feel in control but then she wasn't anymore, and unsurprisingly none of it mattered.

The main road was ahead and Hannah attempted to indicate right but instead of reaching the indicators she had flicked on the windscreen wipers, which began swiping furiously at the screen in front of her, obscuring her vision. The sound of a lorry's horn, loud and constant, aggressively sounded out and Hannah realised she must have cut right in front of it without seeing it coming.

'Concentrate, Hannah,' she told herself. 'Just get yourself to Lauren.'

Her phone started to buzz on the passenger seat and she looked down to see Dom's name appear on the screen. 'No,' she murmured as she reached for the phone and tapped the red button to cancel the call before throwing it back onto the seat. Her eyes flicked back to the road and then back to the phone as she waited to see if he would call back. A beep indicated he'd left a message.

Hannah reached for the phone again and pressed the voicemail button, taking her eyes off the road for a second too long, unaware of the red braking lights of the cars in front that had come to a sudden halt.

– Twenty-Five –

Kathryn hung her head over the toilet and threw up for a third time. Standing up to wipe her mouth, she stared at the reflection gaping back at her. She no longer recognised the woman in the mirror. That woman was pale, with such dark rings beneath her eyes they suggested utter exhaustion with life. The whites of her eyes were now red, making her look like a wild animal.

'What have you done, you stupid woman?' Kathryn asked. 'You stupid, *stupid* old woman! What do we do now?'

She clutched the sink and continued to stare, waiting for a response.

She had never been good at discovering answers for herself. Eleanor had always been on hand to provide those. At the slightest suggestion of something going wrong Kathryn was on the phone to her mother, asking her, begging her to tell her what to do. Now everything was falling apart and she had no idea how to stick it back together again.

'You should learn to stand on your own two feet!' Peter once snarled at her. That could have been on any one of a number of occasions, all of them blurred into one long tragic life. 'She rules you, Kathryn, but the saddest thing is you let her.'

'Yes,' she told the ghost in the mirror. 'Well, you were right, Peter. And don't you worry because I'm paying the price now.'

She'd seen the disgust in his eyes as he spat out the words at her. He might have been a useless father and abandoned his daughters, but she was worse. She was a mother – no mother should do that.

'Why do you have to be so weak?' Abigail once said to her. 'Why can't you stand up to her, put me first for a change?' When had that been? Kathryn searched her memories. Not that it mattered. None of it mattered, but she wanted to remember. It was when Robert died. No, Abigail was too young. It was when she fell pregnant. Yes, that was probably it. Abigail had needed Kathryn, and Kathryn in turn had found herself a cupboard and hidden herself away.

'The girls will never know the truth,' her mother had said.

Kathryn started to laugh. How adamant Eleanor had been, that it was right to leave.

'But they do, Mother,' she shouted at the mirror. 'And where are you now when I need you to tell me what to do about it? That's right, now the shit's hit the fan you've checked yourself out. But you created this mess, not me. You did this.'

Eleanor hadn't been right. The real truth was alarming, and once she had worked it out, it all seemed so obvious. The thought had been haunting her for a while, but since seeing Peter it was practically jumping into her head and kicking away at her skull. Eleanor hadn't told Kathryn what to do for the best. Not for Kathryn anyway. Not for the girls, and definitely not for Abigail.

Eleanor had been so scared everyone would find out about the girls. When it came to the end she had been adamant what they had done would never be revealed. She had said she was worried they would take Hannah away, and Kathryn believed her. Because of the way Abigail was being, she had thought her mother was right, and she was scared too.

But what if it really wasn't like that? What if she remembered wrong? After what Peter had told her, Eleanor certainly had other things to lose.

Kathryn slammed her fist against the mirror. 'You stupid, *stupid* woman!' she screamed again, pounding harder and harder until the mirror shattered and she yelled in pain, her balled fist sliced with a shard of glass. Blood quickly rushed to the surface, dripping into the basin. For a moment she watched, mesmerised by the bright red drops splattering against the stark contrast of the white porcelain. Pulling a piece of toilet paper from the holder and wrapping it around her fist, she haphazardly created a bandage to soak up the blood that still flowed.

Hannah would tell Lauren what she now knew.

Hannah would want to find Abigail.

None of them would forgive her; none of them would want to know her. She would never forgive herself.

She would be all alone; she would have no one. That was too unbearable to think about. She had to to do something, anything – but what?

Kathryn backed out of the bathroom. She couldn't look at herself any longer without the rush of bile rising in her throat. Running down the stairs, she picked up her jacket and fled through the front door. She had to get out, to where she didn't know; she just had to go somewhere.

*****

It was five hours later when Kathryn returned to the house. The church bell was chiming two o'clock as she unlatched the gate and shuffled up the path. She couldn't explain how she'd passed five hours walking, trying to make sense of what had happened, how much truth there was in what Peter had told her, what the future held in store. She had decided to come back and call Peter; to get that call out of the way.

Inside the house she hung her keys on the hook and picked up her mobile that she'd left behind in the rush to escape. It was flashing away at her angrily. She pressed a button and the screen lit up. *You have 14 missed calls*, it told her, all from numbers she didn't recognise. Her fingers unsteadily jabbed at the Voicemail button when the shrill ring of the landline made her jump. Grabbing it from its cradle she called into the receiver.

'Hello?'

'Mum?' the voice cried out. 'Where have you been? I've been trying to get hold of you for hours.'

'I've been out, I've been walking, I was … Lauren, what's happened, is everything OK?'

'No, it's not,' she sobbed. 'I'm at the hospital. I, oh, Mum! You need to get here. You need to be here! I even had Morrie looking for you. No one could find you.'

'Lauren, tell me what's happened,' Kathryn begged.

'Hannah was in an accident. The car went into a tree and—' She broke off, crying.

'What do you mean, car? What's happened? Is she OK?'

'I don't know all the details but I think it's serious.'

'How do you mean, serious? She's going to be OK, isn't she?'

'I don't know, they're doing a scan on her at the moment to find out what's wrong. They said something about internal bleeding. She looks awful, Mum. Her face is so swollen I hardly recognised her and they said she might have concussion. I'm sorry,' Lauren wept. 'I really don't know what they were saying, it's all too much.'

'No,' Kathryn cried. 'God, *no!*'

This was all her fault. It was karma coming right back round for her with a vengeance.

'Don't take away Hannah,' she sobbed as she hung up the phone.

– Twenty-Six –

Dear Adam,

I've found Eleanor. I took the plunge and figuring my grandmother would be the easiest person to start with, I looked on Rightmove for her house in Yorkshire. Lordavale, it came up straight away. Turns out all you need is a postcode and you can find any property that's been put on the market in the last few years. I didn't expect to see it because I hadn't believed she would leave her precious house, but there it was, clear as day in all its eerie glory. Photos of each room, as stark and cold as they were in reality. I felt as if a ghost had swept through me when I saw it again.

Another few clicks and it appeared her neighbour, Doris, hadn't put her house on the market. I say 'neighbour', she lived a good five hundred metres from the haunted house, but anyway, Doris, whose telephone number is still listed, was easy to get hold of. I told her I was an old school friend of Kathryn's, that we'd lost touch years ago, and I was trying to trace her to invite her to a reunion. Doris told me she knew all about what had happened to Eleanor, yet didn't manage to be very specific.

'My memory,' she kept telling me. 'It's not what it was.'

Doris is in her mid-eighties and couldn't hear well. She kept asking for my name so eventually I made up the name Nancy, and she said, 'Oh, yes, dear, I remember you.' She couldn't recall much about Kathryn and didn't know what had happened to her but told me she could probably find the address for Eleanor, if that would help.

I told her it definitely would. 'Well, hold on a moment, dear, and I'll have a look in my drawer,' she said. Her voice went in and out of earshot as she carried the phone with her. I could hear her rummaging and tutting, 'No, no, maybe I don't have it anymore.' As she searched, she peppered me with snippets about the family.

'Of course when dear Charles passed away four years ago it took its toll on her,' she said. 'The big house was such an upkeep.'

It threw me to hear my grandpa had died. I hadn't really thought through what I might learn from the call, so when she dropped in his death it was a shock. Grandpa was an elusive presence flitting between his office and the dinner table, always absorbed by his work. He wasn't an unkind man – he just had absolutely no interest in anything other than business. So I wouldn't say I was particularly sad to hear about him dying, I just hadn't given him any thought.

'And then it was about a year ago she moved to the home.'

'The home?' I asked. 'Do you mean a care home?'

'Yes, dear. And Lordavale was sold to a young family. Bit of a saga all that was of course, with all Charles's debts. I don't think Eleanor saw much money in the end.'

'He had debts?' I asked.

But Doris didn't answer me. 'Oh dear, I can't find this address. I'm really not being too helpful, am I?' she said.

'Don't worry,' I sighed. 'It was a long shot anyway.'

'It's in a place just to the West of Darlington,' she said. 'I can't remember the name, a grand place though.'

'That's great, Doris,' I said. 'Thank you.'

I hung up the receiver and took a deep breath. My hands were shaking; I hadn't realised how nervous I was. But it had been easy – too easy. I felt a fluttering of excitement as I tapped another search into Google. There are twenty care homes in that area and so I starting calling each one in turn. By the fifth I struck lucky. Eleanor, they told me, was in Elms Home. A huge Victorian building and, according to their website, 'the pinnacle of all care homes, where everyone wants their loved ones to be looked after'.

The person I spoke to asked who I was. 'I'm a granddaughter,' I said, 'of her cousin Mabel. My name is Katie.'

Another lie, though Mabel did exist: she died when I was young and her family then moved to America, so even if Eleanor had no interest in seeing her cousin's granddaughter, I hoped she'd believe the story. I told the nurse I was in the area and wanted to see Eleanor, and the woman said she was happy for me to visit as long as I made an appointment.

I put the phone down and reality hit me: I had found my grandmother. A major link to the girls, and my mother, yet I didn't know if I could face her. What would I say? Hello, Grandma, remember me? Well, it's been a while, but here I am and I just wondered if you wouldn't mind being awfully kind and giving me my mother's address. You wouldn't mind? How wonderful! Well, I'll just pop along and say hello to her, then.

This was Eleanor. But this wasn't any ordinary grandmother: this was the force behind our lives, the woman who had dictated everything. This was the evil bitch who had made me hand over my baby daughter.

But then if I didn't go and see her, what would I do?

*****

And so I am going today, Adam. Right now I am sitting in a hotel room, surrounded by a sea of beige and mustard. There are putrid yellow plaid curtains and a dull carpet covered in stains. I dread to think what they might be and have to hotfoot it over them to get from the bathroom to the bed.

I have been pacing the room since 6 a.m. this morning and

knew if I only had myself to talk to, most likely I'd get cold feet, which is why I'm talking to you. I'm hoping you'll give me some courage. I need to keep my end goal in mind, finding the girls. I can't let Eleanor win again without even confronting her. I only hope that when I do, I don't fall apart – I don't want all my hard work with Maggie to be pulled from under my feet the moment I lay eyes on Eleanor. Because she has a way of doing that, making me feel like I'm nothing.

Eleanor ruled all of us. She ruled my mother because Kathryn was weak and because she allowed herself to be controlled. She ruled me because I feared her. Whatever Eleanor wanted, Eleanor usually got, whatever the cost.

The night my mother left, when Eleanor turned up and pushed past me into the living room, she told the police officers she knew exactly where my mother was and I should never have called them in the first place.

'Abigail is being dramatic,' she said, gesturing a hand towards me. 'As always.'

The policeman nodded, as if he knew exactly the type of girl I was. He had, after all, already made up his mind about me the first time we had crossed paths.

I was in shock but tried telling them I had no idea, pleading for them to believe me. But Eleanor shot me a look, her steely eyes piercing through me, and I was scared. There was something about her that night, like nothing would stop her, and I found myself clamping my mouth shut and waiting for her to get rid of them so I could hear what she knew about my mother.

The two police officers shuffled beside me, neither knowing what to do. But this was Eleanor Bretton, wife of Lord Charles Bretton, and I was just a kid who had been in trouble with them the week before, and so wholeheartedly they swallowed up her lies.

I knew I should have told them the truth – that I had no idea where my mother had gone with the girls. But as Eleanor glared at me, almost goading me to speak, I couldn't, Adam. I just couldn't.

'I'll be sorting this out,' she said to me once they had left.

'Where have they gone?' I begged her. 'Just tell me.'

'They have gone away,' she said simply. 'And it's up to you what happens next, but things have to change, Abigail, because I will not tolerate you trying to orchestrate what happens around here.'

And I didn't stand up to her – I let her tell me what to do, to wait, to leave well alone, because that's what Eleanor makes you do. But the funny thing was, when Eleanor had turned up on my doorstep that evening I'd seen the surprise in her face. She hadn't known my mother had left – she had been as shocked as me. Yet over the course of the following days I had forgotten that and allowed myself to believe she had been responsible.

*****

While my mother's disappearance was out of the blue there had been some build-up. Our relationship had hit rock bottom and I shouldn't have been surprised that she did something crazy. There were times before the girls came along when I got home from school expecting to find her swinging from the rafters, so I guess her going was the preferable outcome. I shouldn't make light of it but that's the way it was – Kathryn was pretty mental. And Eleanor would take advantage of it.

All Eleanor wanted was to make sure she came out on top and that no one stood in the way of her doing that. In her eyes I was an obstacle. Everything I did was one major hurdle after another for her. She despised me for the amount of complication I brought to her life.

In February 2001, Hannah had hit the terrible twos and wasn't averse to throwing tantrums. Every time she didn't get her own way she threw herself to the floor and kicked at the air, screaming. If anyone approached her they would often get struck on the shins, so I found the best way to deal with it was to leave her well alone until it passed. It usually did within ten minutes. If I was on my own with the girls I would roll my eyes at Lauren and say, 'What's she like, eh?' and we would ignore her. Then as soon as Hannah had stopped, she would pick herself up and join us. By contrast, Lauren was amazingly placid. Nothing provoked her into a bad mood.

It was clear Kathryn found Hannah and her moods harder to cope with. She would fuss and get agitated, fanning herself like she was overheating. Her arms waving about her, she would parrot, 'Please just stop that. What is it you want? I just don't understand what you are crying for.'

'Leave her alone,' I'd say. 'Stop trying to calm her down, you're obviously making things worse.'

My mother would then get defensive. 'I'm perfectly capable of raising my daughter,' she'd say, always a slight emphasis on the word 'my', but never a confident one.

If Eleanor was around when Hannah was having a tantrum, her eyebrows would rise to a point and her shoulders arch back further and further before she almost screamed at my mother to do something about it. 'I would never let you throw yourself about like that,' I often heard her say. 'Your children should be controlled.' She always said 'children', with one never differentiated from the other, careful not to point out that one was any worse behaved than the other. I expect she would have taken great delight in pointing out it was Hannah who was the uncontrollable child, but she never did. Eleanor was much too measured for that.

Then one day I came out of the bathroom to find Hannah lying on her back in the hallway, screaming and kicking the front door with Kathryn about to lose it. My mother was shaking, her arms flailing around the top of her head like some crazy woman. Meanwhile Lauren was cowering in a corner, one watchful eye trained on Hannah to make sure her sister was OK.

I don't know what Kathryn was about to do but I wasn't going to find out. 'Leave her alone!' I shouted as I raced down the stairs, standing in front of Hannah to block Kathryn. She glared at me and told me to move.

'No,' I said. 'I won't let you anywhere near my daughter if you're going to be like that.'

Kathryn inhaled a deep breath and said, 'She's not your daughter, Abigail. She is my daughter. Step aside.'

But I refused. 'You don't know how to handle her,' I said. 'Just like you can't handle anything.'

That was the second and last time she slapped me round the face. I didn't care that time. I wanted to slap her right back but I could hear Lauren whimpering in the corner. Hannah had by then stopped screaming and was staring at us both, wide-eyed with fear.

Kathryn held out her hand as if she was trying to take her slap back, but I pulled away. 'You aren't fit to bring up any more children,' I said through clenched teeth. 'I should never have let you do what you did.'

She didn't respond, which only gave me more ammunition. 'I'm going to make sure everyone knows whose child she really is,' I said, and left the house.

*****

'I'm going to take Hannah,' I told Cara, full of confidence. 'I should never have handed her over.'

But by the time I had left Cara, I was less assured. She reminded me Hannah had been legally adopted, that I'd have no money, and would probably never see Lauren again. But I also knew I didn't want to carry on living the life I'd unwillingly signed up to.

At home backup had already arrived. Eleanor was standing at the door when I got there and pulled me in with force, shutting the door behind me. 'Don't you ever refer to yourself as that child's mother again,' she warned me. 'She is no longer yours, she is your sister and nothing more.'

Her eyes bore into mine as her words sliced through me. I'd signed documents the day Hannah was born. Dr Edgar Simmonds had pushed them in front of me the moment Mae had taken Hannah to be weighed. I was so tired and my hand was trembling as I put my childish signature next to where Eleanor's bony finger pointed. In that moment I had signed away any right I had over Hannah and I knew that. I was also aware, as Cara pointed out, that should I ever run off with Hannah, I'd get nothing from them. Financially I'd be broken and I couldn't support a daughter on fresh air and love.

My life wasn't suitable for looking after a baby and I was well aware of that. I spent my evenings drinking and smoking in alleyways with my mates, and days in school trying to scrape by as best I could. I was aware I couldn't look after a child, even when I loved her as much as I did Hannah. So I knew I wouldn't take her away, but that didn't stop me from threatening it. I enjoyed the reactions I got. Every time my mother pissed me off, I told her I would tell the world Hannah was my daughter and I was made to give her up. She would shrivel into herself before my eyes. It gave me a wonderful feeling to see the power I had over her. That with those few words I could send shivers down her spine. Of course every time I made a threat it wasn't long before Eleanor arrived to reprimand me, but I didn't care: it was all just words.

Three days before they left me, and just after I'd made more threats, I'd left Kathryn sobbing on the kitchen floor like a child. Eleanor had at that moment walked in and I gave her a smug look as I passed her in the hallway and went upstairs to my bedroom. I was naïve, too young to realise I was playing a game against a woman who would never lose.

'This cannot continue,' I heard her say to Mother. 'I am going to put an end to this.'

But I had smirked as I went into my room.

Three days later they were all gone. I wondered how much of it was my fault, if I'd pushed Kathryn to the brink. Yet I also couldn't imagine it was her decision. She would have needed help and that help would always come from Eleanor. The truth was I was sure Eleanor had somehow been behind it, I just didn't know how.

So Eleanor won. It didn't matter her opponent was her seventeen-year-old granddaughter.

That's the woman I'm up against today, Adam. My only hope of finding the girls rests with the very person I suspect took them away from me in the first place.

– Twenty-Seven –

Kathryn pushed through the main doors to the hospital and stood in the entrance. The signs faded in and out of focus as she searched for the ward where her daughter would be. Around and around she looked, but the more signs she saw, the less clear they became. Panic coursed through her body: it was happening again. They had taken Robert, and now Hannah.

But she couldn't go there. Couldn't believe she might lose Hannah too. Yet still Kathryn heard the threatening voice telling her it was all her fault, all her doing.

She had prayed in the car on the way to the hospital. Made a bargain with God. 'Keep Hannah safe,' she had said. 'And I'll—' What was it she could do? Come on, Kathryn, think! What could possibly make any of this better? 'I'll put it all right, I'll find Abigail, I'll tell everyone the truth,' she had cried out. 'Just keep her safe.'

'Can I help you?' a voice asked. Kathryn turned round, still rooted to the spot in the middle of the foyer. A man in his early twenties surveyed her over the top of his frameless glasses. He wore a badge that said Jenson Turner.

'My daughter,' she said.

'Would you like me to see if I can find out?' he asked kindly.

Kathryn nodded and gave him Hannah's name. She watched him walk to the reception desk and speak to the girl behind its counter, gesturing vaguely behind him in her direction. When he returned, he said, 'She's in Ward 23. Through those doors to the left, and it's the first ward on the right-hand side.'

'Thank you,' Kathryn mumbled, but didn't move.

'I'll take you there if you like?' the young man said as he nodded towards the doors. 'I'm going that way.'

Kathryn allowed the stranger to lead her to the ward, where he left her at the door, telling her she was in the right place and nodding towards the nurses' station.

'Can I help you?' a nurse asked, barely looking up from her paperwork.

'My daughter ...' Kathryn started again.

'What's her name?'

'Hannah Webb.'

'Oh, Mrs Webb,' the nurse said, looking up before standing and walking round the desk. 'Hannah's through here.' She pointed to a closed door and walked towards it, one hand on Kathryn's arm. 'She's stable, but I think she might be sleeping.' They stopped at the door and the nurse turned to Kathryn. 'Your other daughter, Lauren, is in there with her. She's very upset so she'll be glad you're here. And I'll try and get hold of the doctor for you to speak to.'

Kathryn nodded and gazed through the small window on Hannah's door as the nurse retreated to her station. Lauren wasn't aware of her presence and for the moment Kathryn preferred it that way: she wanted to watch them. There was something about the girls, the way they moved around each other, that had always captivated her. They were as close as real twins could ever be, moving as one, always in tune with the other. Sometimes Kathryn felt a small pinch of jealousy, as if she was an outsider. But there wasn't room for jealousy today, it was superseded by the knowledge she was ripping that bond apart for ever.

Kathryn couldn't see much of Hannah's face from where she stood. It was masked by the angle of the bed and a drip with one line feeding into her wrist. But she saw what Lauren meant when she'd said she barely recognised her. The right side of her face was noticeably swollen, distorting her features. It made her eye look black, as if she had been beaten up. Kathryn wanted to run her hands over Hannah's face and wipe away the bruising; her daughter shouldn't look like this.

Lauren held Hannah's hand in her own, using the other to stroke her sister's hair, pushing it away from her face. She bent to kiss Hannah on the forehead and then stood and walked around the bed to the table, where she poured herself a cup of water from the jug. She drank the water and crushed the cup in her hand before throwing it into a bin then went back around the bed, sitting next to Hannah again, once more taking her hand and placing it back within her own as she stroked her fingertips over Hannah's. There was plenty of space at the other side of Hannah, even an empty chair. But Kathryn knew why Lauren was on the other side of her: she needed to be on the right, just the way she always was.

Kathryn knew she should go in. Just push open the door and be there with her girls. She held her hand up to the glass window on the door. Everything was playing out in slow motion. Her precious Hannah, lying deadly still. Hannah had been trying to get away from her, running away. How long had she been trying to do that for? 'But look where's it got you,' she whispered to Hannah. 'It's so unsafe.'

Then there was Lauren: sweet, oblivious Lauren. Kathryn felt an overwhelming need to keep it that way.

Taking her hand away from the glass she stepped back, her eyes sweeping across the room. It was so empty, unsurprisingly, as Hannah had only been brought in that afternoon, but the lack of cards and flowers felt wrong. The room needed colour, Kathryn decided. That was it, she would go to the shop and buy balloons, flowers … Anything to distract from the stark white clinical box her daughter was lying in. It was a good idea that almost made her smile. Turning away, she began walking back down the corridor when the nurse called, 'Aren't you going in to see your daughter, Mrs Webb?'

'I'm going to the shop first,' Kathryn told her. 'To buy balloons, I think.'

'But Mrs Webb, Lauren's been waiting for you. She needs you to be with her. I really think you should—'

'I will in a minute,' Kathryn snapped. 'But first I need to brighten up that room, it's far too drab.' She turned on her heels and walked away before the nurse could intervene further but not before she heard them whispering.

'What was all that about? Has she even been in there?' another voice asked.

'No, she's gone to the bloody shop.'

A sigh, and then, 'I just don't get some people.'

Kathryn picked up pace and turned left into the main corridor leading back to the entrance. She knew the nurses would think she was a bad mother. They were probably right. But the truth was she couldn't face going in and seeing Hannah, knowing she herself was the reason her daughter was lying in hospital with internal bleeding, her face in pieces. Kathryn kept her eyes trained forwards, not wanting to look anyone else in the eye. She didn't see the boy with the huge bunch of flowers as he turned the corner and walked straight into her.

'Sorry,' he mumbled as he knocked against her left arm. Kathryn didn't respond.

'Mrs Webb?'

She turned and saw the face behind the flowers. 'Dominic,' she said coldly. 'What are you doing here?'

'I just came to see Hannah.'

'I can take those to her.' Kathryn held out her hand for the flowers. 'This time is for family only. We don't want any other visitors.'

Dominic looked uncertain. 'Oh,' he said, 'if that's what you want.' He handed the flowers to Kathryn. Yellow, pink and white carnations sprayed with gypsophila. They were a pretty choice.

'How's she doing?' he asked.

'She's—' Kathryn stopped. 'How did you know she was here?'

'Erm …' Dominic paused and looked down, contemplating his shoes as he shuffled from one foot to the other. 'Well, when my dad got the call.' He shrugged.

'What do you mean? What's your dad got to do with it?'

'Oh,' he said. 'You don't know what happened?'

'Just tell me.'

'Well, I thought she was just waving at me, when I was in the sea, you know.' He shrugged again. 'I guess she must have needed me pretty urgently, though. I didn't see her text until I got out and by then she'd taken off in Dad's car.'

'She took your dad's car? What are you saying? She was driving?'

Dominic nodded. 'Yeah, Cal saw the car speeding off, and he—'

'Just shut up for a moment,' Kathryn said, holding up a hand to stop him. 'You're saying Hannah took your dad's car and drove off – where? Where was she going?'

'I think she was looking for Lauren,' he said, his head hung to one side as if considering whether Kathryn actually knew anything at all. 'The police called my dad when they got to the accident. Then he called me.'

Kathryn rubbed at her temple with her free hand. This couldn't be happening. Her sixteen-year-old daughter, who couldn't drive, had stolen a car and crashed it.

'I don't think he'll press charges, though,' he added.

Kathryn nodded. 'Good,' she snapped. Her head was beginning to throb. She wanted to ask the boy if he thought the lights were too bright in the hospital because they were spearing her eyes so much it was becoming difficult to focus. He hadn't seemed to notice, though. In fact he was still staring at her intently as if waiting for something. Maybe he had asked her a question and she hadn't heard. The lights really were too bright.

'What did you say?' she murmured.

'I didn't say anything,' he said.

'OK, well, I've got things to do, if you don't mind.'

She really did need to get to the shop or maybe sit down for a bit. Somewhere dark.

'It was me that got hold of Lauren,' he carried on talking. 'Hannah said in her text she was at the shopping centre so I called them and they put out a tannoy.' He sounded so pleased with himself, she thought, as if waiting for her to thank him when all she wanted was to grab him by the arms and shout, '*Get out of my bloody way!*'

'I didn't say anything to Lauren, obviously,' Dominic said.

'What?'

'Well, you know,' he said. 'Hannah said something about finding something out—' he tailed off. 'Anyway, I didn't say anything.'

'Now you listen here,' Kathryn lurched towards him, grabbing a handful of his shirt, the flowers dropping to the floor beside them. 'Whatever you think you might know it has nothing to do with you. Nothing.'

But Dominic stared back at her; his head gave a fraction of a nod, his mouth the glimmer of a smirk. She pulled her hands away and held her clenched fists in front of her stomach, her eyes quickly scanning the empty corridor. Dominic reached down to pick up the flowers and pushed them back at Kathryn, who by reflex took hold of them.

'Let Hannah know I was asking after her,' he said.

– Twenty-Eight –

'I wish you could tell me what you so badly wanted to,' Lauren murmured to her sleeping sister, squeezing her hand. 'What made you take a car and come looking for me?'

Lauren had been queuing to pay for a pair of jeans when the tannoy came booming across the speakers: '*Will Lauren Webb please report to the main office on the ground floor immediately?*' Sophie looked at her, gaping. Something awful had happened, of course it had. They didn't put out messages like that if it wasn't an accident, or someone had died.

'You'd have had a phone call if it was something bad,' Sophie said. 'Check your phone. It's probably something to do with your bank card.'

Lauren scrabbled in her bag for her phone and found it at the bottom. 'It's dead,' she said, pressing the button. 'It must have run out of battery.'

Sophie took the jeans and dumped them on the floor, grabbing Lauren's arm. 'Come on, then, we'd better get down there.'

My mum's had an accident, she thought. *Or maybe it's Grandma. That's more likely it*, she reasoned, with guilty relief. Grandma's ill, or dead. No, she's just had an accident. It will be awful and her mum would be in pieces, but it was still a preferable option. Not once did she think it was Hannah. Not once did she remember that, of course, Hannah was the only one who even knew she'd gone to the shopping centre that morning.

When they gave her the message, that her sister was in hospital, they told her to call Dom. Lauren felt as if all the breath had been sucked out of her. Nothing could happen to Hannah; she wouldn't let it. Not her little sister. 'We need to go,' she turned to Sophie. 'I've got to be with her.'

'Of course. Do you think your mum knows? You'd better try calling her from my phone on the way.'

No, she didn't think her mum knew, because Kathryn would have been the one to call the shopping centre and leave the message. Lauren tried her but she wasn't answering the phone. Her mum could wait, as long as she was there with her sister. Lauren would be the one Hannah would want to see when she opened her eyes. It was always each other they first saw when they woke up, no one else.

And now she was watching her sister, slowly breathing in, out, in, out. Tubes feeding her veins and her face so swollen and sore. 'Wake up, sis,' she pleaded with her. 'Talk to me, tell me what you wanted to say so badly.'

She couldn't bear to see her sister so empty of life. Sometimes Hannah's bubbling moods drove her mad; she was always looking for the next thing, never pausing for breath. Lauren envied Hannah's take on life, how she always knew what she wanted out of it and would make sure it happened. One day she would have to let her go, she knew that. Hannah wouldn't settle in the Bay as she herself most likely would. But none of that mattered right now, because all she wanted was for Hannah to open her eyes and laugh and joke about something, then leap out of bed announcing her next crazy plan.

Lauren heard the door click and turned around to see her mum standing in the doorway, armed with at least half a dozen pink and purple balloons, a giant teddy bear and a bunch of flowers. *Don't say anything*, she told herself. *Don't ask what's taken her so long.*

'Come and sit down,' Lauren said, pulling up another seat next to her. Kathryn looked awful. Her face was ghostly pale and her hair a mess. Her hand shook as she took hold of the chair and sat down next to her. Not once did she look at Lauren, nor at Hannah, it seemed. Instead she stared intently at the bed.

'Are you OK, Mum? The doctor's going to come by in a bit and speak to us. We'll know more then,' Lauren told her.

Kathryn nodded and Lauren shifted on her chair. She would have liked her mum to tell her everything was going to be OK and to hold her in her arms, but she could see she wasn't going to get that. Yet again, Lauren would have to be mother.

'Why was she trying to get hold of me?' she asked her mum. 'Do you know what she wanted? I've got no idea why she would take Dom's car. It must have been something urgent.'

Kathryn turned and gazed at Lauren. 'Do you need a drink?' she asked, a forced spring in her voice. 'Shall I get us both a cup of tea, or maybe some soup. I fancy soup, I think. There's a machine just out there.'

'*Mum*! Will you just stay here with me for a bit; you've only just got here. I was asking you if you knew what Hannah wanted.'

'No, I don't, I'm afraid,' Kathryn murmured.

'Well, aren't you in the least bit curious?' Lauren asked. 'She stole a car; she can't drive. She was desperate to see me for some reason because she couldn't get hold of me.' Lauren started to cry. 'It's my fault, Mum. It's my fault she's in here because my phone wasn't on.'

'No, no, it's not your fault,' said Kathryn. 'It's definitely not your fault.' But her words were flat and either she didn't believe what she was saying or she knew something. Lauren watched as Kathryn idly twisted her ring around her middle finger, then stared blankly at the bed again. *That was more likely it: her mum knew exactly why Hannah wanted to see her but she couldn't bring herself to tell her.*

– Twenty-Nine –

Lauren was asking questions and all Kathryn wanted was to get out of the room. A rap at the door made her jump as a doctor walked in, smiling at her. He looked older than her, maybe in his sixties, which she liked because that meant he would know what he was talking about. Much more than all those young ones swanning about in their pristine white coats, barely out of college.

'Mrs Webb?' His voice was soft. She nodded and stood up. 'I'm Dr Emmett.' He held out a hand, which she shook. He had large hands that enveloped her own and a nice firm handshake. *Yes, Hannah would quite literally be in good hands with him*, she thought, stifling an unwanted giggle. There it was again, that urge to laugh in the midst of a horrific situation. Kathryn shook her head, ridding herself of the thought.

'Shall we step outside the room for a moment?' he asked, motioning to the corridor.

'Hannah's car collided head-on with a tree,' Dr Emmett said, once they were outside the room. He had glasses that might be for reading, Kathryn thought, because they were perched on top of his head, making his white hair spring out either side. 'The force of the impact meant that Hannah was thrown against the steering wheel,' he continued. 'Her stomach was very swollen when she arrived at the hospital and she was complaining of pain in the top right side, so we ran some blood tests. There were indications of internal bleeding so we carried out a CT scan too, which shows the impact of the crash has caused a laceration to her liver.'

'A *what*? What does that mean?' said Kathryn.

'Well, the cut to the liver is about three centimetres in depth, which is significant. About 25 per cent of the surface area of her liver is damaged but the good news is that there doesn't appear to be too much bleeding. That means, at present, we don't need to do a blood transfusion. She'll be monitored closely and if she remains stable, the liver should be able to heal itself.'

'Oh God!' Kathryn shook her head. 'But she's my baby,' she said, turning to look at Hannah through the open door. 'When will you know more? When will you know if she's stable?'

'We'll run more tests in a few hours.'

Kathryn turned back to look at the doctor. 'She will be OK, won't she, Doctor? You'll make sure she's OK?'

'Mrs Webb, rest assured we're doing everything we can to help your daughter.'

'My other daughter, Lauren,' she said, pointing into the room. 'She mentioned concussion.'

'It appears Hannah knocked her head on the side window. We believe she was probably unconscious for a few minutes, and there is evidence of concussion, yes. When she was awake earlier she was very drowsy and confused. But the best thing you can do for now is let your daughter rest. It's going to take a bit of time for her to fully recover.'

'What do you mean by confused? Does she remember anything at all?'

'We don't know how much she remembers at the moment. There's a chance she might have some amnesia. But as I said, we don't know for sure. We just need to monitor her progress for now. Your daughter's sleeping still,' he nodded towards Hannah's bed. 'Why don't you go and get yourself a coffee, have a break and come back in a bit? She might have woken by then.'

Kathryn grabbed the doctor's arm. 'Yes, I will, but are you saying there's a chance she might not remember things?'

'Well, maybe, but I really can't say any more at the moment.'

'Mum?' Lauren was standing behind her. She hadn't heard her daughter join them. 'What might she not remember?'

'Let's see how the next couple of hours go,' Dr Emmett said calmly. 'I just suggested you both might like to take a break, get something to eat. Let Hannah sleep for a bit.'

But Lauren shook her head. 'You go, Mum. I'm not leaving her.'

*****

It was too wrong to even think it but maybe if Hannah could just not remember what had happened that morning ... It was a sick thought and something she should never wish upon her daughter – a sick, sick thought. But say she didn't remember it, then Hannah and Lauren need never know and Kathryn could put it all right. She would make them happy; even let Hannah go away, if that's what she wanted. But then of course she had made a deal with God earlier. And He was probably looking down on her right now and thinking, *It didn't take you long to forget your end of the bargain, so maybe I won't keep mine.*

And of course that Dominic boy knew something. Maybe Hannah had told him all of it. Or maybe she hadn't.

What would you do, Mother? Kathryn closed her eyes as she leaned against the wall, waiting for the lift. *How would you handle this shitty mess I'm in?*

'Kathryn!'

She opened her eyes and saw Morrie coming towards her, just as the lift pinged next to her.

'Wait for me.'

'It's good of you to come,' she said as he reached the lift, his breath short and sharp, as if any exertion was a shock to his body.

'Of course I was going to come. As soon as Lauren called me I told her I'd try and find you, then come over.'

They found the cafeteria on the second floor. Kathryn scanned the room, for what she didn't really know. Maybe in case she saw someone she knew, perhaps that Dominic. But she didn't recognise anyone and chose a small table by the window overlooking the car park, where she sat waiting for Morrie to bring tea for them both.

'You don't look good,' he remarked when he'd joined her. She watched him open a sachet of sugar and tap it into his cup, transfixed on his spoon as it swirled his tea in decreasing circles. 'Tell me what's happening with Hannah. Have you spoken to the doctor?'

'Just now,' Kathryn said, wrapping her fingers around her own cup and looping a thumb through the handle as she relayed to Morrie what the doctor had told her.

'I think it sounds like good news, considering. And you're bound to worry, but she's in a great place and they'll tell you—'

'I've ruined everything, Morrie,' she interrupted.

The spoon stooped swirling and she felt his gaze rest on her. 'What do you mean?' he asked.

Morrie knew her well. She didn't know if he would even be surprised when he heard what she had done. He might have suspected for years there was something oddly secretive about her.

'I told Hannah something this morning. That's why she took off like she did. She's in here because of me.'

'Oh, and this thing you told her,' he paused and rested his spoon on the table, laying his hands out flat. 'I take it, this was something pretty bad?'

Kathryn nodded.

'Do you want to tell me what it is?'

'Oh, Morrie,' Kathryn groaned, burying her face in the palms of her hands, 'I've done something so awful!' And before she could stop herself, she told him all about Hannah and Abigail. When she'd finished she couldn't bear to look at his face, to see his shock or disgust staring back at her.

But he didn't say a word. Not even an intake of breath or a sigh gave away what he thought about Kathryn. When his silence became too hard to bear and she had nothing more to say, she chanced a glance at him.

Morrie's eyes always gave him away. They were deep blue with flecks of grey and when he laughed she saw the sea sparkle in them. But when he was unsettled they clouded over and the grey deepened, making him look sad. Kathryn was with Morrie when he took the call telling him his father had died. The two hadn't had a relationship for twenty years and Morrie always professed to feel nothing towards the man who had left his mother. When he'd hung up the phone, he straightened up and turned back to hauling the fishing nets into the boat. But Kathryn had seen the dullness in his eyes, and she could feel the depth of sadness and regret in them. That day in the hospital cafeteria was no different.

'I don't expect you to stay,' she whispered, tears she hadn't even realised she had been crying choking her words.

Morrie reached over and took hold of her hand. 'I'm just trying to take it all in,' he said, shaking his head. 'Out of everything you've just told me the hardest thing to get my head around is that the girls aren't twins, not even sisters, they look so—'

Kathryn waited for him to continue. They didn't look alike at all but no one had ever questioned it, barely remarked on it. She herself saw it every time Lauren came back from the beach, though, her pale skin freckled and often blemished with patches of red where the sun cream hadn't been evenly spread, while Hannah's was brushed gold. How Lauren's hair curled at the ends ever so softly, but Hannah's was poker-straight. Little reminders that the girls could never be the twins everyone thought them to be.

'I guess they just behave like twins,' he said sadly. 'So what are you going to do about Lauren? She might not know yet but she's going to need to. Something like this can't be contained. You do know that, don't you?'

Kathryn sighed and looked out of the window.

'Don't let her hear it from someone else.'

'I need to see my mother,' she announced.

'What, now?' Morrie asked.

'I have to,' she said calmly. 'There's things I need to ask her. She's the only one who can tell me what I need to do.'

'But Kathryn, Eleanor can't do that,' he said, gripping her hand tighter as she made to stand. 'And you need to be here,' he added. 'Hannah needs you, they both need you.'

'But I have to.' Kathryn nodded her head in confirmation that seeing Eleanor was her only option. 'Don't you see, she got me into this, she needs to tell me how to get out of it.'

'I can't admit I have any idea why you think you need to run off to your mother, but just stay put for a moment, will you? Let's see how we can work this through together.' Morrie let go of his grip on her hand and sat back in his own seat. 'Your mother won't be able to help you, Kathryn. This is something you have to deal with yourself.'

Kathryn nodded, trying to reassure Morrie that she agreed with him. 'I'm just going to the bathroom,' she said, and before he could say another word she hurried out of the restaurant.

At the top of the stairs she patted her pockets to check for her keys. Throwing a quick glance towards the restaurant behind her, Kathryn turned and took the two flights of stairs down to the main entrance and out to the car park. She couldn't expect anyone to understand but it was the only thing she could think of doing.

– Thirty –

Dear Adam,

The last time I saw my grandmother was in 2003, two years after my mother left me. I was living in a shared house in North London. The night she turned up I had already been drinking. She stood at the door cloaked in a long cashmere coat and fur hat, and could not have looked more out of place.

'Why do you keep turning up, Eleanor?' I said to her. 'Can't you just leave me alone?'

'I'm just checking on you,' she said, peering over my shoulder.

'Well, I would invite you in,' I said. 'But I don't know if it's quite your scene.'

'So, do you need any more money?' she asked, wrapping her coat tighter around her as if to ward off any germs that might have come out of the house.

'What is this? A Christmas bonus for being a good girl?' I laughed. 'No, Eleanor, you can take your money and you can sod off! And don't come back again,' I shouted as she retreated down the path.

*****

I waited in my car outside Elms Home, sick with the anticipation of seeing her again. For fifteen minutes I stared at the large building, with its perfectly manicured bushes decorating the front. I had the same feelings swishing through my stomach that I'd had twelve years ago. It was as if I was walking into an examination and I hadn't prepared enough.

'I assume you're aware of her condition?' The woman who opened the door asked, ushering me into the expansive entrance hall. Home from home, I thought. Eleanor was still living in luxury even in a care home.

'No,' I said. 'Is it serious?'

'Oh,' she replied. 'I thought you would know. Most of our residents here suffer from some form of dementia.'

'Dementia?'

'Yes. Eleanor has Alzheimer's.'

I couldn't believe it. Did that mean she might not remember me? If that was the case I could stop panicking – I would have a plausible story if she didn't recognise me. But then what was the point in seeing her if she couldn't tell me where the girls were living?

'Katie?' the woman was asking. 'Katie, are you OK, dear?'

'What? Oh, yes! I'm fine, sorry. I just don't know what I expected, but it wasn't that.'

Actually I did know what I expected: an older, even more bitter version of the grandmother I remembered from my past, shrunk into a chair in a nursing home maybe, but definitely still with a very clear and commanding mind.

'Well, go and sit yourself through there,' she said, nodding towards a lounge. 'Someone is collecting her. Can I get you a drink?'

I asked for water and she scurried off, leaving me to find a seat, to wait and watch. There were at least a dozen residents in the lounge, mostly women. All of them sat alone, contemplating the garden. The air was still and deathly quiet and anticipation hung above the room like smog, gradually falling lower until I felt it would smother me. I practised taking deep breaths, counting One Mississippi, Two Mississippi, just as Mae had once taught me.

It's amazing how such a simple technique can actually make you feel calmer.

But then I saw her.

A young girl entered a door at the far side of the room and holding onto her arm was Eleanor. She was shuffling along slowly, her back bending her body into a 'C', her slippers scuffing against the carpet. I could hear each step she made as she moved towards a chair right in front of me, before dropping into it with a heavy fall. At first glance it could have been any old woman. I might have walked straight past her on the street. She looked so frail. The last time I saw her she stood tall, her stature making her presence felt, but the years had moulded her body and caused her to shrink. Her hair was white and no longer streaked with the gold highlights religiously threaded into her coarse bob. The skin on her hands was paper-thin. Her long bony fingers draped over the arm of the chair and I recognised the emerald ring that now hung loosely on her wedding finger. A grotesque thing in its size and shape, I'd never liked it.

I stood up, my legs jelly-like. I thought they might not hold my weight, but they did as I slowly walked over to her. Once I reached her chair, the same woman who had let me in appeared with my glass of water and announced to Eleanor, 'Look, dear, you have a visitor to see you. Katie.' She turned to me as she said, 'Your cousin's granddaughter?'

I nodded and waited for Eleanor's reaction. She was in no hurry to look up at me and when she did, she moved her head only slightly to the right to look at me. Her face remained impassive. The woman took hold of my arm and leaned in to me.

'She might not recognise you, dear,' she said quietly. 'She has days when she doesn't recognise anyone.'

'Anyone?' I asked.

'Sometimes not even her own daughter.'

Her daughter – my mother. So she was still alive and visiting Eleanor. The mention of Kathryn sent a jolt through me. They must all come here; she and the girls would sit in this very room. They may have only been yesterday. A sickening thought struck me: they may all be coming that day. I looked around me, suddenly expecting my mother to appear.

'Anyway, I'll leave you two to it,' the woman said. 'Just give me a shout if there's anything you need.'

'Actually,' I told her, 'you might be able to help me locate the rest of my family. Kathryn, isn't it, the daughter?'

'That's it. Lovely lady,' she said.

Was there a hint of sarcasm or had I imagined it?

'Would you be able to help?' I asked, hopefully.

'I could pass on your number,' she smiled. 'But obviously I wouldn't be able to give you any confidential details.' She walked away, leaving me alone with the old woman, who was still staring at me, although Eleanor's expression had by now changed to one of curiosity.

'Who are you really?' she asked.

'As they said, my name's Katie,' I told her.

She shook her head. 'No.'

Her face was covered in a thick layer of powder and her gaze pierced right into me. She didn't once take her eyes off me, summing me up, trying to figure out if she knew who I was or not. They flickered occasionally as if a memory swam through her mind, but her cold blue irises didn't once drift. I tried to maintain eye contact, to not let her win this one. I had something over her, I told myself: I have my mind.

'What are you here for?' she asked me.

'I wanted to ask you something,' I replied. Watching her

shuffling across the lounge only moments earlier I'd been less afraid of her, but now I was so close to her, I felt uneasy. My grandmother might have dementia and have lost that once so powerful mind but she was still able to make it look as though her mind was her strongest weapon.

'Go ahead,' she said.

'I'm looking to trace some of our family and I wondered if you knew where I could find them?' I asked. 'Kathryn, in particular.'

'You remind me of someone,' she said, ignoring my question.

At this I shifted uncomfortably, wishing her eyes would stop boring through me.

'Of who?'

Eleanor cocked her head slightly to one side as if searching through the files of a long past memory. Her eyes narrowed marginally when nothing came. The old Eleanor would be angry with herself for forgetting something she desperately wanted to know. I imagined this one would be too.

'So,' I continued when she didn't speak. 'Kathryn, your daughter. Does she come and see you here often?'

'No,' she said abruptly. 'She never comes.'

'Oh? But they said—'

'Patricia makes things up. She has nothing better to do with her time and it amuses her to tell stories. You can't believe a word she says,' she snapped.

Take the word of an old woman with Alzheimer's or the friendly nurse who cares for her? I know where your bets would be, Adam, but then you never met Eleanor.

'So when was the last time you saw her?' I asked.

'Are you a reporter?'

I shook my head.

'The police?'

'No, I'm Katie. I'm your—'

'I know who you said you are,' she said, leaning towards me.

'Do you ever see the girls?' I asked. 'Hannah and Lauren, the twins?'

I was increasingly desperate to get out and I could feel her gaining control over me. If she suddenly clocked who I was, I didn't think I would be able to stand her confrontation, so I was ready to run.

The faintest of smiles broke onto her face – maybe less of a smile, more of a smirk. It was only a flicker but the corners of her mouth twitched upwards and her eyes briefly sparkled.

'The girls?' I repeated, shuffling from foot to foot, ready to sprint out of the room any moment. 'Do they come here?'

She was making me impatient, and I knew she could probably see the flush of burning red spreading up my throat. I glanced at my watch to see how much time I had before Patricia would return. I had the feeling Eleanor was playing mind games with me although I wasn't sure she was aware she was doing it. By then I had little doubt that she'd never tell me where the girls were, even if she knew.

'I told you, no one visits me.'

I sighed and grabbed the handle of my bag. It was useless and I needed little encouragement to leave.

Eleanor turned away from me and looked out of the window. 'I know exactly who you are,' she said in a cold flat tone. 'Abigail.'

At this, I froze. My body pricked cold as if someone had thrown a bucket of ice over me, the follicles on my arms and legs pinching my skin.

'So tell me why you're really here, Abigail,' she said slowly, turning back to face me.

'I want to find the girls,' I told her, with all the strength I could summon.

'Patricia,' she suddenly called out, and like a genie, the woman who had let me in appeared. 'I need the bathroom. Please take me back up to my room,' she told the nurse, not once taking her cold, hard stare off me.

Patricia ushered another nurse over and walked me back towards the hallway. 'I'm sorry,' she said. 'She sometimes gets like that when she's had enough. It drives her daughter mad. Not that Kathryn ever lets on, of course. She smiles her way through her visits, but you can see the sadness in her eyes. We see it all the time with relatives. The disappointment.'

'Really?'

She still cares about the old witch then, I thought.

'She has the patience of a saint that lady. I shouldn't really say, but Eleanor can be a little ...' Patricia paused, 'testing sometimes, but I've never once heard her daughter raise her voice, or seem offended by it.'

My mother, the saint. How I would have loved to tell Patricia a thing or two about Kathryn that would make her seem far from godly, although it didn't surprise me that she was still keeping up her pretence that everything was fine. She probably even believed it was, despite her own mother crumbling away in front of her eyes.

'And the girls?' I asked. I had so many questions. I wondered how well Patricia knew them, if she saw them every week. What they looked like. How they behaved with Eleanor. If she thought they liked their grandmother or couldn't stand her.

'Ah yes, the lovely girls. Such pretty young things.'

'Are they?' I smiled, a surge of emotion rising within me. My body was swelling with pride to hear them described as lovely and pretty, and my heart ached so heavily with a desperate need to see it for myself.

I was about to ask more when a voice called from the top of the stairs.

'Patricia, Eleanor's asking for the lady visiting her to come up to her room.'

Patricia glanced at me quizzically. 'That's unusual,' she said. 'But I guess you'd better go up, if you want to. Suzanne can show you the way when you get up there,' she said, gesturing towards the girl who was waiting.

I looked up at Suzanne hovering at the top of the stairwell. It was the last thing I wanted to do; I had almost felt relief at the thought of getting out of there, yet I couldn't leave without hearing what she wanted to say. I let Suzanne lead me to her room at the far end of the corridor.

The door was ajar, and she tapped lightly on it, pushing it open as she did so.

'Your visitor's here, Eleanor,' she announced loudly, as if Eleanor were deaf.

I held my breath as I stepped in. It was a large room overlooking the back gardens, with minimal furniture: a double bed, wardrobe, a dressing table and a bedside table. It reminded me of a plush hotel rather than a nursing home. I remembered what Doris had said about Charles's debts and how little money had been left, and wondered how Eleanor could afford to keep herself plumped in comfort. Was the home draining every penny she had left?

Eleanor was perched on the end of her bed facing a mirror. She held a hairbrush in one hand, although it drooped towards her lap, as if forgotten about. She didn't acknowledge Suzanne or me, and as Suzanne retreated back down the corridor I cautiously took another step nearer her bed.

'Abigail,' she said, testing the name.

'Yes.'

'Why are you here, Abigail?'

'You know why I'm here. I want to find the girls.'

'They're gone,' she said. 'They all went away because you can't be trusted.'

'What are you talking about?'

'They left days ago now. I told her she had no choice. Silly woman, though. I didn't tell her to do that.'

'What do you—?'

I stopped suddenly, realising she had no idea how much time had passed. Eleanor must have thought it had only just happened. I don't know if seeing me had confused her, maybe taken her back to when my mother left, but I could tell she was getting agitated. She was tapping the brush on her knee rhythmically, her other hand scratching at her leg.

Play her game then, I thought.

'You can trust me,' I said calmly. 'I won't say anything.'

'I knew I had to do something,' she continued, 'but to leave just like that …' Eleanor shook her head. 'Never did know what that woman would do next.'

'Are you talking about my mother, still?' I asked.

'It couldn't come out,' she said, shaking her head as she stared at her reflection in the mirror. 'It couldn't come out. I wouldn't let them say I was involved in a cover-up.'

'You weren't just involved, you manipulated the whole thing!' I cried.

Eleanor lifted her brush and started running it through her hair.

'Where are they?' I begged. 'Please just tell me where they are.'

There was a knock at the door and Patricia came in, slowly looking at both of us in turn. I wondered how long she had been

– 264 –

standing outside because her eyes were watching us carefully, waiting for some explanation.

'I'm very tired, Patricia. Please show this girl out. I need to rest.' Eleanor threw her hairbrush onto the dressing table.

Patricia nodded and gently took hold of my arm. I tried pulling away – I couldn't walk out with nothing, not when I had put myself through so much. But Patricia's firm grip was already steering me out of the door.

'Just tell me,' I called out, but already I knew Eleanor would say nothing more.

I wanted to run back and hurl myself at her, pummel her with my fists and beat the truth out of her. How dare she still do this to me? Ruling my life as if it was her authority to do so. I turned back one last time to see the woman who ruined my life and realised there was still nothing I could do to pay my grandmother back for the years of hurt she'd thrown at me.

Patricia closed the door behind us. As I blinked back tears of frustration, I was shaking. I didn't know what to do next. I suspected Patricia wanted to coax me down the stairs but I couldn't move. I was contemplating my next step, whether or not to barge back into Eleanor's room, demanding the truth, or to relent and leave. Because she'd tell me nothing I wanted to hear, and the nurses would soon be bustling me out of the home like a criminal.

'Abigail,' Patricia said softly, leaning in so she could keep her voice low.

'Yes,' I snapped back. I didn't want to answer her questions.

She nodded, all the time her eyes scrutinising me. I was about to tell her to let me go when she held up a hand to stop me.

'Mull Bay,' she said, gently smiling. 'They're living in a place called Mull Bay.'

– Thirty-One –

Kathryn pulled down the visor but it didn't help block the sun from piercing through the side window. She couldn't see the road in front of her clearly and it didn't help that her hands were shaking against the wheel. Determined not to pull over, she carried on: she needed to get to her mother quickly.

Everything her life was built upon had been ripped apart and she could see no way through it. Her mother had orchestrated her life for her, so it seemed fitting that only Eleanor could tell her what she should do now all those cleverly made plans were falling apart and she was about to lose two more of her daughters. She had never wanted to lose her first.

She needed her mother to tell her the truth. For once she wished Eleanor could look into her eyes and tell her what happened. Had she really covered up an illness because she was ashamed? Kathryn so wanted her to deny it, and to believe her, because it was such an unthinkably cruel thing to have done. To refuse her daughter the help she needed and all because she didn't want people knowing. But deep down, Kathryn knew Peter was telling her the truth.

Who was she kidding, anyway? She knew the possibility of having such a conversation was negligible.

It didn't stop Kathryn hoping, though. Because there were also all the other things she needed answers to. Large chunks of the time she walked away from Abigail were missing in her mind and she needed her mother to fill them in for her.

'Why did I just leave?' Kathryn shouted, banging the heels of her palms against the steering wheel. It had been a hard time, there was a lot going on. The girls were demanding, Hannah always throwing tantrums, and Kathryn never knew what to do about it.

Abigail would sneer at her whenever she tried to calm Hannah down, letting her know what she herself already knew – that she was a useless mother. Peter barely spoke to her. She had wanted to scream at all of them that she didn't belong there. Kathryn hadn't belonged anywhere since Robert had died. He had taken her heart and her soul with him that day but Eleanor had never let her grieve. Instead she had bustled her on to the next husband. And Edgar Simmonds had been there, with more medication, which Kathryn had accepted without even asking what it was for because she hadn't really cared, and she had trusted they were doing the right thing for her.

Then Abigail threatened to expose their secret about Hannah. She remembered that much. Kathryn was scared; she didn't want to lose Hannah. Eleanor was adamant it never got out, that the situation must be resolved, and Kathryn never really knew what her mother meant by that.

Eleanor pounded it into her, mentally tap-tap tapping away at Kathryn's empty shell as if cracking an egg.

Abigail will ruin everything, she kept chanting.

She will tell people we took her baby.

Tap, tap on her shell.

You will lose Hannah, of course.

Another hard tap.

Something needs to be done about her, and you said yourself she's threatening you.

Had she? Kathryn vaguely remembered something, but had Abigail actually made threats against them?

Look what's she's capable of.

Eleanor had pointed to the deep cut down her face. And crack, Kathryn's thin shell was broken.

No, she knew deep down Abigail would never have caused that.

But she's deranged, her mother had said. *She would do anything to any of them. She could hurt the children. And take Hannah back and ...*

But Hannah was hers now, wasn't she, Mother? It was legal; Abigail couldn't take her.

A swipe of Eleanor's hand in the air.

It is legal, isn't it, Mother? she had asked again. *I did adopt her?*

All technicalities or something, Eleanor had said.

Technicalities? Kathryn thumped her fist against the steering wheel again. Why had she forgotten that conversation before now? She couldn't remember how she'd responded. Most likely she had let it pass over her.

But did that mean she hadn't legally adopted Hannah? Had Eleanor faked the whole thing, just to get it dealt with quickly? Like she had made them fake the fact that the girls were twins. Like she had covered up that her daughter was sick, and didn't get her the help she needed.

But she could see her mother pointing to that cut again. That awful, ugly cut running down her face. This is what she is capable of, Eleanor had said to her, and she had taken her mother's word for it.

The sun was creeping into the window again, the road blurring ahead of her. Kathryn's head was swimming. She should probably pull over but she had to keep going.

Her mother had told her about the house in Mull Bay. Kathryn assumed it was for them: a safe house. In her rush she had packed their bags hastily the day they left for Mull Bay, scooped up every single thing the girls had before scurrying away. Just until things settled down, of course. Because she knew she had heard Abigail telling her she would do something awful.

But had she heard that? Only now she couldn't actually remember Abigail saying anything like that at all.

'I've written this for Abigail.' Kathryn had passed her mother an envelope when Eleanor turned up, a day later. She still wanted to explain herself to her daughter.

There was fog ahead. They didn't usually get fog in July; everything was hazy, it felt like she was in a desert. Kathryn really couldn't see that well at all.

Eleanor had stuffed the envelope in her pocket. She had later told Kathryn that Abigail wasn't interested.

A horn blasted her. Not just one, they were all doing it, drivers staring at her and waving their arms as they overtook on the inside lane.

'Slow down,' she mouthed back.

In her heart she had known she shouldn't leave, not really, and yet she had.

'What is it?' she screamed, swerving back into the inside lane, narrowly missing a red fiesta. 'You get out of my way then,' she called to the young girl sticking a finger up at her.

*****

Kathryn wasn't sure how she made it to Elms Home. Getting out of the car, she stretched her arms above her head, locking her hands behind her neck, and took a moment to calm herself down before going into the home. She watched a girl run out of the home and back to her car. Her long dark hair swished behind her as she sank into the driver's seat and closed the door behind her. The girl looked so like Abigail. There was something about her movements so familiar they took Kathryn's breath away. But of course it couldn't be her: it must be her mind, playing its usual tricks.

The car drove off and Kathryn made her way to the front door. She sensed both Patricia's surprise and irritation when she opened the door, but Kathryn cut her off before she was able to say anything.

'I need to see my mother.'

'She's resting. I've just left her room. Eleanor's exhausted so I think it's best if you let her sleep.'

'But I need to see her,' said Kathryn, pushing past her into the hallway.

'I said she needs to rest. She's had a very busy day and looks quite pale. I don't think—'

'I *have* to. You can't stop me. Hannah's in hospital and … I have to see her.'

Kathryn knew her voice was rising but she would shout if she had to.

'Hannah's in hospital?' Patricia's voice softened. 'What happened? Is she OK?'

'No.' Kathryn waved her hand dismissively. 'I don't know. That's not why I'm here, I need to talk to her about something else.'

Patricia bent her head to one side. 'Not today, Kathryn,' she said firmly.

Kathryn was about to shove past her and go up to her mother's room anyway when her mobile started ringing. She fumbled in her bag and pulled it out: Morrie's name flashed across the screen.

'Morrie?'

'Hannah's awake. You really need to come back.'

'Why, has something happened?'

'No, she's been down for another scan and the bleeding has decreased, which is really good news, but it shouldn't be me telling you this. You need to be here,' he continued. 'This isn't fair on either of them. You can't keep running, Kathryn.'

'They won't let me see my mother,' she cried out.

There was a deep sigh at the other end of the line. 'You don't need to.'

'But—'

'Your responsibility is right here, at the hospital. Hannah is asking where you are,' he said. 'This is your chance to make it right, Kathryn. You *have* to come back for the girls.'

Kathryn looked at Patricia determinedly watching her, glanced up the stairs towards her mother's room and wavered. She knew what she should do and that was turn back and put her daughters first, however hard that might be, yet she still didn't know if she could.

– Thirty-Two –

Dear Adam,

Kathryn never spoke of the sea. We had always lived in London and our holidays were mostly spent at Eleanor's house in the country. The sea wasn't part of her – I don't think I ever saw her swim. Yet she chose to build herself a life beside it in a bay so beautiful and idyllic. What a perfect contrast to the life she left me living.

You used to say to me, 'One day, Abi, we should leave this city behind us and find ourselves a little shack away from the bustle and smog.' Of course you saw us surrounded by a flock of little Abigails and Adams and so I could never fully buy into the picture, but I liked the idea, and I would let you draw me our future from your imagination.

You would love Mull Bay. I would like it if we could move to the sea now and live in your dream. If we lived in Mull Bay we could sit on the clifftop every evening and watch the sea as the sun set over the hills behind us.

*****

After my visit to Eleanor yesterday I looked up Mull Bay. It was a tiny dot on the map and when I pulled up directions I knew I would have to be careful not to miss it. I left the hotel early this morning and drove north. It took me two hours by the time I'd taken a few wrong turns and twice circled another village.

As soon as I entered Mull Bay I was drawn to its heart: the bay itself. All roads lead to it. I parked the car and walked down to the beach. It was cathartic to finally be clearing my head of Eleanor and focusing on what to do next. But as soon as I reached the sea, I realised I didn't know what to do next. I needed to think carefully before I threw myself back into their lives.

I wore my sunglasses and the straw hat I had bought three years ago in Crete – I didn't want her recognising me before I knew what I wanted to say. I sat down on a cluster of rocks where I intended to make my plan, and watched the sea gently roll in and out again. It was mesmerising. Two surfers ambled down the steps, chatting, oblivious to me watching them. Apart from a couple of fishermen at the other end of the bay they were the first people I'd seen. They were young and carefree and I found myself envying them the life they had.

They paddled out to sea lying on their boards, waiting for something to happen, and even though the sea wasn't as calm as now, I still didn't know what they were waiting for. It didn't seem like the type of day to be surfing. The waves that sporadically rolled to shore were low and when the one with blond hair jumped onto his board it carried him only metres before he slipped back into the water. I watched them for at least half an hour, wondering if this was all they had to do in Mull Bay – surf on calm waters.

When they eventually came out they were deep in conversation, the blond animatedly waving his arms about as if making a point. And then I heard her name: Hannah. My head snapped up and I strained to hear him because they were walking away, towards a pile of clothes strewn on the sand. 'Hannah,' he said it again. I got up and followed. 'I want to go back and see her but her mother won't let me anywhere near,' he added.

Was this my Hannah they were talking about?

'Yeah, well, she always was a mad old cow,' the shorter one piped up. 'Maybe you should speak to Lauren.'

I held my breath, picking up step so I could get closer to them.

'Look, there's Morrie,' said the first. I followed his gaze towards the fishing boats and caught sight of a man bending over a boat. 'I'll see if he can pass Hannah a message, he's bound to go in later.'

The shorter guy turned and noticed me lingering. 'All right?' he said.

'Yes. Morning,' I said and scurried past them to the steps, where I waited until they'd spoken to Morrie, deciding I would then speak to him myself. Wherever they were, it sounded like he would be seeing them himself, even if Kathryn was keeping the boys away.

*****

Morrie is the double of your Uncle Mitch. I couldn't believe how similar they look. Grey wisps of hair against a tanned, weathered face. Bushy eyebrows I'd love to get my tweezers on. Deep blue eyes that pierced through me. As soon as he turned and smiled at me I felt at ease. Not many people have such a warm and open face as Mitch but I was pleased to have found another one.

He saw me approaching his boat and stopped what he was doing, stretching and rubbing the base of his spine as if it was causing him pain.

'Hello,' I said, 'I'm looking for an old friend, and I heard you might be able to help me.'

'I'll be happy to see what I can do,' he said, holding his hand out for me to shake. 'Morrie.'

'Abi,' I said, taking it. 'Do you have some time?' I asked. 'I don't want to disturb you if you're in the middle of something.' I nodded towards the pot of paint perched on the side of his boat, brushes poking out of it.

'Nothing that can't wait,' he smiled, grabbing a paper towel and rubbing it over his hands. 'Now who is it you're looking for?'

'Her name's Kathryn,' I said. 'She's got two daughters, and I know they live here, I'm just not sure where exactly.'

'Oh,' he said, before adding, 'Oh? And you said your name was—?'

'Abi.'

Morrie nodded, and his smile faltered slightly. 'Abigail,' he said eventually. 'That's what Kathryn called you so it didn't click at first. But I can see it,' he said. 'You look like her.' He carried on nodding. 'You're also the image of Hannah.'

I realised my mouth had dropped open as I stared at him, but I didn't have a clue what to say. Had Kathryn told him? I couldn't believe she would. Yet ...

'Tell you what, Abi,' he said. 'I was just thinking I could do with a bite to eat. How about we head to the diner up there and we can chat? I could do with an excuse to take a break.'

I nodded mutely and waited for him to tidy his paintbrushes, wiping them against the paper towel he had used on his hands before wrapping them in a plastic bag and setting them carefully on the deck of his boat.

We walked up the steps to the top of the cliff and towards the diner he had pointed out from the beach. All the while he talked to me, telling me they hadn't seen a summer so hot in years and how the kids still didn't realise they needed to top up the sun cream. He pointed out a boy with a sunburnt chest to prove his point and then changed the subject, asking me what I did for a living and where I lived.

At the diner the woman behind the counter laughed when he placed our order.

'Morrie, that has to be the third time you've ordered a bacon sarnie this week! Oh, and by the way, are you OK to look at our garage tonight?'

I took my Diet Coke and thanked him, all the while wanting to say, 'Will you just tell me what you know,' but at the same time I knew I had to pace myself. He knew my family and I needed him to help me.

'So, Kathryn's talked about me?' I asked, when we found a table outside.

Morrie nodded. 'Only yesterday.'

'Are you friends?'

'I've known the family a long time. I've got a lot of time for them – the girls are lovely.'

'I guess you know who I am, then?' I asked.

'I believe you're Kathryn's daughter,' he replied.

'What else did she tell you?'

'I hope she told me the truth. That you're Hannah's mother?'

I nodded. 'And she only told you this yesterday? That's a big coincidence.'

'It does feel odd,' Morrie agreed. 'But sadly it all came about because Hannah found out the truth,' he said. 'Yesterday morning.'

'So she knows about me?' I gasped

'Yes.' He looked out to the sea. 'As you can imagine she was extremely upset. She took off and had an accident. Hannah's in hospital, I'm afraid,' he said, turning back. 'She's going to be fine but she's been through the mill a bit.'

'What happened?'

'She took a car belonging to her boyfriend's father and drove it off. I don't know where she was going. But she can't drive.'

It was too much to take in.

'Where's the hospital?' I asked. All I could think of was my baby finding out about me and ending up in hospital. I had to see her. She must be so frightened; I needed to tell her it was going to be OK.

Morrie took a sip of his tea and carefully placed the mug back on the table.

'This isn't my place to say, but I think the last thing you should do is turn up now.'

'But I have to see her,' I said. 'I've finally found them and you tell me she's in hospital. You can't expect me to walk away.'

'No, but she's poorly, and if you want all this to work out OK, I'm just saying I don't think now is the right time.'

'Is there ever going to be a right time?'

'Maybe not, but here's what I know. Hannah didn't know anything about you until yesterday morning. As soon as she did, she ended up in hospital. She needs time to get her head around what she found out and also to recover physically. Then there's Lauren – she doesn't know any of it yet. She will, but Kathryn needs to tell her. Lauren is devastated by her sister's accident. Those girls are as close as real twins could ever be and they're going to need time to adjust to this.'

'But what if they don't adjust?'

'They will,' said Morrie, smiling gently at me.

'You don't know that.'

'I know them,' he said. 'And I know that once they can work this out, you'll all be in a much better place to meet.'

'But I'm so close,' I cried out. 'I don't know how I can leave again, not now I'm here and I know they're—' I sighed and shook my head. 'I need to see them.'

Morrie leant across the table to hold my hand and squeezed it. 'I don't know what happened all those years ago. Kathryn didn't *tell me why you haven't seen each other in so long. I can't begin to understand what life you've led, but if only for the girls, you need to give this some more time.'*

How was it possible to give it more time? I haven't seen the girls in fourteen years, and there I was so close – close to where they live and breathe, to where Hannah is lying in hospital and where Lauren is most likely sitting by her bedside.

'I'll stay in touch with you,' he continued. 'You have my word that when I think the time is right, I'll let you know.'

*****

I was so torn, Adam. In the end I told Morrie I'd take his advice. I said goodbye and left, hoping he would keep his end of the bargain. Then I drove out of Mull Bay and straight to the hospital.

But now I'm here, Adam, I don't think I can go in. Inside is my daughter – my girls. If I walk through that door now, I might ruin everything. If they aren't ready to see me I could lose them for ever all over again. And on top of all that Morrie was right about one thing: he knows them – I don't.

So maybe if being a good mum is putting Hannah first, then I should walk away. Maybe that's what will set me apart from Kathryn and Eleanor. Maybe I can finally break the chain of broken mothers.

– Thirty-Three –

Lauren was by the door. She looked blurry but then Hannah felt so tired, it could just be that her eyes weren't focusing. Her mum still wasn't there. If she had the strength Hannah would pull the tubes and wires out of her arms and pace the corridors until she found her. Kathryn was probably hiding somewhere, in case Hannah remembered what had happened right before the accident. Which of course she did: Hannah remembered every word of it.

Lauren looked tired. She was rubbing her face and yawning, her eyes were bloodshot and watery. Every time Hannah woke, Lauren was in the room with her. Her sister hadn't left her side.

'Hannah, you're awake.'

Hannah smiled back. 'Where's Mum?' she asked. Every time she thought of Kathryn as 'Mum' it sent a sharp stab to her stomach. She felt her eyes filling with tears but she couldn't lift her hand to wipe them.

'Don't cry,' Lauren said, rushing to her side, gently holding her arm. 'You'll be fine, everything's going to be OK. The doctor was only just saying they were pleased with your progress. He says you're strong.'

Hannah tried turning her head away but it hurt too much. She couldn't bear to look at Lauren, who knew nothing of what their mum had done to them.

'I said in that case it was better it was you and not me.' Lauren gave a short laugh. 'Because I'm not nearly as strong as you.'

'Where's Mum?' Hannah asked again.

'She's on her way. Morrie's just spoken to her so she'll be here soon. I didn't mean that, by the way,' she added. 'I'd swap places with you in a heartbeat.'

Hannah gave her sister a weak smile. 'Has she been here at all?'

'God yes, of course she has, but you know what she's like.' Lauren shrugged. 'She had to go.'

'Go where?'

But Lauren didn't answer. They were silent for a while, each sister watching the other. There was nothing to say, yet at the same time there was everything, but Hannah couldn't bring herself to do it. She felt tired again, her eyelids were heavy and as much as she wanted to keep them open the pressure was too much and she let them drop shut.

'Mum.' Lauren's voice broke the silence and Hannah managed to flicker her lids open to see her mum at the door.

Her mum. Kathryn. Whoever.

'You've come back,' said Lauren.

Kathryn looked concerned, her eyes dark, their lids hooded, but she had a glimmer of a smile on her face when she saw Hannah's eyes open.

She still cares about you, Hannah told herself. *It's all over her face.* And as much as Hannah wanted to shout at her and cry and tell Lauren the truth, it was good to see her mum still cared.

Then Hannah couldn't stop herself from falling back into a deep sleep.

– Thirty-Four –

'Lauren's here,' Morrie said to Kathryn gently. 'I can wait in your kitchen if you like.'

'Don't go, Morrie,' Kathryn begged. 'Stay here, please.'

She wasn't ready; it was ridiculous she was going through this already.

But he shook his head. 'You must do this on your own, Kathryn. Don't back out, will you?'

'I don't think I can do it.' Her whole body trembled with fear.

'You *have* to,' he said calmly, backing out of the room.

Kathryn grabbed her glass of water but couldn't keep her hands still. Water splashed over the top, wetting her skirt, and she tried to rub it away roughly with her hands.

'Mum?' Lauren came into the living room, looking at her with wide eyes.

Kathryn's mouth still felt dry so she reached for another sip of water, but again it splashed, this time over her hand.

Lauren sat down on the chair opposite and leaned forward, her face a mixture of worry and anticipation. 'What is it?' she asked. 'Is it Grandma?'

'No. No, it's not Grandma,' Kathryn said. 'Well, not really. Maybe it is.'

'Mum, you're not making sense, just tell me what it is, please. I'm getting worried now.'

Kathryn took a deep breath, trying to look at her daughter,

but she found her eyes drifting towards her lap. 'There's something I did, a long, long time ago,' she said finally, 'and it's something I should never have done.'

'OK, well, we all make mistakes.'

'Yes, I suppose we do ...' Kathryn paused, shaking her head. 'But this was big, a very big thing I did and I've never told anyone.' As she lay her hands across her lap, her legs were jiggling up and down and she wished she could make them stop. Kathryn closed her eyes. It was impossible, there was no way she could tell Lauren the truth.

But what if she didn't? Someone else would tell her. Though maybe that was preferable, maybe she could let someone else do it. Who would that be, though?

'Mum?' Lauren sounded impatient.

'Kathryn?' Morrie was now calling her, standing in the doorway, glaring at her. She hadn't ever seen him glare. Only one day had passed since Hannah's accident and he had been repeating himself over and over that she needed to speak to Lauren.

Fine, I'll just come out with it then he might stop glaring.

'I have another daughter. Her name is Abigail.'

'Abigail?' This was Lauren.

Don't answer questions. Breathe. Remember what you practised. Talk again before she asks anything else.

'I left her when you and Hannah were two, because I believed she was very out of control and was going to ruin everything for us and I was scared.'

I had believed that, hadn't I? But was it true? Because only now I don't actually remember what she had said and ...

'What do you mean, ruin things? What are you on about, Mum?'

Ignore her. Now I can't think of the next line. Think, Kathryn, think.

'Abigail had a baby at fourteen, the baby was Hannah and she couldn't look after her, so I looked after her and brought you both up as twins. Then she said she was going to tell everyone and take her away from me and I couldn't let that happen, and oh God, Lauren, I really don't feel very well.'

Breathe, Kathryn, Breathe.

Kathryn grabbed a magazine from the side table and started fanning herself.

'What the hell are you talking about? This is ridiculous! Are you making this up?'

'No, Lauren, she isn't.'

Kathryn heard Morrie's voice, which was good, she thought, because she needed to lie down now. He sat down on the sofa next to Lauren and took hold of her daughter's hand, rubbing it gently. Maybe she could lie out on the floor and Morrie could take it from there.

Kathryn shuffled forward to the edge of the sofa but Lauren's questions came one after the other. She heard her own voice answering them, but it all sounded like it was happening very far away. She heard Morrie's voice too; he sounded like an interpreter.

The room was swimming in and out; she felt as if she was being dragged under the surface of water. Everyone's voices were muffled and unreal. In a way it was a pleasant feeling. But then Lauren started crying before shouting. Kathryn desperately wanted to close her eyes because there was so much noise and she couldn't make any sense of it. Then Lauren stood up and cried out, 'I'm going to be with my sister!'

Was that it? Was it over?

'Do you want to know more?' Kathryn stood up, her legs wobbling. She needed to grab hold of the chair to steady herself, but Lauren was already out of the room. Kathryn desperately wanted to do the right thing for her girls. It was just so very, very hard.

The front door slammed behind Lauren.

'Oh, I think I've ruined everything,' said Kathryn.

'No, you haven't. That's the hardest part over,' Morrie told her softly. 'Whatever happens from now on, you'll cope with it because you've told them the truth and that's all that matters.'

She heard his words but she didn't believe them. 'They'll talk about it together,' she said, biting the corner of her thumbnail. 'About how much they both hate me for what I did. They won't want anything more to do with me.' She should stop because she had reached the skin and it was hurting now.

'That's not true.'

'I can't blame them. What kind of mother am I? What kind of mother abandons one child and lies to the others their whole lives? Oh, Morrie, why did all this have to come out? Why couldn't we have carried on as we were? And now it's bleeding again.' She held up her thumb.

Morrie looked down at his feet, shuffled on the spot and she knew he wanted to say something.

'What? There's something you're not telling me.'

Still he said nothing.

Kathryn felt a blinding stab of pain across her forehead. 'I'm going to lie down,' she said. 'I think I'm getting a migraine.'

'OK—' He paused. She wished he'd just say whatever was on his mind, but instead he turned his back and told her he would make them both a cup of tea.

Kathryn went up to her bedroom. The light was streaming in through the window, its glare bright. She moved to pull the curtains, stopping briefly to look out onto the lane. If she craned her neck to the right she could glimpse the sea. It had surprised her the morning after they'd arrived in Mull Bay. So different to what she was used to in London, the rows and rows of houses overlooked from every side. Mull Bay was isolated in comparison. She had always hoped they could have a happy life in the Bay, the three of them. And they had. But she had also hoped that one day Abigail would join them too. That's what she had written in her letter to her: that once it had all blown over, Abigail could join them. Only Eleanor always said it never had.

Abigail, Kathryn mouthed her daughter's name. Abigail. 'Abigail,' she gasped, peering to see the figure against the wall, further down the lane. Dark brown hair that hung poker-straight, falling onto her shoulders. White shorts showing off tanned legs, and a bright pink top. Kathryn closed her eyes and shook the image out of her head, but when she looked again the girl was still there.

'Here's your tea,' Morrie said, appearing in the room. 'Shall I leave it on your table?'

Kathryn pressed both hands against the windowpane and leant in closer.

'Kathryn, what are you looking at?'

He joined her at the window and gazed in the direction she was staring.

'Oh.'

'It's Abigail,' she whispered. 'It looks exactly like Abigail. I saw her the other day too, at Mother's home.'

There was an ache in her chest. A dull pain that felt like her insides were being tugged. The girl looked so much like her daughter.

'Yes,' Morrie said.

'But it can't be her.'

'Well … Actually, it is.' Morrie coughed and took hold of her arm as if he thought she would fall at any moment.

Kathryn turned to him. 'What do you mean, it's her?'

'I met her yesterday,' he explained. 'She came to the Bay looking for you and the girls.'

Kathryn tried opening her mouth to speak but every muscle in her body was too numb for movement. It couldn't be true. Abigail was here?

'I don't know how she found you in Mull Bay and I don't know why now, but she's here, and she obviously wants to see them. I told her it wasn't a good time,' he added. 'I thought she'd gone. She said she would.'

Kathryn looked back out of the window but the girl had disappeared. *Was this it?* she wondered. *Was this the point when her life crumbled into dust around her? Yet Abigail was here – she'd finally come.*

'This will all be fine,' Morrie was saying to her.

'No, no, it won't be,' she said. 'It isn't fine. It won't be fine because I'm not strong enough to deal with any of this. I never have been, Morrie, and I don't know how to be.'

*****

There were points in Kathryn's life when everything built up to such a crescendo she felt her whole world would explode with the pressure of it. Robert's death was the first. Leaving the hospital without the man she had given her heart to meant her life would never be the same again. She had looked down at the little dark-haired girl clutching her hand tightly and thought, now it's just you and me, and a cold shiver had run through her spine. Why God had chosen to take Robert and not her she could never fathom. Robert was the better parent for Abigail. He knew what to do when she cried, or when she was hurt. Not her. She relied on him to guide her through parenting, just as she relied on her mother to guide her through the rest of her life.

Once in a Religious Studies class at school, Kathryn had dabbled with the idea that God had forgotten to fill her with anything. He had put in all the necessary bits for her to operate, bones and major organs, but He had forgotten all the extras that made her human. Maybe that was why her mother was so frustrated with her all the time, she had considered. Why Eleanor was so angry when Kathryn didn't seem to be able to do anything as well as her mother hoped. Like the time she had sat a spelling bee, even though she had pleaded with her mother that spelling wasn't her strongest subject. Eleanor had pushed her onto the stage with all the other little girls, wearing their glasses and clips holding down the sides of their hair, every one of them looking smarter than Kathryn. Mischievous. M I S C H I E O ... No, there was no 'O' that side of the 'V'; she wouldn't forget that again.

Kathryn, her face beetroot red, had run off the stage crying and into her mother's stiff arms. 'Everyone's going to laugh at me,' she had said, waiting and hoping for some comfort.

'*You*?' said Eleanor through gritted teeth. 'What about *me*? I don't know why you entered.'

'But I didn't want to enter,' Kathryn whined. But looking up at Eleanor's face, set so rigid with determined anger, she had wondered, *Did I*?

And now this was the final crescendo, the one when everything that had happened came crashing down around her, closing in on her. A black storm engulfed her.

And still, Mother, where are you to tell me what to do? Just like I've been asking. You're not answering me, Kathryn shouted inside her head.

– Thirty-Five –

'What is it?' Hannah opened her eyes to see Lauren standing over her bed again, but Lauren looked ill. Her face was drained of its colour, except for her eyes so red and raw. Hannah tried to shuffle upwards into a sitting position. Over the last twenty-four hours she had been awake more and the doctors told her they were pleased with how well she was doing.

Lauren's fingers played with the stiff white sheet. Hannah was looking forward to getting back into her own bed, and her nice, soft duvet. She took her sister's hand.

'You know, don't you?' Hannah asked, quietly. 'Has she told you?' Lauren nodded and Hannah squeezed tighter. 'This doesn't change us,' she said, but she needed to hear Lauren say it too. 'Nothing changes.'

'I'm so sorry,' Lauren cried, tears tumbling down her cheeks and onto their hands. 'I can't believe any of it.'

'No, me neither. But there you go.'

'She lied to us.'

'I know.'

'Made us believe we were twins.'

'We *are* twins, Lauren. Don't ever say that. We are, aren't we?'

'Yes,' Lauren whispered. 'Always.'

'Well, then nothing else matters,' Hannah smiled weakly, her own tears sliding down her face.

'Where do we go from here? I mean, what's going to happen?'

'About what?' Hannah asked.

'I don't know. Mum. Kathryn,' she choked on the word. 'Abigail. I'm frightened, Hannah. Everything's going to be different and I don't want it to be.'

'I know. But all we have to do is make sure nothing comes between us.'

'But how are you going to deal with Mum? Knowing she lied to you about, you know—'

'About being my real mum?' Hannah shook her head. 'I have no idea. I guess it depends how she deals with it too. But I'm angry with her, Lauren. I can't just let her walk away from this. You know that, don't you?'

Lauren nodded. 'I know, just—'

'Just what?'

'I'm scared.'

Hannah dipped her head, focusing her attention on their hands, so tightly clasped, holding on for everything they still had. 'I need to see Abigail.'

'Of course. One day …'

'No, not one day! I need to see her soon. I want to know who she is, what she looks like. I want to hear her side of the story.'

'We have no idea where she is,' said Lauren, and Hannah felt her shift uncomfortably at the side of her.

'No, but we can find her. We'll ask Dom to help. Or Morrie. I'll speak to him when he next comes in.'

'OK, if that's what you want.'

'Of course it's what I want. But we do this together, right? We deal with Mum and we deal with Abigail together. Or else neither of us will get through it.'

– Thirty-Six –

Dear Adam,

I watched her for a moment through the window of her door. She was sitting up at a table by her bed, sketching on a pad, her head bent low, her tongue sticking out of the corner of her mouth in concentration. Just as you used to joke I did.

My heart ached at the sight of her. She looked like a younger version of me. Kathryn must have seen it every time she saw her. Hannah had to be a constant reminder of the daughter she left behind.

I pressed my fingers against the window and traced the outline of her face, glad for those few minutes so I could take everything in. Her chestnut brown eyes, her rosebud mouth. At certain angles there were glimpses of the baby I had held in my arms and promised I'd never let go of. But at the same time my daughter was a complete stranger to me.

I was filled with such overpowering emotions, love for my girl, but at the same time a fierce anger that I'd lost so many years watching her grow up. That she had been ripped away from me and I was never given the chance.

Hannah looked up and saw me. She took a deep breath and smiled, her eyes anxiously watching me. I needed to push my anger aside because I was about to meet my daughter again for the first time in fourteen years.

Morrie had called me three nights ago, and told me Hannah had asked to see me, and we agreed I would visit her at the weekend. 'She couldn't believe it when I told her I had met you,' he chuckled. 'She nearly leapt out of bed and hugged me, firing a barrage of questions about what you look like.' He warned me that whilst she was excited, he didn't think Hannah understood what she was thinking or feeling about everything yet, and I promised him I would take things slowly.

I noticed Lauren wasn't in the room. Morrie had said she might not be. Still, I prayed she would come. I didn't want to break their bond, I hoped I could be a part of it.

Tentatively I opened the door and stepped into the room.

'Hi, Hannah,' I said. Tears dripped down my cheeks and however much I tried brushing them away, I wasn't quick enough.

Hannah giggled nervously, her eyes filling up too. I knelt beside her chair.

'I'm Abigail.'

'I know that,' she laughed. 'I don't recognise you, though.'

'I recognise you,' I smiled. 'You look exactly how I thought you would look.'

'I did always think I remembered someone else,' she said. 'It must have been you.'

'Yes, probably.'

'I didn't find out about you until the other day,' she said, nervously fiddling with the pen in her hand. 'I didn't know any of it.'

'I know that, Hannah. You don't need to explain anything.'

'I don't even know why Mum, I mean—' She looked away and her cheeks flushed red.

'You can still call her Mum. Don't feel embarrassed about anything,' I told her. 'Just do whatever feels right.'

'I don't really know what feels right, if I'm honest.' She smiled. 'I was going to say I don't know why she left you.'

'No, well … we can talk about all that some other time,' I said. 'But let's not worry about it right now.'

Hannah smiled at me again, her eyes twinkled and I could see she looked more relaxed.

'Does this feel weird to you? Because it does to me.'

'Yep, totally weird! But it also feels incredibly wonderful,' I laughed.

I had so many questions toppling over themselves to get out. Did you have a good childhood, Hannah? Have you been happy? Has Kathryn always treated you OK? What do you like doing? How do you get on with Lauren? But I didn't ask any of them. Instead we made small talk, and spoke about the little things, like how she was getting on at school, who her friends were; her boyfriend, Dom. We circled each other cautiously; it would take time to get to know one another. But I had all the time in the world for my little girl. Right then I was enjoying building up a picture with all the small but significant details that made up my daughter.

'There's so much I want to ask you, and I don't think I'll ever find it all out from my mum,' Hannah said after we had exhausted those subjects. 'Are you, I mean, are we—' She stopped and shifted in her seat.

'Go on, what is it you want to know?'

'What happens next?' she asked.

'Well, that's up to both of us to decide what we want to do. But from my point of view, I've lost fourteen years of your life and I don't want to lose any more.'

'So we carry on seeing each other?'

'Would you like to?'

Hannah nodded. 'Yes, I really do, I just … I just don't know what we're supposed to do,' she said. 'Or even what I call you. Do I call you Abigail?'

'You can call me Abi,' I said simply. 'And if you like, you can see me as your big sister.'

'That sounds like a perfect idea,' she said.

I waited as a nurse came in and took Hannah's blood pressure and temperature. 'How are you doing today?' she asked, peering at Hannah over the top of her notes. 'Don't go tiring yourself out, will you?' She smiled.

'When will I see you again?' Hannah asked me when the nurse had finished and left the room.

'Whenever you want to,' I told her. 'I'm here at your beck and call, you and Lauren.'

'Lauren,' she said.

'Yes, Lauren too,' I said.

'No, Lauren,' she replied, nodding towards the door, a smile spreading across her face that was so wide, I realised I hadn't seen her so happy in the time I'd been there. 'Lauren's turned up. I knew she would,' she said, almost bouncing in her chair. 'Lauren, come in,' she called. 'Come and meet Abi.'

I turned to see Lauren hovering by the open door. Her body was rigid and her face so closed in contrast to Hannah's. I couldn't tell if she was annoyed I was there or just plain frightened.

'Hi, Lauren,' I said, my legs shaky as I stood up. I had been crouching on the floor in one position and my muscles were burning. There was my Lauren, such a contrast to Hannah in looks. She had changed more; I really had to try hard to find pieces of the little girl I remembered in the one standing before me now. I didn't know if I'd have picked her out in a crowd.

'Lauren, come in,' Hannah urged. 'She won't bite.'

Lauren walked over stiffly and sat on the edge of the bed next to Hannah's chair. She looked wary of me, and as much as I knew that was natural, I wanted to tell her it wasn't my fault. None of this was my doing.

Hannah grabbed hold of Lauren's hand and squeezed it, and started to babble, telling me stories about her and Lauren and every so often saying, 'Don't you remember?' or, 'What was it you said to her, Lauren?' Lauren giggled when it was appropriate and I thought she was beginning to relax, but she kept her eyes fixed on Hannah, glancing at me occasionally, as if checking me out and trying to figure out how I was going to fit into their lives. And I couldn't blame her: I was an intruder, Hannah's mother. But she'd forgotten that I was with both of them from when they were a day old and I had loved her too.

Eventually the same nurse came back in and told us visiting time was over. 'You really need some rest, Hannah,' she said, plumping the pillows and encouraging her back into bed.

So we said our goodbyes and made promises of seeing each other soon. I leaned over and hugged Hannah, breathing her in like I had the moment she was born. I didn't want to let her go again, but the nurse was bustling about, asking Hannah what she wanted for tea, and so I grudgingly pulled away. Lauren gave me a hurried hug and then hung back, waiting for me to leave. Outside the door I looked back in on them, Hannah making herself comfy in the bed, Lauren fussing around her with the sheets.

'I'm finding this really hard to get my head around,' I heard Lauren say.

'She says she can be our big sister,' Hannah replied. 'It'll be fine, Lauren. We can do this together.'

My daughter. My girls. They were back in my life again. It was all I'd ever dreamed of. I was so happy in that moment I didn't care about anything else.

I have them back.

Now the only thing missing from my life is you.

– Thirty-Seven –

Kathryn felt the walls closing in on her. It had been that way for days, she didn't know how many. The migraines were getting worse and the new pills Dr Morgan had prescribed weren't working. She found herself wishing Edgar Simmonds was still alive. Whatever he might have done, he had always helped her feel better.

She hadn't spoken to Dr Morgan about what Peter told her yet. And she still hadn't spoken to Peter again. She hadn't told anyone she might have an illness that had been covered up her entire life. She rather hoped it could be ignored, but Kathryn knew it couldn't. She would have to do something about it.

Morrie was downstairs. He had spoken with Lauren earlier but she couldn't make out what about. Kathryn hadn't left her bed since the day the migraine started, after she had told Lauren everything and after she had seen Abigail outside her house.

Morrie was back again now to check on her. He looked concerned when he peered round the door. She had closed her eyes quickly, hoping he would leave her to rot in her own stupidity, which he did. The morning passed and afternoon came quickly. She knew because she had followed the direction of the sun at intervals throughout the day. It crept in through the chinks in her curtains.

Had she taken too many pills? she wondered briefly, because she felt so sluggish. It was possible. No one had counted them out.

The home phone rang. Morrie answered it, speaking in hushed tones to whoever was on the other end. Kathryn wanted to know how Hannah was doing, and waited, hoping that if it was the hospital Morrie would give her some news even if she didn't acknowledge it when he did. But none came, and despite how desperately she needed to know Hannah was OK, she didn't have the strength to walk down the stairs and find out for herself.

Sleep came again. Kathryn woke in a fug, checked the clock to see that only half an hour had passed, then drifted off once more. The longer she stayed in bed, the more tired she became. Each time she woke her body felt heavier and when the clock told her it was 7.30 p.m. she knew it would now be impossible to heave herself out of bed, even if she wanted to.

The phone rang again that evening. She could just about make out Morrie's voice answering it although she had no idea what he said. It was odd for it to ring so often: the home phone rarely rang.

The door to her bedroom slowly opened and Kathryn sensed the presence of someone at the door but wasn't inclined to open her eyes to look.

More murmuring took place, this time on the other side of her door. And then silence. Next, the doorbell sounded, two sharp stabs piercing the stillness of the house, but still she couldn't rouse herself out of the lethargy swallowing her up, keeping her a prisoner in her own bed.

*****

Morning came. Kathryn must have slept through the entire night. Her pillow felt damp and her nightie was clinging to her with sweat. She had to get out of bed; it wasn't helping, sitting there wallowing. Her head had cleared a little too.

The doorbell rang again. Pulling herself up, Kathryn sat back against the headboard and waited for the room to stop spinning before swinging her legs to the floor and going to the window to see who was there. By the time she looked out, the door had already been answered and she could hear the sound of male voices downstairs.

With numb feet she padded back across the wooden floor and slipped her feet into slippers. Wobbling, she held out a hand to steady herself against the wall but instead knocked it against the bedside table, and tumbling back onto the bed watched the open bottle topple, white pills spilling out of it, bouncing across the floor. 'Christ!' she muttered, picking up the now-empty bottle and clutching it in her hands.

The rap on her bedroom door made her jump. It opened slowly and Morrie's head peered around it. 'Ah, you're up,' he said. Opening the door further he came into the room, his eyes sweeping over the tablets scattered across the floor as he stepped over them carefully, approaching the bed. 'Kathryn, there's someone here to see you.'

'Who is it?'

'How many of those did you have last night?' Morrie asked, gesturing to the pills.

'Two, I think.'

Morrie sighed. 'It's Dr Morgan. Is it OK if I bring him up?'

'Why?' she asked.

'Kathryn, let me bring him up. Or maybe you feel well enough to make it downstairs?'

'No,' she said, leaning back against her headboard, staring at the wall ahead. 'I'll stay here.'

Morrie stepped over the pills, back towards the door.

'Where's Lauren?' she asked.

'She's not here at the moment.' Morrie gave her a thin smile and left the room, closing the door behind him. She listened to his footsteps retreating, more low voices and then the sound of two pairs of feet climbing the stairs.

'Hello, Kathryn,' Dr Morgan said as both men entered her bedroom. 'Do you mind if I sit down?' he asked, gesturing to the end of the bed.

Kathryn shook her head and watched the doctor sit down, look at her and then at Morrie as if unsure which of them should speak first.

'We need to find something out,' she said, 'something about me. We need to ask my mother if I'm—' She stopped, catching the look Dr Morgan shot Morrie.

'What is it?' she asked. 'Something's happened. Tell me what it is.'

Morrie crouched beside her bed and rested his hand on her arm. 'Yesterday afternoon your mother had a stroke,' he told her. 'I'm so sorry, Kathryn. She didn't make it. Eleanor died last night.'

*****

Kathryn felt the life whipped out of her in one clean sweep.

'Your mother—' the doctor started.

'She's dead?' Kathryn choked on the words. 'My mother is dead?'

'I'm so sorry,' Morrie whispered.

'She can't be. I don't believe it. I don't believe *you*,' she said, her voice rising as she pointed her finger at Morrie. 'You must be lying, she can't be gone.'

She could feel her heart pounding, though, and knew deep down he was telling her the truth – but a life without Mother?

'It was all very sudden,' Dr Morgan explained. 'She would have felt no pain.'

'They wouldn't let me see her,' Kathryn cried, turning to the doctor. 'I went to see her yesterday. No, not yesterday – the other day, whenever it was. They wouldn't let me. They knew she wasn't well, didn't they?'

'No, I don't believe they did,' he said softly.

'And you told me not to as well,' she said, turning back to Morrie.

'Kathryn, no one knew what was going to happen.'

'But I didn't get to see her,' she cried. 'I didn't get to see her. I knew it! I knew there was something wrong when they told me she was sleeping in the afternoon. Everyone was being so odd with me.'

Morrie rubbed his hand gently against her arm. 'You were upset about Hannah,' he reminded her. 'There was nothing you could have known or done.'

'Oh God, Morrie! What do I do now?' Kathryn was sobbing and shaking as she clawed at the sheets. 'Now she's gone too.'

'The doctor's going to help you get through the next few days,' Morrie said, nodding towards Dr Morgan, who remained helplessly seated at the end of Kathryn's bed. 'You will do this, Kathryn. We'll make sure you do.'

'But she was everything,' Kathryn spoke in a whisper. 'There were things I needed to ask,' she cried. 'And now I might never know.'

Three Months Later

– Thirty-Eight –

That summer had set a number of things in motion for Hannah. All of them starting from the point of finding out her mum had lied their entire lives. If it wasn't for that she wouldn't have had the accident, her relationship with Lauren wouldn't have been shaken, and – well, she really didn't know how things would be with her mum, because they weren't exactly normal anyway.

But as always Hannah could see that good things came out of it too. Like Dom, who ever since bumping into her mum in the hospital that one time had found a way of creeping around her and seeing Hannah, no matter what. He was determined Kathryn wouldn't keep him away; in fact it made him more adamant that Hannah was worth fighting for.

Then there was Abi, her 'big sister', who was now such a huge part of her life she couldn't imagine her ever not being in it.

Of course everything had to change after that moment, and actually Hannah was pleased it had. Because as hard as it was to accept what her mum had done, it had opened up a world of possibilities for her. Already she could see a life ahead of her that didn't have to revolve around the Bay. She had looked into universities in London, where she would study Art. Her future was no longer dictated; it was going to have good times and bad, but the fun of it was the not knowing, the fact that it wasn't all mapped out like her mum had been desperately hoping for.

But Lauren didn't feel the same: she hated change. She was much more similar to Kathryn than Hannah had realised. Abi turning up in their lives had thrown her and Lauren's relationship up in the air and they were still trying to catch the pieces of it as they fell back down. But at least they were both determined they wanted the same thing: they were the sisters they always had been and neither of them would let anything change that.

Hannah knew Lauren wasn't likely to leave the Bay and one day they would go their separate ways. It was something they would both have to come to terms with. But she also knew she wouldn't let anyone stop her from doing what she wanted. This summer had at least taught her that.

In the days after her grandmother had died, her mum had plummeted even more rapidly. She had already taken to her bed while Hannah was still in hospital, but after Grandma, she had sunk even deeper into herself. Hannah remembered looking at her one day, wondering how her skin, so pale and paper-thin, was managing to hold her together.

'She can't go on like this,' she had said to Morrie the morning of Eleanor's funeral. 'She looks like she wants to die too.'

He had nodded, rubbing his bristly chin, his ashen face telling her he agreed.

She and Lauren had carried Kathryn through the funeral, holding her up where every few steps she would stumble. Had they let go of her arm, she would have dropped to the ground, Hannah had thought.

In the funeral car Lauren had taken hold of Hannah's hand and as they watched their mother, Hannah's heart had softened a little. She didn't want to feel sorry for her and she didn't want to lose the anger because if she did it meant she had forgiven Kathryn for what she had done to them. But seeing the sorrow and the grief that plagued her, Hannah couldn't help reaching out and taking her mum's hand in her other one. Soon Lauren did the same and the three of them formed a circle with their hands as the car slowly meandered through the winding lanes of the Bay. Her grandmother's death might just have been the glue holding the three of them together. But once the funeral was over, much to their relief, the following week Kathryn agreed to see a therapist. She was finally acknowledging there was a problem and had agreed to doing so before meeting Abi.

What Hannah hadn't been expecting was the diagnosis that her mum had schizophrenia, but at least things were beginning to make sense so they could understand why she was like she was. Kathryn had taken the diagnosis in her stride, which surprised Hannah. It was almost as if it wasn't a shock to her.

Their relationship was still fragile; they were links in a chain threatening to break apart easily. Kathryn was getting help and Hannah could see she was trying to work through her problems, but it was taking time. And through all that time Hannah still wasn't getting all the answers she needed. She couldn't let go of the things her mum had done, she still didn't know why she had left Abi.

Hannah might always feel like the parent in their relationship and it was something she was going to have to accept. She didn't know how they would work through it, but she promised Lauren she would try. Besides, if Lauren was opening the door for Abi, the least Hannah could do was keep it open for Kathryn.

Hannah pulled her coat tighter as she waited on the platform. It was a cold day and she'd been half an hour early for the train. Now she wished she had put on more layers. In her rush to get out of the house she'd slipped out with only a T-shirt under her coat.

The train pulled around the bend and made its way slowly into the station. Hannah jumped up, peering eagerly into the carriages as they passed, until she saw Abi, pulling down her bag from the overhead rail and making her way to the door. Hannah ran to meet her.

'I'm so excited to see you!' she shrieked when Abi stepped onto the platform.

'You look beautiful,' Abi said. 'I love what you've done with your hair.'

'I had it all chopped.' Hannah swished her head from side to side.

'It suits you.'

Hannah linked her arm through Abi's and they hailed a taxi to the hotel, where Abi would be staying the night. It was a little way out of the Bay; Abi wanted it that way. She was only there for the night and was meeting Kathryn the following day, so she had said she needed some space first, to get her head round things.

'How are you feeling?' Hannah asked as she perched on the edge of the bed, watching Abi unpack her case. Her eyes drifted to the clothes she had packed: dark jeans, a grey sweater, a couple of brightly coloured scarves. It was strange feeling she already knew this person so well, yet in reality she knew so little.

'Weird, nervous, apprehensive ... Wondering how it's going to pan out ... I don't know, there's a whole host of thoughts running through my head. I'm not looking forward to seeing her again. There's a part of me that thinks she might not even turn up.'

'She will,' said Hannah. 'She'll definitely show up. She's doing so much better, really,' she added, although she knew that meant little to Abi.

Abi turned back to the case and pulled out her washbag, revealing a photo frame lying upside down. 'What's this?' Hannah asked pulling it out and turning it over to look at the photo of Abi with a man, standing in front of the Eiffel Tower. His arm was around her shoulder, pulling her in close, and they were both beaming huge smiles for the camera. 'He's gorgeous. Who is he, you've kept him quiet?'

Abi reached for the photo and laid it back in the case, turned upside down. 'He's just ... no one. It's no one. Anyway, what do you want to do this afternoon?' she said as her mobile rang. Grabbing it from the bedside table, she checked the screen. 'Sorry, I'm going to have to take this.'

'It's fine, go ahead.'

'Hi, Maggie, thanks for getting back to me,' Abi said into the phone. Gesturing that she'd go into the bathroom, she took her washbag through and closed the door behind her.

Her voice was muffled and Hannah couldn't make out the conversation on the other side of the wall. She turned back to the case and pulled out the photo. He obviously wasn't no one or Abi wouldn't have brought his photo with her, but why would she want to hide him from her? Hannah traced her finger over the photo. He was gorgeous! If she had a boyfriend like that, she wouldn't hide him from anyone. With a sigh, she placed the frame back in the case, and noticed a large A3 artists' folder at the bottom. Abi had told her she loved to draw, too, but Hannah hadn't seen anything she'd done yet. She pulled out the folder and lifted out sheets of paper, on them sketches of people, observed from afar. Some of them were drinking in coffee shops, others waiting at bus stops, all oblivious to the person capturing a moment of their life for ever.

Abi really was very good, she thought, flicking through them. She'd been under the impression it was nothing more than a hobby, something she did to pass the time, but Hannah could see a skill that she certainly didn't possess yet. Putting the sketches to one side, she dipped back into the folder and pulled out the rest of the paper.

But there were no more drawings. Instead she scanned the lines of neat, slanted handwriting before reading the start:

Dear Adam, I woke at four again this morning.

It was a letter, and there were pages of it. (Then Hannah paused and looked up…deep in conversation.)

She took a deep breath. She knew she shouldn't read it, that this wasn't for her eyes, but then Hannah never did have much self-control. She skimmed through the first couple of paragraphs, telling herself to stop. But the more she read, the more she realised that in Abi's letters was everything she wanted to know and might never get from her mum. There were pages of them, and as she read through them, now taking in every word, the whole of Abi's life formed before her.

'Hannah?'

'Oh, my God! I'm so sorry! I—'

Her cheeks were aflame with the embarrassment of being caught red-handed. There was nothing she could say to defend her actions. With trembling hands she held the letters out to Abi, who took hold of them, staring down at the paper and then back at Hannah.

'Have you read them all?' she asked.

Hannah looked away. She felt sick and wanted to run from the room in shame.

'I'm not angry,' Abi said softly. 'Just tell me the truth.'

Hannah nodded, as tears filled her eyes. She imagined Abi telling her to get out, that she never wanted to speak to her again.

'I'm *so* sorry,' she repeated.

'Don't cry,' Abi whispered, putting an arm around her. 'I would have told you everything, anyway. I want you to know, Hannah,' she urged.

Eventually Hannah looked up. 'Is that Adam in the photo?'

Abi paused. 'Yes, it is.'

'Why didn't you tell me you're married?'

'I was going to, it's just hard for me to talk about it.'

'I guess things didn't work out in the end, then?' Hannah asked.

Abi sat back down on the bed beside her and shook her head.

'I can't believe everything that happened. I feel like I've learned nearly everything I wanted to know in one go,' Hannah continued.

'*Nearly* everything?' Abi joked. 'So, what was missing?'

Hannah shrugged, biting the corner of her fingernail. 'I dunno. I guess maybe more about my real dad. Did he ever know anything about me?' Now it made sense that the man she had found on the internet meant nothing to her, she wasn't related to him: he was Lauren's father but not hers.

'No,' Abi said. 'Jason never found out I was pregnant.'

'It's so weird. I'd just started looking for my dad at the start of the summer, before everything happened. Dom was helping me,' Hannah said. 'But I was looking for the wrong man.'

'Sadly, neither are people you'd want in your life.'

'No, it doesn't sound like they are,' Hannah sighed. Her mum might not have told them the truth about Peter but she was right about one thing, and that was that they really didn't need to find him.

'Of course if you do want to find Jason, I won't stop you. I'll do what I can to help, but I just have no idea where he is.'

Hannah smiled. 'Thanks, but I don't think I will for now.'

The summer had taught her a few things about who she did and didn't need in her life, and she was no longer fuelled by a desire to have a father in it, no matter what. Hannah had had many romantic visions of reuniting with him but it seemed Lauren was right: some things were better left alone.

'So, what did you actually do after we all left?' Hannah asked eventually. 'You said you stayed in the house for a while, and decided you wouldn't come looking for us.'

'I did decide that. I was in a very low place, mixing with the wrong people, drinking too much and all that kind of thing,' Abi replied. 'I started to believe Eleanor was right, that I couldn't be trusted and you were better off without me. It became easier for me to forget. I was only seventeen, remember, not much older than you are now. Obviously I wasn't capable of making good decisions at the time.'

'And Eleanor gave you money? She was blackmailing you?'

'Yes, she was. I guess I knew that at the time too, but the

money was a lifeline and I came to rely on it. It gave me a lot of credence amongst my friends too. All the kids whose parents didn't care where they were started hanging out with me even more. Then one day she handed me a whole pile of cash and I realised that was my cue to get out of the house and out of her life.'

'So you just took it?'

'I was very mixed up – I had no one I could turn to who'd lead me in the right direction. So I took it and rented a room with a bunch of others. I didn't really have a plan other than using the money to get me through each day at a time. Anyway, things got a little messy.'

'Messy how?'

'Oh, you know,' Abi waved a hand in the air. 'Drinking, drugs ... Nothing I'm proud of.'

'I never liked Grandma. And now I know what she did—' Hannah paused. 'I wish I'd never had to waste a single minute visiting the old witch. She used to scare me.'

'She's a scary woman. I guess that didn't help Kathryn; it must have been terrifying as a child to have a mother like that.'

'It was the way she looked too. Those eyes that bore into you, scrutinising your every move. And the scar that made her look so frightening.'

'Scar?' Abi asked. 'I didn't notice a scar when I last saw her.'

'Yes, a deep red line all down here,' Hannah replied, running a finger down her left cheek. 'She used to wear so much make-up that half the time you could barely see it, but when she didn't, it looked like someone had run a red felt tip down her face.'

Abi shifted on the edge of the bed and opened her mouth to speak but didn't say anything.

'What is it? You look like you've seen a ghost.'

'I don't know, I just remembered something. Look, it doesn't matter. Let's not talk about her,' she said, attempting a smile.

'Anyway, look at you now,' Hannah told her. 'You came through it. You're so strong!'

'Well, of course a lot of that was down to Adam,' Abi smiled.

'I saw the way you wrote to him and the things you said. You can't deny you still love him,' Hannah said, clutching Abi's hand and squeezing it.

'I'll never stop loving him.'

'Then you need to do something about it,' she urged.

A knock at the door interrupted them. 'Housekeeping!' a voice called out, 'I've brought your towels.'

Abi stood up and opened the door, thanked the woman and then suggested to Hannah they made the most of the afternoon before it got too dark outside.

Hannah agreed. She'd continue her conversation with Abi some other time. She had an idea brewing, and one that was exciting her, because a love like Abi and Adam's was too precious to throw away, and so she wasn't about to let them do it. Dom would help her look for Adam – he had been so good about finding Peter. And then Hannah could meet him and tell him everything she knew and he would realise what Abi had really been worried about and how much she still loved him, and that it wasn't too late for them to try to be parents and … Hannah knew she was getting carried away, and if Lauren knew what she was up to, she would probably try stopping her. So this time she wouldn't say anything. Not until she found him.

But this time she was convinced it was the right thing to do.

Later that day they hugged goodbye outside the hotel. Morrie had arrived to drive her back to the Bay on her mum's insistence she didn't get a taxi.

'Pick your battles,' he had advised warmly. Some things would take longer than others.

'This is for you,' Abi said, handing over a paper bag tied with ribbon that she'd pulled from her handbag.

'What is it?' Hannah asked, starting to untie the bow.

'Open it later,' Abi laughed.

Hannah slipped into the passenger seat and closed the door behind her, both of them waving to Abi as Morrie pulled off.

'So did you have a nice afternoon?' Morrie asked.

'Yes, it was lovely.'

'And how's she feeling about tomorrow?'

'Nervous, I think.' Hannah shrugged, already distracted by the bag and its contents.

'What have you got there?' Morrie asked, glancing over.

'He's very cute,' she said, taking the blue teddy out and holding it up. 'But why on earth would she give me this? Oh, hold on, there's a label.' Hannah took a moment before reading aloud: 'This is someone I've always looked after for you, but he's yours again now.'

She looked over at Morrie and then back at the bear.

'Well,' she said, 'I guess you're mine now. Whoever you are, Ted.'

– Thirty-Nine –

It had been eighty-nine days since Kathryn's mother had died. Autumn had taken hold; the days and nights were drawing in. The day before they had put the clocks back. It was a date Kathryn usually hated. She didn't like winter approaching because normally it made her feel nervous – all black and dreary and lacking in hope. But it didn't feel so bad that year. Despite everything that had happened, oddly, it didn't seem so bad at all.

She was meeting Abigail the next day. For the first time in over fourteen years she would be sitting in front of her first-born daughter again. Kathryn didn't know what to think about it, she didn't know if she was ready. But since her mother had died, and since she had begun to piece together what had actually happened all those years ago, she was better equipped, she felt. At least she finally had some answers she'd be able to relay to Abi.

If Kathryn was honest, she was a little excited about their meeting. When the nerves moved aside to let the other emotions through, she found a small glimmer of hope lodged deep inside her that maybe, just maybe, she might be able to start again with Abi. Once they had put all the other bits to rest, once she had told her what she now knew, then they could move forward together. That was her plan anyway.

'Kathryn?'

She looked up. Her therapist, Linda Platt, was waiting in the open doorway, her thin lips spread into a flat smile. She wasn't a pretty woman, her lank blonde hair hung shapelessly to her shoulders, but Kathryn liked her.

Linda stood to one side and waited for Kathryn to walk past into the small square room. She didn't make small talk and had no interest in anything that didn't move them forward.

'So you're meeting Abigail tomorrow?' She asked it as a question, so maybe she expected Kathryn to pull out. Kathryn nodded and waited for Linda to sit down on the faded brown sofa opposite her. She pulled out her familiar pad, full of notes on Kathryn's childhood, husbands and children that she'd gleaned over six sessions.

'I want to come back to you and your mother, today,' Linda said, without pursuing the topic of Abigail any further.

They always came back to her mother, but then Kathryn was beginning to see that everything always did.

'But first I want you to tell me how your conversation with Peter went. You eventually spoke with him last week?'

Kathryn nodded and gazed out of the small window. She could see the dull blue sky and the top of a tree swaying in the wind but little else. The tree moved backwards and forwards like a metronome. It was mesmerising, and she had found herself watching it many times over the past few weeks.

'He told me what happened, when I left,' Kathryn said.

*****

Kathryn had put off speaking to Peter after her mother's death. She knew there were still things she needed to hear but was relieved when Linda suggested they worked through other things first. Over the weeks she and Linda had trawled through Kathryn's relationship with her mother. Bit by bit Kathryn was piecing it all together, how much her mother had controlled her life, how even as a child she was manipulated by her.

'When I was ten she made me do elocution even though I hated it,' Kathryn had mentioned in one of their sessions. 'She made me stand up in front of the school on speech day even though I was trembling with nerves and wanted the ground to swallow me up—'

She paused: it was a memory she hadn't thought about in years, the horrendous day when she had spoken in front of four hundred people, her hands shaking as they held tight to the paper in her hand. Even the teachers had told her she really didn't need to do it, but Eleanor had insisted. It was only ten minutes but the fear she might wet herself had overpowered her. In the end Kathryn had run off the stage on the last word as fast as her jelly legs would take her to the sound of sporadic clapping and a few laughs from the front row.

'Why do you think you let her make you do those things?' Linda had asked.

'Because—' Kathryn paused. *Why had she let her?* 'I don't know, really. It was just the way it always was; I didn't see an alternative. Mother was always there with the answers for me, especially when I didn't think I could cope. She would tell me what to do so I wouldn't need to think for myself and in the end I quite liked that. I didn't always want to think for myself, so it made sense to me that Mother should do so instead.'

That was how it was when Robert died: Mother took over. Some days, following his death, Kathryn would get really angry that he had been taken from her. Some days she even blamed Abigail for it. They had been so happy before Abigail came along, when it was just the two of them. But then he had shared his love with her too. And Kathryn didn't want to share his heart. She thought that Abigail was getting more than half her share and somehow convinced herself that was why it broke in the end, because he was giving too much of it away.

Of course she understood now how ridiculous that was, but at the time it was all she could see. Her mother had dragged in Edgar Simmonds, who plied her with more pills, ones she now knew were for her illness but at the time she had eagerly accepted because they made the voices stop.

No one had helped her; no one had made her understand that all those feelings were normal for someone with schizophrenic episodes, because no one other than her parents and Edgar knew. And they weren't telling anyone.

'What did your mother do?' Linda had asked her. 'When Robert died, what did she do that made you think she helped?'

'She told me to stop being so bloody stupid,' Kathryn let out a small laugh. 'She told me to pull myself together and move on.

'"It's not healthy," she said.'

Well, death isn't healthy, Mother, Kathryn had wanted to say back.

'And you think that helped?'

'Well, she took Abigail to school for me and would lay out clothes for me to wear.' All Kathryn had wanted to do was stay in bed in her pyjamas. 'And she bought food. So yes, I guess she helped.'

Eleanor said baked beans weren't a staple diet, but Kathryn couldn't have cared less if they ate them out of the tin every night of the week.

'Then one day she told me enough was enough.'

Kathryn could remember it clearly. It was mid-morning and she was still in bed. Abigail was at school and her mother had returned, telling her they had something to do.

'Get up,' Eleanor had snapped, pulling back the curtains. She threw a box onto the bed.

'What's that for?' Kathryn asked.

'We're filling it up today.'

She watched her mother sweep around the house, room by room, taking down photographs of Robert, the paintings he had done at college, certificates, a card still standing on the mantelpiece. All traces of him were removed. At first Kathryn did nothing but stare at her mother, speechless.

'Don't throw them away,' she pleaded when the box was full and Eleanor seemed satisfied.

'So what do you suggest we do?'

'I don't know, just don't throw them away.'

Later she had found the box resting against the dustbin, to be collected the following morning, and Kathryn knew her mother would have banked on her not leaving the house and finding them. That night she dug a hole in the back garden and buried the box so Eleanor wouldn't find it.

Maybe it was a good idea, she had told herself as she walked back into the house. It was the right thing to do.

Maybe it wasn't, she realised now.

'So, your mother told you to move on after your husband's death and you did as she told you. Even though you didn't feel it was the right thing to do.' Linda paused. 'Do you think you ever grieved for him?'

Kathryn shook her head. No, she hadn't been allowed. And in turn that meant she hadn't let Abigail either.

In the build-up to Kathryn leaving for the Bay she was

struggling again: her relationship with Abigail all but disintegrated, her marriage to Peter practically over. Not only did she have two toddlers to look after, Kathryn had the added worry that Abigail was going to tell the world one of them was hers.

At first Kathryn hadn't seen the problem. It wouldn't have been ideal, but would it have really mattered? Her mother was convinced otherwise, however. Eleanor seemed to believe that if it came out their lives would be ruined.

In a funny way it was a relief to hear Peter tell her what was going on beneath the surface of the life she had blindly accepted. The fact that Eleanor was so petrified of it coming out that she made her granddaughter hand over her baby. 'Everyone would know her and Edgar had manipulated the whole thing,' Peter told her. 'That they had doctored the papers and as far as Abigail's records showed, she was never even pregnant. And your records were tampered with, too,' he said. 'Remember they had been doing it for years. Edgar would have lost his job over it.'

'And my mother?'

'Public disgrace, I don't know, they could have gone to jail. As payback to my uncle, Charles had used his position to get Edgar private funding for research. Your father was on the Committee for Privileges and Conducts, Kathryn. They would have been finished if they had been found out.'

So Eleanor knew she had to stop Abigail at whatever cost. But the more Eleanor tried to manipulate Abigail, the more it seemed to encourage her daughter to make her threats.

'Mother told me I needed to get away for a bit,' Kathryn told Linda. 'She said it wasn't wise to be around Abigail whilst she was such a danger. I told her Abigail wasn't dangerous, but she insisted I would lose my other daughters if I didn't do something about it.'

Kathryn gazed out of the window. 'Peter and Mother had bought the cottage in Mull Bay from Edgar. Apparently he had been renting it out for years to an old woman who had recently died. Mother thought it was a perfect spot to hide away the family she was so ashamed of.' She turned back to Linda but couldn't see any emotion in the therapist's blank face. 'Peter told me the other day he didn't think Eleanor had really thought through her plan for the cottage but she had this idea they could ship Abigail to the Bay for a while, until she was convinced Abi wouldn't say anything.'

'But Abigail didn't come to the cottage?' Linda asked.

Kathryn shook her head. 'It didn't get to that. I was frightened. My mother had been drilling into me how much of a threat Abigail was and I was scared, so scared they would find out what we had done and take Hannah away. I thought I might never see either of them again. Of course, I even believed I had adopted her back then, which I now realise wasn't the case, but I still thought that wouldn't matter. One night I overheard Mother talking to Peter about the cottage. She called it a safe house and I thought she intended it to be for me. I fell in love with the sound of it, the idea of living near the sea in a tiny village far away from London. All I wanted was for us all to be safe, and suddenly I couldn't get the idea out of my head. I was in such a bad way by then I decided to take matters into my own hands and one day whilst Abigail was at school I packed up all the girls' belongings, a few things of my own and ran away.'

Kathryn wiped the tears from her face. 'I was a dreadful mother, I know that. But I hoped my mother would deal with Abigail and then somehow we could all be together again. Only it didn't work out like that.'

'So what happened?' Linda asked.

'A few days after I had gone I wrote to Abigail and told her where I was, said that I hoped she would come to her senses and then she could move up to be with us. But she didn't respond and so I told Mother I wanted to see her. I said I would go back to London to collect her. That's when my mother turned up with a cut down the side of her face.' Kathryn ran a finger down her own cheek. 'She said to me, *Look what that girl is capable of. If she can do this to me then think what she might do to the girls.* So I didn't go. Instead I wrote her more letters but still I never heard back and eventually –' Kathryn paused – 'Eventually I gave up on her.'

She might never know for sure, but she didn't think Abigail would have taken a knife to Eleanor's face, though it was frightening to think how warped her mother must have been to have done that to herself.

'I guess, in time, Mother grew to like the thought of holing me up in the Bay and once Abigail had gone off her radar she had got away with everything. What a pity I found out too late,' Kathryn said. 'Now she's dead she doesn't have to answer to anything.'

Linda passed her a tissue and Kathryn rubbed her eyes and blew her nose noisily. She didn't want to cry any more tears over her mother, but these were tears for all of them now. And she didn't know if she would ever be able to stop crying for what she had done to Abigail.

'I believed my mother and never gave Abigail a chance. It's too late now, isn't it?'

'That's something you can ask her yourself,' said Linda. 'When you see her tomorrow.'

'I see Morrie is waiting for you outside again.' Linda motioned towards the door at the end of their session.

Kathryn turned and saw him sitting on the sofa in the waiting area, rubbing his beard and browsing through a newspaper. When she turned back, Linda was still watching her.

'He's just a friend,' Kathryn said, feeling the need to justify his presence. 'He's been very good to me. He's even been to the home today to collect some of my mother's things for me. And of course he's letting me use his house to meet Abigail.'

Linda nodded. 'I look forward to hearing how it goes.' They shook hands and Kathryn turned back towards Morrie. He was just a friend but sometimes, maybe more than ever, she had a little hope there could be more. She had always had three obstacles, she thought, automatically stretching three fingers out inside her pocket, but none of them were relevant any longer. Not her lies, not Peter, and certainly not her mother.

*****

'I'll bring the box in, but then I have to rush off, I'm afraid,' Morrie said when they pulled up outside Kathryn's cottage. 'It's quite heavy.'

'I've no idea what's in it, but I can't imagine it's anything too important,' she said, leading him to the house and letting him inside. 'Just leave it in there, and thank you, Morrie. I feel like I've relied on you too much lately. You've been so good to me over the years. I dread to think what I would have done over the last couple of months if you hadn't been around.'

Morrie smiled.

'Why do you do it?' she persisted. 'Is it because of the girls?'

But Morrie didn't answer; he simply leant forward and squeezed her hand.

As soon as he'd left, Kathryn pulled the box towards her. After removing the lid, she started rummaging through its contents. A few books, some of which she recognised from the shelves of their library: a very used dictionary, old copies of Dickens and Brontë. None of it meant much to her but she would see if the girls could make use of them.

Underneath the books was a photograph album. Its pages had lost their stick and had turned brown over time, holding photos that had slipped out of place, loosely held by transparent sheets. The photos were mainly of Eleanor and Charles, taken before Kathryn was born. Her mother had been a beautiful woman to look at.

Kathryn closed the album and thumbed through the rest of the belongings: a half-completed tapestry still attached to its loom, newspaper cuttings about Charles, a couple of Order of Services from weddings and one from a funeral. It was a sad collection of pieces to sum up her mother's life.

She was about to close the box when she saw a bundle of letters tucked at the bottom, held together with string that was loosely wrapped around them. Pulling one free, she turned it over to read the front of the envelope. Her heart plummeted as she saw her own familiar handwriting on the front. The letter addressed to Abigail was still sealed. Kathryn pulled out another, and then another, until all ten lay in front of her, unopened and unsent.

Kathryn clasped a hand to her mouth, trying to take in what this meant.

'You really *did* lie to me, Mother,' she said into the empty air, 'you told me you'd given them all to her.'

– Forty –

Dear Adam,

I saw my mother again today. For the first time in over fourteen years I saw Kathryn.

I have often played out this day in my head. Sometimes I would wind up crying, clawing at her to give me the answers I suspected I might not actually want to hear. After all, what exactly could she say? She left me fourteen years ago; nothing could make up for that time. At other times I was fuelled by anger, pumped up with determination that she would pay for what she did to me, and I would find myself coiled up tightly, fists clenched so hard, my knuckles had turned white. Whatever I had played out, it was always determined by my mood that day, and I soon realised I had no idea how I would actually feel when the time came.

This morning I woke feeling numb. Anything I had planned to say to her had blanked out of my head. I couldn't predict what would happen, how she would look, or how I would feel, but still, walking into Morrie's living room and seeing her again was a shock.

'Your mother has made an effort today,' he whispered in my ear as he stood aside to let me walk through. My first sight of her took my breath. She looked so much younger than I'd imagined, so much like the mother I remember from my childhood. Her hair was neatly trimmed and blow-dried, her nails were short and painted cream and she was wearing a soft blue sweater and black trousers.

In an instant I was pulled back to a time before my daddy died, when we were in our small living room in London, waiting for him to come home from work.

'Mummy,' I could hear a tiny voice inside me saying, 'can you help me with my buttons?'

Kathryn stood up and took a step towards me and I almost found myself waiting for her to kneel down and button up my cardigan again. The air filled with her perfume, its scent so overpowering and familiar, and I felt a pull, like I wanted to move closer to her. I wanted her to tell me it was all OK and she was back.

'Abigail,' she said. I hadn't heard her voice in fourteen years – was that how it had always sounded?

I took a step back, my legs shook as I found the armchair behind me and slumped into it.

Kathryn sat back down on the sofa, balancing on the edge. She held out her hands to me, then dropped them back in her lap and started playing with the seam on her trousers. Neither of us knew what to say. I was sure the look of panic on her face mirrored my own.

You must want to know what was going through my head but I'm not sure I can articulate it. You see I was such a ball of mixed emotions I don't actually remember thinking anything. I remember staring at her – the new lines on her face, the way the skin on her neck ruffled now, the silver ball earrings she had in her ears that I'd never seen before. She always used to wear gold. I wanted to feel something; anger, bitterness, sadness, anything, but I didn't in that moment.

'I like the way you have your hair,' Kathryn said to me eventually.

My hand automatically reached out to touch the ends before I pulled it away again. We weren't there to talk about my hair, and *even though I don't know what I expected her to say, it wasn't that.*

'And your sandals are pretty,' she smiled, peering over the top of her knees to get a better look at my feet.

'Don't do this, Kathryn,' I said, pulling my feet back.

'Do what?' She looked surprised. Was she expecting to spend the time making small talk?

I sighed and looked out of Morrie's small window onto his back garden, studying the tubs of perfectly manicured bushes as I took deep breaths.

'I read your letters,' I said, looking back at her. The night before, when Morrie had picked up Hannah, he'd handed me a package, asking if I could read its contents before meeting Kathryn, telling me they were important. There were ten letters that Kathryn had relied upon Eleanor to pass on, but of course she had never done so.

Kathryn nodded. 'I hope they went some way towards explaining that I hadn't wanted to leave you.'

'Yet you did,' I said simply.

'Yes, but—' she stopped. 'She made me believe things that weren't true.'

'You never stopped to ask me. You just ran off and left me in the worst way possible,' I cried.

Her hands trembled and I could see her trying to hold one still with the other.

'I wasn't well,' she said. 'I realise that now, I never knew.'

'She told me you were threatening the girls,' she continued when I didn't respond. 'She said you'd cut her.' Kathryn looked at me, imploring me to believe how awful that must have been for her. 'I was scared, I didn't know what to do.'

'That was the scar wasn't it? Hannah said she had one. She turned up one day with a gaping cut and told me it was a tree

branch.' Abi laughed. 'Oh my God, the mad woman must have done that to herself. I never cut her, Kathryn.'

'I'm so sorry—'

'You never stopped to ask me,' I said again. 'Not once did you listen to me, you always took her word for it.'

'I know, I realise that now, I—'

'She ruled you, Kathryn. And you let her,' I said.

'If I could turn back the clock, I would,' she cried, holding her hands out to me. 'I'm sorry, Abigail, I'm so sorry for what happened.'

I stared at her outstretched hands, her futile attempt at an olive branch and resisted the urge to slap them away.

'Well, sadly, we can't,' I said calmly.

Do you know what I realised then, Adam? That no matter what words were spoken, I would never get what I needed because that was impossible. My mother left me, she took my girls away, and yes, she might have tried to contact me, but the fact was, she lived another life without me for fourteen years. So whatever we said to each other then it didn't really matter because what had happened was unthinkable, it had changed my life too much and there was no going back. No explanation would ever be good enough.

Maggie had asked me yesterday if I wanted her back in my life.

'I never wanted her out of it,' I told her honestly. 'But I don't know if I could take her back.'

She asked me what I hoped to get out of the meeting, and I said I didn't really know, maybe it was just to be able to move on.

Kathryn had started rummaging in her handbag and I half-expected her to pull out a strip of pills, but instead she produced another large padded envelope. 'I've got something for you,' she said, holding it tightly in her hands for a moment before passing it over to me.

'What is it?' I took it off her cautiously.

'Some things I took away that I should have left out,' she said.

I looked inside and pulled out a photo, and then another and another: all pictures of my dad.

'Oh!' I threw my hand to my mouth. 'Daddy!' Tears rolled down my face.

'I have a boxful – they're yours when you would like them. I never threw them away,' she said. 'I couldn't.'

'Why?' I gasped, 'why did you take them all away from me?'

'I don't know,' Kathryn was shaking her head. 'I … I thought I needed to move on.'

'You thought?' I cried out. 'Or she did?' I stared at my daddy's face, pictures I hadn't seen for so many years. He looked so full of life and hope. 'It could have been so different,' I said.

My mother stared into her lap, twisting the bottom of her sweater into a tight ball. Under the cover of her pretty clothes and neat haircut her nerves were still fragile. Those were snatches of my mother when I was a teenager that I saw: the one who let me down again and again.

'Maybe we could start—' Her mouth snapped shut without finishing the sentence, and her brow was furrowed as if she was trying to find the right words to explain what she wanted from me.

'Start what?' I asked coldly. 'Not start again, surely?' Suddenly her appearance, her words felt like a charade. Did she really think we could brush over what had happened so easily?

'Well, maybe we could talk about—' she drifted off again. 'Or you could tell me about yourself. Or, I don't know, there must be so many things we could tell each other about our lives over the years.'

Like the fact I ended up sharing a house with drug addicts and spent most of Eleanor's money on alcohol and clubbing, or that I *didn't allow myself to trust anyone for years for fear that they would leave me like she did. Or that I ruined my marriage because I was too scared to have children with the man I loved. Yes, Kathryn, I could have screamed, there are many things I could tell you, but do you know what? I actually don't want you to be part of any of it. Not the good times or the bad times. Not the really, really low times when I thought there was no way out, or when Adam came into my life and showed me there was.*

'No,' I shook my head. In the end all I could say was, 'I can't do it.'

Kathryn looked up at me, wide eyes searching for a reason why. 'But now you know about me, and that I didn't know I had—' she stopped, hands reaching out as if she truly believed she had given me a good enough reason to rebuild a relationship.

'But you left me,' I spluttered. 'You walked away from me when I was the same age as the girls are now. And I had to grow up all on my own and along the way I've made some shitty choices that I'll have to live with forever because of you.

'I'm sorry you were kept in the dark,' I went on. 'I'm sorry you were never told you're schizophrenic, and I know that goes a long way to explaining many things – but not everything. Because you could still have come looking for me.'

Kathryn looked up at me, her eyes so full of remorse and longing.

'You still shouldn't have left me. You were so controlled by that woman,' I cried.

'I can see it now,' she said quietly.

I gave a short laugh and shaking my head, sat back in my chair, my heart thumping wildly.

'Can't we move on from here?' Her eyes pleaded with me, so full of hope. 'We can take it slowly and see how things go.'

*****

I'd be lying if I said there wasn't a tiny part of me that was tempted: she's my mother. She was supposed to be my role model, the one person I could turn to and rely on, no matter what. Every daughter wants a mum in their life if they have the chance, surely?

But I couldn't forget, and to be honest, I don't think I can ever forgive her for what she did. So actually it's too late for her to be a mother to me now. I spent fourteen years wishing she was still in my life but now I realise that isn't what I need.

I told my mother I wished her well and for the sake of the girls I hoped she would look after herself and accept the help she'd so obviously needed for many years. But I said I couldn't have her in my life. We were too broken for that, and I didn't have the energy or even the wish to fix a relationship that had shattered so far beyond repair.

Maybe one day I might change my mind, I don't know. Maybe one day I might want to talk to her about what happened, but to be honest I don't think she has the answers any more than I do.

There are many things I will never know for sure. Like why my mother let Eleanor rule her life. I imagine her condition played a huge part in that. It is a sad thing she was never allowed to get the help she needed – I believe if she had then our lives would have been very different. I imagine my mum was desperate for a love she never received as a child, and in her skewed mind believed that in letting Eleanor control her, she might earn it.

Strangely, I find Eleanor easier to understand. Everything about her was unambiguous. I believe she was a narcissistic woman, heady with the lifestyle, the money and the power her marriage brought her. She was ashamed of her daughter's condition, so much so she would do anything to make sure no one found out about it.

My grandmother thought about no one but herself. She was never cut out to have a child; she was far too selfish to be a mother. I hope that in climbing to the top of her ladder she never actually made herself happy. I hope that she at least had a moment of realisation that it wasn't worth it if you didn't love and be loved in return. But I accept I will never know that for sure.

*****

I will miss talking to you, Adam. It's a cathartic process, laying your life out in black and white, but it's time for me to stop because I need to move on. I have Hannah in my life. And Lauren too, of course – we are both working at our relationship, and I have no doubt we'll get there.

I still feel sad I've missed out on so much of them. Every time I see them I picture them as babies, curled towards each other, Lauren on the right, Hannah on the left. I can't believe I haven't seen them grow into the beautiful girls they are today, and that breaks my heart. Time is one thing you can never get back.

I try not to let the past control me anymore, but I still regret never giving us the chance to be parents. I always knew you would make a wonderful dad, but now I know I could have been a good mum too. I have it in my heart, I always did. At first I wasn't given the chance to show it, but then with you, I no longer had the confidence to try.

*****

I didn't know Hannah was going to look for you, Adam. If I had, I would have stopped her long before she found you, and told her what happened at the end.

The last time I saw you in St James's Park, you kissed me on the cheek and said, 'Look after yourself, Abs.'

We'd been through so much in those last few months, after you told me you wanted to work things out. At first I couldn't see how we could because I knew I still couldn't give you the baby you wanted. But you didn't push me, saying that we were more important. And so I finally believed that it could be OK.

The moment you kissed me and walked away I had a sense that something was wrong. I told myself not to be stupid, what a ridiculous notion, I couldn't possibly know anything like that. You were only going on a business trip – you were coming home. But still I couldn't shake the unease. I stood up and almost ran after you, begging you not to go. How I wish I'd done that, Adam. But I knew you wouldn't have taken me seriously – you would have held my face in your hands and laughed and told me not to be so silly. Then you would have kissed my forehead and walked away, as you did, leaving me in St James's Park to watch the back of you fade into the distance. Watching you run your fingers through your hair and put your other hand in the back pocket of your jeans, turning round as you were about to walk out of sight to grin and wave at me.

I replay that moment again and again and again in my head until it hurts so much, I need it to stop.

The following day, when I saw your father at the front door I knew immediately something was wrong. His face was grey, his eyes heavy with sorrow. He could barely look me in the eye and when he spoke my name his voice cracked through the ball of grief lodged inside his throat.

'Let's go inside,' he said, leading me into the kitchen.

'Don't,' I cried once inside. 'Don't tell me.'

I didn't want to hear what he was about to say. Because if I didn't hear it, I didn't have to believe it and then I didn't have to deal with it.

'There's been an accident,' he said, ignoring my plea.

'No,' I said. 'No!' I remember saying that over and over: no, no, no. It couldn't be true.

'He was in a taxi,' your dad told me. 'A lorry swerved around the corner too quickly.' He was shaking his head and I watched the tears slipping down his cheeks, thinking it was the first time I had ever seen him cry. His words pierced through the fug surrounding me. The lorry hit the taxi head-on. You weren't wearing a seat belt; you died on impact.

'Stop,' I begged him, as I felt his arms grip my own to stop me from falling to the floor. I needed their strength yet even then I knew he himself couldn't have had any left. He was as broken as I was, so filled with the grief of losing his only child.

*****

It's taken me a long time but I do now accept there was nothing I could have done to stop what happened. And finally I realise that many things weren't my fault.

I didn't start seeing Maggie because of my past; I went because I couldn't see a future without everyone I ever loved in it. But I can now. I can see a really bright one and for the first time in a very long while I'm excited about it. So I'm going to let you go now. And I'm going to let myself go, too. Because I have two beautiful girls in my life again and I can finally see the future I was so desperately searching for.

Thank you for listening to me, Adam. I will always love you.

    Abigail

      xxx

Acknowledgements

Writing a book is something I have always wanted to do, and along the way there have been many people who have given me the encouragement to get on and do it. From everyone at the school gate who asks how the book is going, to friends who have given me feedback and helped in other ways, I am grateful to all of you.

In particular I have some wonderful friends who have helped me on my journey to publication: Lucy Emery, Donna Cross, Deborah Dorman, Becci Holland and Kevan Kelsey. Thank you all, I know I am very lucky to have such good friends in my life.

My many early readers who encouraged me with enthusiasm and direction: Vanessa Edkins, Sandra Clayton, Fran Moore and all the Hinchley Wood Literary Ladies: Jennifer Plant, Jane Worsley, Vasiliki Arvaniti, Roisin McHugh, Larisa Strickland, Liz Sabell and Rach Hyams. Thank you Kate Bradford for your medical input (any mistakes are entirely my own) and Kate Chisman for all your insights into the world of social media!

Without my wonderful support group of writers there were plenty of times I wouldn't have known which way to turn. Your thoughts, comments and motivation kept me going and I feel very grateful to have made some good friends along the way. Thank you Alice Clark-Platts, Catherine Bennetto, Julietta Henderson, Dawn Goodwin, Alex Tyler, Moyette Gibbons, Grace Coleman and Elin Daniels.

Thank you to Sheila Crowley and Becky Ritchie who believed in me and the book from the start. And to Christopher Wakling and Anna Davis for your support and guidance.

Thanks to Clare Christian and Heather Boisseau who have given me much help in getting my book published. I am so pleased I found you both.

Mum, you have shown more love and encouragement for everything I do than I could ever hope for. You inspire me to be the best mother I can be. I know I don't have to say I hope you are proud. But I hope you are!

My wonderful husband, John, who has the eye of a hawk when it comes to a misplaced comma. You never once stopped believing in me and I truly wouldn't have been able to do this if it weren't for you. Thank you for giving me the time, patience and love that enabled me to follow my dream.

And my two amazing children, who I do this for: Bethany and Joseph, you make me proud every single day. Mummy loves you to the moon and back.

About the Author

Heidi Perks is a full-time writer and mum of two. She is fascinated by what makes people tick and how they interact with others, especially when those people or their relationships are slightly dysfunctional. One of the very first books she fell in love with was Enid Blyton's *Island of Adventure*, which sparked her passion for telling stories. She is a graduate of the Curtis Brown Creative Novel Writing course and studied Marketing at Bournemouth University before enjoying a fifteen-year career in marketing. She has since returned to set up home by the sea with her husband and their two young children. Heidi's passion for the beach and the sea always makes its way into her writing, and her happiest times are spent on the sand and in the waves with her family.

www.heidiperksauthor.co.uk